John Simp … tic
Editor, has reported extensively in the past fifteen years on foreign affairs – including the abuse of human rights in Eastern Europe and the Soviet Union as well as in South America.

Jana Bennett is a producer and an Editor of the Day on BBC-2's *Newsnight*. Since joining the BBC in 1979 she has specialised in foreign affairs and defence subjects.

# *The Disappeared*

**JOHN SIMPSON AND JANA BENNETT**

SPHERE BOOKS LIMITED

First published in Great Britain by
Robson Books Ltd 1985

Published by Sphere Books Ltd, 1986
27 Wright's Lane, London W8 5SW

TRADE
MARK



Set in 10 on 11pt Linotron Times

Printed and bound in Great Britain by
Collins, Glasgow

*To those who did not remain silent*

# CONTENTS

# PREFACE

One of the first acts of the democratic government headed by Dr Raúl Alfonsín, which came to power in Argentina on 10 December 1983, was to set up a national commission to inquire into the fate of the thousands of people who disappeared under the military régime that had ruled the country since 1976. Members of the Commission, known from its initials as CONADEP, have estimated that eleven thousand people had been abducted by the armed forces, and that they had almost certainly been murdered. The identities of 8,960 people who disappeared were established. In addition, the Commission found that about twenty thousand people were arrested during the period of military rule, and that many of them were tortured or raped; and that two million fled the country to escape the possibility of death or imprisonment. Of those who are known to have disappeared, 52 were aged between fifty-five and seventy-seven, 160 were adolescents of thirteen to eighteen, and 172 were children who were either taken from their parents or were born in captivity. An unknown number of these children were sold or given to childless couples; the rest were murdered.

The vast majority of the remainder were young adults: men and women from twenty to thirty-five, usually educated and politically aware, whom the military murdered as part of a concerted plan to rid the country of the left-wing terrorism which had plagued it for six years before the coup on 23 March 1976. But of the estimated eleven thousand who disappeared, no more than a few hundred were terrorists; the military came to power with the intention of rooting out the propensity to left-wing thought, and they selected as targets anyone who looked as though he or she might sympathize with terrorism. And so corrupting was their campaign that they were eventually kidnapping people for their money or their property, and treating the Argentine economy as though it were their private fiefdom, to plunder at will.

What happened in Argentina under the military government of 1976 to 1983 constitutes one of the worst examples of state repression since the end of the Second World War. But Argentina under

Videla cannot be put in the same category as Cambodia under Pol Pot or Uganda under Idi Amin: it is a highly developed country with an almost entirely European population, and a capital city which has a higher standard of living than that of many other capitals in what is loosely termed 'the West'. A street in Buenos Aires looks like any street in Brussels or Paris or London, except that the passers-by are likely to be better dressed. But in any developed society there are people who believe that the battle against crime and social discontent can best be fought by throwing the rule-book away, and Argentina provides a textbook example of the results: by setting aside the rule of law in order to be freer to deal with society's enemies, the generals and admirals who controlled the State infected it with a political, economic and moral gangrene which rotted every organ of government through and through. And while the process of decay was at its height, the great majority of Argentines insisted that nothing was wrong; and countries as varied as the Soviet Union and Great Britain ignored the symptoms and did their level best to keep in with the men who had introduced the disease. It is one of the arguments of this book that by deliberately ignoring what was happening in Argentina, successive British governments managed to convince the junta in Buenos Aires that no matter what it might do, they would not react: even if it came to invading British territory in the Falklands. It is one of the curiosities of the Anglo-Argentine relationship that Britain, having exerted herself to defeat the Argentines and regain possession of the islands, should have brought about the overthrow of the military government and then proceeded to cold-shoulder the democratic government whose members had earlier disapproved of the junta's military adventure in the disputed islands.

This is not intended as a comprehensive history of what Argentina's rulers called, Orwell-fashion, the Process of National Reorganization: it is too soon for that. Instead, this book is something of a study in political pathology, and we have concentrated as much as possible on looking at the disastrous years from 1976 to 1983 through the eyes of individuals who witnessed, in one form or another, the crimes and disasters of the period. A mere recitation of the facts of what happened seemed to us insufficient; it was the experience that we wanted to convey.

The victims of the Process of National Reorganization have not all been accounted for; the guilty have not all been brought to account. It is not even clear, at the time of writing, whether the government of President Alfonsín will be allowed to run its full course, facing as it does the immense problems of an economy apparently out of control, an immense foreign debt, and a recent history of all-pervading violence which has not been properly exorcized. Alfonsín's ultra-cautious policy of bringing to book only those who gave the orders during the military's campaign to stamp out all political opposition and those who exceeded their orders, and to allow those who simply obeyed orders to go free, has brought him into increasing conflict with human rights groups like the Mothers of the Plaza de Mayo who played a part in the moral defeat of the military dictatorship. On the other hand, the military and their apologists are already accusing Alfonsín of carrying out a policy of vengeance. The myths are growing: the figures for those who were murdered, are, it is being said, exaggerated, in spite of the clear evidence provided by CONADEP, a summary of whose findings forms the appendix to this book. The military themselves maintain a museum in Buenos Aires to display examples of the campaign of terror carried out by the far left before and after the 1976 coup, as part of their argument that nothing they did while in power was as bad as the crimes committed by the guerrillas. That, at least, is demonstrably untrue: vicious and stupid though the guerrillas were, the military's counter-campaign was far worse, and cost the lives of many thousands who never had the slightest sympathy for the bombings and murders carried out by the Montoneros and the ERP. Comparisons with Nazism are dangerously easy to make, and made far too often, but what happened in Argentina in the years that followed 1976 was probably closer to what happened in Germany after 1933 than anything else in the Western world during the past four decades.

This book had its genesis in the various reporting assignments which its authors undertook in Argentina between October 1983 and April 1984 for BBC Television News and the 'Newsnight' programme; our thanks go therefore initially to the relevant editors, Peter Woon and David Dickinson, for sending us there in the first place and for giving us time to write this account. Carmen Stefani-Gari was our constant guide, researcher and adviser, and arranged most of our interviews for the book. Guillermo Makin of Girton College, Cambridge, gave us invaluable and generous help, and his insights into Argentine history, the British connection, and the present government shaped our entire view of the subject. Tricia Feeney, who watched over Argentina for Amnesty International, helped us greatly, and so did the members and officials of CONADEP, the Permanent Assembly for Human Rights, the Catholic Institute of International Relations, CELS (the Centre for Legal and Social Studies), the Human Rights Commission of the Organization of American States, the United Nations High Commission for Refugees in Buenos Aires, the Mothers of the Plaza de Mayo, the Families of the Disappeared and Detained, and the Centre for Ex-Combatants from the Malvinas. Dante Caputo, Foreign Minister in the Alfonsín government, Carlos Gorostiza, Secretary of Culture, Hipólito Solari Yrigoyen, roving ambassador, and Professor Alfredo Bravo, permanent secretary at the Education Ministry, all gave us interviews, and so did senior officials at the Ministry of Defence and large State corporations who preferred not to be identified. Gabriel Levinas of the magazine *El Porteño* gave us a great deal of help and practical information, as did James Neilson of the *Buenos Aires Herald*, and the reporting staff of *Siete Días, Gente, La Semana, Clarín, La Razón* and *La Nación* as well as the management of the news agency 'Noticias Argentinas' and Channel Seven TV. A number of foreign embassies in Buenos Aires were helpful to us, including the French, the Mexican and the British Interests section of the Swiss Embassy. The Foreign Office in London and the State Department in Washington both helped us in their different ways.

David Stephen, a long-time friend of Argentina, was particularly helpful and his advice always worth taking. Nicanor Costa Méndez was most courteous and forthcoming, and Captain Nicholas Barker, RN, Philip Whitehead and the French yachtsman Serge Briez each gave us useful nuggets of information, as did a number of journalists including our BBC colleagues Harold Briley and John Humphrys, Jimmy Burns of the *Financial Times*, John Arden, Jorge Casal, and Jorge Fonderbrider.

Allen 'Tex' Harris, Rear-Admiral Horacio Zaratiegui, Ragnar Hagelin, Marcelo Sturbrin, Vice-president of the Radical Group in the Chamber of Deputies, the historians and writers Dr José Enrique Miguens, Dr Emilio Mignone, and Dr Fermín Chávez, Herminio Iglesias of the Justicialist Party, Cecilio Madanes, director of the Theátre Colón, the actor Luis Brandoni, Colonel Luis Perlinguer, Judge Luis Córdoba of San Martín, Mgr. Plaza, Archbishop of La Plata, Bishop Jaime Nevares of Neuquén, Nehemias Reznizky, Rabbi Marshall Meyer, and Jacobo Timerman all gave us their help, as did former members of the ERP and the Montoneros.

A large number of people gave us details of their experiences at the hands of the military; of whom we should, perhaps, single out the following for particular thanks: Mrs María Adela Antokaletz, Mrs Hebe Bonafini, Mrs Juanita Pargament, Mrs Blanca Carrieri, Ms Sara Méndez, Ms Ana Quadros, Dante Gullo, Mrs Edith Gardey Walker, Mrs Nelva Falcone, and Richard Whitecross.

Noel Rankin read large sections of the manuscript and provided a digest of one lengthy personal account; Tira Shubart read other large sections and went through some of the printed sources; while Deborah Carruthers went through others, translating and summarizing them. Shelley and Kim Bennett and Elizabeth Cushing were all especially helpful in reading and commenting on sections of the book. Finally, we must register our thanks to the librarians and staff of the London Library, the Canning House Library, the Library of the London School of Economics, and the library of the *Buenos Aires Herald*.

January 1986

*John Simpson*
*Jana Bennett*

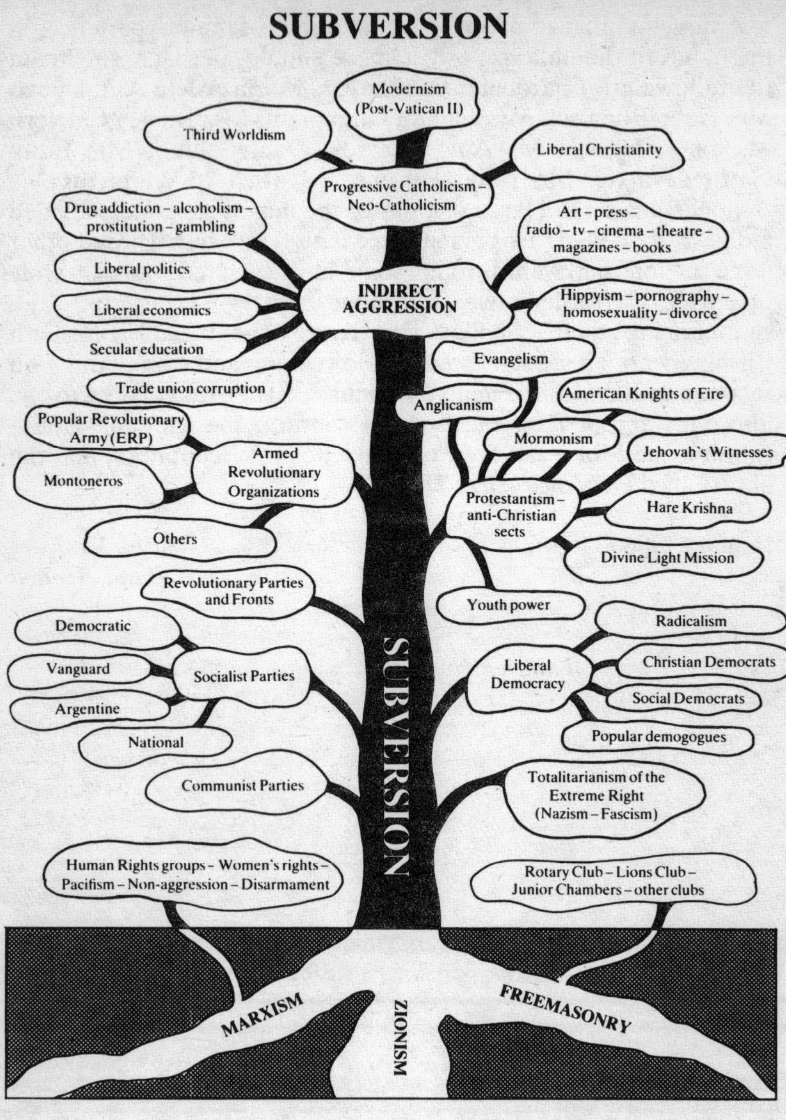


To destroy the tree, it is not enough to cut the branches

The Tree of Subversion: a genealogy of political opposition, as seen by the instructors at the Air Force Academy in Buenos Aires (see p. 242).

# 1 AFTER THE STORM

*'Tiempos mejores, tiempos peores viví,*
*Y estoy aquí.*
*Champagne, a veces, otras cervezas o anís,*
*Y estoy aquí.*
*De las Tres A a las tres Z fui,*
*Bombas y bombones, c'est la vie.*
*Resistí todo el año anterior,*
*Y aquí estoy, todavía;*
*Sólo Dios sabe lo que viví,*
*Ayer y hoy, y aquí estoy.*
*Mírame – que aquí estoy.'*

*(I've lived through good times and bad, and here I am. Champagne at times, beer or anis at others, and here I am. I went from the Triple A to triple Z: bombs and bonbons, c'est la vie. I put up with everything that last year, and I'm still here. God alone knows what I've lived through, yesterday and today, and here I am. Look at me – here I am.)* - Nacha Guevara.

One evening towards the end of March 1984, the Coliseo Theatre in Buenos Aires was filling up with a well-dressed audience mostly in their thirties and forties, talking and calling out to each other with a particular gaiety. There was a sense of anticipation in the air, and yet the audience were in no particular hurry; the show, which was scheduled for nine o'clock, did not begin until nearer nine-thirty. Even when the lights went down and the dim shapes of chairs and desks and less distinguishable props could be made out on the darkened stage, the buzz of chatter and expectation continued. It stopped only when a spotlight snapped on and a thin woman of forty-three walked into the glare and stood looking out at the audience that was now clapping and cheering her ecstatically. The long white mask of her face inclined briefly in acknowledgement, and the wide mouth opened in a sudden smile of recognition and gratitude. After eight years, Nacha Guevara, one of the most admired of all Argentina's political exiles, was home.

In her mannish black and white costume, the red hair pulled back sharply from her forehead, she sang and danced and high-stepped her way through an evening's repertory of songs. Some were comic or satirical, and had her audience laughing loudly at the personal and political references. But most had some element of melancholy, even if only the show-business melancholy of 'Send In The Clowns', sung in Spanish. At the end, when she had run through her planned encores, the audience would not let her go until she had sung one of the songs about freedom for which she had once been famous. The theatre was packed with precisely the kind of people who had suffered most heavily in the so-called 'Dirty War', during which the Argentine military had tried to root out not just left-wing extremism, but the very instincts for liberalism and political moderation, by kidnapping and murdering thousands of educated middle-class men and women in their twenties and thirties and thousands more working-class people from factories, offices and farms. Nacha Guevara sang her last song, calling on her audience, in the name of liberty, to remember all the nameless people tortured, executed, exploited, suppressed, deprived of justice, or killed in war. The survivors of a generation which had been decimated listened to her in silence. When she finished, the applause was, for the first time that evening, muted: Nacha Guevara left the stage, and the audience filed out quietly. Many still had tears in their eyes.

The 97 months since she had last appeared in an Argentine theatre had been the worst period in the country's history. Nacha Guevara's exile began a little before the military coup of March 1976, but it had been impelled by the men who carried out the coup and the repression which followed. She had been due to appear at the Estrellas Theatre in Buenos Aires, and the audience had been as slow in taking its seats then as now. While the theatre was still only half full, a bomb went off among the stalls, killing two people and injuring dozens of others. Nacha Guevara, still in her dressing-room, was unhurt. Everyone knew at once who had carried out the attack – the so-called 'Triple A', or *Alianza Anti-Comunista Argentina*, a para-military group of right-wing extremists. The Triple A was mostly composed of policemen but there were a few servicemen as well. The purpose of the bomb had been to punish Nacha Guevara, whose songs contained too many political comments and whose very surname sounded revolutionary (though she was not, in fact, related to her fellow-Argentine, Che Guevara). It was also meant as a warning to the kind of people who went to hear her sing.

Nacha Guevara left Argentina at once, and spent the following years in Europe and the United States, appearing in famous theatres and attracting critical attention by her sexuality and her expressive sadness. Her range as a performer grew, and the sixtyish songs about liberation and freedom gave way to a more witty, satirical style. In the country she had left, eleven thousand people disappeared in the clandestine gaols of the military, and all but a handful of them were murdered. The evidence CONADEP (the National Commission on the Disappeared) was to find was that the great majority were kidnapped or arrested in 1976 and 1977, tortured repeatedly, and then murdered in 1978 when the international demand for information about their fate was at its height. A further twenty thousand were gaoled officially, and many of them were tortured as well. Two million people left the country, fearful for their own or their family's safety. This systematic attempt to eradicate a way of thinking was accompanied by a gross mismanagement of the nation's affairs, and a degree of corruption that was almost unprecedented in a Westernized society. What happened in Argentina was worse, in every way, than what happened in Chile after Pinochet's coup in 1973. A distinctive quality of the Argentine terror was the strong element of the purely slapdash about it. You could be kidnapped and tortured, and most likely murdered, simply because you had the same surname as someone the military murder gangs were looking for, or you drove the same kind of car, or you lived nearby and might know something.

'It's our Italian blood,' people would say, self-deprecatingly. 'You can't have six million immigrants arriving suddenly in a country of three million, as we did at the end of the last century, and not expect it to have some effect. That's why we don't have any self-discipline, and are always changing our minds.' 'Perón distorts all our politics, even now,' others would suggest. 'His legacy makes everything impossible. Instead of a normal division between right and left, like you get in every sensible country, we've got the centre on one side and the left wing and the right wing both together in the one Peronist Party on the other. No wonder we're so crazy.' 'With a military tradition like ours, what can you expect? They think they're the only ones who can run the place efficiently. Of course they're ashamed of what they've done, for the time being. But the military never really change. They'll invent some story to show it wasn't their fault, or that the disappeared never did really disappear, and then they'll be back, worse than before. You wait and see.'

In the Plaza de Mayo, the long, elegant square which is almost all that has survived in Buenos Aires from the beginning of the nineteenth century, the focus of attention, on every Thursday afternoon at three-thirty, is on the centre of the square. There, the charming white obelisk which is surmounted by an allegorical figure with Athenian helmet and spear, celebrating the first steps towards an Argentinian republic on 25 May 1810, is completely encircled by a wide, broad ring of slowly shuffling women: the Mothers of the Plaza de Mayo. The ring must be about 60 yards in diameter, as the women follow with their feet a decorative circular pathway of white tiles, laid out round the monument. Nowadays plenty of other people walk with them: men and women of all ages, who join them out of solidarity. But the older women represent the core of the demonstration, as they have on most Thursdays since they started coming here in 1977, when the Dirty War was at its height. Many of them are well-dressed, in tweeds or expensive sweaters; not at all the kind of women who normally appear at demonstrations. Others have the brown complexions and broad faces that show their Indian origins; they come perhaps from the provinces bordering on Paraguay or Brazil. But the majority are unremarkable in their appearance, wearing heavy-heeled flat shoes and sensible clothes, and the white scarves which have become their symbol. Only a few now carry placards round their necks with the details of their missing children: a name in capitals, a blurred incongruously smiling photograph, a date, and the words 'desaparecido' – disappeared. The purpose of the slow shuffle around the monument is the same now that there is a democratic government in Argentina as it was when the military were still in power: to demand details of those who are missing, and to make it impossible for people to forget about them.

Once, photographers used to hang around the circle of women, hired by the various security forces to get pictures of anyone new who turned up to join it; it was a crudely effective form of deterrent. Nowadays there are photographers again, but they are either tourists or sympathizers. Two or three women skirt round the outside of the circle, asking for the signatures of passers-by on the latest of the Mothers' petitions. Many people refuse. One man walks away fast from the woman who has approached him, making little brushing movements of his hands to emphasize his unwillingness. For the cautious, it is still too soon to commit oneself. A signature might one day turn out to be difficult to explain away. No doubt even this man would sympathize with the aims of the demonstrators; most people do, now that everything is out in the open. But sympathy is one thing: taking chances is another.

Times have changed, even for the Mothers. As they walk slowly round, their feet seeking out the pathway of white tiles, they smile and joke with one another in the warm sunshine. The dangers of turning up here, week after week, are gone; now there is the pleasure of greeting friends and acquaintances who have also stayed the course. Gathering here during the difficult times turned out to be, after all, a kind of therapy. It gave them a purpose, and a ready-made set of friends and allies who had suffered similar misery and uncertainty. The value of the therapy is clear, now that the tide of repressive government has turned. It can only be a guess, but the mothers who did something when their children disappeared may have come to terms with their loss better than those who stayed quiet and did nothing.

At the far end of the Plaza de Mayo, gleaming pleasantly in the sun, lies the Casa Rosada, the Pink Palace where Argentina's presidents have their offices, and hold their receptions and – if they are that way inclined – make their speeches. From the balcony of the Casa Rosada, which is indeed painted a thick coral pink, as deep in colour as nail varnish, Perón and Evita would thunder out their challenges to the hereditary wealth of Argentina, addressing a crowd of a million or so which packed the Plaza de Mayo; and from the roof a helicopter took Perón's last wife, Isabelita, to imprisonment and eventual exile in 1976 – leaving the palace empty for the military junta to take over, and use as their headquarters in the Dirty War. In front of the Casa Rosada the big demonstrations took place against the government in the days before the invasion of the Falklands; and in the weeks that followed there were passionate demonstrations, at first in favour of the Argentine take-over of the islands, and then to show the people's contempt for a government which had shown itself as incompetent at fighting a war against Britain as it had been at running the country.

Compared with such major set-pieces, the regular hounding of the Mothers of the Plaza de Mayo out of the square was no more than a small-scale police action. But the name of the square where the tear gas and vomit gas once billowed out to envelop them, and where the riot police weighed in with their heavy night-sticks to beat them about the head and kidneys, is now identified firmly with the Mothers, not with their tormentors. They outlasted the men in the Casa Rosada who set the police on them.

After forty minutes of slow circling, without any noticeable signals, the demonstration breaks up for the week, and the people who formed it head off into smallish groups of twenty or so each: the better dressed with the better dressed, the poorer with the poorer, men with men, students with students; and not long afterwards these groups themselves disperse, as people wave goodbye to one another or call out promises to see each other there next week. Within twenty minutes other ordinary people, who have not lost their children, can start using the piazza as a thoroughfare again, now that it is safe for them to do so, and no one might mistake them for someone dangerous.

The large, white-painted block of the Ministry of Education had, within weeks of being redecorated by the incoming civilian politicians, been covered with slogans to a height of eight feet or so by rival groups of university students and schoolchildren. Now the building seems to be hovering on a cloud of words: angry words, encouraging words, uncomprehending words. Two floors above the cloud is the grand office of a small, unremarkable man, slightly round-shouldered, who walks with a pronounced limp. Professor Alfredo Bravo was appointed to the post of senior civil servant in the ministry within days of the inauguration of President Alfonsín in December 1983, making him responsible for teachers' professional affairs throughout Argentina. He had been a personal friend of the President since before the coup of 1976, when with other leading figures of a liberal persuasion they set up the Permanent Assembly for Human Rights to combat the growing number of kidnappings, murders and cases of torture which were taking place under the government of Isabel Perón. Bravo was the secretary-general of the teachers' union CTERA at that point: a moderate man with no sympathy for revolutionary or violent politics of any kind. During the first year or so of military government he had considerable difficulties, like other members of the Permanent Assembly and other trade union leaders. But he was not a Peronist, and was not therefore a primary target for the military, and his prominence gave him a certain amount of protection.

That came to an end in September 1977, just at the time when General Videla, Argentina's military leader, was in Washington explaining to President Carter how the campaign of kidnapping and murder was being stamped out by his government. Two policemen came to the school where Professor Bravo was teaching an adult education class, arrested him, and drove him away. Over the next few days, Professor Bravo was tortured as badly as anyone who has survived to tell the tale. His teeth were broken by hammers, he was half-drowned several times in baths of water, he was tortured with an electrical cattle prod by other prisoners and forced to torture them in his turn. Finally he was crucified upside down.

Nowadays, seated at his large mahogany desk in one of the best rooms in the ministry, with officials to usher in visitors and bring in trays of black coffee, it is hard to imagine him as a prisoner standing in line, blindfolded, resting his hand on the shoulder of the man in front of him, and waiting for the hand to drop when that man was taken away – the sign that Bravo himself would be the next to be tortured. At the end of the interview, Bravo gets up and walks courteously over to the door to say goodbye to his visitor, and await the next in a busy schedule. Only his limp is an irreversible reminder of what happened to him in September 1977.

Behind a barricade composed of old magazines, back copies of newspapers and yellowing sheets of discarded copy, James Neilson fiddles with his pipe and reads over what he has just written on a large electric typewriter. The theme for tomorrow's editorial is the economic mess facing President Alfonsín and the slim prospect that it will be dealt with successfully. It is the kind of office which the editors of small newspapers the world over occupy, with a few reference books, some out of date, lined up untidily on the shelves, a filing cabinet or two, a couple of suspect chairs, and the editorial desk itself – a vast plateau covered with the evidence of past projects. Uncharacteristically, a vaguely North American strain of piped music issues soothingly out of a speaker high up on the wall, leaving a formless version of 'Moon River' hanging in the air, above the layer of James Neilson's pipe smoke. The editorial he is composing will be in a language foreign to the country in which it is published: the *Buenos Aires Herald* is an old-established newspaper in English, owned by an American company and run by a British editor.

During the Dirty War, the *Herald*'s foreign status was its chief protection. Under Neilson and his predecessor, Robert Cox, it showed a far greater degree of courage than any other newspaper in Argentina by drawing attention to the abuses of human rights that were being committed daily; indeed, Neilson and Cox are two of the small number of heroes the Dirty War created. When Professor Alfredo Bravo was arrested, on Thursday, 8 September 1977, the *Herald* reported the fact on its front page the next morning. No other newspaper in the country so much as mentioned it at that stage. On each of the following days the *Herald* carried some reference to the case, but it was only on 14 September that two other papers reported it, and then only because a government official had met Professor Bravo's wife to discuss what had happened to her husband. When it came to the everyday victims of the Dirty War, young men and women whose names were unknown outside their immediate circle, scarcely anyone in Argentine journalism took an interest in them. Except the *Herald*. Nowadays, many of the parents of people who disappeared talk enthusiastically and gratefully about the interest Robert Cox and James Neilson took in their cases, and the practical advice they gave them, about where to go and whom to contact for information. But since the military have gone from power, the *Herald* has been free to slip out of its heroic role, and back into its former, more congenial one: that of being the noticeboard for the English-speaking and English-reading population of Buenos Aires. Its readers prefer it that way. James Neilson looks carefully at his pipe and admits that when it did what he and Cox believed to be the right thing by bringing to light the evils of the military junta, it was highly unpopular with many of the people who bought it. And now that the time for powerful editorials on the need to stop the death squads and the torture has passed, Neilson as editor is free to concentrate on writing about Argentina's troubled economy and the problem of external indebtedness. He, too, seems more at home with that.

Mrs Blanca Carrieri's five grandchildren play quietly and rather seriously on a balding patch of grass that serves them as a garden, acting out a game that seems to involve various acts of obedience by each of the children in turn as they slowly pass a coloured rubber ball round and round. Their house is a wooden hut on the outskirts of the city of La Plata, the capital of Buenos Aires Province and a particular centre of repression during the Dirty War. Like most shanty-towns, this one is laid out along the same lines as much better-off places, where there are bungalows and well-tended lawns, and the children have tricycles and paddling pools. The houses here are for the most part kept carefully, with orderly flower-beds and neat front rooms. Mrs Carrieri walks past the children, smiling and wiping the perspiration from her forehead, as she carries a couple of buckets to the stand-pipe in the lane in front of the house. She must fill the buckets six or seven times a day.

Mrs Carrieri is fifty-nine, and a handsome woman despite her shabby clothes and brown, broken teeth. She has always been poor, especially since her husband left her, but she works hard, and now, even with five grandchildren to look after, she manages to keep the small cabin they live in neat and clean. The eldest children help her, but the workload is much greater nowadays. Mrs Carrieri has looked after the five of them since the night in 1977 when a group of armed men came and took her son and daughter-in-law away from their house some distance from the city of La Plata. Mrs Carrieri does not make it clear whether they were, or were not, involved in left-wing politics. Possibly they were; the Young Peronist movement, which had close links with the Montonero guerrillas, was strong in La Plata, and they came from the sort of background that provided the Young Peronists with the greatest number of their supporters. All Mrs Carrieri will say is that her son was asked to go somewhere to meet somebody; clearly, like so many people, she is not too prepared, even now, to go into details. What happened after that was the kind of thing that happened in thousands of cases: the security men arrived, the couple were taken away, and nothing, or next to nothing, was heard of them again. In this case, though, there was the complication of the children. They were taken too.

By this time, as Mrs Carrieri is telling her story, the children are grouped round her in the kitchen, listening as she goes through the experiences they themselves still remember: the rough voices, the lights shining on their faces, the journey through the darkness, the police station somewhere, the people they do not recognize. In the end, the children were dumped outside Mrs Carrieri's house, and there was no one else to look after them. In a way, she and they were lucky; other children, left after their parents had been abducted, were given away, like the secret spoils of war, to childless policemen and their wives or military families. In one case, the kidnappers took the children of their victims to another country altogether – several thousand miles away – and left them standing in the main square of a small market town, where they were admitted to an orphanage and eventually adopted by local families.

The experience was bad enough for Mrs Carrieri's grandchildren, who were kept for only a night. Several of them suffer from what is already being called the forced abandonment syndrome: they are unable to learn quickly at school, they suffer from nightmares, they even pick up infections more easily than other children. Most of the children sit quietly, listlessly even, at the kitchen table; but one of the boys has started playing with a couple of building blocks, and he props up a photograph of his missing parents against them like a drawbridge, taking it from a little pile of pictures Mrs Carrieri has brought out. The couple are looking at each other and smiling; it is the best picture Mrs Carrieri has of them. The second eldest girl, meanwhile, is leaning against her shoulder, listening to everything that is being said. At the end, she starts talking for the first time. 'I like living with my grandmother here; she's like a second mother to me. But what I really want is for my parents to come back.' The words sound pre-arranged, almost rehearsed, but the girl seems unaware of it. Sometimes reality itself sounds too artificial.

Four thousand, five hundred miles away, in the depths of a particularly sombre northern hemisphere winter, an official of the US State Department sits in his overheated office in the ugly 1950s architecture of the building at Foggy Bottom, and sets aside a pile of papers and reports connected with refugee programmes. With perhaps a sense of relief, and certainly of interest, he turns to the day's newspapers and cuts out several articles on events in Argentina. The major American newspapers have usually maintained staff correspondents in Buenos Aires, unlike the majority of the European press, and at the moment, particularly, the coverage is considerable. Each day seems to bring news of more clandestine torture centres uncovered, more graves of the military's victims found, more generals arrested or accused of complicity in the Dirty War. The State Department official reads it all with satisfaction, clipping out the most useful articles for a personal file of his own. It makes a welcome change from the intractable problems of refugees in Africa and South-East Asia.

Allen Harris, who is never called by that name but always by his nickname, 'Tex', dominates the small office. He is an outsized figure of a man, around two hundred and forty pounds in weight, overflowing a crumpled grey suit, his massive forearms seeming to stretch the sleeves of his jacket. Now in his early forties, his last foreign posting was in Buenos Aires, from 1977 to 1979; since then, he has been back at the State Department at Foggy Bottom in Washington. He is careful never to comment on his relations with the other officials in the US Embassy in Buenos Aires, and he will not accept that his career has been affected in any way by what he did while he was in Argentina; but colleagues in the State Department believe that it has. The State Department, like most foreign services, wants its diplomats to be 'team players' but Tex Harris, with his bulk and his Texas accent and his general approach to the way things are supposed to be done, cannot merge easily into the team. The State Department, to its credit, has accepted this in part, by giving him something called the Rifkin Award for creative dissent. It is difficult to believe that a more conventional service, like the Foreign Office in London or the Quai d'Orsay in Paris, would accept the notion that dissent was particularly creative; even so, since his days in Argentina, Tex Harris has not been given another posting abroad to the small conformist world of an embassy.

Tex Harris was one of the heroes of the dangerous and frightening period of the Process of National Reorganization. As a first secretary at the US Embassy, he was given the task of monitoring the human rights violations being committed by the military government; and in spite of the intimidation and pressure to which he was subjected, he and his assistants catalogued no fewer than fifteen thousand cases, the details of which were sent to Washington for President Jimmy Carter's Administration to use as part of its wider human rights campaign in the world. It is even possible to maintain that the information from Tex Harris played an essential part in bringing the worst of the military's campaign to an end. As part of a deal agreed between Vice-President Walter Mondale and President Videla in Rome in 1979, the Organization of American States was allowed to go to Argentina to investigate the human rights situation, and the hand of so-called 'moderates' like Videla was strengthened within the military régime to the point where some of the worst offenders were eased out. Pressure from Washington had had its effect; and the pressure was made possible by a careful observation of detailed case histories of repression, as Tex Harris compiled them.

He, however, is not at all enthusiastic about the label of hero; apart from the civil servant's instinctive dislike of the personality cult, it does not, probably, help his career within a Republican administration which was prepared to tolerate the military régime in Argentina and even to reward it for its anti-Communist credentials, to have too much attention paid to his part in a Democratic administration's crusade. And anyway it is not his style. He is conspicuous – it would be hard for a man of his build not to be – but there is a lack of ostentation about him which suits his Texas accent and his use of slangy, informal language. If he were British, and a hundred pounds lighter, it would be classed as understatement; in his case, it is the self-congratulation implicit in the notion of heroism that he seems to dislike most.

It was Tex Harris who discovered the true nature of the repression in Argentina: that far from being a revenge war between shadowy gangs of left- and right-wing terrorists, it was a battle waged by the armed forces of the country, on the orders of the military government, to wipe out not simply terrorism but the propensity to opposition. 'They killed some real terrorists in shoot-outs early on, sure enough, and they captured some too.' The Texas-accented voice pauses, as he searches for a phrase. 'But those ones had cyanide pills, so when they were caught it was a race between the stomach-pumps and dying, if the military wanted to get information out of them. But the great majority of the ones they arrested were just wine and coffee subversives – kids who sat in cafés talking about socialist ideals and how the country ought to be changed. They were easy meat: if they'd sent a hundred of them postcards asking them to come in and surrender, ninety-five of them would have shown up.'

The style is reminiscent of Raymond Chandler, but the mean streets of Buenos Aires under the Process of National Reorganization, where Tex Harris once drove in his conspicuous American station-wagon, are far behind him nowadays. He checks the watch on his massive wrist, and calculates perhaps the length of time before he rejoins his large and noisy family in the Washington suburbs. Then his mind goes back to Argentina. 'There was even a guy from Army Intelligence who told me in person that the real tragedy of their operations was that half the people eliminated were innocent even by their own criteria. But it was easier to kill them because it was less risky and less compromising than going through the legal procedures. Easier,' he repeats, shaking his head, 'to handcuff them to a lamppost and just shoot them.'

'Our mistakes were very great.' The speaker is a studious-looking man of thirty-eight, who could have passed for ten years younger, with his high colour and his long, lank hair and thick-lensed glasses. The judgement he makes is a considered one; he has put long hours – years, even – into the process of arriving at it, but it contains no apparent element of remorse. Merely acknowledging the fact that there were mistakes seems to be sufficient for him. Pedro has been a member of the urban guerrilla movement *Ejército Revolucionario del Pueblo*, the People's Revolutionary Army, which fought alongside the Montoneros from the beginning of the Seventies until both movements were effectively wiped out by the savagery of the Dirty War. He himself spent nearly ten years in prison, captured long before the military seized power; and that was his protection. As an ERP guerrilla, he was a political prisoner and was recognized as such. He was tortured, and once had his eyelids pierced with needles; and for two years he was kept in cells reserved for people who would be taken out from time to time and shot. But his captors were careless: ten out of the fifty held with him were executed, but they never got round to him. Eventually, when the new civilian government came in at the end of 1983, Pedro, like most of the other official political prisoners, had been released.

The ERP and the Montoneros were, in their way, responsible for creating the climate of lawlessness and random violence which made the overwhelming retaliation of the military government almost inevitable after 1976. Between them, the two movements killed nearly two thousand people: soldiers, policemen, senior officers and their families, innocent civilians who got in the way, businessmen they disapproved of. They began their campaign of violence under the military governments of the late Sixties; and when the Lanusse régime decided it could no longer control the country and allowed elections to take place in 1973, the ERP and the Montoneros decided to carry on their campaign under the duly elected government of Héctor Cámpora, a Peronist who soon stepped down in favour of Juan Perón himself. Their violence created the climate of instability in which, three years later, the military seized power and began the Dirty War. Despite the bombings and murders they continued for a time to carry out, the

ERP and the Montoneros were destroyed as a fighting force by the middle of 1978.

When Pedro and the other survivors of the ERP talk of their mistakes, they mean chiefly the mistake of fighting on when the Peronist government of Héctor Cámpora was elected in 1973 – even though they broadly supported Peronism:

> We had the idea that from the first days of the Cámpora administration the forces of reaction were plotting to bring about its downfall. It was a very real danger. But the way we decided to combat it was to continue fighting the Argentine armed forces and the structure of big business. Those aims of our organization weren't clear to the people. That was our mistake. It was clear to us what we were doing, but it wasn't clear to other people outside. It was a big mistake, not because people like me spent years in gaol and some of us were killed, but because thousands of people who had nothing to do with our struggle are now missing.

But neither Pedro nor the other men sitting at the table beside him would be prepared to accept that their original campaign was a mistake as well; and somehow, when they talk about it, their campaign takes on a nobler aspect and it is cleansed of its unpleasantness. The bespectacled man of thirty-eight whose ten years in prison have left no apparent mark on him talks of the struggle to get weapons, and to distribute food to the poor; he makes no mention of what happened to the original owners of the weapons, nor of the shopkeepers or delivery men who did not want to give up the foodstuffs.

But now that is all over, and the mistakes have been made, there is no discernible desire to go back to some form of underground struggle, no matter what happens under the civilian government of Dr Alfonsín. Pedro and the others accept that it was their actions that made the military coup possible, and having destroyed one civilian administration they do not want to take up arms again now that there is at last another one in power. But the years that have left so few outward marks on Pedro have left ones that are savage enough on Argentina as a whole. Nowadays he is a pharmacologist, working at the job he trained for as a student and never fully practised before he went underground. In his innocent expression, in the full red lips and the weak eyes behind the thick lenses, there is still a kind of surprise, as though even now he finds it hard to believe that he should be alive when so many other people died.

Dust-sheets cover everything in the expensive room, and give the place a mournful atmosphere, as though someone has died. The general's wife hovers in the background, apologizing meekly for everything. 'We're just off on our holiday to Mar del Plata,' she keeps repeating, though the explanation seems somehow lame: there is an air of permanence about the way everything has been covered up. The general takes no notice of his wife's apologies. A pale man in his early fifties, overweight, there is little of the military man about his appearance. Perched on the edge of one of his shrouded armchairs, in an open-necked shirt and slacks – the temperature this January day is 94 degrees – he chain-smokes, making swift motions with his small, neatly manicured hands. His face seems somehow absurd, with the heavy bags under his eyes and the receding chin which, when he is sitting down, rests on the folds of his neck; he could be a character actor from one of Argentine television's comedy soap operas. Instead, he was the man who had had direct, daily responsibility for some of the worst excesses of the Dirty War. General Guillermo Suárez Mason was the commanding officer of the First Army Corps, which controlled Greater Buenos Aires. The task forces which went out every day in their unmarked Ford Falcon cars, hunting down suspected left-wingers in the city and taking them away for torture and almost certain death – together with an unknown number of people who were by no means left wing, but who looked suspicious in some way – all came under his orders. So did some of the worst of the clandestine prisons where the torture was carried out: Olimpo, Club Atlético, El Campo, Omega, La Cacha, La Salada, and many others. Perhaps as many as six thousand people lost their lives at the instigation of this man.

There is nothing absurd or comic about General Suárez Mason's manner: whatever his reasons for agreeing to be interviewed, he is often angered by the direct line of questioning, and answers in short, imperious sentences. His whole approach is threatening, and there are long moments when he says nothing, and the silence hangs in the hot, sombre air. Even in retirement, with the military out of power and the threat of arrest and imprisonment hanging over him, Suárez Mason is an intimidating man. And yet he is anxious to deflect the blame. Asked whose was the guilt for the Dirty War, he explodes at once: 'Look here, I'm not taking the political responsibility. That's a matter for the military junta. I'm not going to be the scapegoat who gets all the blame.' Did he know that torture was being used? 'No one said anything about torture.

The important thing was to get information. That, for me, was what mattered.' And what about the wholesale robbery of people's goods, and the evidence that some people were kidnapped and murdered simply because they were well-off? All thefts were investigated, he says. There were penalties for men who stole things like radios, and so on; as for the theft of money, that was more difficult to prevent. Like other senior officers involved in the Dirty War, Suárez Mason is primarily concerned with trying to give the impression that everything was under control; it might be a better defence to admit what was actually the case: that the task forces were a law unto themselves, with no apparent requirement to report on their exact duties. But the habit of command is too strong with men like Suárez Mason. 'You must remember that the subversives were operating in cells, and in order to combat them we had to give our commando groups a certain independence. At the end of 1977 things calmed down and they could be better controlled.' Why, finally, had the Dirty War gone so wrcng? Why had it rebounded on the armed forces? 'That's simple.' For General Suárez Mason, most of these questions have been simple. 'Here you've got a military victory against subversion, and a political defeat, beause an economic policy was followed which people didn't like, and there was all that idiocy about the Malvinas.' The dark brown, almost black, eyes stare accusingly at the interviewer, the last cigarette is ground into the ashtray. The self-evidently simple problems of the previous eight years have been explained in a matter of a few sentences, and the interview is over. Suárez Mason is clearly not disposed to talk about the other accusations that have been made against him: accusations of wholesale embezzlement at the state oil company, YPF, which he ran under the military government. Nor is he prepared to discuss the question of his membership of Propaganda-2, the secret Masonic lodge which linked politicians and some less creditable figures in Italy and elsewhere.

When the Italian police broke into the expensive mansion which the Italian financier and political fixer Licio Gelli owned in the town of Arezzo, near Florence, they found that the Grand Master of P-2 had disappeared, but that he had left behind a file which contained the names of 963 people, many of them in high positions in Italian politics. In the ensuing scandal the Italian government fell, and the Banco Ambrosiano crashed. But in the file were details of twenty-nine Argentines as well – and among them, under the code-number F 1877/0609 was the name Carlos Guillermo

Suárez Mason. The Argentine section of P-2, which was called Pro Patria, constituted an elaborate web of political, business and military contacts, including two members of the 1976 junta, General Videla and Admiral Massera, and the infamous José López Rega, who had found the Triple A murder gangs and was Mrs Perón's leading minister from the time she became President until he fled the country to escape charges of corruption. There were strong allegations of links between members of Pro Patria and the illegal trade in arms and oil; and the Italian Defence Ministry paid $240 million as commission on an arms sale to a group of Argentines which included several close contacts of Suárez Mason.

As it turned out, the interview Suárez Mason gave on 5 January 1984 was not only his first but his last as well. The furniture, carefully swathed in white sheeting by his wife, was being protected not for a short stay at the resort of Mar del Plata, but for an indefinite escape. On 18 January a judge in the town of San Martín issued a warrant for him, in the case of a scientist, Dr Alfredo Giorgi, who was kidnapped in November 1978. Suárez Mason did not turn up in court, and apparently slipped out of the country. It was said at the time that P-2 or one of its offshoots had helped in his escape, much as in Licio Gelli's breakout from gaol in Switzerland not long before. Perhaps the interview which General Suárez Mason gave in his flat on Posadas Street and Montevideo, in one of the wealthier parts of Buenos Aires, was intended as a final clearing up of unfinished business: the chance to put one or two things on the record before he vanished. Whether that is true or not, Suárez Mason had one final threat to make. 'You're a young man,' he told his interviewer, as they stood in the hallway waiting for the lift. 'I'll give you a warning. Don't do anything silly, because this is a country where history changes back and forth like a pendulum. And it always repeats itself.' What he meant was that no matter how pleasant it might be to have the freedom to speak and write openly and without fear, one day the military would come back. It was a powerful exit line, as the doors of the elevator closed, blocking out the pale, puffy face and the hard dark eyes.

The director of the cemetery at San Martín, a small town outside Buenos Aires, is also apologetic. There is no doubting his own political orientation: the large picture of President Alfonsín in a dark suit with the azure and white sash of office across his chest is there because he is a government servant. He gestures towards the heavy volumes which record the burials in his cemetery, and which have a section for the anonymous burials of the Process of National Reorganization ushered in by General Videla. His gesture has a clear meaning: times are difficult, even though the government has changed. Nevertheless, he is prepared to show his visitors where the anonymous burials took place. The little group heads out, past the more expensive graves in a cemetery which serves a town without much wealth. There are few statues here, mostly just brown or black photographs in oval frames set into the marble, though on the left hand are the fantastical temples and tabernacles of the richer families, side by side like houses in some miniature suburb, each family competing in death with the rest. As the director and his deputy walk on they are joined by several workers, tagging along more from interest than anything else. The day is hot and the crickets shriek as loud as distant klaxons in the still air. The director turns off onto a pathway between the cheaper graves, where there are few trees and fewer bushes and where wooden markers in the shape of crosses act as substitutes for marble tombstones. Argentine cemeteries are as well divided as Argentine society, and the path leads between the graves in the lower middle-class section, heading towards the cheapest and least sheltered area of all, close to the outer wall. When the party reaches that zone, the director stops, and asks his deputy to point out the place where the mass graves of the disappeared are. The man outlines with his pointing finger a small area of brown earth, ten yards by eight. 'Sixty burials there,' he says, with the matter-of-fact assurance of a man who knows how many bodies can be buried in a particular plot of land and how many can be laid one upon the other. The director is more concerned about the brutal reality of what took place, and he pauses for a brief consultation with his deputy. 'There are more down this way,' he says at last.

Only the Army buried people in graveyards. The Navy and the Air Force, with greater common sense and less faith, perhaps, that military rule in Argentina would last for ever, preferred to dump the bodies of their victims at sea. After a while the Army, too, chose other methods of disposal, and helicopters would take off every day from some bases with bodies which would be dropped over the jungle of Tucumán Province, or far out into the River Plate – the joke among officers was that they were bringing 'food for the fishes'. But virtually every cemetery in Argentina had its quota of 'NN' graves – NN standing for '*Nihil Nomen*' or 'No Name'. Sometimes the soldiers would bury the bodies themselves, sometimes it was done by the graveyard workers. Everyone knew why the bodies were there, but the directors and the graveyard workers alike knew also that it was essential not to say anything about them; and even after the change of government the habit lingers.

Further on, the director points out a very different area from the first we looked at: a rich profusion of oleander bushes and carefully tended flowering shrubs, the earth under them a blackish brown that shows the regular use of mulch and daily watering in the hot sunshine of midsummer. As before, small wooden pegs marked the various plots where the NN bodies lay. There is no question of asking the director why there is such a difference between the one plot and the other; the subject is not one which he or his staff want to talk about. It is as though they feel, with a superstitiousness which belies their smart suits and obvious education, that harm can come from discussing so unlucky a subject. It is only by chance that the reason emerges: the man who tends that particular area of the cemetery himself lost a daughter to the military death squads some years before, in the town of Córdoba – where the Dirty War was waged with particular ferocity. Not even he is prepared to talk openly about it, but carefully tending the plot where other NN bodies lie under the hot summer sun is one way of expressing his feelings.

# 2 THE WELCOME REVOLUTION

*'Now we are governed by gentlemen'* – Jorge Luis Borges, late March 1976.

The morning of 23 March 1976 was overcast and cool, and it was to prove the quietest day in terms of crime on the streets for several years. By 7 a.m. tanks from the armoured division based at Magdalena on the outskirts of Bueno Aires had occupied all the important points of the city, and their crews sat quietly in the open turrets, or gathered in small groups on the ground between their vehicles. Troops from the Campo de Mayo base set up roadblocks at every main intersection in the city centre, and in front of every government ministry. Key towns and cities elsewhere in Argentina – La Plata, Córdoba, Mendoza, Rosario and others – had been taken over at the same time. *Operación Aries* had achieved all its objectives, and not a shot had been fired.

By and large, people carried on their daily lives as though nothing unusual was happening. Occasionally they stopped to speak to the soldiers, usually in order to congratulate them; otherwise they would cross the street to avoid the tanks and the roadblocks, much as they would have done if the cobblestones were being dug up by workmen. None of the newspapers the following morning reported any cases of hostility to the military in Buenos Aires; in Rosario there had been a shootout, but it might have been purely criminal, not political. On the morning that the tanks rolled in a radio station had given its listeners a sly, joking indication of what was going on, when it started to broadcast music from the film *The Sting*. In Spanish, the title is *El Golpe* – and *golpe* is the equivalent of the French word 'coup'. Otherwise the broadcasting services mostly ignored what was happening on the streets.

By early evening the same day, those streets were almost empty. Most people were indoors, watching the soccer team River Plate beat Union Portuguesa 2–1 in a Liberator's Cup of the Americas game that was being televised live. Fifty women gathered in the Plaza de Mayo outside the Casa Rosada where President Isabelita Perón was a virtual prisoner, but she did not show herself on the balcony and did not seem to know that they were there, offering her their moral support. Her evening was spent in hectic discussion with her advisors and with emissaries of the armed forces on the question of whether she should step down as President of the nation. Otherwise, the capital city of the country she still nominally ruled was wrapped in unusual calm. *The Godfather, Part II* ended a successful run at the Metro cinema, playing for the first time to an almost empty house. *Earthquake* was showing at the Beta in Lavalle Street, and *Towering Inferno* at the Opera in Corrientes Avenue, but there too the takings were low. Restaurants shut early. There were almost no cars on the streets. Elsewhere in the world, the outgoing British Prime Minister Harold Wilson, having recently announced his surprise resignation, was giving a farewell dinner for the Queen at Number 10 Downing Street; the United States had reported a huge trading surplus, and Patty Hearst's lawyers had declared that she would plead innocent to the charges against her of kidnapping and armed robbery. In Argentina itself, the Central Bank had announced that the new one-million peso note (confusingly equal to ten thousand pesos which were still called 'new pesos') would feature the picture of a sunset over the palm trees of Colón; by now, a million pesos were worth seventy US dollars. The mayor of Buenos Aires, on hearing the news that the tanks were rolling into his city, had resigned, and the mayor of the dormitory town of San Isidro had vanished, together with the communal treasury. The big Peronist unions, whose bosses had been promising a general strike if there were a coup against Mrs Perón, failed to take any action whatsoever. And on that first, deceptively peaceful, day of the military takeover, several hundred lower-ranking union officials had been arrested and taken to vessels moored out in the River Plate.

It was the quiet start to a campaign of kidnapping and murder which would be worse than any Argentina had suffered before; and yet at that stage, if it had been announced publicly that a major purge was under way, the chances are that most people would have welcomed it. As for the democratic politicians, they had failed abysmally to come up with any practical alternative to military rule. During the day a meeting of the various party leaders, called by the ineffectual head of the Radical Party, Dr Ricardo Balbín, had broken up after a few hours, calling for 'a permanent dialogue of all the different political expressions' as the best way of achieving the moral and material recuperation of the state. But the words were hollow, used for form's sake only, to cover the politicians' retreat from any position that might have some force or meaning. The entire Argentine system, political, economic, social, had found itself in a dead end, unable to cope with the immensity of the problems confronting it. There was no serious alternative to military government, and almost everyone realized it.

The final weeks of the presidency of María Estela Martínez Cartas de Perón, whom her supporters called 'Isabelita', had had an almost hallucinatory quality about them. Isabelita had been in office for nineteen months since the death of her husband Juan Perón, who had been President to her Vice-President. None of the major difficulties she faced had been of her making, and she was often nothing more than a figurehead; as a former nightclub dancer with no experience of government she brought nothing whatever to the task of coping with the nation's problems. Under her, the downward spiral which had begun half a dozen years before became irreversible. In 1975 inflation had reached 335 per cent a year; but if the figures were taken from March 1975 to March 1976, inflation was 566 per cent and in the first quarter of 1976 it was running at an annual rate of nearly 800 per cent. It was a faster increase even than in Germany in 1921–2.

On the streets the guerrilla war which had begun under the military government of 1966–73 was being fought out openly. By the start of 1976 there were major incidents every day: bombings, kidnappings, murders and attacks on military camps and police stations by the left-wing Montoneros and the ERP; and retaliatory murders of left-wing figures or people believed to sympathize with them which were carried out by the right-wing gangs such as the Triple A, the group that had bombed Nacha Guevara's theatre, not long before.

By February things were worse still. On the 4th Argentina began a foreign imbroglio with Britain when the destroyer *Almirante Storni* was ordered by Bueno Aires to fire across the bows of the British research and communication ship HMS *Shackleton* off the southern coast of the Falkland Islands, which the Argentines have always known as las Malvinas. Soon afterwards, ambassadors were withdrawn from London and Buenos Aires in mutual protests. On the 5th, her forty-fifth birthday, Isabelita Perón appointed a new economics minister, her sixth since she took over as President in July 1974: this represents an average of one every 73 days. During the week that followed, the daughter-in-law of General Lanusse, President from 1970 to 1973, was murdered by left-wing guerrillas in her Buenos Aires flat. A few days later Father Francisco Suárez, one of the last surviving members of the Third World Movement of Catholic priests, was shot dead at his house in Tigre by a group of men who had driven up to the house in a green Ford Falcon without number-plates and rung the doorbell. As they ran off, his brother, who had been crippled in an accident, shouted out at the murderers. One of them turned, almost casually, and shot him in the stomach. Elsewhere, the army announced the deaths of several dozen guerrillas in the hills and jungles of Tucumán Province, in the north of the country, and the bodies of a number of people who had been tortured and shot by the right-wing murder gangs were found by the side of the road on the outskirts of Buenos Aires. Between the beginning of January and the end of February there were 32 kidnappings in the city of Córdoba alone. Like the economy, the fabric of society was coming apart.

The Navy had been making plans for a coup ever since the previous November. The Army commander, General Videla, was more cautious, preferring to frighten the politicians into doing something themselves to stop the slide into anarchy. On Christmas Day he had issued a statement saying that only profound changes could now save the government of Mrs Perón and 'what is left of Peronism'. On 16 February he and his eight most senior generals held a much-publicized conference to discuss the timing and method of a coup; but he still preferred to hold back. By this time the Navy commander, Admiral Massera, was pressing him strongly to take action, and there was no doubt that a great many ordinary people agreed. At the beginning of March the defence minister was greeted with cool silence when he represented the Perón government at a public wreath-laying ceremony in Buenos Aires. By contrast, the military leaders were loudly applauded by the crowd. That day, a headline in one of the morning newspapers read, 'Bombs, Shots and Abductions Everywhere'.

On 15 March General Videla himself narrowly escaped death when a bomb exploded in the carpark in front of the military headquarters in Buenos Aires. His car was sufficiently far away to escape the shock of the explosion, but one man was killed and 29 people injured. Two days later, Videla told a group of journalists, 'My watch has stopped,' meaning that his deadline for action from the politicians had now been reached. The decision to go ahead with the coup was taken, and Mrs Perón was unable to do anything to head it off. It was, perhaps, the most plainly signalled revolution in Argentine history.

The other political parties were as powerless as the government itself. Dr Balbín, the radical leader, made a radio broadcast on 16 March in which he admitted he had no solutions to the nation's difficulties. All he could do was to make yet another call for national reconciliation. The following weekend, many members of Congress went to their offices to clear out their desks; they knew what was coming, and there was no good reason to leave sensitive papers lying around. The leader of the Peronist union movement, Lorenzo Miguel, announced plans for a general strike if the coup took place, and he warned of serious consequences if workers confronted the armed forces on the streets. But the threat was empty; the union leaders wanted to keep Mrs Perón in government, but the rank-and-file members showed no such enthusiasm. Like everyone else, they were frightened and disoriented by the state of the country. Argentina was collapsing in front of their eyes. In the seven days that led up to the coup on the 24 March, forty-three people were murdered by the guerrillas or the right-wing death squads.

By late evening, every street that led to the Plaza de Mayo was blocked by tanks, and the only sound came from the fifty women demonstrators who from time to time took up their cry of 'Isabel, Isabel'. A military delegation composed of a general, a rear-admiral and an air force brigadier had been admitted to the Casa Rosada and was trying to persuade Mrs Perón to stand down. The hope was that she would step down of her own accord, ensuring that it would be, in the words of one officer, 'a decorous operation'. In the Plaza de Mayo the journalists and cameramen who had gathered there outnumbered the police, as they waited for some sign of Isabelita's intentions. Throughout the day, leading figures from the big Peronist unions had been escaping to Uruguay in private aircraft, but in public the party officials blandly refused to admit what was happening. A statement issued several hours after the tanks had moved in that morning condemned 'the intolerable rumour campaign about an imminent coup, unleashed by the usual enemies of the country acting in the service of left-wing and right-wing antinational interests'. The flight from reality seemed complete.

The military delegation left without saying anything to the reporters, and Mrs Perón remained inside the Casa Rosada with a few diehards, still the nominal President of Argentina. For some time there was no sign of movement. Then, soon after 12.30 a.m., the labour leader Lorenzo Miguel emerged from the side door of the palace. The journalists crowded round to hear what he had to say, thrusting microphones forward to catch every word. 'There is no coup, and no ultimatum,' he said wearily. 'Everything has been suspended until the morning, when we will meet again.'

A few minutes later a helicopter lifted off from the roof of the Casa Rosada. As it rose, its rotors drowned out the final chant of 'Isabel, Isabel' by the loyalist women craning their necks to watch. Even now, Mrs Perón had not resigned as President; she was intending to go to her official residence to spend the night, and was flying rather than going by car because of the innumerable roadblocks. But a new plan by the coup leaders had now been put into force: *Operación Bolsa* (*bolsa* meaning 'bag'). It was 12.45 a.m.

As they flew away from the palace and headed across the city the helicopter's pilot, a serving Air Force officer, turned to Mrs Perón and told her that one of the engines was not functioning correctly. It would be necessary, he said, to make an emergency landing at Ezeiza, the main Buenos Aires airport. As she and her small party climbed out and stood on the tarmac, they were met by three senior officers, one from each service. (The Air Force representative was Brigadier Basilio Lami Dozo, who was later to serve in the junta which carried out the invasion of the Falklands in 1982.) Mrs Perón's secretary asked them bitterly, 'What time are the executions?' The Army general turned to him and said, 'You must have a bad conscience.' Mrs Perón, for her part, said nothing, and her calmness impressed her captors. But when she was told that she would be transferred to a plane which would fly her to the province of Neuquén, in the southern foothills of the Andes, she pointed out that she had no clothes with her except the light-coloured two-piece outfit she was wearing. It was, somehow, unsurprising that the military men who had planned *Operación Bolsa* so carefully should have forgotten about the small details of taking their prisoner from a warm climate to a cool one – and that Mrs Perón's first words on being deposed should have been about what clothes she would wear. She was permitted to write out a list of things she wanted, and they were brought to her from her residence. Then, later than planned, the aircraft for Neuquén took off. Mrs Perón's final destination was to be a vast, turreted mansion called El Messidor, which overlooked the beautiful and remote Lake Nahuel Huapi.

Spain was the first country to recognize the new government in Argentina, followed quickly by Peru and by the Sovereign Order of Knights of Malta. Within hours of Mrs Perón's departure, Argentine embassies around the world were issuing a statement which promised that the régime which had just come to power in Buenos Aires would have full respect for 'law, human dignity, and Argentina's international obligations . . . The fundamental objective will be to ensure essential values in leadership, assuring the full development of the country's natural and human potential.' After the months and years of wild disorder in the country, it was precisely the message that everyone wanted to hear, and the newspapers which were going to press while Mrs Perón was still on her way south-east to the Andes were almost unanimous in the welcome they gave to General Videla and his colleagues. The *Buenos Aires Herald*, for instance, which was to be the most outspoken and consistent critic of the military in the following years, spoke of their 'laudable moderation in language and actions', and had considerable hopes that 'the new government will be able to guarantee the basic requirements of a civilized society – honesty, decency, concern for human life, and the will to uphold the law and justice – that will make it possible to rebuild democracy once again, this time on firmer foundations.'

Almost everything the new junta said and did in its earliest hours seemed intended to reinforce this view. Shortly after it was sworn in at a quick and plain ceremony at Army headquarters, Videla asked for the nation's prayers to help him in his task as the thirty-eighth President of Argentina. An announcement followed within hours that military officers holding government posts would not be drawing their government salaries, but would simply continue to receive their military pay. It was carefully calculated to appeal to a nation which had become sickened by the corruption of government under Perón and Isabelita. Videla also showed his skill in creating a good impression when he asked the national press to be frank in its coverage of his government, and not obsequious. The public stance of the new régime was remarkably encouraging. Even the tough measures it took at the very start of assuming power could be excused on the grounds of national emergency. Union activities were immediately suspended and their funds frozen, but the new authorities maintained that they were not hostile to any particular social sector, but were simply reorganizing the unions so that they would operate within the bounds of order and justice, in the national interest. Political parties were ordered to remove the signs over their offices, but a temporary ban on political activity was part of the price of having the military take over the country and set it to rights. Judges and provincial governors were dismissed, but that had happened after past military coups.

The entire country was quiet that night and during most of the next day. Radio and television resumed their normal programmes, and Harrods, the store in Florida Street which had once been connected with the British one, went ahead with announcing its autumn and winter collections. In the morning the government extended the list of regulations it had already issued to take charge of the situation. Communiqué number 17 warned that terrorists would be shot on sight; number 18 said the same penalty would apply to anyone contaminating drinking-water supplies. Number 19 ordained a ten-year gaol sentence for anyone who propagated subversive material or material that was offensive to the military. The machinery that would be used in the progressive militarization of Argentine society was being assembled. The assumption was, though, that the purpose of the coup was to deal with the internal security situation in the country, and with the collapsing economy. No one asked the three junta members, General Videla, Admiral Emilio Eduardo Massera and Air Force Brigadier Orlando Ramón Agosti, how long their régime would last; indeed, it was a year or more before any of the military leaders addressed himself publicly to the question and when one of them did – it was the notorious Interior Minister, General Albano Harguindeguy – he said, apparently pulling the date out of the air, that military rule would last until 1999.

It soon became clear to everyone in Argentina that to criticize the military government was to court trouble; nevertheless, people were more than ready to make sacrifices, especially with the rights of others. On the second anniversary of the coup, with the full machinery of repression in force, the magazine *La Semana* carried out an opinion poll whose findings seem to have been genuine. They were that 45 per cent of people thought the régime's first two years had been 'good', while 42 per cent thought they had been 'fair'; only 13 per cent regarded them, or wanted to be quoted as regarding them, as 'bad'. It was probably an accurate enough guide to public opinion. Almost certainly, if the military had not wrecked the economy they would have been forgiven for their corruption and their wholesale trampling on human rights, so strong was the yearning for peace and quiet.

But for the time being, in the first days and weeks after the coup, it was perfectly reasonable for people to believe that the new government had brought a return to decency and common sense. A huge cache of weapons which the incoming authorities had discovered in the building of the Ministry of Social Welfare was put on show, to demonstrate the lawlessness of the deposed régime; there was talk in the papers that several of Isabelita's ministers would be brought to trial for corruption, and that she herself was under investigation. It seemed a good start. Less than a month after the coup, there was little or no protest when the government issued the following directive: 'As from 22 April 1976, it is forbidden to report, comment on, or make reference to subjects related to subversive incidents, the appearance of bodies and the deaths of subversive elements and/or members of the armed and security forces, unless these are announced by a high official source. This includes kidnappings and disappearances.' 'We are in a state of war', one of the newspapers quoted a government official as saying, 'and the government has the right to use this method to prevent enemy propaganda.' The Process of National Reorganization had begun in earnest.

# 3 SAVIOURS OF THE NATION

> *'When the country, as a result of bad rulers, is put into a situation where there are no constitutional solutions, the military have a duty to fulfil: to put the nation in order.'* – General Franklin Rawson, 1943.

La Recoleta is a city of the rich and great in the heart of Buenos Aires: a city divided from the world of the living by a high wall and ornate iron gates. Away from the chatter of the open-air cafés and the noise of the traffic, the quiet intricate paths between the marble houses where the rich and great lie buried have a life of their own. A small army of attendants keeps the paths swept and free of weeds, and they have little huts in between the elaborate tombs where they keep the weapons they fight with – spades, brooms, wheelbarrows, trowels. Burying people in La Recoleta is not a matter of digging the earth; instead, the doors of long-unopened marble and granite tombs have to be prised open, and the new coffin laid on a stone shelf or on older, rotting coffins inside. Sometimes, with families that have died out or that lack the necessary devotion, the tomb that bears their name is allowed to crumble: the doors rust, the glass falls in, rain floods the marble floor. But for the most part the families of the Recoletans are house-proud on their behalf, and visiting the tomb of the clan is a regular duty. The cemetery is a showplace for those who want to seek out the memorials of the famous, to admire the statuary by forgotten, disregarded sculptors which marks the grave of some general who lasted his entire career without hearing a shot fired in anger, some lawyer who rose to be his country's foreign minister and played the British off against the Americans or the Americans against the British, some engineer who studied in Paris and spent his life evoking French inventions. La Recoleta is a great Argentine invention, but the people who inhabit it came mostly from a class which looked outside Argentina for their models and their influences. Nowadays there are few burials here: just the widows who have come to be reunited with husbands dead for thirty years, or the last surviving sons of famous parents. A small brass plaque low down on an undistinguished tomb in a side-alley marks the place where Eva Perón's body was brought for its final rest in the Duarte family mausoleum after two decades of being carted around as a mummified possession of her husband. After the years of being cold-shouldered in life by the rich and famous of Argentina, Evita is now numbered among them.

In a cemetery where wealth and status are denoted by the size and magnificence of one's tomb, the Illia family is commemorated in a way that is at once grand and rather modest. The tomb itself is set far from the main entrance, almost at the outer edge of La Recoleta; not an easy place to find. The generals and the lieutenant-colonels, the ambassadors and the engineers, lie along the main avenues, but the less ostentatious Illias have to be sought out. Nevertheless their tomb is gloomily imposing: dark marble, with the family name in deep-cut gold letters on the face of the great upper-works of the construction, and two sets of steps to take the mourners below ground-level to the entrance of the tomb itself. Here, on a sweltering January evening, President Alfonsín, after a month in office, came to pay homage to the previous Radical President, Arturo Umberto Illia, and to lay a splendid wreath beside the more modest ones of Illia's own family in the little ante-chamber at the base of the monument.

His voice, relayed by loudspeakers, ringing off the shiny marble of ten thousand graves, Alfonsín had already praised the achievements of Illia's brief time in office, from October 1963 to June 1966, during which time the previously little-known doctor from Córdoba had provided Argentina with a period of calm and recuperation: his 32 months in office were one of the few intervals in Argentina's twentieth-century history when no state of siege was in force. He was a decent, constitutional leader, even if he had not been elected in a fully democratic way; the military who had been in power before him, and had laid down the rules for the presidential election, had forbidden the Peronists from taking part. The economy, damaged by the continuing strife between the military and the Peronists, gradually improved under Illia's care; unemployment was down, the buying power of working-class and middle-class incomes rose, the manufacturing sector expanded by 18.9 per cent in 1964 and by 13.8 per cent in 1965.

Alfonsín recounted many of these achievements. And then he recalled briefly the military's campaign against Illia in the newspapers and by the television and radio stations: how he had been ridiculed and trivialized, how the feeling had grown that the country was in a state of paralysis and the economy in decline; how his slow-moving, country-doctor manners had been caricatured to the point where cartoonists and editorial writers, and particularly those who sympathized with the military, portrayed him, with his wrinkled face and stiff neck, as a tortoise, tardy in reaction, clumsy in style. Argentines, whose self-image is of being swift and fast-minded and changeable, quickly found Illia a figure of fun; and the military, who had come to miss the privileges of being in power and to worry about the possibility that Illia would not be the man to load the system against Peronism in the next election, began to consider the idea of coming back to power.

On Army Day, in May 1966, the Commander-in-Chief, General Pistarini, finally made the military's discontent public. Referring obliquely to the strength of the Peronist cause and Illia's unwillingness to counter it by unconstitutional means, Pistarini said, 'Freedom is placed in danger when, for the sake of convenience, decisions are delayed, encouraging the persistence of outmoded totalitarian myths.' From that moment it was clear that the armed forces would, sooner or later, take back the power they had briefly allowed Illia to wield. It was, as it turned out, sooner. On the morning of 28 June 1966, General Alsogaray of the first Army Corps walked into Illia's office in the Casa Rosada and asked for his resignation.

Knowing that the coup was about to take place, a group of twenty or thirty young Radicals had stayed all night with Illia in his office, not to guard him, since they were unarmed, but to show their solidarity. One of them was a young man with a famous name: Hipólito Solari Yrigoyen, whose uncle, Hipólito Yrigoyen, was elected President in 1916, and was overthrown before the end of his second term in the first military coup in Argentina, in 1930. Solari Yrigoyen, a senator whose life was often in danger during the 1970s from extremists of the left and right, remembers his reason for being there with Illia: 'It was just that I did not want to see him pushed aside like that, in such a frivolous, irresponsible way.' He recalls, too, seeing the dawn come up, and General Alsogaray arriving imperiously at the President's door, with a small group of officers and civilians. Illia was signing photographs as mementos for the young men who had kept him company during the last night of his presidency, and did not look up. Alsogaray swept the photographs aside and told Illia he had come on behalf of the armed forces to request his resignation.

'The armed forces,' Illia replied, in words that were later to be echoed by Alfonsín during his speech in the cemetery at La Recoleta, 'are represented by me. You are making use of a force which should be at the disposal of the Constitution and the law. You cannot invoke a representation which is not yours.' There was no question about the legal position, but the military had tired of being out of office, and they wanted power and prestige again. It was a frivolous coup, which had had the support of many people who might have been expected to know better: the Jewish newspaper editor Jacobo Timerman, for instance, who was later to become one of the victims of the 1976 military coup, but who, ten years earlier, joked about renting himself out like Xerox, and built up the political identity of the man behind the coup against Illia, General Juan Carlos Onganía. 'Let's manufacture intelligent generals,' Timerman is alleged to have said; and he certainly helped greatly in the campaign which brought Illia down.

Solari Yrigoyen and his Young Radical friends were gradually pushed out of the President's office, as they clustered protectively around Illia's small, unfashionable figure, and were forced out into the Plaza de Mayo. The riot police who got rid of them had been ordered not to use force against the President himself, and not to arrest any of his self-appointed bodyguards. Solari Yrigoyen found himself standing, with the others, in the chill of a winter's morning that was still not properly light, with no clear idea of what to do next, or where to go. Illia, though, with the pawky, self-effacing style which had cost him his presidency and Argentina its last decent political leader for years, knew exactly what he should do. He brushed aside an offer of the presidential car to take him home, and hailed a passing taxi.

The day after the coup against Isabelita Perón ten years later, a statement was broadcast on radio and television on behalf of the armed forces. The three commanders, Lieutenant General Videla, Admiral Massera, and Air Force Brigadier Agosti, declared solemnly that they would work together as a junta, a coalition, and that no one service would be supreme. The presidency would be rotated, to ensure that disunity and internal coups would be avoided. The reasons for the decision to assume the direction of the state had a familiar ring to them:

> Since all constitutional mechanisms have been exhausted, and since the impossibility of recovery through normal processes

> has been irrefutably demonstrated, the armed forces must put an end to the situation which has burdened the nation . . . This government will be imbued with a profound national spirit, and will respond only to the most sacred interests of the nation and its inhabitants.

The rhetoric was now in place, like the foundation-stone of a building. Each new coup over the previous 46 years had been built around similar phrases, and each time the fundamental decency of the armed forces was believed in and trusted in by a majority of civilians, because there was no real alternative: the political parties had, or were believed to have, fallen down on the job of controlling the destinies of the state. The military were all that was left. The problem was, that the facts of military rule did not live up to the rhetoric; and what the armed forces were beginning to want, more than anything, was power. Without it they were restless, and found the business of defending a state with no real enemies dull in the extreme.

Between 1930, when the military first intervened in government in Argentina, and the overthrow of Isabelita Perón in 1976, there had been six coups and 21 years of military dictatorship. No civilian administration had lasted its full term, with the single exception of General Perón's first period in office. After the Second World War, each period of military rule had lasted longer and longer, with the 1976 coup ushering in the longest military régime of all. Perón was President for nine years, until he was overthrown in 1955; Frondizi was in power for four years until the coup of 1962; and Illia for less than three years until 1966. After their triumphal return in 1973, Juan Perón, and Isabelita who briefly succeeded him, lasted only two years and six months between them.

And yet, time after time, the military believed its own rhetoric and persuaded the people of Argentina to believe it too; the saviours of the nation found it both pleasurable and profitable to step in from time to time. And the longer they existed as a political force, the more their privileges grew: the privilege of being tried only by military courts, for instance, whatever crime they might have committed. Until recent reforms, a soldier who committed murder was answerable, not to a civil court, but to 'a court of his peers'; and in cases where the soldier can plead that he killed in pursuit of the ideals of the nation, a military court is likely to listen to him with sympathy. The education of cadets is in the hands of the military too, so that doctrines of national security, and the concept of fighting the Third World War against Communism are drummed into young officers right at the start of their professional lives. Not surprisingly, the ideas which people who feel themselves to be in a country which is distant and isolated find attractive – ideas about their strategic importance in the world, and the significance which other nations attach to them – found ready acceptance in the military academies of Argentina. The nation, cadets were taught, had a duty to protect the South Atlantic for the free, Christian West to which Argentina by right belonged. It had a duty, too, to control as much of Antarctica as possible, in order to preserve the mineral riches there from Communist control. And the Falkland Islands, apart from their historical importance to the fatherland, acted as the gateway to the control of Antarctica. At the military academies, rhetoric and reality became so interwoven that it took great independence of mind to pull the two apart – and the cadets were not trained in independence of mind.

Argentina had started out as a 'nation in arms', fighting in order to gain its independence from Spain at the start of the nineteenth century. But after political independence had been declared in 1816 the country was hardly a nation state; it remained a loose grouping of provinces, with the port of Buenos Aires as its link with the world. Right from the start, the only method of turning all this into a governable entity was to control it by force. From 1835 to 1852 the task was performed by Juan Manuel de Rosas, a local chieftain or *caudillo* who had started as a gaucho and built up a prosperous cattle-ranching business. As governor of Buenos Aires – the closest Argentina had at that stage to the post of national President – he ruthlessly stamped on his opponents, brought the Catholic hierarchy to heel and obliged it to hang his portrait next to the altar in the city's churches, fended off aggressive neighbours and defeated France and Britain together in the first Battle of the River Plate. And at the end of it all, he was himself defeated by the governor of a rival province in 1852, and ended his days in exile in a heavily-furnished villa at Burgess Farm near Southampton, on the English south coast. But he had created the prototype for strong government in Argentina; an unruly, individualistic nation like that could only, the argument ran, be governed by force, not by persuasion.

In the 1880s, with the help of the railways and the Remington rifle, both newly arrived in Argentina, President Julio Roca began to unify the country still further, subordinating the regional governors, the *caudillos*, to his highly personal style of leadership by using the national army he had created as a personal tool of the Presidency. Looking to Europe for a model on which to base his army, Roca selected the Prussian system. Argentine soldiers accordingly changed their French képis for the pointed helmets of Prussia. Prussianization was sweeping through South America at the time, and in Argentina the training which the officer corps received from its German instructors was designed to instil a sense of national duty and a pride in professional standards which would protect the new cadet from political aspirations or conspiracies. The idea of the Army as an instrument of efficiency, separate from and above the petty squabbles of civilian politicians, was born.

One of the first graduates to emerge from the newly Prussianized war school was a young officer named José Uriburu. The product of a wealthy landed family, he graduated in 1902 with top honours, having absorbed the German influence with enthusiasm. He served a tour of duty with the Imperial Guard in Germany, and made a good impression on the Emperor Wilhelm II. In his case, the notion of the Army as a disciplined, superior entity encouraged him to take a hand in the relatively stable politics of the 1920s, when he had reached the rank of general. In 1930 he staged the first military coup in the country's history.

By the time of the First World War, Argentina had changed out of all recognition. From being a small nation of fiercely independent ranchers, mostly from old-established Spanish families, it had become in three decades an urban society in which immigrants, the majority of them from Italy and Central Europe and of working-class or peasant origin, outnumbered the people who had been born there. Today, 60 per cent of Argentines are estimated to bear Italian surnames. In the 1920s, the social changes which the influx had brought were already creating increasing anxiety in the Army and causing it to become politicized. The process was unwittingly encouraged by the Radical Party government of President Hipólito Yrigoyen, who, *caudillo*-like, used the Army to get rid of corrupt local politicians and replace them with Radicals. And he went further by promoting Radical officers who had suffered for their loyalty to the Party in the past. Twelve years after first being elected President, Yrigoyen won office again in 1928, taking over from the conservative Marcelo Alvear. Yrigoyen was hugely popular, having introduced universal male suffrage and opened up the universities to a much wider section of society. But once again he involved himself in Army affairs, giving backdated pensions and retroactive promotions to officers, particularly Radical ones, who had been dismissed under the Conservatives. And he was unfortunate enough to be in office at the time of the Great Depression, when the prices for Argentina's exports collapsed and the government appeared increasingly ineffective.

In September 1930 General Uriburu, who had been forced into retirement by the Yrigoyen administration, staged his coup. Nationalistic and conservative groups were loud in their praise of the new régime, which came to power promising an elimination of 'personalist' government and its replacement by an administration that would respect the constitution and achieve national harmony. Over the following decades the same sort of pledges would be repeated many times. And yet for all the talk about efficiency and putting the national interest first, it was the military government which signed the deeply humiliating Roca-Runciman Pact with Britain in 1933, under which Argentine beef was supplied to the British market at unrealistically low prices, and the ad hoc tram and bus services in Buenos Aires were dismantled so that British firms would have the exclusive right to run a transport system in the city. The British negotiators were surprised to find that many of the concessions were first suggested by the Argentine side.

The country's second military coup came in 1943, after a decade in which elections had been rigged and politics brought once again into disrepute. As before, those sectors of society and the economy which were suffering from the mixture of ineffective-seeming government and a recession caused by world conditions welcomed it. But this time the military régime was overtly sympathetic to Fascism and Nazism, and its tone was stridently nationalistic. One of its most prominent members was an ambitious young officer in his early forties who had briefly served as a junior minister in the toppled Conservative Government, and was switched by the newcomers to the relatively harmless department of Social Welfare and Labour. But Juan Domingo Perón could see the opportunities which such a post would provide from someone with political, rather than strictly military, ambitions, and from this base he built up the biggest and most effective political movement Argentina had ever seen, coming to power first by a popular counter-coup of his own and then legalizing it by the ballot box.

By 1955 the standard justification for military intervention in politics was being made again. This time, however, the armed forces had their own sectional reasons for wanting to overthrow Perón. It was the first coup in which the Navy played an important part; not surprisingly, since most of the naval officers belonged to the 'oligarchy' which Perón and his late wife Evita had attacked so stridently during their years in power. In June 1955 the Navy, with the support of the Air Force, attacked the Casa Rosada and the Plaza de Mayo, dropping fragmentation bombs which caused two hundred civilian deaths. The attempt failed; but a few months later a more effective operation by all three services turned Perón out of office.

Each time the armed forces intervened in politics they became more and more of a sectional interest group, a political entity which had the necessary muscle to impose its will, when it chose, on everyone else. From 1955 onwards, the earlier justifications began to fade away. The praetorian rhetoric was the same in the ritual public statement, the morning after each new coup, but the military themselves believed in it less and less. The Prussianization process had faded, and with it the atmosphere of being above, or purer than, politics; all that was left was the consciousness of superiority. The men who had casually carried out the bombing of their fellow-citizens in 1955 came in again in 1962 to overthrow President Frondizi for being too left-wing, and yet again in 1966, when they staged their frivolous coup against the slow-moving but decent government of President Illia.

Military governments from 1955 onwards were no more successful, by and large, than civilian ones, especially in economic terms. But political memories are notoriously short in Argentina, and each time the armed forces came to power they were welcomed by large sections of society which saw them in much the same terms as the military saw themselves: the disciplined, effective force needed to replace the dithering civilians. The illusion was a comfort to many people; but by the time of the 1976 coup against Mrs Perón, it was to be a dangerous one. The constitutional process had all but collapsed, the economy was in ruins, there was fighting on the streets – but the military were to prove as incapable of dealing with the problems as the civilians.

Before 1976, military governments had seized power with a clear-cut attitude of mind – a general feeling of superiority to inefficient civilian rule, a sense of their own esprit de corps – but they had nothing that approximated to a distinct ideology. For a whole succession of military rulers, from 1930 to 1972, the important thing had been to govern for a time, and then (so the usual rationale went) to hand over the country in better shape to the civilian politicians once again. In 1976, by contrast, the military had an ideology; and there were many among them who believed that this time they were in power to impose that ideology on Argentina for good.

By no means all the military leadership felt the same way, and it seems clear that the new President himself, General Videla, saw his rôle mostly in more conventional terms. But he was not a free agent, and among the topmost ranks of the military the strongest and most influential men – Suárez Mason, Saint Jean, Vilas, Luciano Menéndez, Galtieri, and so on – believed that the military government would be permanent, and that its first task was to destroy every vestige of opposition to their rule. Undoubtedly the psychological conditions which made such an ideology possible had been created during the previous six years by the activities of the Montoneros and the ERP, in attacking not just servicemen and officers, but their families and the places where they lived. It does not require a psychopathologist to work out the likely effects of a frightening and deeply unsettling campaign of that kind on the minds of men who were already authoritarian by nature. But the guerrillas simply created the atmosphere in which it was possible for the military leadership to insist that nothing short of a policy of extermination would be sufficient to rid society of left-wing violence. Almost all senior military men shared that view, it seems; but by no means all of them agreed how far, and for how long, the policy of extermination should be allowed to go. There were those, who, like Videla, saw it as a necessary cleansing process, after which the control of the state could be handed back to the duly chastened civilians; the others saw it as a permanent revolution which had to remain in the hands of the only men with the necessary toughness of purpose to carry it out – the military authorities.

This amounted, in practical terms, to an ideology in itself; but as it happened, there was a ready-made set of ideas which helped to flesh it out and give it a kind of intellectual basis. These ideas went by the name of the Doctrine of National Security, and they had arisen in their present form seventeen years earlier, when Castro's 'people's war' brought down the right-wing dictatorship of Fulgencio Batista in Cuba. Castro's friend, the Argentine Ernesto 'Che' Guevara, warned the rest of Latin America that its turn was next: 'We have shown that a small group of resolute men, supported by the people, and not afraid to die if necessary, can take on a disciplined regular army and defeat it.' From that moment on, the first priority in every war school in Central and South America was to work out ways in which those small groups of resolute men could be defeated.

John F. Kennedy's administration in the United States formulated its own answer to the problem. Known as the Alliance for Progress, its major thrust was to combat poverty and thus ward off social unrest in Latin America. But it also encouraged the armed forces of Latin American countries to become involved in areas of government – education, agriculture, health and so on – in order to improve the standing of the armed forces in the eyes of the ordinary population. And this 'civic action' programme was accompanied by improved methods of counter-insurgency, on the grounds that if revolution seemed likely to encompass all sectors of society, then so must the military response to it. The Alliance for Progress, although intended by a Democratic President in the United States as a positive and humane answer to the problems of the hemisphere, provided a generation of military leaders in Latin America with the training, and the excuse, to take political power into their own hands.

Under the terms of the Alliance for Progress, US counter-insurgency programmes at bases in the Panama Canal Zone and at the special forces centre of Fort Bragg, North Carolina, were thrown open to the armed forces of friendly Latin American countries. In 1963, for instance, the US Army Caribbean School at Fort Gulick in the Canal Zone was renamed 'The US Army School of the Americas', and by the late Sixties every Latin American country except Cuba, Costa Rica, Haiti and Mexico was sending officers there.

Argentina's military command took up the opportunities offered with particular enthusiasm. By 1976 six hundred Argentine officers had graduated from the School, having undergone training which lasted for up to forty weeks, concentrating on the techniques of irregular warfare and counter-intelligence. The methods and theory of torture were an important feature of the course, and students were reportedly hardened to the idea by being tortured themselves, usually by being hung up by the arms for hours at a time. Other courses available for Argentine officers were held at the Washington Police Academy and the Academy for Border Control at Los Fresnos, Texas, where there was training in counter-terrorism techniques and methods of dealing with bombs and electrical devices. And when the Argentine officers returned to the Argentine War School in Buenos Aires, duly trained, they usually became instructors in their turn, joining a group which included a number of Frenchmen who had served in the Foreign Legion in Indo-China and Algeria; men, that is, who took the American counter-insurgency theories further by teaching that torture was the essential method to be used in obtaining information.

By the time of the 1976 coup, therefore, a very different kind of officer-corps had been built up in Argentina: men who had been trained, not to emulate the officers and gentlemen of Europe who had once provided the rôle-models for the Argentine armed forces, but to see themselves as being in the front line of a particularly dirty form of warfare. They had the techniques; and ideas, half-digested, from President Kennedy's Alliance for Progress, with older military notions of defending Christianity, were pumped into them assiduously at the various military training schools of Argentina. A civilian professor of sociology who was attached to the military school for officers in Buenos Aires, says for instance that a kind of psychosis was deliberately built up in the minds of the officers who passed through the school: an obsession with the defence of Christianity and the coming Third World War, in which Argentina was believed to be playing a starring rôle. 'It was a kind of joke politics,' the professor says, 'except that the officers who learned it didn't think it was a joke.'

There was, however, enough of an objective reality to the ideas the military were imbibing to make them seem convincing. A war was indeed being fought in Argentina in the early 1970s, and it was against a savage enemy from the far left. For almost every single individual in the Argentine armed forces, it was the first war they had ever been involved in, and the battlefield was their own country. No previous military régime in Argentina had faced anything approaching the challenge, and no previous military régime had found itself and the families of its men in the firing line before. The Videla government seized power in March 1976 with a ferocity of purpose which owed a great deal to the years of training in obsessive anti-Communism; but it owed even more to the psychotic pressures created by the guerrilla war. This time, unlike all the previous coups in Argentina since Uriburu's in 1930, the military were determined to finish the job once and for all.

# 4 THE SHADOW OF PERÓN

*'Detrás de mí vendrán,*
*Los que bueno me harán.'*
*(After I've gone, those who replace me will make me seem good)* – Spanish song, quoted by General Juan Domingo Perón, Madrid, 1971.

On 20 June 1973, the largest crowd ever to assemble in Argentina was gathered at Ezeiza airport, on the outskirts of Buenos Aires, to greet Juan Perón on his final return to the country after 18 years of political exile. It was to prove one of the most significant moments in the country's history. The enormous crowd had begun to assemble the previous day, and the atmosphere was consistently good-tempered. The sellers of Party favours and of cheap portraits of the general and his dead wife Evita did good business. The drums were out in force too – the big *bombos* that required a strong man to carry them and beat them, with lengths of sand-filled hosepipe. As the time for *El Líder*'s arrival came nearer, the crowd of two million or more, generating its own heat in spite of the coolness of the southern winter, was working itself up to a pitch of almost religious fervour.

But what seemed like a unified multitude was in fact composed of three entirely different groups. First of all, there were the ordinary enthusiasts: working-class people mostly, who had been won for ever by Evita's commitment to the masses, and the sense of release and opportunity she and her husband gave them during the years when Perón had been President before from 1946 to 1955. Secondly, there was the *Tendencia Revolucionaria*, the grouping which covered the various Peronist youth movements and organizations which worked with slum-dwellers and poor tenants; the Revolutionary Tendency had taken Evita's message to heart, and its prime movers were the far left-wing Montoneros, whose campaign of guerrilla warfare had helped to bring the military dictatorship to an end, and Perón back as President. But there was an even more powerful force within Peronism, a right-wing extremism which complemented the left-wing extremism of the Montoneros and their allies. The true structure of Perón's power lay with the leadership of the big Peronist unions. Their political principle was 'verticalism': the direction of the masses from the top; and they saw in the rise of the Montoneros a serious threat which had to be stamped out by force.

Hundreds of thousands of the people who had converged on Ezeiza had been mobilized by the Revolutionary Tendency, and ahead of them as they marched were the red and black banners that proclaimed their allied organizations. But they had been outmanoeuvred, politically and in terms of crowd tactics. The right-wingers had packed the committee which was organizing Perón's return, and they had ensured that their supporters were already occupying the area in front of the platform from which Perón would address the crowd. By the time the Revolutionary Tendency reached the field, the supporters of the right-wing were in full possession of it.

After an hour's hard struggling, the left-wingers forced their way through in a phalanx, and managed eventually to establish themselves directly in front of the platform. As soon as they did so, a fusillade of shots met them. The right-wing had not, after all, tried to exclude them: it had arranged an ambush. Several dozen people on the speakers' platform, having assembled there to greet Perón, fired rifles and sub-machine guns into the densely packed ranks of the Montoneros. Twenty-five were killed outright, and hundreds more were wounded. Among the people who directed the ambush was a retired Army lieutenant-colonel, Jorge Osinde, who had been appointed by Perón 18 months before to be his military adviser.

Perón's plane was still in the air when the ambush took place, and it was never clear how much he knew beforehand of the attempt to destroy the left. It ruined the effect of his homecoming, and the plane had to be diverted. But he bore no grudge against the right-wing of his party for what it had done. On the contrary, he attacked the left savagely over the following thirteen months, and the campaign of persecution against the Revolutionary Tendency which he began formed the blueprint for the far worse campaign that followed the military coup of 1976.

The National Justicialist Movement which Perón formed remains an extraordinary phenomenon. It has profoundly changed Argentina, without having had the slightest effect on any other country. Apart from a certain sense of nationalism, there is no single element common to all its conflicting sectors, apart from reverence for Perón himself. It is reminiscent of other movements founded by military men at times of upheaval: Bonapartism and Gaullism in France, Francoism in Spain, Titoism in Yugoslavia, even de Valera's Fianna Fáil Party in Ireland. All were political movements, rather than parties, with a vague philosophy which allowed the founder to change tack as his ambitions and requirements dictated. Military men prefer to remain flexible; and because the body of doctrine and decisions they leave behind them is often contradictory, the leadership passes after their death to followers who prefer to make their appeals to the memory of the great man and to their personal links with him. But none of the other movements contained anything approaching the wide variation of thought and action of the movement founded by Juan Domingo Perón.

In a pleasantly cultured study, with the shelves crammed with books in Spanish and English, and two photographs of Evita among the other pictures on the walls, a Peronist intellectual who had been close to Perón during his later years of exile and flew back to Argentina with him on the day of the ambush at Ezeiza, talked with considerable frankness about the movement which had grown up around *El Líder*, as Perón was nicknamed: its power structure, its failings, the corruption and violence which had taken root in various of its nooks and crannies. He saw it all with the eyes of a professional historian rather than those of an enthusiast. Nevertheless, when at the end of a couple of hours' discussion the subject switched to the character of Perón himself, his whole expression changed. The impersonality, the careful precision left him; his face became gentler, more relaxed; the power that Perón could exert over his followers was still effective.

> He was very amiable, very likeable – an outgoing and pleasant man, much more so than the average military man. And he was extremely persuasive. He was, you see, not only highly intelligent, but very well-read. And that surprised people, because he never used long or difficult words: he would always speak in terms that were easily understood. He was particularly good at summarizing what other people told him, translating complicated ideas into simple terms. When he was in exile in Spain he took on more relaxed ways – perhaps it was

the Spanish influence. He became funnier, more ironic. He was a marvellous man to be with.

A marvellous man.

Argentina never had an industrial revolution. Its wealth lay in land – three-quarters of it owned by fewer than two thousand individuals, as late as 1970. Industrialization came unplanned and haphazardly; even now, there is little steel-making capacity. Because of the powerful influence of big international companies, many of them British, industrial growth was restricted during the Second World War at a time when conditions should have favoured it. Nevertheless, by the early 1940s there was a large new urban working class, whose conditions were bad in every way – low wages, long hours, poor housing – and yet because of the suddenness with which it had emerged, there was no political party to represent its interests, no equivalent of a British Labour Party or the United States Democrats. It was not a revolutionary force: there was no anger, simply misery and a lack of understanding.

In the military government of 1943, the post of Labour and Welfare Secretary – not a popular job among senior officers – went to the 48-year-old Colonel Juan Perón. He already knew the political benefits that could be extracted from gaining the support of the working class: he had served as military attaché in Rome, and watched Mussolini at work. Soon, he was angering his colleagues by raising the minimum wage and shortening working hours – and was gaoled for his pains in 1945. His mistress, the radio actress Eva Duarte, twenty years his junior, reacted with energy and speed, rallying the union leaders who had become his allies and organizing a strike and a rally, hundreds of thousands strong, which marched on his gaol and freed him. Then they swept him into power.

Perón repaid his debt to them handsomely. Living standards were increased as they had never been before, and would never be again. Evita indulged in countless acts of heavily publicized kindnesss, sponsoring vast gifts of money, clothes and food to the poor, and sending chartered planes to bring sick women to Buenos Aires for treatment. She ensured that women were given the vote. At the 1951 election, it paid off handsomely; Perón won 62 per cent of the vote, a 10 per cent increase over the 1946 result. But it was all, essentially, a form of charity. Perón made working-class people feel they had a dignity and an importance in the national life of Argentina, but the dignity and importance were hand-outs, like the food and clothing from the Fundación Eva Perón. The purpose was not to give power to the working class, but to encourage the working class to give power to Juan Perón. Perón was no revolutionary; he was a product of the Argentine military hierarchy, and although he was not strictly a Fascist either, he shared Mussolini's vision of how society ought to be run. He called it not the corporate state but the organized community. Nevertheless, from time to time he used just enough of the language of revolution to keep the far left of his Party believing that his heart was with them. In the last days before the coup against him in 1955, Perón considered and then rejected Evita's idea of several years before, that of arming the workers in his support. 'Imagine,' he said in his first interview after going into exile, 'what would have happened if I had handed weapons from the arsenals to workers who were only too eager to grasp them.' But from the viewpoint of his base in exile, in the Madrid suburb known as the Iron Gate, the idea of a campaign of violence, carried out on his behalf in Argentina, had obvious attractions. And so, in carefully ambiguous language, he gave his support year after year to the revolutionaries of the far left who were fighting for his return. 'Our solution is to free our country in the way Fidel freed his,' he told one interviewer. He was talking about Castro's methods, not his ideology, but for those who wanted to believe in him as an Argentine Castro, it was just what they were hoping to hear. After 1968, he called his doctrine 'Socialismo Nacional', and the left put the emphasis on the socialism while the right took the phrase as a whole and thought of Mussolini. But the right wing could not bring down the military dictatorship in Argentina, and the left wing could, and so Perón encouraged the fast-growing guerrilla movements with the taped speeches which were smuggled into the country from the Iron Gate, telling them in 1971, 'We have a marvellous youth movement which every day demonstrates without equivocation its capacity and its greatness . . . I have absolute faith in our boys who have learned to die for their ideals.' And, he might have added, how to kill for them. The year before, the Montoneros, with a membership of only a dozen at the time, had staged a spectacular murder which had demonstrated that a war, and not just a law and order problem, had begun.

General Pedro Eugenio Aramburu, who had helped to overthrow Perón in 1955, was a subtle and ambitious man who had been

President for three years and was showing signs of wanting another term in power. One morning in May 1970, he answered the entry-phone of his flat in the centre of Buenos Aires and a voice declared that two army officers had arrived to guard him. He invited them in and gave them coffee, and when they had finished it they told the General he must go with them. The operation soon took on the popular name of the *Aramburazo*, the '-azo' ending being an untranslatable term indicating a coup, a stroke of some kind. Aramburu was a particular figure of hatred for the Peronists because of his execution of some Peronist officers and his responsibility for exhuming Evita and sending her body to a secret resting place in Milan. After the Montoneros had tried to discover from Aramburu where the body was hidden, they staged a 'people's trial' and found him guilty. The man who had rung his doorbell shot him through the heart three days later at 7 a.m. on 1 June 1970. The communiqué announcing his death ended with a curiously Christian flourish – 'May God have mercy on his soul' – which owed a good deal to the ultra-Catholic background of some of the original Montoneros.

The *Aramburazo* marked the beginning of a campaign which within three years turned the Montoneros into a genuine mass movement. Their exploits in kidnapping the wealthy and forcing them to give money for the distribution of food to the poor attracted public attention and public sympathy, whilst the military government was putting its efforts into supporting the power of big business, and often foreign-owned big business at that. The middle class, from which so much Montonero support sprang, found the increasing number of bankruptcies and the continuing fall in real incomes a serious cause for disaffection; and so the very people who would normally provide the government with the backbone of its support had more than a sneaking sympathy for the Montoneros in their attacks against the impersonal organs of the state and the unlovable haunts of the very wealthy, golf courses and country clubs in particular. In their first three years, the Montoneros killed only about a dozen people, most of them policemen, and their own losses were much higher. In the heyday of radical chic, what the Montoneros were doing seemed like a breath of fresh air in a tired, conservative country. By 1973, active membership of the Montoneros was well over a thousand, and their supporters were numbered in hundreds of thousands.

The pattern of modern Argentine politics was established in the unlikely surroundings of a Panama City nightclub in 1956. Perón, gloomy, exiled, and a widower, would make his way into the Happy Land Bar each evening, and would sit down to watch the floorshow. The star, in what was not a particularly elevated form of show business, was a 25-year-old dancer, María Estela Martínez. She was handsome in something of the way Evita had been handsome, and the ex-President, at sixty, found her sharp-witted and amusing. Her friends called her Isabelita, and she was later to marry him and one day to succeed him as President of Argentina. But as Perón sat at his accustomed table and watched her go through her routines, the Happy Land Bar contained, not two future Presidents of Argentina, but three – the third being the bar's manager, Raúl Lastiri. He allied himself with Isabelita, and shared in the rise of her fortunes and those of Perón; and eventually, before *El Líder* returned, he became head of the Chamber of Deputies. In 1973, when Héctor Cámpora had been elected President and stood down in Perón's favour, Lastiri served as a stand-in for the four months from July to October. The former manager of the Happy Land Bar was indirectly to have a baleful influence on his country's future.

Lastiri's father-in-law, José López Rega, was an obscure ex-corporal in the Argentine police who left the force in 1960 and started writing books about the occult, one of which he declared had been co-authored by the Archangel Gabriel. He went bankrupt, and escaped to Brazil, where a business partner of his introduced him to Brazilian-African magic: a variety of voodoo. By 1966 he was ready for higher things, and, banking on the link between his son-in-law Raúl Lastiri and Perón, he travelled to the Iron Gate in Madrid and was taken on as a kind of servant. Soon he was carrying out more delicate tasks: once, for instance, he persuaded Isabelita to return to Perón after their marriage had broken down. Later, when a scandal erupted in an Argentine bank run by the Peronist unions, he turned up with a suitcase full of money and smoothed out the problem. After the triumphant return from exile, López Rega's influence grew even more. Now he was in charge of Perón's medical treatment, and there were stories that he and Isabelita, his close ally, would force Perón to sign documents, refusing to give him the rich caramel delicacy, *dulce de leche*, unless he agreed. From the beginning of 1974 to Perón's death the following July, only the two of them had access to him.

By now, López Rega was the most powerful man in the country.

His sleek, well-groomed head appears in countless photographs of the time, usually a little behind Isabelita's, ready at any moment to proffer advice and suggestions. His post as Minister of Social Welfare, Perón's old job, gave him access to a large budget and a nationwide network of officials; and it was at the Ministry, together with his police contacts, that he began to put together a powerful death squad, with the aim of eliminating the left wing of the Peronist movement. In the following year it would be christened the 'Triple A'. Its first operation was at Ezeiza airport on 20 June 1973 – the day of Perón's return. And the man who directed the rifles and sub-machineguns which fired at the crowd of Montoneros, Colonel Osinde, was an under-secretary at López Rega's ministry.

On May Day, 1974, a hundred thousand people filled the Plaza de Mayo, more than half of them mobilized by the Montoneros. It was, they felt, their last chance to make contact with Perón, to show him their devotion and to beg him to put an end to the constant campaign of violence directed against them by Perón's own government. The official rally organizers had laid down that only two chants would be allowed: 'Argentina, Argentina' and 'Perón, Perón.' But the Montoneros had prepared a chant of their own, and when Perón appeared on the balcony of the Casa Rosada they used it to ask him the one question they had not been prepared to answer themselves: '*Qué pasa, qué pasa, qué pasa, General? Está lleno de gorilas el gobierno popular*' ('What's happening, General? the popular government is full of gorillas' – 'gorillas' being the long-standing Peronist nickname for anti-Peronists among the military and the right wing). Perón was furious, and shouted out at 'those stupid beardless fools who keep on chanting' to shut up. Finally he told the people whom he had once called the 'marvellous youth movement' that they were mercenaries in the service of foreign money. The insult was too much for the Montoneros, and they marched out of the Plaza, leaving Perón still shouting angrily into the microphone, haranguing a crowd that had dwindled to less than half its original size. It was the end of the Montoneros' hero-worship. Two months later *El Líder* was dead of a heart attack, and his carelessly embalmed body was swelling and decaying visibly even during its lying-in-state.

The Montoneros, for their part, were free to declare all-out war on the government of Isabelita and López Rega, and this time they had thousands of activists and a vast network of safe houses, workshops, and printing presses. They also had money. By kidnapping the two brothers who ran Argentina's biggest industrial concern, Bunge y Born, they received the largest ransom ever extorted in any country: sixty million dollars. But the Robin Hood days were over. From now on the Montoneros and their partial allies, the ERP, became involved in an increasingly bloody war with the government. The ERP, trying to imitate the Cuban model, had solemnly established themselves in the region of Argentina which seemed most like Cuba: the province of Tucumán, which grows sugar and has the kind of valleys and jungle that looked, in ERP eyes, like the Sierra Maestra range where Fidel Castro began his campaign. But the Argentine Army was not obliging enough to play the part of Bastista, and ERP found it was up against a well-equipped and ruthless enemy which consistently won the setpiece engagements and hunted the guerrillas down in the deep valleys where they had taken shelter. But the killings carried out by the Montoneros and the ERP had anyway begun to sicken the people who had once thought that blowing up the club-house at a golf course was rather amusing. Now the Montoneros were too busy attacking police stations to be able to hand out food to the poor, and the idea of involving the masses in their struggle was something that appeared only in Montonero discussion documents and no longer in real life.

Their attacks on individual Army officers and their families increased, as the Army was brought more and more into the fight to control the Montoneros. But the guerrillas seem to have had little idea of the effect their campaign might have on the attitude of the military. They assumed that there would be a military coup at some stage, but they thought it would be on the old model, with stringent new laws and new efficiency, but also an adherence to the rules of the game, whereby people would be arrested and tortured for a while, but would then 'surface' as legal prisoners with certain minimum rights: the right to go on living, for instance. It does not seem to have occurred to anyone in the movement's leadership that they might instead be frightening and angering the armed forces to the point where any action – and particularly the introduction of mass 'disappearances' as a weapon – would be considered justified.

In the meantime, the death squads were preparing themselves. In 1974 two hundred murders, mostly of left-wing sympathizers, were reported in the Argentine press; during 1975 there were 850.

In the last month of Isabelita's government, March 1976, the newspaper *La Opinión* estimated that there was a political killing every five hours and a bomb attack every three. López Rega had fled the country, and Isabelita had signed a secret instruction to the armed forces to take any action they deemed fit in dealing with terrorism. They now knew exactly what form that action would take.

# 5 WAGING WORLD WAR THREE

'*First we will kill all the subversives; then we will kill their collaborators; then . . . their sympathizers, then . . . those who remain indifferent; and finally we will kill the timid.*' – General Iberico Saint Jean, Governor of Buenos Aires, May 1976.

Mrs Walker started a fire at the place in the garden behind the house where the family held their *asado* parties. To any neighbours who might have been looking on, it would have seemed an odd time of year to cook an *asado* – the Argentine equivalent of a barbecue – because it was June, Argentina's winter, in the year of the coup. But Edith Gardey Walker, a small woman in her late sixties, stayed out in her garden for some time, her slight figure bent over the barbecue pit, keeping the coals stoked up and piling on more fuel. She made a number of trips back and forth between her house and the garden, her arms full of material to burn. She carried stacks of magazines, scrapbooks and letters. Inside, shelves were cleared and the books were brought out to be burned; boxes were taken out of storage and emptied, their contents put on the *asador*. In the grey overcast light of a winter afternoon, Mrs Walker sadly turned the tangible proofs of her son's life and career into ashes and smoke. To encourage the papers to burn more quickly, she doused the bundles with petrol; as they burst into flames, she eliminated all traces of the work of her son, the journalist, Enrique Walker.

She says:

> He came to my house that June day, saying, they're after me now. He knew. 'Burn everything,' he said. 'Burn my papers, everything about me and things I've written and get rid of any dangerous books, and articles. And if they ever come to ask after me, just tell them that you haven't seen me for years,

because I'm a bad son. Tell them that I'm a rotter, that I've been a bad son to you.'

The Walkers, an Anglo-Argentine family who lived in the wealthy suburb of San Isidro about six miles outside of Buenos Aires, were fond of holding outdoor parties with their friends, children and grandchildren. An *asado* is one of those social occasions which all levels of Argentine society enjoy: it centres on the staple food of the pampas, beef. It is a simple meal of special cuts of beef, preferably sliced from the ribs of the cow so that each piece has a bit of bone attached for extra flavour when it is roasted on an open fire, accompanied with fresh pimento and onion. It was an ideal way for the Walkers to get their family together. They enjoyed each other's company enormously, since they were a collection of witty and argumentative individuals who sparred with one another over politics, sport, or any issue. Mrs Walker was the head of the household: a handsome woman with silver hair, a dark complexion and bright, dark eyes. She exuded a restless energy and determination, and at her age she had to have a certain amount of both in order to continue teaching boisterous schoolchildren every schoolday. In contrast, her husband was rather reserved and quiet. An Englishman who had come to Argentina as a young man, he belonged to the large Anglo-Argentine business community in Buenos Aires, working for a refrigeration company owned by the Vestey family in England. As a businessman and foreigner, he was conservative and therefore unlikely to dissent from the widely held view that the new military government was to be welcomed, given the previous violence and chaos. But the family stayed out of politics on the whole, though they had political connections. The Walkers' daughter, Vicky, who was thirty in 1976, had married into the Alsogaray family.

Dr Alsogaray had been Argentina's Economy Minister in the previous military government, and one of his brothers was a commander in the Army. Vicky had followed her mother into the teaching profession; they both worked at private English-language schools which spend almost as much time teaching junior schoolchildren about England's kings and queens as about the great Spanish conquistadors. Vicky also took after her mother in her talkative, argumentative character. But it was the older brother, Enrique, who really held the centre of attention when the family met. At thirty-five, he was a well-known journalist with a good sense of humour and an intense interest in what was happening in the world. He was close to his sister and parents but was not afraid to disagree with them about politics. He was also active in sports, excelling at rugby and polo.

They were a model upper-middle class family, and apparently typical supporters of the coup which had been carried out, in Videla's words, 'not to trample on liberty, but to consolidate it; not to twist justice, but to impose it.' But the family could not view events after the coup with equanimity, because Enrique was neither quiet nor cautious in voicing his increasing criticisms of the military.

He had started off as a law student, but gave his studies up when he became disenchanted with the devious methods lawyers often used to win their cases. His idealism convinced him that journalism would suit his character better, and he started in 1964 on the popular news magazine *Gente* as a reporter. Soon he became a star, and his personal accounts of visits to exotic places were given front-page treatment. *Gente* would make great play of the fact that it was Enrique Walker covering the story: 'Enrique Walker in the Siberian wastes', 'Enrique Walker in Rome', and in the mid-Sixties, at the height of the Vietnam War, 'Enrique reporting from Saigon'. His mother remembers this as a turning point:

> Saigon changed his life. I always blame his English blood for his travels – if he'd had a bit more of the Italian or Spanish blood in him, he would have stayed with his mother. But he was restless. When he went to Vietnam on a story about another Argentine journalist who had been killed there, he travelled from Paris on a plane which had four or five Americans on it. I was struck by what an impression that made on him; they were businessmen in some automobile business or other and they were only going there for the money they could make and weren't at all interested in those poor boys who were dying out there. The drugs problem, the attitude of the officers, the dead being sorted out in numbered bags, it all disgusted him. The experience made him more radical, less satisfied with the way society was.

In 1969 Enrique left *Gente* which was proving too establishment. The break came because the magazine timidly refused to publish pictures Enrique had taken of the *cordobazo*, the popular uprising in the city of Córdoba in May that year. His photographs of students' and workers' protests showed policemen acting as agents provocateurs, dressed as revolutionaries and carrying guns, apparently to bolster the government's claims that in killing some fourteen people during the unrest, they were defending the state against terrorism. When the magazine refused to print these highly damaging pictures or to run Enrique's exposé, he handed in his resignation. Soon he helped to start a weekly, *Nuevo Hombre*, which began as a left-wing independent paper and ended by reflecting Trotskyist views.

Enrique had moved further to the left because of Vietnam, according to his mother, but it was also conditions in Argentina itself which made him more radical.

> I think he became a socialist without realizing it. He was very critical of what was going on here in Argentina, although he was never a communist because he thought it wouldn't lead to more freedom, but less. We never used to believe the things he used to say about corruption scandals, the military men, things like that. He told us at the beginning of 1976 that there was a price-fixing deal which involved selling petrol to Paraguay which had gone on for seven years, with people high up pocketing the profits. He wasn't afraid. There was nothing he wouldn't publish. He would write about all of them; López Rega, Massera, even Videla.

After the distributors refused to handle copies of *Nuevo Hombre*, Enrique became a freelance writer, contributing to the left-wing Peronist paper *El Descamisado*. That was closed down by the government in April 1974, but Enrique continued to write in spite of the difficulties of finding editors who would accept his work. It was becoming nearly impossible for a mainstream left-wing journalist to carry on working, but no one in the Walker family was prepared for the onslaught which followed the coup of March 1976; no one, that is, except Enrique.

> He knew they were looking for him by June. I just don't know how he dared to come and see me that day, there were so many police around the neighbourhood. They were standing at every street corner in those months. After all, the former President General Onganía had his house just down the street from us and he was an obvious target for the guerrillas. Onganía's secret service men were investigating everyone who lived around here and were watching all of us, but Enrique still came to warn me.

> And I did as he told me; I burnt nearly everything, I'm afraid I don't have much of his work left – just a few copies of the early *Gentes*.

Four weeks later, Enrique disappeared. It was the evening of 17 July 1976, a Saturday night. He went to the cinema, possibly to meet a contact. It was safer to meet in public places than at home, because the intelligence services were less likely to be watching him away from his house. Enrique went to the Cinema Moreno at 5050 Rivadavia St, in Buenos Aires. He was watching the film when suddenly the lights of the cinema were turned on. A group of men, some in plain clothes and some in police uniforms, walked up and down the aisles looking for him. Enrique got out of his seat and tried to escape from the cinema, but the men grabbed him and dragged him outside. As he was taken out, he managed to shout out his name and telephone number to the people inside the cinema. No one attempted to interfere with the officers as he was shoved into a station-wagon and driven away, followed by another car full of men. There had been no arrest, no charges; no identification was shown by the officers or the men dressed in civilian clothes; everyone who witnessed Enrique's capture, though, knew what the operation meant: it was another action against a 'subversive', part of the round-up of terrorists and their collaborators.

Mrs Walker saw Enrique for the last time when he came to the school where she taught to see his son. He was separated from his wife, and the boy lived with her. Mrs Walker remembers that Enrique was nervous but apparently fatalistic about the chances of being picked up; several of his friends had already disappeared. Before he left, he reminded her to say that he was a bad son if anything happened to him, so that she would not get into trouble herself. At about one o'clock the following morning, the woman Enrique lived with, Helena Medici, telephoned Mrs Walker to say that Enrique had not returned home from the cinema, though she told her not to worry. But Mrs Walker did worry, and her fears were confirmed six hours later when Helena telephoned again to say that she had heard of Enrique's arrest. But no one knew which police station might have been involved, or whether it was the armed forces or an unofficial death squad like the Triple A who had taken him. There was no report on the kidnapping from any government office or security service and no one contacted the family to say he was under arrest. Enrique Walker had just disappeared.

> I couldn't believe it. You always think it won't happen to you, though I know it seems silly to say that; it was happening to other people maybe, but not to us. And it's still a mystery to me: Enrique must have said something to protect the rest of the family because they never came here to question us or look at what was in the house, or his wife's house. There's no answer to it.

Mrs Walker speaks without self-pity but with anger and sadness after the years of waiting, searching and hoping for some answers about her son's fate. But answers were very hard to come by. The temptation was to say nothing about the affair in public, in the hope that he might reappear, as occasionally happened. And there were other pressures to make her stay silent; neighbours and friends would often be afraid to be associated with a 'subversive', in case they too, came under suspicion. Like so many other people who found themselves in the same position, Mrs Walker felt completely alone. The day after the news of her son's abduction, she sent a telegram to President Videla's office and went to Buenos Aires to the Ministry of the Interior to report that he had been kidnapped. There was no reply from the President, and the Ministry simply made a note of her son's name, saying that there was no record of any charges against Enrique, and no notification of his arrest. But Mrs Walker noticed that she was not the only person asking for information; and by this time the government was receiving an average of ten complaints a day about disappearances. The following month, the Ministry of the Interior opened an official register where the names of missing persons could be entered by relatives, though they set a limit of forty complaints a day. When the Ministry was asked by an Amnesty International delegation who visited Argentina in 1976 how many of these complaints had been officially taken up, they were told that 150 were being investigated out of perhaps 2,000 officially registered by that time. Enrique Walker was not one of the 150 cases.

Mrs Walker decided to file a writ of habeas corpus with the central law court in the capital, demanding that her son either be charged by the government or freed. She went to a lawyer who was a friend of the family and he showed her how to write out a habeas corpus, and agreed to accompany her to the law courts. She couldn't use his name or identify him, because lawyers came under suspicion if they helped the families of missing persons, and might well join the ranks of the disappeared themselves. It was courageous of her friend to go with Mrs Walker to the courts, crowded as they were with police guards. '1976 was a very bad year for lawyers,' Mrs Walker recalls. 'No lawyers would take a habeas corpus writ to court. You had to do it yourself. So I went to the court and handed it to the judge in person.' Ten days later the writ came back: 'rechazado' – refused. The writ was not accepted because Enrique Walker had not been picked up according to the records of the police and military, so charges were obviously not being laid against him. Habeas corpus came to have no meaning, and offered no protection, because the authorities refused to admit that they were holding the people named. The ploy was foolproof.

Two hundred writs were filed at the central court of Buenos Aires in one week during May 1976, each relating to a case in the city. Elsewhere in Argentina, university towns were particularly affected by the wave of disappearances, and so were areas where there were big naval or military bases, or where there had been a record of labour militancy. Sometimes, though, the severity or otherwise of the military's campaign depended on the character of the general in command of a particular area; under extremists like Suárez Mason or Luciano Menéndez, the toll was always high. But in spite of the growing evidence for what was going on, Mrs Walker's husband, like the great majority of well-to-do Anglo-Argentines, refused to believe what she told him.

> I wasn't afraid myself, but he was. He was a real conservative Englishman, and he didn't want to know anything about what was going on in Argentina then. So I did everything myself. Every Friday I would go into town to ask about my son. I would hear rumours about him – that he was being held in an official prison, or maybe at some Army camp. I would get these rumours from his friends, but they came to nothing. I tried family contacts; for instance I went to a cousin who was in the Navy, because I knew that the Navy was picking people up. But people like that often used to refuse to help. You see, if someone in the military got involved, they could disappear too. Even people with really good connections got nowhere – the Press Secretary to one of our military Presidents, Lanusse, disappeared, and so did his car. When you heard of people like that disappearing, you really felt helpless. My own friends didn't want to help. Sometimes they would invent little stories

to explain why they could not do anything, and so I decided not to ask them to help because I didn't want to put myself in the position of losing friends because they said 'no'. Even when you heard of other families losing someone, they were still afraid and usually didn't talk about it.

Mrs Walker also tried the press, going to the independent newspaper *La Opinión* edited by Jacobo Timerman, who printed a story about her son the week he disappeared. She also went to the English-language newspaper, the *Buenos Aires Herald*.

They were marvellous. Nothing was ever too much trouble for them. The editor, Bob Cox, was always helpful. But I didn't go to the British Embassy for help, even though we had English connections through my husband. I would have been told to go there if they were any help, but I never considered them because I knew they weren't doing anything for anyone then.

The United States Embassy took up the case and there was help from abroad over the years that followed, including representations to the Argentine government from the US Congress, the United Nations, international journalists' unions, and the Organization of American States. But in Argentina itself, it was an isolated search with few results.

Three months after Enrique had been kidnapped, the woman he had been living with, Helena Medici, disappeared too. Her military contacts were closer than most people's – her father worked as a legal adviser to one of the departments of the Defence Ministry – and a few days later she telephoned the Walkers to say that she was all right, but that she was being held in custody somewhere. In spite of rumours that her father had managed to get her out of the country, it seems that she was being held at the Navy Mechanics School, and that she was later murdered.

In spite of his determination to ignore the situation as much as possible, Enrique's father was becoming increasingly affected by the thought of his son's disappearance. His daughter Vicky says it was gnawing away at him.

He was troubled in his conscience because of the disappearance but also because he had disagreed with Enrique's views and had been against subversives. Enrique was never with the ERP or the other guerrillas, but he probably supported some of their views. My father, I would say, suffered more than the rest of us because he hadn't liked Enrique being mixed up in these things and had opposed him but felt guilty about it. He was reserved and withdrawn, he didn't help with the search, he didn't want to know; he was like an ostrich. But the sorrow was gradually killing him. Then one day, the former President, Frondizi, said publicly that he didn't think any of the disappeared were still alive. The next day, my father died of a heart attack. The thought that Enrique was dead killea him.

After her husband's death, a man contacted Mrs Walker and said he could find out about Enrique for them; that he had ways of discovering where he was being held. He looked like a security man, they thought, tall, with fair hair, very Germanic-looking; but they decided to give him the money he asked for, so that he would make special enquiries for them. He kept stringing them along, promising that he would be in contact soon, but would always say that more money was necessary. For a long time they gave it to him, and Vicky, unknown to her mother, came up with extra funds as the blackmail terms grew harder to meet. He finally said that he could get a letter from Enrique out of the place where he was being kept, but asked Mrs Walker to write the first letter. That was enough for the family. They told him not to come back. But he did come back; he made one last attempt to extort money from them, turning up at their house, demanding money. It was Mothers' Day, Mrs Walker remembers. They told him to get out.

'My son was born in 1941, so now he's forty-three': she speaks as though he is still alive, while at other times, Enrique's mother slips into the past tense. The difficult thing is there is no final certainty – there is always some room for the remotest of hopes that he might be found.

After a time, Mrs Walker gets out of her armchair and goes back to the patio to call in her daughter and grandchildren. As the children are served cold drinks in the playroom she sits down once more and, looking down at the few cuttings and magazines she has left showing her son's career, she says, speaking quickly before she can change her mind: 'It is terrible to say it, but I have thought many times that he must be dead; maybe they killed him on the spot outside the cinema or after they took him away in the car; if he was killed early on, that would explain why they never came here to question us.' Vicky, listening on the other side of the room as she speaks, realizes that it is the first time her mother has ever admitted out loud that Enrique might no longer be alive. Eight years after his abduction it might, she believes, mark an end to her mother's torment of uncertainty: a torment worse than the certain knowledge of his death would ever have been.

Enrique Walker was one of the first victims of a new and improved way of dealing with political dissidents. Under Isabelita Perón, the Triple A had carried out its murders and dumped the victims' bodies in the streets as a warning to others. Under the new régime there would be few bodies, and the full extent of the repression would remain hidden. The combined leadership of the armed forces had various useful examples from which they could learn. In Chile, for example, General Pinochet had murdered a thousand or more of the Allende government's supporters within days of his coup in 1973. The action was known all over the world, as the bodies floated down the River Mapocho that runs through the centre of Santiago, or piled up along the sides of the roads. As a result there were protests throughout the Western world, Chilean goods were boycotted, and Chilean representatives vilified. In Uruguay, after the military coup in the same year, the military had gone in for the mass imprisonment of left-wing suspects – only to find that other prisoners and even some of the warders were being converted by them. Equally, in Argentina there was a strategy of mass detention, but there could be no question of allowing the detainees to live. When Héctor Cámpora had been elected President, three years before, his general amnesty of political prisoners had released six hundred hard-core urban guerrillas on to the streets and their campaign started all over again; this time there would be no publicity, and no one left alive to release. Suspects would be captured in secret, and put to death in secret, and no one would know who had done it.

The strategy was worked out in detail a good six months before the coup of March 1976 took place. General Videla, who had just taken over as commander-in-chief of the armed forces, called a meeting of officers of the rank of brigadier and above in conditions of great secrecy in August 1975. Accounts of it are sketchy, and sometimes conflicting, but they agree on the broad outlines. The conference was presented with the plan drawn up at Videla's request by the chiefs of staff of the three armed forces and their intelligence committees. It was read out and described at some length, and there was a debate. Three generals, one of whom is thought to have been Roberto Viola, briefly Videla's successor as

President in 1981 before being forced aside by Galtieri, argued against the plan, and voted against it when it came to a show of hands. In view of the otherwise unanimous acceptance, however, they gave in and accepted it themselves. On 23 October, two months later, Videla made a speech in Montevideo, the capital of Uruguay in which he was quoted as saying, 'In order to guarantee the security of the state, all the necessary people will die.' Later, questioned by a foreign journalist, he said he defined a subversive as 'anyone who opposes the Argentine way of life'.

The police, who had played an important part in the activities of the Triple A, would from now on be subordinated to the three armed forces in the campaign against subversion, as Videla defined it. The Ministry of the Interior co-ordinated the overall campaign, from the very building where the register of the names of people who had disappeared was based. There was a congruence about it all which may have pleased the military mind. The lists of suspects, from which the various task forces of the three services worked, had been drawn up by the different intelligence organizations, of which there was a proliferation. SIDE, the Service of State Information, was the chief security service, covering both internal and external intelligence, and had its headquarters on the Avenue of 25 May, in the centre of Buenos Aires. Each of the armed forces had its own intelligence service: SIE for the Army, SIN for the Navy, SIA for the Air Force. Each of these bodies had its own list of suspects, which was rarely if ever made available to other services, since all felt themselves to be in competition for the prestige – and increasingly the financial profit – of carrying out arrests. In addition, the federal police, the provincial police forces, the National Gendarmerie and the city police, all had their own independent intelligence operations and its own separate list of suspects. Several government ministries had intelligence services – the Interior Ministry, the Foreign Ministry, and so on. The state oil company, YPF, had one of its own, and presumably a list of suspects. Not surprisingly, since there was competition rather than co-operation between each of these groups, there was often little warning that an undercover operation was being staged by one or other of them; the service bodies would tell the police, but not each other. And since most operations were carried out by men dressed in civilian clothes, there were a number of cases of shoot-outs between the members of different security forces. The Ministry of the Interior, it has been said, held a master list of everyone arrested by the various intelligence services, and of what happened to them afterwards. Given the habitual carelessness of the security forces, the list was probably unreliable and it was almost certainly destroyed before the military left power.

The green, four-door, Ford Falcon saloon, standard issue for the police and government ministries, became the chief symbol of the terror. They would cruise slowly along the streets keeping a watch for suspects, or career down the middle of the road in convoys of three or more, packed with the men of the *patotas*, the arresting squads. *Patotas* varied in number from six to twenty or so, and the men in them usually carried pistols, as well as heavier arms such as sub-machine guns. Sometimes the Falcons they used had false markings, to make it look as though they belonged to state corporations like ENTEL, the state telephone company. Others had no markings, and no number plates. Not all the *patotas* used Falcons, however; some even used ambulances. Each *patota* belonging to a larger task force, or *grupo de tareas* (GT). GT 1 took its orders from the federal police and operated throughout Buenos Aires Province. GT 2 came under the Army, and received its orders from Army Intelligence. GT 3 belonged to the Navy, and one of its sub-divisions had the worst reputation of all: based at the Naval Mechanics School or ESMA, it counted among its members Lieutenant (later Lt Cdr) Alfredo Astiz. Finally, GT 4 belonged to the Air Force, and had its principal centre of operations at the Palomar Air Base, west of Buenos Aires.

Once the *patotas* has received their orders, they would carry out a reconnaissance and then move in. Most arrests were made late at night. The cars would wait down the street, while the driver stayed in communication with the others by radio, as well as feeding information to his base. The main group would hammer on the door, or simply break in; sometimes they showed their identity cards and even gave their real names, but for the most part there was no need: the people inside would be too frightened to ask. Because there had been occasional resistance from genuine members of urban guerrilla groups, the arresting officers would usually be on edge, and inclined to use violence at the slightest provocation. If there was resistance, they might be shot in what would later be reported as a 'shootout with terrorists'. The whole family, children and all, might be taken away, or simply the husband or perhaps his wife. They would be handcuffed and hooded or blindfolded, and taken down to the waiting car, where the normal practice was to shove them into the boot. While the prisoners were being taken away, the other members of the *patota* would get down to the congenial business of ransacking the home, usually taking anything that was resaleable or useful: clothes in particular. The smaller items, jewellery or silver, would be kept by the men themselves, but the larger objects and the clothes would be taken back for the group's 'war chest'; the clothes would be used for people who were already imprisoned. Relatives who witnessed what had happened would be told to say nothing, or perhaps that they would hear from the victims soon. The whole operation could always be denied by the authorities, or blamed on some left-wing group. When the police admitted that they had been told about an operation, which happened only occasionally, they would always say they could not intervene. It had taken place in what was known as 'the free zone' – an action which was authorized, and yet unofficial.

A new vocabulary grew up around the nightmarish state of affairs in which completely illegal actions were being carried out by the forces of law and order. Since there were no longer any unofficial kidnappings by guerrilla groups, the word *sucuestro*, or abduction, came to mean only the arrests carried out by the *patotas*. *Chupaderos*, coming from the word for 'suck', were the detention centres used by the security forces, in which the emphasis was often on the numbers arrested, not their importance as suspects. *Desaparecidos* were not simply missing persons any longer: they were specifically the victims of a strategy that ensured they would disappear for ever. The explanations occasionally produced by the authorities about those who had died, and whose death or disappearance could not for some reason be hidden, were cynical: they had faked their own abductions in order to go underground as terrorists; they had gone abroad for training; they had died in shoot-outs with other terrorists; they had been innocent bystanders killed during a battle between the security forces and the guerrillas; or they had been shot while attacking a police station or a military installation. The parents of a twenty-year-old agricultural student, Rosa Ana Frigerio, were told that their daughter was being held at Mar del Plata Naval Base after her arrest in August 1976. She was taken there in an ambulance, since she was in a plaster cast from her waist to her knees after a spinal operation. Later that year, the Navy informed them that she was no longer at the base, and when they filed a writ of habeas corpus in February 1977 the base commander told them that she was now being held at the disposal of the national executive power because of her involvement in subversive activities. A month later, her parents were telephoned again to be told that Rosa Ana had died in an 'armed confrontation' on 8 March and was buried in a cemetery nearby. The death certificate said she had died of 'cardiac arrest' and 'cardio-thoracic traumatism', but the Frigerio family was unable to get any explanation of how she came to be at liberty, or how she could have been fit enough to take part in a gun battle. The authorities refused to allow an exhumation of the body or to give a full account of the circumstances of her death.

After a Montonero attack on a national police headquarters, 30 corpses riddled with bullets were left near the town of Pilar. All were supposedly killed during the guerrilla attack, but the evidence pointed to their having been prisoners inside the police headquarters. They didn't look as if they had seen active combat, and their ties, shoelaces and belts had been removed – customary when someone is placed under police arrest.

But the fact that the Montoneros and the ERP were still active after the military coup helped to make the military's version of such events a little more credible. Since there were genuine subversives, the arrest and disappearance of innocent people became that much easier to accept. There were a number of horrific attacks in the first year of military rule, while the Montonero organization was still reasonably intact, which led to an even more savage backlash. The attacks were directed mainly against the police; the Montoneros did not at first realize that the Army and other military forces had assumed control over the counter-subversive campaign and that the police were no longer the prime actors. The bombing campaign struck down the Chief of Federal Police, General Césareo Cardozo, in the middle of June, after Ana Maria González, an eighteen-year-old Montonero, had made friends with the general's daughter. She gained entry to their house, and planted a bomb which exploded underneath the general's bed, killing him. Early in July, a nine-kilogram bomb went off at the federal police headquarters killing 25 policemen and injuring more than 60 officers in the dining-room. In September, a car bomb was detonated as a police bus passed alongside it, killing eleven policemen and two bystanders. The following month another police officer died when a bomb went off in La Plata provincial police headquarters.

There were also some attacks on the military during this time. In May 1976 the military man heading the committee which was organizing the 1978 World Cup was shot by five gunmen while walking across the street; President Videla was nearly assassinated by a bomb which had been placed underneath a platform at the Campo de Mayo Army Barracks: it exploded at the precise spot where he had been standing, minutes after he had moved on. Two weeks after that, there was an explosion at an officers' club cinema which injured at least 50 retired officers. On 15 December a large fragmentation bomb killed 14 senior military and intelligence men attending an anti-subversion conference in a Defence Ministry building in Buenos Aires. These attacks, although carried out by relatively few guerrillas, gave an exaggerated impression of a big underground organization which was still capable of striking at the very heart of the state. They were audacious and well-planned, and often relied on infiltration for their success, and this shook the confidence of the military, briefly.

The Montoneros' own publicity, and the dramatic attacks they carried out, appeared to justify the way the military were setting aside legality and going for the quickest, most ruthless methods. This in itself would not have been too disturbing for most people, as long as the terrorist threat was dealt with – they had become used to violence under the previous government. What the public did not realize was just how wide the meaning of 'subversive' had become. And when the evidence showed that it meant ordinary civilians, trade unionists, students, journalists, lawyers, doctors, artists and politicians, the majority of people still chose to believe the military's version of events. And even when the number of victims multiplied and stories circulated that few if any of them were reappearing, people still clutched at the idea that they must have been guilty of some kind of anti-state activity, and that the military were somehow right.

But it gradually became clear that the military's idea of subversion was not at all limited to left-wing terrorism. General Videla, in one speech, expressed the thought this way: 'A terrorist is not just someone with a gun or a bomb; he can also be someone who spreads ideas that are contrary to Western and Christian civilization.' Occasionally, the crimes that were being committed were ascribed to the 'excesses' of the military, as though they had simply been a little too enthusiastic in obeying orders. But there was always a clear division in the minds of the country's military leaders between the activities of the left-wing guerrillas and of those who were combatting them. In August 1976, at the United Nations, the Minister of Foreign Affairs, Admiral César Guzetti, put the military's excesses into context: 'My idea of subversion is that of the left-wing terrorist organizations. Subversion or terrorism of the right is not the same thing. When the social body of the country has been contaminated by a disease which eats away at its entrails, it forms antibodies. These antibodies cannot be considered in the same way as the microbes. As the government controls and destroys the guerrillas, the actions of the antibodies will disappear. This is already happening. It is only the reaction of a sick body.'

The windows are shuttered, and the curtains are drawn even in the daytime, so that there is not much light from the hallway; but the door is seldom opened. The rest of the house, a nineteenth-century building which has so far survived the Argentine mania for demolition and the construction of apartment blocks, is worn and comfortable. It is shabby and disregarded, but there is a certain elegance to it all the same. But the front room, to the right of the entrance hall, has an odd feeling of modernity about it; it is the best cared for, and yet the least lived in. The books on the shelves are dusty, and the papers piled on the desk have remained unread for years. Many of the papers are dated November 1976. A calendar hanging on the wall shows the same month, the same year. Next to the desk is a reclining chair; on the wall, a diploma in the name of Dr Alberto José Pargament. Tne books include Jung and Freud, and more modern American works on psychology and medicine.

Alberto Pargament, a practising psychiatrist, worked from his mother's house, and the room doubled as his office and his surgery. He was well known in his field, writing frequently for foreign publications, and he lived for his work, sometimes staying at his desk until midnight. Some of the bundles of papers stacked on it bear dates later than 1976. There are ten of them, all signed by Mrs Juanita Pargament, his mother, and they are all writs of habeas corpus, issued in the name of her son, who was arrested on 10 November 1976. Not one of them has been accepted by the courts. The bundles of paper are the only things Alberto Pargament would not recognize about the room; everything else has been kept exactly as he left it that evening.

It was half-past ten at night when Alberto finished with the last patient of the day. He cleared up hurriedly, knowing that he had promised to be at home by now, in another part of the city. His mother said goodnight to him. She enjoyed the fact that he worked at her house, because she had been very close to Alberto; he was her only son and her husband had died when the boy was very young. Four hours later, at two in the morning, nine heavily-armed men knocked at the door of Alberto's apartment. When he got to the door, they pushed it open, asking whether a doctor lived there. Alberto said he was a doctor, and some of the men seized him; the others searched the apartment, going into the bedroom where Alberto's wife was lying in bed, listening anxiously to the conversation out in the hall. They left her alone, telling her not to take any notice and to stay in bed. She obeyed their instructions and Alberto was taken away. His wife left the house later, guessing that the men might return. They did, the next afternoon, breaking the door down and ransacking the apartment. All of Alberto's books were taken away.

Earlier that year, the Pargament family had listened to radio broadcasts in which military and academic speakers had warned that psychiatrists were ideologically dangerous because they had a tendency to subversive ideas. The military, it seemed, associated psychiatry with Freud, and Freud with foreign, especially Jewish interests; at some stage in the complex process, they had decided that Freud was linked with Communism. The only type of psychoanalysis which it was safe to practice in Argentina after the coup was a version which took no account whatever of Freud. But Pargament continued to practise as before, deciding that it wasn't necessary to leave the country, as many of his colleagues had. He may have been taken because his name was noted down in the diary of one of his patients who had been picked up as a subversive. Or perhaps his name was on a list compiled by one of the intelligence services because he had contacts abroad, read foreign literature and practised a questionable occupation. What is certain is that he had no association with guerrillas or left-wing organizations.

The family could discover nothing about where Alberto had been taken, despite the habeas corpus writs and the visits to the authorities. But when Mrs Pargament sought information about her son, and continued to go to the Interior Ministry and police, her persistence began to irritate someone. The outside of her house was painted one night with slogans saying 'Beware of subversives inside' and 'Terrorists', which made her neighbours nervous of associating with her, let alone of giving her any support. 'Everyone behaved as if they had a wall around them. People were afraid to give sympathy,' she remembers. 'And no one would say anything about what they had seen. No one at the police station or in the military would help. They had a *pacto de sangre*, a blood pact, so everyone was involved and nobody would say what was happening.' Both Alberto's wife and Mrs Pargament moved out of their homes for a time after the disappearance because they were frightened of being taken themselves.

When Mrs Pargament went back to her house to pick up some clothes a few days after Alberto's abduction she found a group of former patients waiting outside for their normal appointments. 'They said to me, "Where is Dr Pargament today? Why doesn't he want to see me anymore? Explain it to me, I can't believe that he would go away and not tell me!" I couldn't tell them anything about it. I couldn't explain anything, all I knew was that a group of men had taken him at two in the morning. That's all.' She had heard nothing since and knew nothing more. It wasn't until one and a half months later that a phone call came to a member of her family. The call was taken by a servant. It was a voice from the interior, from the country, a provincial voice. 'I am calling in the name of Dr José Pargament. I want you to take a note that the doctor has had a little accident but now he's alright,' the voice said. The servant asked, 'Do you mean Alberto?' The reply was, 'No, I'm talking about José Pargament. He's had a little accident but now he's all right. I will be calling again with more details.' There was nothing else. Mrs Pargament hoped this call was about her son; his middle name was José, so that might explain the muddle, but it was a strange message. They never heard from the mystery caller again and got no more information.

> I am sure it was the military, with the police from the federal headquarters, who took my son. But I want to know the actual criminals who kidnapped him. Alberto's boy will want to know some day who his father was; he'll want to know the real story when he is older. I want to know for him. From the time they took my son I have always hoped he would return; and I cleaned his room for him, then shut it, leaving everything here for him as it was when he went away. Every day has passed slowly. Now it is so many years, but a mother has some hopes that she will some day hear about her son.

Mrs Pargament spreads out her photographs of Alberto on the beach, Alberto posing with his friends, Alberto as a small boy gazing solemnly at the camera. She also holds out a picture of herself. In the years since his disappearance she has aged a good deal. Now her hair is almost entirely grey, her sight has worsened and she wears green-tinted glasses to shade her eyes from the sun, much as she shades her son's empty room by the use of curtains and shutters. She is embarrassed about the change in her appearance, and realizes that it is necessary to mention it in some way. She holds out the family album. 'That's me,' she says with a note almost of apology in her voice, pointing to her younger, happier self.

# 6 THE MURDER MACHINE

*'These people – they tortured and murdered and stole, they were an occupying army which spoke our language.'* – Mrs Nelva Falcone.

Eight months after the coup, in November 1976, Amnesty International was finally allowed to visit Argentina. The purpose of the mission was to gather facts about the abuses of human rights and the conditions in which prisoners there were being held. The report which Amnesty produced, several months later, was a model of its kind: in spite of the official restrictions which had been placed on the mission, it proved possible to give a picture of conditions in Argentina which was startlingly accurate, and which stands up well to examination even after all the disclosures which followed the final collapse of the military government. Its only failing is that, dreadful though many of the cases which it documented were, what was happening in the clandestine gaols where the Amnesty mission was not permitted to go, and from which few people had emerged alive at that stage, was more dreadful still.

But there was no shortage of people prepared to come forward and give details of the treatment they had received, in spite of the likelihood of reprisals. And even when Lord Avebury, who was heading the Amnesty mission, was allowed to visit the official detention centre at Villa Devoto outside Buenos Aires, several of the women who were held there gave him detailed accounts of the torture and ill-treatment they and others had suffered, even though they were obliged to speak to him in the presence of prison officials. For them, clearly, it was more important that the world at large should know what was happening, than that they should try to keep out of trouble with their captors.

There were other official detention centres at La Plata, Olmos, and Sierra Chica (all in the province of Buenos Aires), together with three in the province of Córdoba and one each in Santa Fe, Chubut and Chaco. Conditions were bad at most of them, and brutality was commonplace. Prisoners complained in particular about their treatment when they were being transferred from one prison to another. One woman described how she was moved from Olmos to Villa Devoto in October 1976: they were beaten repeatedly with truncheons and forced to stand up in the meat vans they were transported in. Throughout the day, from six in the morning to six at night, they were given nothing to eat. Another woman who had a newborn baby with her was unable to feed it during the journey because she was handcuffed. A man who had been held at Sierra Chica said that when they arrived by plane at Azul airport they were taken off and showered with blows, and had to lie face down on the ground until the lorry which was to take them to their prison arrived. They were beaten as they ran to the lorry, and at Sierra Chica they were beaten again, with truncheons and gun butts. The savagery of the beating was so great that while one of the guards was hitting a prisoner with his gun, it went off accidentally and killed another guard beside him. Inside, the brutality continued:

> Naked, flat on our backs in the corridors, prohibited from looking at one another, we were questioned about our activities outside: trade unions, political parties, etc. We were beaten with rubber sticks with steel centres. They would pick us out at random for prolonged beating. These night-time disturbances created an apprehensive and nervous silence among us. We never knew which of us would be beaten that night.

But it has to be stressed that these were, to some extent, official prisoners: people whose arrest and detention was officially registered, and who therefore had to be accounted for in some way. There were, it is true, a number of cases of summary executions, disguised as shooting during the course of an attempt at escape or a riot as at Villa Devoto; but for the most part those who were held in prison, though systematically maltreated, were likely to survive. For those who had simply 'disappeared', who had been kidnapped by an unknown group of men and taken to an unknown destination, there were no restraints at all. People could be tortured there until they died, and many of them were.

It is possible that the names of all the clandestine gaols may never be known; there are believed to have been more than three hundred altogether. Many have been located only by vague indications: the fact that guard dogs could be heard barking nearby, or that planes flew overhead, or that trains passed close to the buildings, or that guards' conversations were overheard. In some of the clandestine gaols prisoners passed their whole time, from the moment they arrived to the moment they left, with their heads covered by hoods or their eyes blindfolded; and it is possible that no one at all emerged alive from one or two of the gaols. Nevertheless, the following are the main ones:

In Buenos Aires itself: Escuela de Mecánica de la Armada, or ESMA – the Navy Mechanics School – which was called, without too much hyperbole, the Auschwitz of Argentina, and was probably the worst, both in terms of treatment and of numbers; the Navy Prefecture; the Police Superintendencia, or headquarters; Orletti and the Club Atlético, both run by the police as well; Olimpo and Palermo, run by the First Army Corps; and a number of police stations around the city.

In the province of Buenos Aires: El Banco, Vesubio, and Ezeiza, which were also run by the First Army Corps: Quilmes, Banfield and Villa Budge, all run by the provincial police; La Cacha (First Army Corps), Arana and two police stations in the provincial capital, La Plata (all run by the provincial police), and several others which were run variously by the Marines, the Army Command, the First Air Brigade, and so on; as well as centres of Mar del Plata, Puerto Belgrano and elsewhere, which were under the Navy's control.

In the other provinces of Argentina there were fifteen camps.

It is impossible to know how many prisoners were held altogether, or even how many might be held at any one time, but at the Navy Mechanics School, which was probably the biggest, there were about fifty or sixty prisoners at any one time, and after a big series of raids there might be as many as a hundred. The population at ESMA, as at the other clandestine gaols, was continually changing, as prisoners were brought in, tortured, and then taken out for execution. Only a small proportion stayed for any great length of time, or indeed survived at all.

The methods of torture varied, from prison to prison and from torturer to torturer. But there were a number which were common to all. The electric cattle prod, the *picana*, for instance, was used in all the official as well as the clandestine prisons. So was the method known as the *submarino*, in which the prisoner was lowered into a bath of water with his or her head covered by a cloth hood which stuck to the nose and mouth when it became wet and made breathing almost impossible. In a number of places, police dogs were set on prisoners; some people died in this way. In almost all the clandestine prisons, men as well as women were liable to be sexually abused and raped by their guards, and many of the torturers paid a particular and sadistic attention to women who were pregnant.

A nursery school teacher of 27, Isabel Gamba de Negrotti, who was kidnapped from her home together with her husband, was taken to a police station, *Comisaria* 39, in the Buenos Aires suburb of Villa Urquiza. She was beaten, although she was pregnant, and began to have cramp spasms. She could hear her husband screaming in another part of the building. The next day she was taken to the police headquarters in Buenos Aires:

> They took me to another room where they kicked me and punched me in the head. Then they undressed me and beat me on the legs, buttocks and shoulders with something made of rubber. This lasted a long time. I fell down several times and they made me stand by supporting myself on a table. They carried on beating me. While all this was going on they talked to me, insulted me and asked me about people I didn't know and things I didn't understand. I pleaded with them to leave me alone, or else I would lose my baby. I hadn't the strength to speak, the pain was so bad.
>
> They started to give me electric shocks on my breasts, the side of my body, and under my arms. They kept questioning me. They gave me electric shocks in the vagina and put a pillow over my mouth to stop me screaming. Someone they called the 'colonel' came and said they were going to increase the voltage until I talked. They kept throwing water over my body and applying electric shocks all over.

Two days later, Isabel Negrotti miscarried.

Two men, Oscar González and Horacio Cid de la Paz, have given an account of their treatment at the secret detention centre known as 'Club Atlético', which was on Independencia Street and Paseo Colón in Buenos Aires. The building, like those of many other clandestine centres, was later destroyed, presumably to cover the traces of those who had used it. It was in operation from mid-1976 to the end of 1977. Both men were tortured on various occasions in one of the camp's three 'operating theatres'. Each operating theatre contained simply a table and the *picana* – the electric prod. It was, they said, a sinister place, the walls splashed with blood, and the air filled with the stench of burning flesh, blood, sweat and excrement. There was no ventilation. The torturers maintained a curiously efficient shift pattern, and on the door was pinned a notice which read as follows:

| *Interrogator* | *Group* | *Case no.* | *Time of starting* | *Finishing* | *State* |
|---|---|---|---|---|---|
| 'Blanco' | GT3 | X–15 | 5/4/77–1100 | 1900 | Normal |
| 'Turco' | GT3 | H–23 | 6/4/77–0800 | 2100 | Dead |
| 'Raúl' | ICIA | L–70 | 6/4/77–1200 | 1700 | Normal |

González and de la Paz also reconstructed from memory an even more disturbing document, a 'Notice of Final Resolution'; this carried the name and details of each person's case, and then listed thirteen different types of offence or subversive experience which were supposed to have applied to him or her. These included knowledge of weapons, painting slogans on walls, hiding people in their houses, belonging to political groups and taking part in murders. Another form graded them into one of three degrees: potentially dangerous, dangerous, and extremely dangerous. The last document dealt with the 'Final Resolution' itself:

| | *D.F.* (*destino final*, presumably death) | *P.E.N.* (*Poder Ejecutivo Nacional*, meaning imprisonment) | *Otras* (Others) |
|---|---|---|---|
| Interrogator | | | |
| Chief of Sub-Zone | | | |
| Commander, 1 Army Corps | | | |

The clandestine gaols were not intended to be places where people would be held indefinitely; they were interrogation centres, and on the basis – so the theory went – of what was learned during their interrogation, the prisoners' fate was decided. But so many innocent people were taken there, and the mutilations inflicted on them were often so great, that there was no alternative but to kill them. The business of grading the prisoners seems to have been more the result of a desire to appear to be working to a clearly-defined system than an exercise that had real value in itself. Nevertheless there was a degree of efficiency in the transmission of the details of each case to the Interior Ministry. The Ministry is said to have drawn up daily lists of people arrested, tortured and killed, though every one of those lists later disappeared. There was a considerable amount of disorganization in practice, but in general terms the military government had a clear idea of what was happening from day to day. And even if the hard evidence to prove it no longer exists, the incoming civilian government found one or two documents which had survived the otherwise thorough process of weeding out: a letter received by the President's office in June 1976, for instance, which says that a group of military men based at the morgue in Córdoba had been doing a good job, but that the morticians there wanted their work regraded as hazardous because the bodies they had to deal with were those of people who had been executed by shooting after torture. And at La Pampa a careful official had filed his copy of a general order which said that every document to do with disappearances and executions must be destroyed.

The basic principle behind the 1976 coup was to smash subversion in all its forms, and right from the start it was clear to the military leadership that subversion could not be adequately smashed if people were simply held in prison. Previous governments had tried that, and the problem simply arose again. This time the subversives would be physically exterminated. A good deal of planning went into working out the methods: shooting was the most common, though the Navy favoured dropping people alive, and sometimes conscious, out of planes; the nickname for that solution was 'doorless flights'. A former member of the armed forces who took refuge in Bolivia claimed that bodies were also packed into containers, the living with the dead, and dumped out at sea; but this has not been verified. The Army, too, dropped some bodies from planes, mostly in the province of Tucumán where the ERP guerrillas were fighting their losing campaign: it was a way of disheartening the guerrillas, as well as of providing an explanation of sorts for the bodies, which could always be passed off as those of terrorists killed in action.

But for the Army, the simplest if not the most secret method was to drive the corpses of the dead to the cemeteries in trucks, and have them registered there as 'NN' – no name. A certain number of bodies come in this way to every cemetery, the victims of 'road accidents' or of some other circumstance which makes it impossible for them to be identified. In Argentina, these bodies would be buried, usually by the cemetery workers themselves, in the poorest and least cared-for plots. So there was no difficulty in locating them when the military left power and the democratic government of Dr Alfonsín took over. The digging-up of remains went on all over Argentina for two or three months at the end of 1983 and the beginning of 1984; and the various human rights groups put out a call to the relatives of people who had disappeared, asking them for details of bone fractures which their sons or daughters, husbands or wives, might have suffered in the past. It was one faint possibility for identifying the otherwise anonymous remains. Otherwise, most people are still left not knowing how those they have lost met their deaths.

The régime which wrecked the Argentine economy and fought an unnecessary war so badly that it was forced out of office in disgrace nevertheless managed to kill eleven thousand people and hide the evidence. The NN graves, the doorless flights, the operating theatres where the instruments were the *picana* and the butcher's knife, were the symbols of the régime's sole success.

On the edge of a noisy, assertive group of people, several of whom are talking at once, stands a woman in her middle fifties; quiet, distracted, slightly ineffectual, she looks from one face to another and listens to what is being said, but says nothing herself. She is a large woman, handsome and well turned out. She has the build and the looks to dominate the conversation, but not the necessary bent of mind. She is the kind of woman you might see walking down Hampstead High Street, or the Boulevard Saint Germain: the well-to-do middle-class matron, on her way to a coffee morning or an expensive shop of some kind, perhaps trailing a sleek little dog on a lead. Nelva Falcone is precisely the Argentine equivalent. Her husband was a doctor and the mayor of La Plata, near Buenos Aires, a provincial capital and a university town. He suffered from a bad heart, but otherwise they lived a pleasant, affluent life with their two children, a son of twenty-two and a daughter of sixteen: a close-knit family group, well protected from the economic problems that the country as a whole was experiencing. Not, however, particularly well protected from political vicissitudes: her husband was a Peronist, and was therefore liable for immediate dismissal from office when the military took over government in 1976. But that was the price which politicians expected to pay in Argentina. On past experience, they would simply have to keep their heads down and wait for the return of civilian rule – nothing more unpleasant than that. Times, however, had changed. The violence between left and right during the early Seventies had forced a great many people to take sides; and given that Dr Falcone was himself on the left wing of the Peronist movement it is not surprising that the two Falcone children should have been Montonero supporters. But their support was moral rather than active. Jorge Falcone, the twenty-two-year old, who was married, and an artist, had been a member of the Peronist University Youth, the JUP, and directly after the coup took place he and his wife went into hiding in Buenos Aires. The Falcones' daughter, María Claudia, was also involved in politics: she was the delegate from her school to the Union of Secondary School Students. On 16 September 1976 María Claudia was arrested and taken to an unknown place of imprisonment. Her parents never saw her again.

Nelva Falcone sits in a bare, dusty office in Buenos Aires, with the noise of voices coming from downstairs as the other mothers of disappeared children carry on their loud discussions without her. Talking about what happened to her small, happy, conventional family during the year that followed María Claudia's arrest is not easy for her. Her hands, well-manicured and with rings on most of the fingers, are rarely still as she talks; she clasps and unclasps them, looking absently at them, twisting the rings around, and examining the carefully painted nails without being aware of it. It seems impossible that a woman like this should have undergone anything more difficult in her life than having to sack a housemaid who is careless with the china; but the stress which is plainly present when she speaks, and the left eyelid which droops and closes independently of the other from time to time, tell a story of their own. For a woman like Mrs Falcone to undergo the experiences she related, all the restraints on a society, moral or practical, would have to be removed. No one would be secure. For the next seven months, their daughter missing and their son in hiding, the Falcones lived an unhappy and uncertain life alone; though they were not afraid, since they had nothing to be afraid of: the worst, they assumed, had already happened. But it had not. On 13 April 1977 a group of heavily-armed men – two three-men *patotas* – came to the house. The Falcones let them in without question, and they began immediately to ransack the house. They did it professionally, hardly speaking to Dr Falcone, or his wife, and taking no notice of their outraged complaints. Then they separated them, and hooded them, and drove them off in different cars to a place fifteen minutes' drive away, which they were never able to identify. Dr Falcone was questioned immediately; his wife was left alone, still hooded, sitting on a chair and listening to the terrifying sounds of a detention centre, and trying to work out what they meant. Her husband meanwhile was faced with two interrogators, who wanted to know where their son Jorge was, and what had happened to two friends of the family, a man and a woman, who were doctors: the woman, who was pregnant, was later arrested and shot, while the man managed to escape to Spain. Dr Falcone told his questioners nothing about any of them, in spite of occasional threats of physical ill-treatment.

For the next five days they were held in a place which Mrs Falcone even now finds it hard to describe: a large room divided into a number of small barbed-wire hutches, with mattresses in each to which they were handcuffed. There appeared to be no windows or doors in the room. The other hutches were occupied by people who were hooded, like themselves, but who were mostly a good deal younger: the age of their children. The Falcones were not tortured or physically ill-treated, and they were reasonably well fed while they were there. Eventually they were told they would be released. The gang that came to arrest them had, it turned out, locked up the house, and the keys, together with the things that had been taken from them when they arrived at the detention centre – watches, rings, a cross Mrs Falcone wore around her neck – were handed back to them. They were once again put into separate cars and driven round for fifteen minutes or so, still hooded, and then finally pushed out at a place only about two blocks away from where they lived.

It had been an unpleasant and frightening experience; still, no real harm had come to them. Their house had been roughly searched and some small things were missing, but they were easily able to settle down again into their lonely, melancholy routine together. They had not been held prisoner for long enough or treated badly enough for Dr Falcone's heart condition to have been aggravated by what had happened. They may have considered leaving the country, though not with any seriousness; their children were still presumably in Argentina, and would at some stage need their help, assuming they saw them again. Besides, there was the feeling that they had already suffered for the fact that their son and daughter were regarded as subversive; lightning, they argued, did not strike in the same place twice.

Their son Jorge remained free in Buenos Aires. He and his wife had found somewhere else to live, and had taken another name. From time to time Mrs Falcone or her husband would meet them, or Jorge alone, always in a different place, always carefully and secretly arranged in advance. Then on 14 January 1978 they had a call from him: he had to meet them urgently. When they arrived at the rendezvous, he and his wife were both there. He explained that the man who ran a local food-store had tipped him off that the police had been around, asking questions, and looking for an artist whose wife was pregnant. Jorge, his cover gone, knew that he would have to move away fast. He had made arrangements for the pair of them to go and live with friends, but he wanted his parents to go to the house where they had been living and pick up some clothes and other things for them. They had both left the place directly Jorge had heard that the police were closing in on him.

Mrs Falcone and her husband decided that they would move everything out of the house, because it belonged to friends and they did not want them to get into trouble. And perhaps because they were that kind of people, they called in a removals firm to take the things away, on the assumption that the police did not know the exact address where Jorge and his wife had been living. The removal men emptied the house, furniture and all, and the Falcones supervised them, or else sat in their car outside and waited. When everything was packed into the van it drove off, and they followed it.

A short way down the street they ran into an ambush. They were forced out of their car at gunpoint, searched, blindfolded and put into another car. The suddenness of the operation, after the nervous business of clearing the house and the tension that followed, was terrifying. Mrs Falcone shouted out at one point that her husband had a bad heart, and they should treat him gently, but they took no notice. This time it was a long drive, through the city streets and along one of the networks of motorways that the military government was building. In spite of the blindfold, that at least was obvious to Mrs Falcone because of the long stretch of open road and the toll-gate they passed through. She later discovered that the place they were being taken to was a police barracks called El Banco.

A short spur road off the motorway to Ezeiza airport leads to El Banco: a conventional police barracks with a high gateway guarded by stocky, dark-faced policemen and a main block painted white with a grimy Argentine flag flying from the flagpole. Set some way away from the main building, and over to the right as you face the gateway, lie the barracks proper – a rectangle with single-storey buildings surrounding a central square of beaten earth and a little scrubby grass. The whole complex is easily visible from the motorway, which it overlooks. Even under a civilian government and a new approach altogether to the question of human rights and the past, El Banco is a difficult place to enter. When the Government Commission on the Disappeared paid a formal visit to it in April 1984, five months after the change of government, the atmosphere was so tense that the Commission members decided not to allow any journalists to accompany them in case the officers there should use that as an excuse to cancel the visit.

Mrs Falcone and her husband felt the jolting of the car and the slowing of speed which indicated that they had left the motorway and were on the spur which would take them into the barracks. When they were pushed out of the car and stood in the courtyard, they could tell in spite of their blindfolds that it was a big place. They went through a form of registration in which they were asked their names. When they replied to the questioner they could not see, they were told that they were no longer Dr and Mrs Falcone, but simply 'D 86' and 'D 87'. They were ordered to take off all their clothes, and Mrs Falcone was given a dress to wear, while her husband was given back his underpants but nothing more. One of the men in charge of registering them called out to someone else, 'One is okay, the other isn't'; and even at that stage Mrs Falcone realized that it was likely that he was talking about their suitability for torture, and that her husband's heart condition had been noted. It was the beginning of perhaps the worst two hours of her life.

Her husband was taken away and put in a cell, while she was taken to what the police called the 'surgery ward', which was where they did the torturing. The thin dress was taken off her and she was put down naked on to a table with a metal top, and a metal ring was put on the little finger of her left hand and the little toe of her left foot. She did not struggle. The shame of lying there naked, and the paralysing effect of the suddenness and the fear left her with no strength to resist physically; but even at that moment, she decided that she would say nothing whatsoever about her son's whereabouts.

They began by running the electric prod, the *picana*, up and down her legs, asking her as she jolted and shook on the metal table where her son was, and when she had last seen him. She scarcely answered, too shocked by the pain to say anything coherent.

'You've been collaborating with the enemy,' one of the men shouted.

'I only helped him to move because I love him, because he's my son,' she said. It angered them, and they changed their tactics, using the *picana* on her genitals, her breasts, her eyes, her gums. Her mouth started bleeding from the strength of the current, and they hit her as she lay there, shouting out questions at her, accusing her, threatening her. All she did was to repeat that she had nothing to do with politics, that she was just behaving as any mother would. 'I can't understand what you want,' she cried out in between the continuing shocks and the blows. 'Why are you doing this to me?'

Recalling it, in the dusty office with the voices of her friends still floating up from the main meeting room below, Mrs Falcone goes through her account carefully, repeating what she has repeated many times before, but pulling at her necklace and frowning hard as she talks about the pain and the humiliation, her left eyelid twitching and closing. The details are clear and settled in her mind, but the feelings it aroused have not been exorcized.

Her husband had been checked by a doctor in the meantime, and it had been decided at the examination that if he were tortured there would be a strong likelihood that he would die immediately, and would as a result have nothing to say. But the doctor had confirmed that there was no such objection to Dr Falcone's being forced to watch his wife while she was being tortured. So as Mrs Falcone lay on the metal table the door opened and her husband was brought into the 'surgery ward'. She could see that he was getting paler and paler, and looked very ill, but for them to be in the same room gave each of them a greater strength to resist the questioning. The torturers plied the electric prod, and Mrs Falcone lay on the table and screamed, and the urine she could not control flowed down her legs, but neither of them would say anything about their son. Perhaps if they had simply threatened to torture his wife, Falcone might have broken down; but since she withstood it, he withstood it as well. At the end of two hours the torturers gave up in disgust. They disconnected the *picana* and took the rings off her finger and her toe, and threw her the dress she had been given. Her body aching and sweaty, she put it on, ashamed of being soiled and dirty, but proud that in spite of everything she had not given way. She was taken to a cell, where she could hear her husband being questioned in the cubicle next door. Later, someone came in with a mattress that stank of urine and was stained with blood, and threw it on the floor. At first she was too appalled to touch it, but eventually she decided that she was feeling so bad she would have to lie down on it.

For the next two days she was not tortured, but her captors would come into her cell from time to time and ask the kind of questions that made her feel that she, and they, and everything else had become insane. Did she speak French to her children at home? Did she speak English to them? What religion was she? Did she practise her Catholicism? Was she Jewish? They had a particular hatred for Jews, it seemed. Some of the questions were so bizarre it was hard to answer them. As for the language that she used when at home with her children, she explained that she had been a teacher and knew some French and English, but did not speak them to her children. Then the questioners would leave her. Opposite her cell, across the corridor, someone else was being tortured, and the screams were more than Nelva Falcone could bear. She shouted out loud, 'Please stop it, for God's sake,' and the footsteps came in the corridor and the door opened, and the questioners were back again. Did she know the person who was being tortured? Why had she cried out, if she didn't know them? Was she Jewish? Did she know any of the Mothers of the Plaza de Mayo? Was she a supporter of the Mothers?

On 16 January, two days after their arrest, Dr Falcone was taken back to their house in La Plata by three men from the federal police. He did not realize why at first, but the purpose was for him to answer the telephone if his son tried to get through. They waited in the house for two full days, but Jorge didn't ring. On the 18th, the policemen decided to give it up, and the four of them were just leaving, with the front door open, when the phone sounded. It was Jorge. By this time his father had been coached as to what he should say: that Nelva Falcone had had a car accident, and was in such and such a hospital. Dr Falcone had worked out what he was going to do, and as he went through the concocted story for Jorge's benefit he confused the details so much that it was obvious it was phoney. One of the policemen, losing his temper, banged his fist down on the phone to cut it off, and he and his two companions set about Falcone in revenge. They seemed to concentrate on his chest, and beat him so severely that it was later found they had ruptured his aorta vein. Then they took him back to El Banco.

Mrs Falcone, in the meantime, had been suffering further torment. On 17 January they announced to her that she was going in front of a firing squad. They took her to 'the war chest', where they kept clothes which had been stolen from people held at the barracks, and told her to get something to cover herself. But she found that most of the other women prisoners were young, and thinner and smaller than she was, and all that she could come up with was a skimpy nightgown. It increased the sense of humiliation and misery in a way that the guards had perhaps not realized. They took her into the yard at the back of the barracks, away from the motorway, and although she was hooded she could feel the grass under her bare feet, and smell the distinctive odour of washing drying on a clothes line. In what she believed to be her last minutes, her senses were particularly acute. The police went through an elaborate charade, pretending to telephone a Buenos Aires cemetery to let them know that another body was on its way. Someone else said something about giving her the 'Nirvana treatment'. Beside her, another policeman started talking to her, and perhaps because she felt she was about to die she started to pour out everything she felt to him. It was horrifying, what they had done to her, she said; she was entirely innocent, and she knew nothing about where her son was. Why were they doing all this to a mother? 'You're going home,' he said. It wasn't a euphemism; he meant it literally, perhaps he was touched by her outburst, but she assumed that he was telling her she was about to die. He gave her a glass of water, but she refused to drink it, thinking that it might be drugged; she had heard about the 'doorless flights' even at that stage – the helicopters loaded with unconscious bodies which were dropped over the Plate estuary. By this time she was standing against a wall. The policeman realized that she had misunderstood him. 'We've changed the policy now,' he said. 'We aren't killing relations or neighbours any more.'

She was taken back to the 'surgery ward', dreading that at any moment she would be tortured again. But she was left alone there for two days, at the end of which her husband was brought in, looking very ill. After that, they were transferred to another cell which was called 'the Tube': two metres long, two metres high, and only eighty centimetres wide – the width and length of a single bed. They lay there, side by side, talking occasionally in whispers but too afraid of attracting the notice and the anger of the guards to say much. Once a day, at noon, they were allowed out to a meal. They had to line up with other prisoners, all of them blindfolded, their hands on the shoulders of the person in front of them. Sometimes they heard people talking in low whispers, and they learned that the others were being held in cells underneath the barracks, that they called 'the hole', because it was such a clandestine, forgotten, hidden place that it was like being out of sight of the whole world. The younger, more active prisoners wore leg-irons; Mrs Falcone could hear the metal clinking as they walked. They sat around a table to eat their meal, guarded by four policemen who were armed with night-sticks. Often the guards would lash out at them with the sticks, screaming insults at them and knocking their plates to the ground on the slightest pretext. But even when they were left in peace to eat their food, it was poor stuff: watery soup with rice or noodles, and occasionally a small piece of meat floating in it.

One of the guards was nicknamed 'the Fuehrer' because of his small moustache, and his habit of forcing prisoners to salute him, Nazi-style. One night, an hour or two before dawn, they were jolted awake by a recording of a speech by Hitler, played at full blast over the camp loudspeakers. Mrs Falcone did not recognize it as such, hearing only the abominably loud 'squeaking, squealing voice', as she put it, and not understanding the words; but a prisoner, who did menial tasks around the barracks and was allowed to take off his blindfold, told them it was Hitler's voice, played in order to undermine the prisoners.

The Falcones stayed in the Tube for another three weeks, Dr Falcone's heart condition deteriorating all the time. By the middle of February, in the stifling heat of summer, his health took a serious turn for the worse. A guard asked if he wanted a shower (neither of them had washed since being brought there a month before) and when he said he would he was taken to a bathroom and the shower was switched on. The water was ice-cold, and Dr Falcone was badly shocked. Realizing that his condition was now dangerous, he told the guards that they must get him the drug Trinatron. To his surprise they did, and he improved a little. But in the middle of the following night he was taken ill again.

This time the guards transferred them both at once to the camp infirmary for treatment. When they got there, they found that only four beds were occupied: one by a man of seventy, who had once been a trade unionist, and the others by three women, one of whom was seven months pregnant. The infirmary was run by a prisoner who was a trained nurse. It should have been preferable to the heat and claustrophobic discomfort of the Tube, but it wasn't. The infirmary was right beside the rooms where the guards tortured their prisoners, and screams filled the place continually. One day a blonde girl of twenty was brought into the infirmary in a semi-coma. It appeared that she had been suffering from a heart condition which neither she nor the guards had known about, and they had tried out a new invention of theirs on her – an automatic version of the *picana*, which gave her shocks at regular intervals. She had been subjected to particular ill-treatment partly no doubt because she was an attractive blonde, but more especially because her brother and fiancé were both being hunted by the police, and she was refusing to give any information about them in order to allow them time to get completely away. She lay in the infirmary in a state of delirium, saying again and again (according to Mrs Falcone), 'Father, father, why is this happening to me?' Dr Falcone examined her and gave instructions about her treatment, and after two days she was better. When they saw that, the guards took her back and began torturing her again, though she survived and was still alive when the Falcones were released a few days later.

The guards could see that Mrs Falcone and her husband were very close to each other, and that other prisoners, particularly the ones in the infirmary, looked to them for advice and help; and in a curious reversal of their former cruelty the guards would come to them and talk about their sexual or family problems, asking for their opinion. They would also try clumsily to explain why they were doing what they did: it was for Argentina, or the flag, or because of their relatives and friends who had suffered in the guerrilla war; some, for instance, had known people who were killed in a Montonero bomb explosion at a police station not far away. The Falcones were educated people who had managed to withstand the treatment they had received, and some at least of the men who had been responsible for it were now turning to them as stronger personalities. Other prisoners who had a similar experience found that in this mood the guards would reveal themselves as weak and dependent, searching for approval and sometimes for forgiveness.

On 22 February, 39 days after their arrest, the Falcones were told they would be released. They were given their original clothes back, washed and pressed. As they left, people tried to give them facts about themselves – their names, or phone numbers of their relatives and friends, in the hope that they would remember some at least of the details and pass them on. Dr Falcone and his wife expected, however, that it would turn out to be a trick, and that they would be taken out and executed: it never occurred to them that they would be allowed to return to society, knowing what they did. They were taken outside in a heavy downpour of rain, and heard the planes flying overhead in the direction of the nearby airport; then, to their astonishment, they were put in a car, dropped off in Buenos Aires, and even given money for the fare to La Plata. The car drove off, and the two of them were left standing in the darkness and the rain, still blindfolded, obeying their guards' instructions to wait for ten minutes before taking off their blindfolds and heading home.

The following year, Dr Falcone died of the heart condition which had been so badly aggravated during his time in police custody. Jorge, their son, had realized at once what had happened when he telephoned his father and the policeman had cut the line. He and his wife managed to escape from Argentina, and took refuge first in Sweden and then in Spain. Mrs Falcone, having lost her husband, her daughter and her son, was left alone in their once happy home in La Plata.

Her story told, the loneliness and unhappiness of the years after the death of her husband seem to settle on her. 'The military destroyed our perfect family,' she says, not in a spirit of self-pity particularly, but in a tone of quiet resignation. There is no particular malice when she says, 'It was an occupying army which spoke our language.'

Hannah Arendt, in writing about the extermination camps of Nazi Germany and the men and women who ran them, uses the phrase 'the banality of evil'. That would also fit the most detailed account which has yet been given by a man who himself took part in the Argentine campaign of extermination. More than a thousand men, all told, took part in the business of interrogating, torturing and murdering the victims of the Dirty War. One of them, a thick-set former petty officer in the Navy, contacted the office of the weekly magazine *La Semana* one day in early December 1983, and said he wanted to make a clean breast of everything he had done. Raúl David Vilariño was an ugly, broad-faced man with dark, crinkly hair who was born in 1948 but looked a good deal older than his thirty-five years when he met the journalists from the magazine whose job it was to work with him on his story; he could easily have passed for forty-five. His story was a long one, filling nearly two hundred pages when it was printed in book form: a rambling, jerky account of the kidnappings and murders he confessed to having carried out, filled with stories which began and ended abruptly and without apparent consequences – so much so that some of them seem more like fantasies than real experience. Nevertheless, it is highly likely that he did the things he confessed to; there is sufficient circumstantial evidence to prove it. In all, Vilariño thinks he carried out two hundred kidnappings for his bosses at ESMA – the Navy Mechanics School in Buenos Aires. He estimates that five thousand prisoners passed through the School altogether, and almost all of them were tortured. At most, he says, 4 or 5 per cent – two hundred people – survived.

Vilariño first became involved with the men who ran ESMA on 5 November 1975, four days after his twenty-seventh birthday. At that stage Mrs Perón was still nominally President of Argentina, but the Navy in the person of its commander, the ambitious Admiral Massera, was already planning to take over the government. Vilariño had met Massera on a couple of occasions in the past: once in 1970, when Massera was still a captain, and then two years later when he had accompanied him on an official trip to Italy. At that time, perhaps with his eye already on the outline of a final solution to Argentina's problems, Massera had asked Vilariño if he would be prepared to take on special duties. Vilariño said he would.

In November 1975, then, he was given his chance. He was called to Navy headquarters and to his amazement was shown into Massera's own private lift. He waited patiently with six other men, mostly naval petty officers, for several hours outside Massera's office before they were told to go in. Even now, the special duties were not clearly outlined, but the seven of them must have had a fairly clear understanding of what was meant: the guerrilla war was at its height, and there was the example of the Triple A, which was busy kidnapping and murdering suspected left-wingers. Massera told the men ranged in front of him that he was setting up a paramilitary group, and that they were going to be the core of it. They would have to operate outside the protection of the Navy; if they ran into trouble, they could expect no help. They would, he said, be under the orders of Rear-Admiral Rubén Chamorro, the head of the Navy Mechanics School. Then came the clearest indications of all: they would frequently not be in Navy uniform, and would often have to follow procedures which were at variance with the Navy's way of doing things. And if it were necessary to arrest people, or even to commit murder, the Navy, once again, would not accept any responsibility. Admiral Chamorro was sitting alongside Massera when he said this, and there were nine or ten other officers there as well. The meeting lasted for three hours, and at the end of it Vilariño and the other six men agreed to take part in Massera's scheme. A major step in the process which was to turn ESMA into Argentina's worst camp for torture and murder over the next few years had been taken.

The seven men went off, and were given six months' salary in advance, without having to sign receipts for it. For 20 days they underwent training in weapons and unarmed combat, and after a final test on 18 December they and the other men who had been selected were divided up into task forces, the *grupos de tareas* (GTs), four men in each. From then on they moved into the officers' quarters at the Navy Mechanics School, and a few days afterwards Chamorro sent Vilariño's group out on its first mission: to arrest a couple in a house in Buenos Aires where there was a good deal of subversive literature.

ESMA is a splendidly smart set of buildings in one of the better districts of Buenos Aires. Its white walls and brown wooden shutters have an aura of intelligently applied discipline – very much the Argentine Navy's self-image – and its trim lawns and pleasant flower-beds appear to indicate a greater sense of humanity than would be found at, say, an Army barracks.

The site is a huge one, stretching for three hundred yards or so along the road, and covering altogether several acres when its sports ground and training areas are taken into account. At each corner are watch-towers, with alert naval ratings in them, helmeted and with rifles in their hands, watching out for any sign of terrorist attack. The School plays an important part in the Navy's training programmes, dealing as it does with the more general technical education of its ratings, petty officers and officers. But it also performs another, less obvious function: it is the Navy's largest troop presence in Buenos Aires, the centre of the nation's political activities. It would make more sense in many ways if the Navy's main training establishment were sited at one of its bases – Puerto Belgrano, for instance, or Mar del Plata. But since each of the Argentine armed forces has believed from 1930 onwards that it had a political persona as well as a purely military one, it is important to be represented in strength in the nation's capital. ESMA was part of that representation.

It was also a concentration camp. As you pass the pleasant front of ESMA, travelling away from the centre of Buenos Aires along the Avenida Libertador General San Martín, the main buildings facing the road end in a small park containing a few ornamental trees. Among them is another watch-tower, and the road which runs along the side of the ESMA complex is shut off by a barrier controlled from a sentry-box. It was this side road that the Ford Falcons and other cars in the GT 3 fleet would take when they brought their prisoners back to be interrogated at ESMA. Halfway down the side road is another long block, painted white and set some way back and scarcely visible from the road itself. Before the start of 1976 it had been an officers' mess and recreation block. Three storeys high, L-shaped and containing forty or fifty rooms altogether, it made an ideal prison. There can be no doubt that everybody in the legitimate part of the Mechanics School knew something about the building and its new function: the screams that emanated from it, the coming and going of cars at midnight, and later the stench of burning bodies from the sports ground would all have been clear signs. And from time to time men from the School proper would be brought in to help with particular cases. It might have been unsafe to talk about it, but for the thousand or so men in the main part of the School the function of that particular area cannot have been a secret.

Raúl Vilariño, as he told his story to *La Semana*, showed himself to be strangely selective in the incidents he could recall. It was not that he shrank from confessing his own involvement in what happened; though with a curious sense of pride which is certainly convincing he maintains that he killed a number of people but never did any torturing himself, and indeed disapproved of much that was done inside the walls of the prison camp. But his stories are strangely fragmented: often he is not there when something important happens, having seen the early stages; for one reason or another he leaves, and then comes back after some particularly horrific assault has been committed. He intervenes time and again to protect the victims of such assaults, and yet somehow is never punished by his superiors for interfering. Perhaps it is all true: but even in a man who proclaims that his conscience has troubled him to the point where he is obliged to come forward and tell everything he knows, there may be a deep-rooted desire to show himself in as good a light as possible. There is little confirmation for much of what Vilariño has to say about the day-to-day horrors inside ESMA; nevertheless, he has confessed enough to make his conviction certain in any trial for kidnapping or murder. And the few who survived their imprisonment at ESMA have shown by their testimony that most of the things Vilariño says happened there are entirely credible.

According to him, it was only at the start of ESMA's time as a clandestine prison that people who were brought in by the kidnap gangs could hope to avoid being tortured. Very soon it became standard practice to torture people directly they arrived, and to castrate the men among them. There were, Vilariño says, ten men who were most involved in torture: Admiral Chamorro himself, and his deputy Captain Jorge Acosta; Captain Francis William Whamond, who was of British descent and had been called in from retirement to act as intelligence officer; Captain Vildoza; Lieutenant – later Lt Cdr – Alfredo Astiz, who was to bcome one of the most important single figures in the military's campaign of murder and kidnapping, and whose name will crop up again and again in this book; three shadowy figures, whom Vilariño seems not to have known very well, José Melián, known as 'La Bruja', the sorcerer, and two others, known only by the names 'Chupitegui' and 'Fenoglio'. Finally, there were the two main torturers, who were also known only by *nommes de guerre*: one was known as 'Magnosco', though Vilariño, whose grasp of names is not strong, thinks his real name might have been something like 'Macganaco'; and the other was known as 'Menguele' – a Spanish version of the name of the most feared man in Auschwitz, Dr Mengele. Vilariño maintains that Magnosco and Menguele were both doctors as well, but it is possible that he is mistaken.

Although these men began as interrogators, rather than torturers, the distinction quickly vanished in face of the work they did. By May and June 1976, only a few months after the School had begun to take in prisoners, Magnosco and Menguele were torturing people, particularly women, for their own sexual gratification. In June, Vilariño says, Astiz brought in a woman in an advanced state of pregnancy, whom he had just happened to come across in the street. There seems to have been no certainty that she was suspected of taking part in guerrilla activity. She had with her a little girl of six or seven. Vilariño, who had been having breakfast, played with the girl, who was frightened and upset. Astiz then came back with Captain Whamond and took the mother and daughter away.

As so often with Vilariño's stories, he says that he went off on a mission. When he returned, he heard screaming, and went into the torture room on the ground floor to find out what was happening.

The pregnant woman was tied to the bed, and Menguele was applying electric shocks to her genitals, while Magnosco was raping, or pretending to rape, the little girl. He was shouting out to the woman to confess, or he would make the child suffer. Vilariño then apparently left the room again, and when two other members of his task force came back he told them what he had seen. They all went into the torture room, and found that the two 'doctors', Menguele and Magnosco, had gone. The woman's breasts and belly had been mutilated, and the little girl appeared to be badly injured as well. Both seemed close to death. Vilariño's friend, Luis Gallio, was very upset and insisted that they should go and report what had happened to Admiral Chamorro, but they could not find him. Instead, they brought a medical assistant from the legal infirmary in the main part of the School with them. But when they got back they found that Menguele and Chamorro were in the torture room, and were told that the two of them would take care of everything. Vilariño and Gallio wanted to make sure that the woman and her daughter were given proper treatment, and offered to go with them, but they were told to leave. The woman and the little girl were put into a Ford truck which belonged to their task force, and Astiz drove it away with the male nurse beside him. The woman, the little girl and the medical assistant were never seen again. A few days later, Vilariño's friend Luis Gallio committed suicide, leaving a note in which he said he was sorry to show himself a coward, but he couldn't go on any longer: he was worried that he would break down in front of the others.

People who met Alfredo Astiz, his victims as well as his colleagues, found it hard to believe he was the kind of man he was. Fair-haired and blue-eyed, he had an alert and sympathetic expression and a pleasant smile, all of which helped to give him the nickname of 'the blond angel'. His father was a senior naval officer, and Astiz himself was a general favourite with his own superiors, who had early on marked him out for quick promotion. His willingness to take on unpleasant jobs – both at ESMA and in various places where he was sent as an infiltrator – ensured that promotion came even faster than he might have expected; he was a lieutenant-commander in the Navy before he was out of his twenties. At ESMA he was given free rein, and made the most of it. He was in charge of all the important kidnapping and arrest operations, and distinguished himself in more than one when there was resistance from genuine guerrillas. But according to Vilariño he, like many of the other officers, involved in killings and kidnappings, was early on engaged in business on his own account. In May 1976, when the military government was only two months old, Vilariño found himself at a house which had belonged to two elderly men. They had, it seemed, been killed by Astiz in a small explosion which had not been large enough to do structural damage to the house. Astiz had found out that they had no heirs. In this particular case Admiral Chamorro took over the house, but he may have shared the proceeds with Astiz.

Later that year, Vilariño heard Astiz betting Whamond that he could bring back a more attractive girl than he could. The next morning Astiz came back to ESMA with two young girls, aged sixteen at the most; one of them had been badly beaten about the face, the other had hurt her arm. Later, Vilariño says, he went to the dormitories for a shower, and found Astiz, Whamond and Captain Vildoza (another of the torturers) naked in one of the cubicles together with the girls, who were tied up. Astiz was raping one of the girls. Vilariño was angry, once again, and went to get one of his colleagues. They came back, having armed themselves, and burst into the shower room. Astiz had a look of terror on his face, and the two girls were sent off to the infirmary with a medical attendant. Vilariño and his friend gave their three senior officers a severe talking-to – or so he says. Like all of his stories, it ends with his own action; we are not told what three of the most senior officers at ESMA thought about being interrupted and told off by a couple of petty officers. Nevertheless, it is not altogether impossible that the normal structures of service discipline had broken down in the dreadful circumstances of ESMA; and what does certainly ring true is Vilariño's rough-and-ready sense of loyalty to his task force section; he would give details of some particularly cruel or violent treatment, and then say that his group, the original ones, would never have done something like that.

Astiz was also, he says, involved in a racket to sell children whose parents had been kidnapped and murdered. Once, Vilariño maintains, Astiz arrived with no fewer than five children, one of about a year and the others aged two or three; this was in August 1976. Two or three days later, Vilariño discovered that Astiz had taken them off to sell to childless policemen or servicemen and their wives; the going rate was a hundred million pesos, which at that time equalled about seven hundred US dollars, or three hundred and thirty pounds, though the precise fee depended on the age of the child and the financial circumstances of the couple involved. Birth certificates could be forged in a laboratory to which Astiz had access, and so could changes to existing marriage certificates. Vilariño estimates that about sixty babies passed through ESMA during this time, and all but two of them were sold. The two which were not had their heads dashed against a wall by 'Dr' Menguele in an attempt to make their mothers talk.

As time went on, Vilariño noticed that the torturers became more and more degenerate. Nominally, as in other camps, the torturers worked a shift pattern; but at ESMA the complete licence they had to do what they wanted with their prisoners seems to have acted on them like an addiction. Sometimes they would stay in the torture room for a full 24 hours, never taking time off or resting; or else they would go home, and then return a couple of hours later, as though the atmosphere of cruelty and violence had drawn them back. It was clear, Vilariño said, that they were often sexually aroused by what they did. And because the need to torture had become their prime concern they were scarcely interested any longer in getting information out of their victims. It ceased to matter whether the people they tortured talked or not, they carried on just the same. Talking, or inventing stories to please their torturers did the unfortunate victims no more good than keeping silent. And since a sizeable number of the people arrested by ESMA groups had committed no offence other than to be wealthy, plenty of people who passed through the torture room had nothing they could possibly confess. Astiz, Chamorro and the others wanted their money, and Menguele and Magnosco wanted to make them suffer.

The military government's final solution was soon producing large numbers of bodies, which had to be dealt with in one way or another. Despising the Army's use of 'NN' graves as being too likely to lead to eventual identification, the Navy devised methods of its own to get rid of them. Some, indeed, were buried at ESMA itself, in the sports ground: the naval authorities presumably thought they would be safe there from exhumation at some time in the future. Most of these bodies came from other naval camps: La Plata, Mar del Plata, Puerto Belgrano. Some were those of people who had died in shoot-outs. Relatively few of those buried were from ESMA itself, since there were only very occasional executions in the camp, and most of those who died did so under torture. But by 1977 the sports ground was too full to take any more burials, though it is bigger than two football pitches, and the practice of burning bodies became more common. It was done at a set time of day, five-thirty in the afternoon, and the bodies were often cut up beforehand with a circular saw. But none of these methods was felt to be very satisfactory, and very soon after the coup the Navy hit on its 'doorless flights'. The great majority of people who had been taken to ESMA after being arrested and who were not earmarked for survival – Vilariño puts their number at around 4,800 – were disposed of in this way.

The first flight was in May 1976, but Vilariño says the bodies they disposed of on that occasion did not come from ESMA, and he never found out where they did come from. The method was adjudged a success, and from then on ESMA got rid of many of its corpses the same way. Hooded people would be put into lorries and taken to a military airport where they would be put on board the so-called 'doorless' planes: doorless, so that the bodies could be thrown out more easily. In the planes they would be stripped of anything that might identify them, their faces were disfigured and their jaws broken to prevent their being recognized even from dental records. At first the prisoners were treated this way when they were conscious, but later the officers began injecting them with penthenol because their victims would struggle too much in the lorries and on the planes. Vilariño and his colleagues called these people 'future corpses', and it is noticeable that in his confession he never gives them their real names or describes them in any way. The whole process required that the victims were dehumanized. At first the Navy dropped them out over the River Plate opposite Martín García Island, which is well upriver from Buenos Aires, but the bodies started to be washed up along the shore at Quilmes, so they switched to an area of the estuary which was farther out. But even that was no good: the bodies were washed up on the Uruguayan side. No one, it seemed, had bothered to work out where the currents flowed. Eventually they flew over Samborombón Bay, at the mouth of the Plate, thirty miles out, and the bodies were not washed up any more. Sometimes, according to Vilariño, the prisoners put up a fight as they were being thrown out, and they had to be beaten over the head or kicked through the open doorway. All around the doors were the marks of people's fingers, made as they tried to hold on and prevent themselves from falling.

Several naval pilots and crews refused to take part in the doorless flights, and were accused of cowardice as a result, often losing their chances of promotion. Vilariño told *La Semana* that he did not feel that the ones who did fly were to blame, since there were so many pressures on them to do so. And he and his colleagues were conditioned to think that what they were doing was right: that it could not possibly count as murder to get rid of the country's internal enemies. He confesses that even when he and some of the others did rebel, it was against particular methods that were being used, not against the whole dreadful business. They didn't want to come to terms with the fact that their superior officers might have been wrong, he says, so they carried on; and the men who gave them their orders, noticing their waning of enthusiasm, would give them less work to do so that they could continue believing in the things Massera had told them when they first sat in his office on 5 November 1975.

Perhaps it was obvious in Vilariño's case, too, that he was no longer one hundred per cent reliable. By January 1978 he ceased to be a member of the task force, though he stayed at ESMA and was still apparently trusted in other ways. As so often in his *La Semana* interviews, he retreats into vagueness, saying only that he left in December 1978 to compile a book about the campaign against insurgency in Argentina; though the book doesn't seem ever to have appeared. He will give no details of his life from then until the day in December 1983 when he made contact with *La Semana*. Since he was officially 'posted to Antarctica' during the entire period from November 1975 onwards, he has no way of proving the truth of what he says in any formal way; but *La Semana* was besieged by calls and requests for information from people who had lost relatives, in the hope that he might perhaps be able to give them some hint, some indication, which would end the pain of not knowing. One man who went to see him when he was being kept in Uruguay by *La Semana* found him anxious to help, as though it were a method of atoning for what he had done. And so the roughly-spoken former petty officer, who had by his own admission kidnapped two hundred people and taken them to their almost certain deaths, became a last source of hope to the kind of people whose families he had destroyed. The banality of evil had turned into a form of irony.

# 7 THE PRISONER AT THE VILLA JOYOSA

*'She was too difficult a package to return to society'* – Admiral Chamorro, referring to Dagmar Hagelin.

In the offices of one of the main human rights groups which sprang up in Argentina during the Process of National Reorganization there is a wall covered with photographs. Some tidy hand has arranged them so that the larger ones surround the smaller, though they are mostly beginning to curl and fade in the sunlight which strikes across them in the afternoons. There are, perhaps, a thousand of them: smiling faces, serious faces, strained faces, staring out at a school photographer, perhaps, or at a society portrait-taker, or the anonymous flashing light of a photo booth. Some are in colour, and show couples at their wedding looking affectionately at each other for the camera. Some are more earnest – official pictures taken for military service or identity cards. Some are snapshots, taken at parties or at *asados*, and the people in them are laughing or fooling around, never guessing that this moment will be the one that they are remembered for. In the middle of the display are the hundreds of small black and white pictures that were all, perhaps, that the relatives of the people who had disappeared were prepared to part with, when they went through their albums and boxes of memorabilia. Each of the pictures on display has a curling snippet of typed paper taped to it, recording the name and the date of disappearance.

As the eye runs along the line, taking in the fact that about 40 per cent of the people commemorated in this matter-of-fact way are women, it stops at a grey, fading snap, which, judging from the background, must have been taken in a photographic booth. The face is that of a girl in her mid-teens: sweet-faced but not particularly beautiful, the greyness of the picture disguising the blonde hair and blue eyes which most people would remember her by. It would have seemed absurd when the photograph was taken, to suggest that the girl whose face it showed would within a year or so be the subject of appeals by the Pope, the American Secretary of State, and a score of governments and organizations around the world. Under the picture appears the girl's name and the date she disappeared: 'Ingrid Dagmar Hagelin, 27.1.77'. The fact that the British Government was not among those which made appeals, and played no discernible part whatever in the campaign either for Dagmar or for the disappeared in general during the years of Argentina's 'Dirty War', meant that Dagmar's father, Ragnar Hagelin, at first refused to see us or talk to us; when eventually he did, he made a point of saying that he disapproved of British policy towards Argentina and believed that Britain had been in the wrong over the issue of the Falkland Islands. But his anger soon passed, and he turned to the question which has dominated his entire life since 1977: the disappearance of his daughter, the search for news of her fate, and the punishment of those responsible for it.

Ragnar Hagelin does not look like a man with Swedish nationality – he is dark-haired and below average height, though powerfully built. His active manner and lively face indicate a tension which the campaign for Dagmar has only intensified; for some time now he has been suffering from a stomach problem which is related to the stress he feels. He is now fifty, though he looks and acts like a younger man. He was once the general manager of the largest meat corporation in Argentina, a job he had to give up in order to devote himelf more fully to the search for news of Dagmar. His father was a Swede, an engineer who came to South America at the start of the Thirties to work in the mining industries of various countries; his mother was also Swedish, but of French and Spanish parents, who provided Ragnar Hagelin with his dark colouring. Dagmar, however, inherited the Nordic looks of her grandfather, as well as his Swedish nationality. She was born in 1959.

The Hagelins were a musical family, and from the age of four or five Dagmar started going to the Colón Theatre in Buenos Aires with her parents for the opera or the ballet. She was almost fanatical in her interest in classical music, and one of her main studies at the Liceo Nacional Sarmiento was singing. Almost certainly she would have made a career of it, though at the time when she was arrested she had not finally decided. She was also good at sports, particularly athletics and gymnastics. Her nature was outgoing and generous, romantic, a little sentimental; and it was that, allied to an unhappy coincidence, that brought about her arrest and serious injury, and her presumed death. At the end of 1975, Dagmar's mother, who had by this time divorced Hagelin and remarried, took her to the seaside resort of Villa Gessell, in the province of Buenos Aires, for a holiday. On the beach one day, they met a woman who at twenty-six was a good eight years older than Dagmar, and had with her a little girl of two. It was the child, rather than the mother, who first attracted Dagmar's interest and sympathy, but the older woman found Dagmar's company pleasant, and they saw each other several times more during the holiday. The woman's name was Norma Susana Burgos, and she was the widow of Carlos Caride, a leading figure in the Montoneros, who had recently been killed in a shoot-out with the police. Dagmar's stepfather, Edgardo Weissman, knew Norma Burgos because he had represented Caride when he was a prisoner in 1974. That indicates a certain support for the revolutionary cause on the part of the stepfather; but Dagmar's real father, Ragnar Hagelin, had no such sympathies, and it was with him that Dagmar lived, and apparently felt closest. Although Dagmar presumably knew about Norma Burgos's background, there was never any sign whatever that she herself had any interest in left-wing politics, or even knew that Norma Burgos, like her husband, was a member of the Montoneros. Burgos confirmed this to Hagelin, after Dagmar's disappearance.

Shortly after Christmas 1976 the little girl who had first attracted Dagmar's attention on the beach at Villa Gessell, Victoria Eva, found a bottle of some poisonous substance in the house of Norma Burgos's parents, where the two of them were living, and swallowed some of it. Dagmar Hagelin was very upset by the news of Victoria's death, and went several times to see Norma Burgos and comfort her. That deepened the friendship between them. The Hagelins were due to go on holiday on 1 February and it occurred to Dagmar to tell Norma Burgos they were going, and to ask her if she was going away too. Since it was the school holidays, Dagmar decided she would make the journey to the township of El Palomar, twenty-five miles away where Norma lived. The date was 27 January 1977. No one knew that Norma Burgos had been arrested in the street the previous day by a group of men from the Navy Mechanics School.

Dagmar left home early, wearing the new blouse her father had bought her for the holiday. She was careful to take her identification card with her, because there was always the danger of being arrested and held for at least 24 hours for not having the necessary papers, and it sometimes happened that girls who were arrested were raped by the police. But her father was not worried about her: a journey by train and bus was safe enough in daytime, even though it was a difficult period, with disappearances occurring every day. He assumed, like everybody else, that people who disappeared were mixed up with politics, and he knew that Dagmar was not.

At 8.30 a.m. Dagmar reached the house of Norma's parents at 317 Sargento Cabral Street, and went up to the porch to ring the bell. She had walked into an ambush. Two men ran around the side of the house to grab her, and others appeared suddenly at the windows, pointing guns at her. Perhaps even then she would have been all right, able to convince her captors that she was not the person they were looking for. But she was athletic, fast on her feet, and she was scared. She ran for it. The two men who had come to take her were fast too, but she got away from them and headed down the street, ignoring the gunfire from the upstairs windows. When she was only fifteen yards from the corner of the street, the senior of the two men chasing her stopped and went down on one knee, a revolver in his hand. He fired once, and Dagmar went down.

It is not clear where the bullet struck her. She tripped over the broken pavement and hit her forehead badly as she fell. The man who had fired at her stood over her, pointing his gun at her as she lay on the ground. Her head was bleeding badly. The other man stopped a taxi and shouted out to the driver that they were federal police and needed his cab. In spite of the driver's protestations that the cab was in poor shape, the man forced him to drive over to where Dagmar lay, and after some difficulty managed to open the boot. The two supposed policeman lifted Dagmar up and put her inside it, but as they were closing the lid of the boot she grabbed it with both hands, unable to talk or call out because of her injuries. The senior of the two men then spoke for the first time. 'Don't worry, *flaca* [little girl]', he said. 'We're going to take you to Churruca hospital.' That was all the cab driver heard, and he watched them drive away with their badly injured prisoner lying in the boot. Churruca was the police hospital, but they did not take Dagmar there; they took her instead across the city to the base they really worked from – the Navy Mechanics School, ESMA. The man who had hijacked the taxi was a naval petty officer called Peralta. The officer who fired the shot was Lieutenant Alfredo Astiz.

Dagmar's father was expecting her back at twelve o'clock; they had a good deal of shopping to do before leaving for their holiday, mostly to buy clothes for Dagmar. She was a punctual girl, and at first Ragnar Hagelin and his second wife, Dagmar's stepmother, waited for her without too much anxiety. By one o'clock they decided to have lunch. But by two-thirty, with Dagmar still not back, Hagelin and his wife were very worried indeed, and he decided to drive out and look for her. Norma Burgos's father was at the house in Sargento Cabral Street when he arrived there, and he heard the whole story from him. Scarcely stopping to look at the place where his daughter had fallen down, he raced back home, knowing now that speed was essential.

As elsewhere in South America, connections are all-important, and a man like Hagelin, in charge of one of the biggest concerns in Argentina, had a good many of them. One was a senior military figure, who had long been a friend of the family. He too knew the importance of speed in a case like this, and directly Hagelin contacted him the officer promised to drive straight to the police station that covered the area of the Burgos house. The two men met outside and walked in together, saying they wanted to speak to the inspector on duty. When the reply came that the inspector was busy the military man said who he was and told the policeman on the desk that the inspector had twenty seconds to come out. He came out, Hagelin recalls with a kind of bitter relish, within twelve. The inspector, by now anxious to help, gave Hagelin the first hard evidence of what had happened: they had received a radio message, he said, informing them that an 'official operation' would be taking place at the Burgos house. (It had proved necessary for the police to be warned about such things, because these operations were always carried out by men in plain clothes, whose actions were often indistinguishable from those of ordinary criminals. More than once there had been shoot-outs between military gangs and the police who had been summoned by passers-by.) The inspector went with them to the scene of Dagmar's injury and kidnapping, and they saw the blood on the ground for themselves. Even now, after telling his daughter's story so many times to so many people, Hagelin's voice trembles when he tells how he felt as he looked at the blood, and how he decided that she could not, perhaps, be too badly hurt since there was not much of it.

For the next six or seven hours Hagelin and his friend from the military went the rounds of the Buenos Aires hospitals, getting access to the special lists which contained the names of people brought in by the police or the military. It was a depressing task: they knew that at that time most of the cases were entered under false names, with the wrong sex recorded against their name, precisely to hinder the kind of search Hagelin was trying to carry out. By 10.30 p.m. they had gone through all the lists, unable to say for certain that she was not there but knowing, at least, that they had done what they could. At that point Hagelin's friend suggested one last possibility: going to the regional police headquarters at Morón – the centre from which radio messages were sent out to all the sub-stations in the area. For Hagelin to go there alone might have been difficult; as the father of someone who had been arrested he stood a good chance of being arrested and beaten up himself, simply for making enquiries. With the military officer, however, he was safe.

It turned out to be the best thing they could have done. Hagelin by this stage was close to breaking down, and was in tears; and that seems to have encouraged the young officer at the regional headquarters to help them. 'You know what it could mean for me if I give you any information,' he said, but nevertheless he took out the book in which radio messages were logged and opened it on the 26th. He ran his finger down the page, and then turned the book round so that they could see what was written there: a message to say that a team from the Navy Mechanics School would be undertaking an operation at the house in Sargento Cabral Street. The colours and registration numbers of the cars that were used in the operation were also listed, to avoid any problems with the police: three Ford Falcons, coloured white, green and grey, and a light-blue Chevrolet, which turned out to have been the private car of the officer commanding the School, Admiral Chamorro. The military man was exultant: 'It's like winning the lottery,' he said. Now, at last, they had a clear lead. Dagmar had not simply vanished, she was being held at the Navy Mechanics School. It was a piece of luck that few parents of people who disappeared experienced.

An hour or so later, Hagelin was at the residence of the Swedish ambassador. His friend from the military had gone home, and Mrs Hagelin was sitting in their car at the side of the road. Hagelin rang the doorbell and at that moment a man came out of the shadows and put a gun to his head. Hagelin, almost too tired by this time to be afraid, explained that he was a Swedish citizen and needed to speak to the ambassador urgently; the man lowered his gun reluctantly, and told him to clear off. It was uncertain whether he had been posted there because of the kidnapping of Dagmar, or whether he was part of some surveillance team which kept an eye on embassies and their staff; if so, the Swedish ambassador knew nothing about it. As for Hagelin, he had to be content with driving home and waiting until morning.

At the first possible moment, directly the Embassy was open, he went round and soon found himself sitting in front of the Swedish ambassador, Dr Walter. Sweden's position in Argentina was a complicated one: as a known supporter of libertarian causes and with a long tradition of Social Democracy, it was suspect to the Argentine military government, and Sweden for its part found everything about the Process abhorrent. All the same, the Argentine military appeared to have a grudging respect for the Swedes, and were anxious to keep on reasonable terms with them as with other countries that could provide a good market. But the Swedish ambassador had no reservations about speaking out firmly in the case of a Swedish citizen who had disappeared; there was nothing very much to be lost by angering the host government, and public opinion in Sweden would expect it; and although Dagmar had Argentine nationality as well as Swedish, and in Argentina would be considered a citizen of Argentina first, he went into action immediately. It was the first time a Swedish citizen had had any serious difficulties under the Process government.

Directly Hagelin had explained the situation to him, he picked up the telephone and told the switchboard to put him through to the police headquarters at Morón. When he had identified himself, they confirmed that the kidnapping of Dagmar had in fact been an official operation. It then became a matter of applying to the competent authorities to release her; and having established what had become of Dagmar, the ambassador knew that the methods to be adopted were clear-cut: a request by him to the Foreign Ministry, a parallel request in Stockholm by the Ministry there to the Argentine Embassy. And since the Argentine Foreign Ministry was controlled by the Navy, which ran the Mechanics School, there was a reasonable chance that they would get Dagmar freed. For the first time since he knew that Dagmar had been kidnapped, Hagelin allowed himself to hope that things might after all turn out all right.

Almost three years later, in Stockholm, Norma Burgos signed her name on the seventh and last page of a deposition she had made to an under-secretary for legal affairs in the Swedish Foreign Ministry.

It provides the clearest indication of what happened to Dagmar after she was taken to the Mechanics School. Norma Burgos remains an elusive character, and the part she played in the whole incident has never been entirely clear. She seems genuinely to have liked Dagmar Hagelin, and to have been grateful for the girl's sympathy after the death of her daughter Victoria; but the deception that was essential to her while she was still free, and the dubious circumstances under which she agreed to co-operate with the naval authorities, have tended to obscure the account she gives at several crucial points. Nevertheless the outline at least is clear enough: she was arrested in the street on the morning of 26 January 1977 by a group from the Navy, and taken directly to the Mechanics School. The assumption is that before she had been tortured badly, or perhaps before she had been tortured at all, she told her interrogators much of what she knew, and decided to help them. That evening they took her to her house at El Palomar, 'in order', she said later in her deposition in Stockholm, 'that she should accompany them while they searched it'. What seems rather more likely is that Norma Burgos had given them detailed information about another woman prominent in the guerrilla movement whom they wanted to capture: María Antonia Berger. And she must have given them some reason to believe that María Berger would be visiting the house. Her statement later puts it as follows: 'Some of the naval personnel remained in her house [after the search] in order to arrest anyone who came to it, according to information which she later received from her captors.' In fact seven men stayed overnight in the El Palomar house, once Norma Burgos had been taken back to the Mechanics School, and it is quite possible that they were waiting for María Berger, a blonde woman of 27 with blue eyes.

It was Dagmar Hagelin's fatal misfortune that she should have come to the house at 8.30 the following morning when there were men waiting there for someone of roughly her description. Ragnar, her father, has long passed the stage of counting the steps which led her to be there at that particular time: the idea of seeing if Norma Burgos was also going on holiday, the speed with which Burgos had agreed to co-operate with the group from the Mechanics School, Dagmar's own split-second decision to run rather than to show her identity card and prove that she was not the person whom Astiz and the others wanted. Like the ready sympathy which created a bond between her and Norma Burgos in the first place, it was a part of her nature that led her to the house, and part of Norma Burgos's nature that meant there was an ambush waiting there; it was the coincidence of these different elements that caused the mistake.

That it was a mistake is clear from the evidence of the other main witness in the case: the naval petty officer Raúl Vilariño, who was not himself part of the gang that captured Dagmar, but knew all about her from the gossip at the Mechanics School. Admiral Chamorro, for instance, was furious at what had happened, and called Astiz into his office to give him a dressing-down. 'You shouldn't be so quick to use your gun,' Vilariño quotes him as saying; 'you've given a foreign government the chance to attack us.' But once the mistake had been made, it was not easy to rectify. In other cases where people had been shot by mistake during kidnappings, the doctors at the Mechanics School and the other centres would give them treatment so that they would recover; then they would be released, on the strict understanding that if they said anything about what had happened to them they would disappear for good. No doubt this is what would have happened in Dagmar's case, but for the serious nature of her wounds. 'She was too difficult a package to return to society', Chamorro is quoted by Vilariño as saying.

Shortly before noon on 27 January – the day Dagmar was captured – Norma Burgos was taken from her cell on the third floor of the Mechanics School down to the basement of the building. She was hooded, and she may have thought she was going to be tortured. Instead, she found herself in the makeshift infirmary and when they took off her blindfold she saw Dagmar lying there on an iron bed, with Astiz and the naval officer of British descent, Francis William Whamond, standing beside her. They clearly intended to confront her with her main Montonero contact, María Berger.

Dagmar was covered with a sheet, her hands chained to the frame of the bed. She had a wound above her left eyebrow, her hair and scalp were sticky with unwashed blood, and she had reddish bruises under her eyes. Directly she was allowed to speak to her, Norma Burgos asked how she was feeling. 'All right, in spite of everything,' Dagmar replied. Norma Burgos, recalling the scene three years later in the Swedish Ministry of Foreign Affairs, said she thought that Dagmar only said it in order to keep the other woman's spirits up.

By this time it was becoming obvious to Astiz and Whamond that they had captured the wrong person; Norma Burgos's own unfeigned surprise at seeing Dagmar must have told them that. Astiz began to question Dagmar, and in doing so told her she was lucky that it had been he who had fired at her. Astiz was famous for his skill with weapons. He also pointed out to her that they were both Nordic types, with their fair hair and blue eyes. 'You're the same type as me,' he said. As Astiz and Whamond took Norma Burgos away, they remarked that the mistake over Dagmar had arisen because 'la suequita', the little Swedish girl, was so like María Berger. Neither apparently expressed any regret about what had happened to her; it was a mistake, nothing more.

Next to Dagmar's bed, Norma Burgos had noticed the girl's clothes lying folded up: a pair of jeans, a blouse, dark-coloured sandals. The blouse was to have a long and curious history: first of all it was put into the general collection of things taken from prisoners or stolen from their houses, which were handed out when the clothes people arrived with at the Mechanics School became too worn. Norma Burgos saw another girl wearing it later. Then she asked for it herself, and when she was released, under curious circumstances, she took it with her.

In Sweden, when she finally met Ragnar Hagelin, she gave the blouse to him, and he recognized it as the one he had bought for Dagmar a few days before the holiday they never took. He has it still – the last link with his daughter.

Two or three days later, Norma Burgos was taken down to the basement room again, this time by Francis Whamond alone. By now there were clear signs that Dagmar was being cared for: although she had one hand handcuffed to the bed, there was a medical dressing over the wound on her head. Her eyes still had bruises under them, though, and she looked thinner. When Whamond took Norma Burgos's blindfold off, he said to Dagmar, 'You see, the lady is still alive, and you're going to live too.' Burgos said in her deposition that it was obvious Dagmar had been complaining, and that he was trying to calm her anxieties; but this time the meeting was very brief, and the two women had scarcely any time to talk to each other. Burgos saw Dagmar again about a week afterwards. By this time Dagmar had been moved to the third floor, and was being kept in a room next to the lavatory which the other prisoners on the third floor used, Burgos among them. When she was being taken there, by a young cadet from the Mechanics School rather than one of the usual guards, Burgos managed to persuade him to let her look through the door, as long as she did not speak to her. Raising a part of her hood for a second or two, Norma Burgos was able to see her standing up in the room, wearing a dressing-gown but not hooded. It was the last time she saw Dagmar.

Two or three days afterwards, on another journey to the lavatory, she took advantage of a moment's lack of attention by her guard to sneak a look from under her hood into Dagmar's room again. She saw the girl's sandals there, but the room was empty. She asked her gaolers several times after that what had happened to the prisoner in the little room next to the lavatory, and eventually one of them told her that she had been taken away some nights before, on her own, but that was all the information she could get out of him. She could not discover from anyone else what Dagmar's fate was. But she did have two other pieces of information to add to her attested statement. Another prisoner told her he had overheard a conversation between two of the officers at the Mechanics School, in which one of them said that the injury which Dagmar had suffered when she was arrested had caused paralysis of the legs and an inability to control her bladder. And a long time afterwards, though exactly when she was unable to say, Norma Burgos was taken to the office of a naval lieutenant at the School, Antonio Pernia. Because Burgos was going to be questioned she was not forced to wear her hood, and she saw lying on top of his attaché case a telex message in which the Swedish Government was asking the Argentine Foreign Ministry for information about Dagmar. The message bore the name of the Argentine Foreign Ministry on top, and in capital letters Dagmar's name. It was clear evidence that although the Argentine Government, from President Videla down, was denying all knowledge of the case, the authorities knew precisely who could best answer questions about her.

Ragnar Hagelin has rebuilt his life, and has three children by his second marriage, the youngest born in 1983 when he was in his fiftieth year. He is also establishing a career once more in Argentina, after the time he spent in Sweden and elsewhere as an exile. But it is not altogether easy; Hagelin is a man whose life is still dominated by the need to know exactly what happened to his daughter, regardless of the pain it costs him.

> The senior military people talked to me about Dagmar's case – though that was just a trick to gain time, because while I was talking to them the Swedish government had to stop its

diplomatic pressure on them – and I said to them, 'Even if my daughter is paralysed, give her back to me, and I'll take her to Europe and get her better again. You'll never see any of us any more if you do that. I know what happened to her was a mistake, and so do you. Give her back to me, and that will be the end of the whole business.' But they didn't react. Once one of them said to me, 'If we take one part of the pyramid out, the whole thing will come crashing down.'

The morning after Dagmar's kidnapping, when he saw the Swedish ambassador, Hagelin decided to give the military authorities two weeks to produce her – and then he would tell his story to the newspapers. But even though the ambassador called the Mechanics School in person and approached General Videla's office within 24 hours of her disappearance, there was no response; so when the two weeks had elapsed, he contacted all the main Swedish papers, as well as the Argentine press. In Argentina, three newspapers published his story: *La Nación, La Opinión*, and the *Buenos Aires Herald*. They were obliged to be fairly discreet about the details, but for the Swedish press it was headline news; Dagmar was the first Swedish citizen to have suffered under what was known to be a savage régime.

On 14 April 1977 Hagelin and his entire family left Argentina for the United States, where they saw a number of politicians and journalists, who gave him considerable help and advice, and from there he went on to Sweden. He had left quietly, without telling anyone. About two weeks later, a group of ten armed men arrived at his flat in the expensive suburb of Belgrano at two o'clock in the morning to arrest him. The Mechanics School had decided that it would be better if he, too, disappeared – in spite of the worldwide outcry it would have caused. But by this stage the men in charge of the murder campaign had clearly decided that it was more important to destroy the evidence of what they were doing than to ensure that no offence was given to foreign governments. Not long before, a girl with West German nationality had disappeared, and when the Bonn Government began to hint that it would block some of the big loans it was providing to Argentina unless it was given some information about her, the Argentine régime handed over the girl's body to the West German Embassy, saying that she had been shot while trying to escape. Hagelin's fear was that the same thing would happen to Dagmar. Nevertheless, he and the Swedish foreign ministry took the calculated decision to continue the pressure on the government in Buenos Aires. The Pope applied three times to the junta for information about Dagmar, and when the US Secretary of State, Cyrus Vance, went to Argentina in November 1977 he asked in person about her. President Videla's officials would only produce the reply that they were searching for her. A formal request from the Organization of American States was answered in the same way. A naval officer was quoted in the newspapers as saying that Dagmar was free, and had gone into hiding; it was an attempt to suggest that she had, after all, been involved in guerrilla activity. But that had no effect whatsoever: the pressure continued, from other Western governments as well as from Sweden and the United States, and there was support from opposition parties in Western Europe and from the International Free Church Committee in Geneva. Inevitably, Hagelin had hopes that it would be effective. 'You can't imagine how many times I would be waiting to hear a telephone call or get a telegram when I was in Sweden, to hear that Dagmar had been found in the street, or at some police station, and that she'd been set free. But it never came.'

Finding some news about her had become the chief task of Dr Walter, the Swedish ambassador, and he brought a determination and a personal commitment to the task. Occasionally he would receive snippets of information, but they were almost always from suspect sources, or were intended to keep him quiet. In March 1978 he heard from a fairly senior officer in military intelligence who had fallen from grace that Dagmar had been given a fifty-fifty chance of recovering from her injuries at the end of the previous January. Three months later he heard from the man again: after treatment, Dagmar had made a full recovery. That was the last Dr Walter heard from his source, or indeed from any source. Not long afterwards, tired out by his struggle against a government which had no interest in being truthful about the case, he asked the Foreign Ministry in Stockholm to transfer him. The Argentines held a special farewell reception for him and offered him a decoration, but he rejected it. After that, newspapers like *La Prensa* which followed an almost slavishly pro-military line ran a series of hostile articles on Dr Walter; *La Prensa* called its story 'A Diplomat Who Does Not Understand Diplomacy'.

Mar del Plata is the Brighton, the Boulogne, the Atlantic City of Argentina: the slightly brash seaside resort that serves the chief city of the country. Women with fat legs and stockings rolled down sit in deckchairs; fast cars drive around, crammed with too many people. The theatres at Mar del Plata are good starting points for plays which will later transfer to Buenos Aires, and the restaurants are almost as good as those in the capital. All along the coast are the vast houses that wealthy families built for themselves from about 1910 onwards: mansions with tiled roofs and balconies and widow's walks overlooking the sea, set in their own grounds.

The Villa Joyosa is just such a house, in the style which Argentines vaguely call 'colonial', painted white, with a large and unnecessary tower at one end of the main building. The road from Mar del Plata separates it from the sea, and it is surrounded by a low wall. In front is a cafeteria which boasts a pool table. Behind, in the grounds, is a four-storey building, also painted white, with an iron staircase on the outside, and beyond that a park opens out, well planted with mature trees. In the past, it belonged to the Jewish community of Buenos Aires, and served as a holiday home. In those days it was not called the Villa Joyosa; that was clearly an estate agent's inspiration, to emphasize the attractiveness of the surroundings and catch a buyer who did not know of the house's recent history. So far it has not been successful; not surprisingly, since the Villa Joyosa was, in effect, an extermination camp used by the Navy. The neighbours reported later that in 1977 and part of 1978 they would hear the sound of shooting coming from the house almost every night, and the tree trunks of the pleasant park are studded with bullet holes. Inside the house, one wall carried a slogan so clearly set out that it required several coats of paint to obscure it: 'We will carry on killing until people understand.' It was a place for torturing and murdering people, not for holding them prisoner for long periods of time; there was a crematorium in the grounds where some of the bodies were disposed of, while others were taken out by rubber dinghy and dropped into the current, which took them well away from the Villa Joyosa and the pleasant holiday resorts along the coast.

It was from here that the last unconfirmed stories about Dagmar were received. She was not, however, brought here as most people were, for quick execution. There was said to be one other person at the Villa who was being held there indefinitely, because he, like Dagmar, was a considerable embarrassment to the Navy and had to be hidden away, since no one wanted to take a decision on their fate. The man had been a member of a kidnap gang himself, and had beaten a prisoner so badly that the man had died; but the horror of his death had sent the Navy man mad, and there may have been some fear that he would talk about the things he had seen and done. The information that Dagmar too was held there comes from the ubiquitous Raúl Vilariño, who says he was sent there in November 1977 on an errand for his superior officers at the Naval Mechanics School in Buenos Aires, whose outstation the Villa was. Vilariño said later that he had been walking round the park when he came across a blonde girl sitting in a wheelchair, one of the wheels of which was stuck in the ground. She asked him to move it for her, and he did so. Her right leg seemed to be paralysed, but otherwise she seemed healthy enough. He asked her name, and when she answered he said it sounded Scandinavian. 'It could be Argentine also,' she said.

When the Argentine magazine *La Semana* arranged a meeting between Vilariño and Ragnar Hagelin in Uruguay, Hagelin brought a photograph of Dagmar with him. Vilariño looked at it for a moment and then said, 'I'm sorry to have to tell you it was your daughter I saw there.' It is possible that as the major source of information about what went on at the Navy's interrogation centres Vilariño simply wanted to make his testimony both more credible and more valuable by linking himself with a well-known case like that of Dagmar. On the other hand, the rest of his evidence about the Villa Joyosa proved to be accurate: he described the house itself, and the grounds, and the buildings in the grounds, including the ovens where the bodies were cremated.

After Hagelin had returned to Argentina, he went with an investigating judge to the Villa in January 1984. He saw the cells and the cremation ovens and was still looking for evidence when a Swedish journalist who had accompanied him on the visit called out excitedly from the park. Hagelin went over to see what it was, and saw the journalist pointing to the trunk of one of the trees. In the bark, someone had cut the initials 'DH'. But like all the evidence about Dagmar Hagelin's fate, it is far from being conclusive: the initials could have been those of someone else, even if 'H' is not a particularly common initial for surnames in a Spanish-speaking country.

A doctor in Mar del Plata later told a newspaper that he had administered drugs to prisoners at the Villa in order to put them into a coma, and he added that he thought that Dagmar might have been among them. A report, less well-founded, said that she had been transferred to a clandestine gaol in Tucumán Province, but when Hagelin went there and searched in all the gaols that had been discovered, he could find no sign of her. If the information which the Swedish ambassador received about her was accurate – and there must be doubt about that as well – she was given only a 50 per cent chance of living in January 1978 – two months after Vilariño claims to have seen her in her wheelchair at the Villa Joyosa, when she appeared to him to be normal apart from the paralysis of her leg. Her father says he received some indication that she had been tortured, but that seems unlikely to have occurred at the Villa, where she was clearly allowed out in the grounds in her wheelchair.

It seems possible that assuming she really was there, Dagmar survived until the last days of the Villa's use by the Navy, before it was closed in June or July of 1978 – shortly before the World Cup was staged in Argentina. There is abundant evidence from other sources that the order went out to kill most of the surviving prisoners held in clandestine gaols around Argentina in the months before the World Cup, perhaps to prevent any damaging disclosures. In that case, the likelihood is that she was given some powerful drug and killed soon afterwards, her body either dropped out at sea or cremated in the grounds were she had taken exercise and may have carved her initials on a tree. She would have been eighteen years old.

But even if that represents the most likely of all the theories, Ragnar Hagelin cannot be certain. For a long time, he was kept going by the thought that she was alive somewhere, perhaps in a coma and kept alive by ventilators and a drip feed. Once during his stay in Sweden, when he was watching television, Dagmar's photograph suddenly appeared on the screen and a newsflash announced that the military authorities in Argentina had assured the Swedish Football Association that Dagmar's case would definitely be solved in August – after the World Cup was over. It was a great shock to him, and it raised his hopes. But it turned out to be just another way of delaying things further, of winning a few more months. Later, the Argentine Embassy contacted him on several occasions, telling him that the only way to get Dagmar back would be for him to return to the country to live. The third time they contacted him, he agreed, and he went back with his new family in June 1979. Even then, with the military still in power, there was an outside chance that she might be alive somewhere. But the military government handed over power to a civilian one which was committed to discovering what had happened to the disappeared; and in some ways for people like Ragnar Hagelin the knowledge that the secret gaols were now open, and the tiny number who had survived was all that would be found, was harder to bear than the years of faint hope.

# 8 WAR WITHOUT FRONTIERS

*'Subversion is not a problem which requires a solely military response. It is a global phenomenon which also demands a global strategy in all aspects of life: political, cultural, economic and military.'* – General Videla, April 1976.

Two young Uruguayan women, living some miles apart from each other in Buenos Aires, each decided to spend the evening of 13 July 1976 at home alone. Ana Inés Quadros was 32, Sara Rita Méndez, 31. They knew each other slightly – most upper middle-class Uruguayans do, since it's such a small country – but as a result of the events of that night they were to become close friends.

Uruguayans have always come to Argentina in large numbers. The journey is a short one: thirty minutes by air from Montevideo to Buenos Aires, an hour from Colonia to the Argentine capital if you take the hydrofoil across the immense River Plate estuary. Historically the two countries are very close, and Uruguay might well still be a large province of Argentina if its history had been slightly different. As it is, Uruguayans feel themselves at home in Buenos Aires, much more than Irish people do in London, say, or Canadians in New York. Ana Quadros and Sara Méndez were both from Uruguay's small and wealthy upper middle class, and both had come to Buenos Aires because of the political situation at home.

Sara was quick-minded and serious, slightly built, and with lively, expressive features. In 1976 she was living in the expensive Buenos Aires suburb of Belgrano with her baby son Simón. He was twenty days old on the night of the 13th. Ana Quadros came from a wealthier family and was a famous beauty, with large, dark eyes, high cheekbones and a delicately shaped mouth. She had been educated in England, at Mayfield School, and, like many people of her class in Uruguay, spoke English almost as well as she spoke Spanish – and she spoke it with a soft, cultured English accent. Her father had been Uruguay's ambassador in London, and at first Ana Quadros seemed destined for the conventional existence of a well-to-do Uruguayan. She married a man even wealthier than herself, and had three children, and spent her summers at Punta del Este, the fashionable resort of the Uruguayan coast, and her winters visiting Europe. But the predictable pattern of life as a hostess and mother was interrupted. Ana Quadros began to find her privileged life boring, and, much against the wishes of her husband and her parents, she announced that she wanted to go to university.

In Uruguay, even more than in Argentina, the urban guerrilla groups of the Sixties and Seventies were composed very largely of middle-class students, who found the sterile, placid course of Uruguayan domestic politics deeply unsatisfying. Some of them had been educated in Europe, and were influenced by the student protests of 1968; though the Tupamaros guerrillas of Uruguay preferred rifles and bombs to the cobble-stones of the French students they tried to emulate. Both Ana Quadros and Sara Méndez, at university in Montevideo in the same years, became converts to many of the ideas current among students at the time. Sara Méndez joined the tiny leftist PVP, the Party for the Victory of the People; Ana Quadros joined a broader and much more moderate group, the Frente Amplio or Broad Front, which included not just communists and socialists but breakaway groups from the two established centrist parties, the Blancos or Whites and the Colorados or Reds, which had alternated in power for years and whose policies were in many ways almost indistinguishable. Neither woman was involved in the activities of the Tupamaros guerrillas, though some of their friends no doubt were. But the increasing political and social dislocation brought about by the Tupamaros' campaign led directly to the military coup of 1973, and to a dictatorship by the armed forces which lasted eleven years and was one of the worst in Latin America in terms of brutal torture and repression. In those circumstances, Ana Quadros's links with the left became a threat to her and even to her establishment-minded family. Her husband divorced her and gained custody of their three children, with her own parents' tacit agreement. She went into hiding, even though the Frente Amplio to which she belonged was still legal, and eventually made her way to Argentina. Thousands of Uruguayans with a left-wing background made the same journey, including Sara Méndez.

At much the same time on the night of 13 July 1976, groups of armed men went to the homes of the two women and took them prisoner. Sara Méndez tried to persuade the men to let her take the baby, but they forced her to leave him behind with no one to look after him. After a drive through the city, they were brought to a place where they could hear a metal door being rolled up, as though they were in a garage. A flight of metal steps led to a big open room where, despite her blindfold, Ana Quadros thought that about thirty or forty people were being held. They were allowed to lie down or sit up as they chose, but they were not allowed to speak. And they were kept blindfolded the entire time they were there – thirteen days. Even so, by picking up small details here and there – an occasional whisper or comment from one of the guards – the two women realized from the accents of those around them that most of the others were Uruguayans too. There had been a widespread operation to pick them up.

Years later, the two women were able to identify the clandestine detention centre where they were held as 'Orletti'; it had been a garage and car repair works, and still bears the name 'Orletti Automobiles' over its metal door. It is in a suburb northwest of Buenos Aires city centre, on the corner of Venancio Flores and Emilio Lamarca streets: an unremarkable sort of place which, when they returned to it, seemed virtually unchanged. While they were looking at it, one or two people came up to them and explained that although they had known what Orletti was used for, they had been too frightened to say anything. One person said the noise and screaming coming from the former garage had been so bad he had been forced to move away. Telling the story now, neither woman feels much anger against such people. 'That's what it was like in Argentina in those days,' they say.

Among the other Uruguayans who were being held there when Ana Quadros and Sara Méndez were brought in was a well-known journalist, Enrique Rodríguez Larreta, who had come to Buenos Aires a week before to search for his son, who had disappeared the previous month. In a way, his search had been successful: he recognized his son's voice among those of his fellow-prisoners in the garage. Through brief, whispered conversations and the occasional overheard remark from their guards, the prisoners also discovered that three of Uruguay's most prominent trades unionists were there too. Gerardo Gatti, Hugo Méndez and León Duarte had all taken refuge in Argentina after the coup in their own country, and all had disappeared a few weeks before Ana Quadros and Sara Méndez were taken.

The two women did not know what would happen to them from

one moment to the next. Sometimes they would be taken in groups for torture, sometimes individually. There was no pattern to it, though the majority of torturing sessions took place at night. What their inquisitors wanted to know were details of other Uruguayans living in Buenos Aires, and of some people who were still living in Uruguay. It became apparent that among the Argentines who were questioning them there were a number of Uruguayans, serving officers in the Uruguayan forces, who gave themselves away by the way they spoke, and above all by their detailed knowledge of Uruguayan politics. To drown out the screams from the people they tortured, the guards switched on the engines of the cars downstairs in the garage, and raced them to a high pitch; on top of that, they would play music very loudly. Sara and Ana were both badly tortured; their wrists were tied together behind their backs and they were hung up by the arms and given electric shocks all over their bodies. The guards spread coarse salt underneath them, so that if the prisoners allowed their feet, covered with perspiration from the torture, to touch the floor the conductivity would be greatly increased. True to their self-image of being quieter and subtler than Argentines, the Uruguayan officers would sometimes whisper to the women that they should be grateful they weren't totally at the mercy of 'those Argentine savages'. Sara Méndez lost the use of her arms, and after the torture sessions when she was back in the main room where everyone was held, another prisoner had to help her to her feet by pushing against her. They were fed only twice during the 13 days they were there, but the two women both felt that was because of a lack of organization on the part of their guards, rather than a deliberate policy. Things were so casual that two Uruguayans who had been part of an earlier batch of prisoners at Orletti had been left behind by mistake when the earlier prisoners were 'transferred'. There was some security in keeping with the newcomers; a conversation between two of the guards indicated that some at least of them would be sent back to Uruguay.

Not by any means all of them, though. Another Uruguayan, Washington Pérez, was taken to Orletti at the same time as Ana Quadros and Sara Méndez, but he was not a prisoner: he was there to act as a negotiator with the three trade union leaders. When Pérez arrived, he recognized several Uruguayan officers, who were setting the captives up as Montonero kidnap victims in an attempt to ransom the union leaders for cash, and Pérez, who knew two of them, was supposed to travel to Europe to raise the money from exiled sympathizers. He saw the union leaders, but they had been broken by torture and were in a pitiful state. As he said goodbye to one of them, León Duarte, and embraced him, Duarte whispered in his ear, 'Just get away from here.' Pérez, frightened for his own safety, sought help from the United Nations High Commission for Refugees in Buenos Aires, and was eventually sent with his family to Sweden, where he made his story public. The three trades unionists were never seen alive again.

The other Uruguayans in Orletti were told on 26 July that they were being transferred. Adhesive tape was stuck over their eyes, their hands were bound, and they were put inside a lorry, together with boxes of stolen goods; earlier, Sara Méndez had caught a glimpse of some of her own furniture in the detention centre – her house had been robbed by the men who abducted her. The lorry, with thirty or so Uruguayans on board, went straight to a military airport, where a plane of the Uruguayan Air Force was waiting for them. Less than an hour later, it landed at an airfield outside the Uruguayan capital, Montevideo. In a way they were safer: the Uruguayans, though notorious for their ill-treatment of prisoners, had no systematic plan for murdering them. They were held prisoner for many months, and then found themselves caught up in an absurd piece of theatre, staged apparently for the benefit of the newly-elected Carter administration in Washington. The United States had announced that it would stop military aid to Latin American countries which had a bad human rights record, unless those countries could show that they were threatened by invasion from abroad. After five months in gaol, 14 of the group which had been brought back from Buenos Aires – including Sara Méndez and Ana Quadros – were taken to a house in the village of Shangri-la, 20 kilometres from Montevideo. Their hands were tied, but their blindfolds were taken off. Directly they arrived, the house was surrounded by soldiers. In the meantime, Uruguayan television and radio were announcing that the security forces had tracked down a group of guerrillas who had arrived in the country as part of an attempt to organize a leftist invasion of the country. The 'terrorist fourteen' were led from the house in full view of the carefully sited cameras, handcuffed and walking in line, and several of them were forced to go through the motions of confessing to the invasion plan for the television cameras.

For Ana and Sara, the advantage was that they were now legalized prisoners who would not be allowed to disappear again. Ana Quadros's father, as ambassador and a partial supporter of the military government, had been unable to obtain any information about her during the months before the televised raid at Shangri-la, and it was only now that her family and Sara's were able to make contact with them. For Sara Méndez, it was a cruel moment: the military had led her to believe that her baby son Simón, less than three weeks old when she was forced to leave him behind at her flat in Buenos Aires, had been handed over to her family. When she finally saw her parents, they told her it was not true; indeed, they had been given the impression that he was with her in prison. Simón's father went to the Chilean capital Santiago when it was reported that two Argentine children had turned up there, but Simón was not one of them. Both Sara Méndez and Ana Quadros spent the next five years in prison, and even from there Sara tried to get information about her son's fate. When the British ambassador was brought to the gaol in August 1977, as part of a carefully devised tour for foreign dignitaries, Sara managed to approach him and ask him for help, but the enquiries were fruitless.

Today, the two women have come through their experiences with few outward signs of what they have endured. Ana Quadros wears expensive, well-tailored clothes and is still beautiful, looking younger than her thirty-nine years; but now that she has left the world of embassy receptions and English public schools behind her, her English is not as good as it once was. Sara Méndez has lost more than a good accent, and she seems more serious – impenetrably serious, as though nothing will ever make her entirely happy again. Her voice, habitually quiet, becomes even softer when she explains that at thirty-eight, after the experiences she has been through, she has been advised not to try to have any more children. Simón she accepts, is probably lost to her for ever, whether he is alive or dead.

The groundwork for the kind of co-operation between Latin American countries which made the arrest, imprisonment and forcible repatriation of Ana Quadros and Sara Méndez possible was laid in Montevideo, as it happens, at a meeting of commanders-in-chief of the armed forces of half a dozen or more countries, with Videla from Argentina prominent among them. They were there to discuss the threat of international Communism, and the means they should use to combat it. The head of the Brazilian Army, General Fritz de Asevedo Manso, told the meeting that they now faced a total war, which was being fought throughout the world; and indeed to military men whose forces were fighting subversion and left-wing opposition in many parts of the continent – the ERP and the Montoneros in Argentina, the Tupamaros in Uruguay, the ELN in Bolivia, the MIR in Chile, and so on – the threat must have seemed very real. The Brazilians seemed well-placed to teach the others what to do, since in 1964 they had taken on an urban guerrilla movement and had brought it under almost complete control by the time of the Montevideo conference, eleven years later. And once there was a meeting of minds over the nature of the problem, it was an easy step to take to decide to help each other out in dealing with it. Even two traditional enemies like Argentina and Chile were happy to co-operate in the persecution of their internal opponents: at the very time when the two countries were mobilizing their armies to go to war over the Beagle Channel in 1978, the same two armies were exchanging information and prisoners – so long as they were political prisoners.

It was not entirely incorrect to portray Latin American guerrilla movements as an 'international' threat. By 1974 a Revolutionary Co-ordinating Council had been formed to link a number of left-wing guerrilla groups and the ERP, the Tupamaros, the MIR and the ELN were all members of it. The Council went so far as to agree on a standard issue machine-gun for its members. But such decisions were mostly for propaganda purposes; in practice, the individual guerrilla movements of Latin America operated largely on their own, with little material support from the others, or, in the main, from Marxist régimes elsewhere in the world. The people who became genuinely international were the political refugees, and Argentina, with its European atmosphere and high standard of living, became a natural settling place for them as country after country in Latin America succumbed to a kind of right-wing domino effect: in 1954, Paraguay fell to the military dictatorship of General Stroessner; Brazil followed, ten years later, and there were military coups in Bolivia in 1971, and Chile and Uruguay in 1973. Argentina was the odd man out, the only reasonable place to go to in the southern part of Latin America, and the military government which eventually took over there too claimed that half a million people entered the country illegally between 1971 and 1976. Only 300 people were officially listed as political refugees, because Argentine governments, while adhering to the relevant international protocols and conventions, nevertheless placed a rigid interpretation on the term, which meant that only people who had been affected by 'events occurring in Europe' were classed as refugees in Argentina: in other words, only people who had come from Europe as a result of the Second World War. All the same, Argentina's record of hospitality to Latin American refugees had in fact been a good one, but it was an ad hoc, informal sort of welcome, which could evaporate at any time.

The time came with Isabel Perón. During 1974, stories began circulating about attacks on refugees by the Triple A. General Carlos Prats, who had been one of the few constitutionalist generals in Chile, and had tried to head off opposition to the Marxist President Salvador Allende, was killed together with his wife by a car bomb in September 1974, after taking refuge in Argentina. The murder was assumed to have been the work of DINA, the Chilean secret police force set up by General Pinochet after he had seized power. The man in charge of General Prats's safety was a future President of Argentina, General Bignone, but since DINA had been provided by the Argentines with office space within the central police headquarters in Buenos Aires, the assassination cannot have been too difficult to organize. About forty Chilean agents are thought to have worked from the office. Before the coup, five Uruguayans were abducted in Buenos Aires in the same month, and their bodies turned up inside Uruguay. In 1975 security men from Paraguay arrested two Paraguayan exiles in Argentina and took them back to face certain death.

Directly the military took power in Argentina, the position became worse for foreign refugees. The new régime promised that they would be left unmolested, but as with so many similar promises made at the time, it was broken immediately. Some arrests were carried out by the Argentine forces on behalf of foreign governments, others by the agents of those governments. Within a month of the Argentine coup, the bodies of five Uruguayans were washed up on the beaches of the River Plate, on the Uruguayan side; all were of people who had last been seen alive in Argentina, across the river. Over the next six months 13 more bodies were found on the Uruguayan shore, all naked and most showing signs of torture. Some were mutilated. The cases were sometimes reported in the press; once, for instance, the Uruguayan authorities announced that the corpses were those of North Korean sailors who had been drinking and fell from a ship. But the faces did not have Asiatic features, and an Argentine woman later identified one of the bodies, which bore a distinctive tattoo, as that of her son.

Chileans, too, continued to be at risk. At one stage, an average of twenty were disappearing each week in Argentina, and there was a particularly active repatriation service conducted along the border in towns like Junin de los Andes and Mendoza. As late as 1981, two Chileans who had been living in Europe during the worst period of repression in their own country and in Argentina were arrested near the border and taken to an unknown destination – probably Chile. In all probability, the Chileans had asked the Argentines to arrest them and hand them over. Not long after the 1976 coup, a former President of Bolivia, General Juan Torres, who had taken refuge in Buenos Aires, was kidnapped in broad daylight in the centre of the city. The area is full of cafés and expensive shops, and there were a number of witnesses, but in answer to the urgent enquiries that were made, the Interior Ministry suggested that it was an example of 'self-kidnapping', whereby someone who wanted to go underground staged his own arrest. General Torres, though a military man, had formed a left-wing alliance to challenge the military government of General Banzer – the man who had replaced him as Bolivia's leader. The Interior Ministry's ingenious suggestion of 'self-kidnapping' was disproved when Torres's body was found dumped in the town of San Antonio de Giles in Buenos Aires Province, some months later.

Political assassination was a weapon aimed at refugees in the centre of the political spectrum, as well as the left. Senator Zelmar Michelini of Uruguay came to Buenos Aires and lived there openly after the coup in his country, and he was much admired by the *émigré* community because he was always ready to help his fellow Uruguayans. Early in the morning of 18 May 1976 he was kidnapped from his home by a group of armed men, while elsewhere in the city another respected politician from Uruguay, Héctor Gutiérrez Ruiz, a former President of the Chamber of Deputies there, was also picked up. The entrance to Ruiz's apartment lay immediately across the street from the office of the Brazilian military attaché, where an armed guard was posted, day and night. During the raid on Ruiz's apartment, the guard heard the noise and came to see what was going on, but left after the kidnappers had shown him their identity cards. Four days later the bodies of Ruiz and Michelini, together with those of two other Uruguayans, were found in an abandoned car. An official at the Ministry of Defence, Brigadier José Klix, told one journalist, 'We're dealing here with a Uruguayan operation. I don't know if it's official or not.' In fact, it seems to have been a joint

Argentine-Uruguayan operation, like the arrest and torture of Ana Quadros and Sara Méndez. Officers from OCOA, the main anti-subversion agency in Uruguay, and others from SID, Uruguayan intelligence, were allowed to function on Argentine soil throughout the Dirty War. There were occasional signs, too, of a three-way link between the various intelligence groups. The two children of a Uruguayan couple who had been murdered after the entire family had been abducted and taken from Argentina to Uruguay were eventually discovered in Chile: the children had been taken across two frontiers and dumped in a square in the town of Valparaiso, with no money and no papers. A Chilean family had taken them in and looked after them. On another occasion, two Uruguayans who had escaped to Paraguay were abducted, sent to Argentina, and handed over to the Uruguayan authorities. For many, it seemed that there was no escape from repression; it was a nightmarish world in which all routes were sealed off. If terrorism was perceived as an international menace by the military at the time of the coup in Argentina, the situation was reversed within two years: by 1978, it was state terror that had become international.

Many people came to the decision that the only way of avoiding the death squads and the increasingly savage repression was simply to leave Argentina altogether. Around two million did just that during the years of the Process. The most popular cities for Argentines abroad were Madrid, Mexico City, Paris and Rome. Madrid and Rome were relatively easy to get visas for, because many Argentines had dual Spanish or Italian nationality. Paris had long been a centre of refugee activity for Latin Americans as well as the favourite city for Argentine students abroad. But the chief base for political exiles during the political repression in Argentina was Mexico City. Well before the 1976 coup, refugees had started arriving in Mexico. More than any other Latin American country, Mexico had the reputation of being a tolerant, even friendly, host for exiles from other countries in Latin America. The first wave of people seeking political asylum came in 1973 following the resignation of Dr Héctor Cámpora and the end of his left-wing Peronist Government. Then, on Perón's death, the growing activities of the Triple A forced many more to go abroad. Certainly, the publication of death lists by the Triple A led to an exodus of leading left-wing Peronists. By the middle of 1975, the Argentine community in Mexico City included two former Rectors of the University of Buenos Aires who had fled the country in September 1974; Peronist journalists, many of whom went to work on the Mexican daily newspaper, *El Día*; a former Governor of the province of Córdoba, Ricardo Obregón Cano, who had been overthrown in a police-led coup; and the former Minister of the Interior under Cámpora, Esteban Righi. Righi left Argentina soon after Dr Cámpora's resignation because he knew he was a target of the Triple A; he had been responsible for the amnesty law which had given many guerrillas their freedom, and had overseen the dismantling of the Department for Anti-Democratic Information which had collated details of left-wing activities. Two years before the military coup, Dr Cámpora himself had taken refuge in Mexico. He had briefly served as Argentina's Ambassador to Mexico but, with the rise of the right-wing Peronists, was no longer welcome in the government, at home or abroad. He went on to run a dental clinic with Obregón Cano in Mexico, but in 1975 returned to Buenos Aires. Dr Cámpora was to find himself still in Argentina when the military took control and was forced, once more, to turn to the Mexicans for protection, but this time he was depending on them for more than just somewhere to live: he needed them to save his life.

The political refugees who flowed into Mexico after the coup included not only politicians but also guerrillas. The Montoneros withdrew from Argentina in large numbers, leaving fairly small groups of commandos to carry out acts against the authorities, and a majority of the thousand or so Montoneros who regrouped beyond Argentina's borders went to Mexico, usually entering as tourists or 'businessmen'. The strategic base for the guerrilla organization became Havana where they were given the protection of the Cuban government, but Mexico City became the Montoneros' foreign political headquarters. The resistance campaign, especially during the run-up to the World Cup of 1978, was organized from Mexico City. For a time, there was even a 'Casa Montonero' in the city which served as a sort of embassy for the guerrillas, until the Argentine government persuaded the Mexicans to close it down.

Peronists, trades unionists, artists, teachers and actors left, too; anyone falling into the category of 'subversive' or 'leftist' was safer outside Argentina than inside it. About a quarter of a million people went to Mexico after the coup – about eight times more than the number who had left in 1973 and 1974. Most of them did not apply for formal status as political refugees; they just made the easy journey from Venezuela or the United States and settled. There was relative security in Mexico, but it was only relative because Argentine intelligence agents travelled abroad looking for exiles and certainly operated in Mexico. Several attempts were made to assassinate or kidnap guerrilla and Peronist leaders there, but they all failed. The most curious plot to come to light was against Obregón Cano, the former governor (and Cámpora's dentistry partner). At the beginning of 1978, a Montonero guerrilla, Tulio Valenzuela, was kidnapped in Argentina together with his wife and son. While his family were being held as hostages, he was apparently forced to co-operate with officers of Naval Intelligence and the Second Army Corps, travelling to Mexico to assist in the kidnapping or murder of Obregón Cano and Montonero leaders. But when Valenzuela got to Mexico, he decided to reveal the plot and called a press conference to disclose the details of the operation, challenging the military to take whatever measures they wished against his wife and child, if they were still alive. This saved Obregón Cano and embarrassed General Galtieri, who was commander of the Army Corps connected with the plot. Valenzuela's case, though, was a complex and mysterious one, and he was treated with great suspicion by the Montonero leadership in Mexico. The regional secretariat of his own guerrilla cell in Argentina had betrayed him, and perhaps the Montoneros thought he had acted as a double agent by collaborating with the Army. Whatever the truth, his superiors in the movement ordered him to go back to Argentina after he had given his news conference revealing the details of 'Operation Mexico', and, as they may have expected, he was shot as he tried to cross the Argentine border – though even then the Montoneros must have considered the theory that Argentine intelligence had disposed of him in order to safeguard other double agents and other operations. His wife and son were found dead some days later.

In spite of such alarming activities, the Mexican Government continued to be lenient towards political exiles from Argentina. In other countries they were less fortunate. At least 12 Montoneros disappeared or were assassinated outside Argentina: four in Peru, two in Uruguay, and others in Rio de Janeiro and Madrid. Argentine agents were active in Spain and in France.

In Argentina, the fear within the refugee community mounted as stories of the actions against them multiplied. The United Nations High Commission for Refugees (UNHCR), which had an office in the capital, had been growing increasingly alarmed at the use of terror against foreigners. It was becoming so bad by 1976 that to be a refugee was tantamount to being subversive. UNHCR set up hostels and refuges for those who were most endangered and to help protect those who were trying to leave the country, but the junta's hostile attitude scared many refugees away from even the UN's protection; to register with them could mean identifying yourself. Such caution seemed justified when, four nights after the coup, a number of UN hostels were raided by the police. Refugees in one Buenos Aires hostel were detained and interrogated. Later, UNHCR's own offices were raided and files were taken, including lists of the names and addresses of refugees and their families. Fortunately, many of those on the lists had already left the country.

UNHCR's efforts to find countries for refugees to go to were made even more difficult because the Argentine authorities arbitrarily changed rules and regulations in order to tighten the net around the refugee community. A decree was passed making foreigners liable to expulsion from Argentina back to their native countries for failing to report previous convictions in their *own* countries and for carrying out activities which affected 'social peace, national security or public order'. Such decrees tended to drive refugees into hiding. But if exiles attempted to go through official procedures and legally obtain residence in Argentina, the immigration office was likely to classify them as illegal residents, immediately making them liable for deportation back to their home countries.

The Commission countered such moves by keeping refugees informed of the current restrictions and the likely tricks being played by the Argentine officials. Hostels and hotel rooms, which were secretly kept with a kind of block bookings system for refugees, were rotated to prevent detection by the police. Those in the greatest danger would be escorted in United Nations cars, and might stay at UN officials' own homes for safety. Twelve thousand refugees were registered with the UN at the time of the coup, but there were many more than that who weren't registered.

Those who were registered were mainly the ones who were interested in leaving the country, but many refugees wished to stay in Argentina, hoping one day to get back to their native countries. UNHCR worked to find countries which were taking people in for people who did want to settle in another country. They managed to place 1,000 refugees a month during 1976. But finding third countries and obtaining visas still left the problem of getting them out of Argentina. If the security forces of a country wanted to detain someone leaving Argentina they would often try to abduct them as they boarded the plane on the way out. This made it imperative to put refugees on flights with an embassy official of the country which was accepting them. But that alone might not be sufficient protection, if the flight touched down for refuelling or to take on passengers in neighbouring countries. Airports and immigration offices and passport control took on a new and frightening aspect for political refugees. In one case, UNHCR put two Uruguayans destined for Belgium onto a Sabena airlines flight out of Argentina, chosen because it was not scheduled to touch down on Uruguayan territory. UNHCR had even taken pains to establish that the plane did not cross Uruguayan airspace in case Uruguayan agents were aboard the flight. Suddenly the flight plans were changed; the aircraft landed in Montevideo to pick up more passengers and the Uruguayans were forcibly taken off the plane. It was only after long, tough negotiations and considerable international pressure that they were allowed back on board. Airports such as Ezeiza in Buenos Aires were under military jurisdiction, with checkpoints and guard posts, so that getting out by air was usually a harrowing experience even with a diplomatic escort.

About forty minutes' drive from the Plaza de Mayo in the centre of the capital is the pleasant suburb of Belgrano. Its quiet, leafy streets are lined with a mixture of expensive high-rise apartments, private schools, small shops and embassies. Belgrano is a favourite residential area for many military officers, particularly naval men, because it's near to many military administrative buildings and a number of offices for weapons production identified only by the letters FM on the doors, which stand for 'Fabricaciones Militares'. The ESMA complex is only a little way down the road, and, during the Process years, a clandestine interrogation centre was even closer. But right in the middle of the suburb on Arcos Street, the Mexican ambassador's residence provided Argentina's safest 'safe house' for people being hunted by the junta. From 1976, the residence was one of the few places where secure asylum could be provided, as well as safe passage out of Argentina.

There were considerable risks involved in actually making it through the streets of Belgrano, and up to the gates of the embassy residence. Many policemen and military officers were operating in the area, and once word spread that the Mexicans were taking people in, police were posted on street corners near the residence and elsewhere in Belgrano suburb. Many decided to run the gauntlet up to the residence's wrought-iron gates anyway. Most arrived at night and rang the bell, hiding near the walls outside the grounds of the residence to avoid being seen. One man came dressed as a woman, with a handkerchief tied around his head because he knew the police were looking for him. Once the bell was rung, a guard would swing open the gates and the new arrival would become a refugee, protected by the diplomatic immunity of the Mexican ambassador. There was nothing the Argentine authorities could do once someone was inside the grounds of the residence. If the junta had disregarded diplomatic protocol, they would have brought the full weight of the international community's indignation down on themselves. And so, for years, the ambassador's residence became a hostel for fugitives – albeit a rather civilized one, as hostels go.

New residents were given a change of clothes, so that one outfit could be worn while the other was washed. Toothpaste and other basic toiletries were handed out. Nobody knew how long their stay would last. It depended on how quickly they would be accepted as refugees by Mexico or another country and on whether the Argentine government would allow them safe conduct out of the country. It was impossible to leave the ambassador's residence without a guarantee of safe conduct through Argentine territory given by the junta, because without it, the moment a refugee set foot outside the confines of the residence, he could be picked up. And the very act of going to the Mexicans ensured that the security forces would have a definite interest in the case. Once inside, then, there was no going back, no changing one's mind, and nothing but the basic necessities of life. The residence staff were the only ones who could go out to buy food and other essentials.

The most famous guest of the period of the Dirty War was Dr Héctor Cámpora. His house was raided in March that year but he and his son escaped arrest and managed to reach the embassy residence before the security services caught up with them. From early 1976 until late November 1979 Dr Cámpora stayed inside the Mexican ambassador's residence. He was, with his son, one of the longest-staying guests of any embassy in Buenos Aires, because the military would not allow the Cámporas to leave the country. Indeed, Dr Cámpora outlasted two of Mexico's ambassadors to Argentina. As subsequent diplomats took up residence in Arcos

Street, Dr Cámpora would make it his job to greet them warmly, then proceed to give them the tour of the Spanish-style colonial building, pointing out its interesting features. His tour would end up on the first floor, where the ambassador and his family were allocated space.

In the early years of military rule, that space was limited. Up to seventy people at any one time were being sheltered by the Mexicans. Although the residence is a substantial house, it is by no means a mansion. The handsome house is set back from the street with a modest garden laid out at the front. Inside on the ground floor are three elegant reception rooms, kitchens and the ambassador's own library. The residence is decorated in simple but good taste; highly polished parquet floors, beautiful carpets, gilded mirrors and marble-topped tables. On the walls hang paintings from Europe and Mexico and on the mantelpiece there is the traditional Mexican symbol of Christian hope, the terracotta Tree of Life. During the tour, Dr Cámpora would explain to the newly arrived ambassador that these ground-floor rooms had been turned into a set of dining and recreation areas for the inhabitants of the residence. The library, too, was opened to refugees. On the first floor, next to the bedroom suites for the ambassador and his family, bedrooms were provided for a few of the refugees. The floor above, which was the attic, housed the rest. Fold-out beds and mattresses filled the attic wall-to-wall, laid out under the eaves. And in the basement, more beds were kept next door to the boiler room.

At mealtimes, small tables were set up in the reception rooms and in an empty garage at the back of the residence. The formal dining-room table only sat 20 people, so dinner was served throughout the ground floor. Extra kitchen staff were taken on to cater for the larger numbers and the embassy's budget for food was quadrupled.

The summer of 1977 was the most uncomfortable one for everyone at the residence as they waited to hear news of when they could leave the country. The ambassador even investigated the possibility of purchasing another house nearby to service as a 'refugee annexe' so that people could sleep in less cramped quarters. The plan was never carried out in the end, because the rate at which refugees were granted asylum abroad picked up soon after 1977.

After dinner, the guests would play cards, listen to the radio, watch television, or read in the library. The previous owners of the residence had been German immigrants to Argentina and they had discreetly attempted to recreate the atmosphere of the 'old country' downstairs in the basement. They built a Bierkeller there, complete with wood panelling and authentic carvings in old German script above the bar. The Bierkeller now served as a table tennis and pool room. At the evening's end, everyone would head for their beds upstairs, like children trooping up to their dormitories.

The other main diversion for those who were waiting at the embassy was the swimming pool at the side of the garden at the back of the residence, shielded by high walls on all sides. But ex-president Cámpora would not go outside for this part of the ambassador's tour; during all the years he stayed at the residence, he refused to use the swimming pool because he was afraid that assassins could be planted on the balconies of any one of the many apartment blocks overlooking the residence and the gardens; he stayed indoors for four years, and inside, he was even wary of standing too close to the windows in case he was spotted by a marksman. But Dr Cámpora was also fighting against a different kind of enemy while he stayed on at the residence. He had developed a tumour in the throat which he knew needed medical care, but while the Argentine authorities refused to guarantee safe conduct out of the country, this was impossible. The military insisted that he prove that he suffered from a medical condition by producing a medical certificate stating the fact, but it was impossible to go to a hospital as long as Dr Cámpora was still being treated as a wanted criminal. Finally, in the middle of November in 1979, the junta agreed to temporarily declare a Buenos Aires hospital Mexican territory so that the former President could go there for a biopsy on his throat. The biopsy confirmed that it was throat cancer that needed urgent treatment. On the 28 November, Dr Cámpora and his son were granted safe conduct out of Argentina and flew to Mexico under heavy diplomatic protection. But the tumour was already far advanced, and despite immediate medical attention, Dr Cámpora had only a year of liberty in Mexico, dying in the town of Cuernavaca in December the following year at the age of seventy-one.

It wasn't quite so difficult for others seeking political asylum; the average length of stay at the residence was one or two months. Some people were offered asylum and given permission to leave the country within ten days or so. But refugees could never be certain how long they would have to wait, or whether the

Argentine government would put up serious objections to the requests for safe conduct. The Ministry of the Interior could deliberately cause delays if it decided that the person should be considered a common criminal. And Argentina's government didn't recognize the existence of 'political' refugees or even political persecution in many of the cases, partly because the military legal code had redefined many previously 'political' activities as criminal ones.

The usual procedure when people arrived at the residence asking for asylum and resettlement abroad was that the ambassador would interview the refugees, asking about their background, their reasons for wanting to leave the country and whether their problems amounted to political persecution and imminent danger. If the ambassador wasn't satisfied with the information he could reject the application for asylum, though in practice this almost never happened. The next stage was to ask the Ministry of the Interior for their side of the story. Predictably, it gave a completely different account of the refugee's activities; usually, in the eyes of the Ministry, they added up to dangerous criminal activities rather than political persecution. The ambassador would decide for himself which account to believe, and would assess whether the danger would be real and imminent if protection wasn't granted. The request for political asylum would then be passed on to the Foreign Ministry in Mexico City or to another country for consideration. The processing of political refugees for asylum was much more drawn out at the Mexican Embassy than at other foreign embassies during the Dirty War. Sweden and France were especially fast in deciding to accept political refugees. But altogether, nearly two hundred and fifty people passed through the Mexican ambassador's residence after the military took power and all but one or two were given asylum abroad. That was on top of tens of thousands more who didn't go to the residence itself for protection, but went by other routes to Mexico for safety.

Once accepted for settlement abroad, there was the final hurdle of actually leaving Argentina. The Mexicans had to formally request safe conduct outside the bounds of the residence because diplomatic immunity, of course, could not protect them once the refugees stepped outside the gates. Refusing to grant safe conduct was therefore a petty but effective stalling tactic on the part of the military, and a tactic contrary to various international agreements which had been signed by the Argentine government regarding the right to political asylum. Any criticism of such behaviour was met with charges that Mexico was interfering in Argentine internal affairs – the usual sort of defence put up by countries with siege mentalities – yet, once the 'common criminals' in the residence were in Mexico, the junta didn't attempt to extradite a single person who had previously been wanted under their criminal code. Mexico paid for its human rights policy. The Mexican government sought to minimize the damage to its relations with Argentina by rigidly adhering to the 'Estrada' doctrine which stated the principle of non-intervention in internal affairs, and the Mexicans never publicly criticized Argentina's military leaders for their record on human rights. But the granting of political asylum and the use of the residence meant that relations between the two countries grew very cold. Although Mexico refused to follow the lead of the United States or Sweden in condemning Argentina publicly, the military still didn't forgive Mexico for what it considered amounted to harbouring subversives. Trade between Mexico and Argentina declined from 1976 onwards; fewer business agreements were signed; a number of scientific and cultural exchanges were cancelled. Student exchange scholarships dropped off from a level of twenty-five or thirty a year to three or four.

It is possible that, by taking a 'non-political' line during the years of military repression, Mexico was more effective in helping those who arrived at the residence in Arcos Street; on the other hand, this approach was limited in its scope and only really helped those who came forward for help at considerable risk to themselves; taking in refugees had little impact on the military régime's behaviour, while a more outspoken position might have done more to force them to slacken off the ferocity of the repression. But for those who joined the community of exiles in their own country, some for months, and some for years, the Mexican ambassadors and the staff of the residence were generous, concerned and helpful; what will never be known is just how many people tried to take advantage of the Mexicans' hospitality, but never made it past the police and up to the residence gates. There are no official figures available on how many 'criminals' were picked up in the quiet streets of Belgrano suburb in the years of the junta.

# 9 THE MOTHERS OF THE PLAZA

*'This is a matter of no concern to us. These women are mad.'* – Official of the Office of the President of the Argentine Republic, questioned about the campaign on behalf of the disappeared, June 1977.

The tactic of making people disappear without trace had proved its effectiveness by the middle of 1977. It had avoided turning people into martyrs around whose names opposition to the military régime could grow; and the proof was that no one was demonstrating in the capitals of the Western world about Argentina as they had four years earlier about Chile. No foreign government had broken off diplomatic relations with the Videla régime, as they had with that of General Pinochet. It was generally known that unpleasant things were happening in Argentina, but since it was impossible to say precisely what the nature of those things was, protest and complaint were difficult to focus. Torture was known to be widespread and the assumption was that many people must have died. The report by Amnesty International in 1976 put a remarkably accurate figure on the number of people who had disappeared, but what had happened to them after they had disappeared was unknown. In a large number of cases it remains and will always remain unknown. Within Argentina itself, some people knew what was happening in considerable detail, and almost everyone, except those who wilfully refused to know, had a good idea of it. But because of the widespread terror and the complete absence of real information, it was impossible to gain any clear picture of the scale and the effect of what the military had done.

Nevertheless, although the calculation which lay behind the decision to deal with dissidents in a clandestine and apparently unofficial way had paid off handsomely, it had overlooked one detail: that some people whose sons or daughters had disappeared might be pushed to the point where they felt that they had nothing more to lose by coming out into the open and demanding to know what had happened. Other countries had shown, of course, that such outbreaks could be perfectly adequately contained: 1977 was the year of Charter '77 in Czechoslovakia, for instance, a movement which was effectively beaten down in the long run by savage police tactics and the slower grind of ensuring that the Charter's signatories would suffer in their jobs and their home lives, and in their relatives' future prospects, for having spoken out. In 1977 the Soviet Union was building up to its most effective campaign yet against dissidents who wanted greater political and religious freedom, or who dared to reveal details of the abuse of psychiatry and drugs. But this was a policy of revenge; by and large, it was impossible even in countries as closed as the Soviet Union and Czechoslovakia to prevent people from demonstrating in full view of Western journalists, and thereby highlighting their complaints.

Argentina went further, by ensuring that people who spoke out would face, not simply arrest and torture, but death; and the greater threat proved undoubtedly more effective. And yet it was not absolutely certain that the people who had been arrested and kidnapped were dead; the threat was a vague one. So there were some people therefore who ignored the dictates of ordinary common sense and self-preservation in order to come out into the open. Not very many of them, at least until the later stages of the campaign; but enough to attract attention.

Two women sit side by side in the office of the Mothers of the Plaza de Mayo, a dark and mildly disorganized place with photographs of people who have disappeared stuck on the walls, together with posters from organizations abroad which sympathize with and support the Mothers: the Greens in West Germany and leftist groups from France, the Netherlands and the United States. The women are the President and Vice-President of the movement, Hebe Bonafini and Adela Antokaletz. They are rumoured not to get along particularly well, and it is certainly true that they are almost complete opposites, physically, socially, and in their way of behaving. Mrs Bonafini is a big woman, with a shrewd face and iron-grey hair, who sits heavily in her chair, her legs apart, the wedding-ring tight on her finger, a man's watch on her wrist. A formidable and strong-minded woman, it was her direction which made a force out of what might otherwise have been nothing more than an emotional reaction. Mrs Antokaletz, the Vice-President, is, at seventy-two, almost ten years older, but she is active and young in her movements, getting up quickly from her chair and walking over with a spring in her step to talk to a latecomer. Her face is plump and brown, and relatively unlined, and she wears a bright checked shirt and a shortish skirt which seem to show that she is aware of her continuing energy. Her husband was a diplomat, whose family originated in Lithuania, and she has lived in various other countries. Mrs Bonafini, by contrast, was the wife of a factory worker, and her two sons, both of whom she has lost, were active trade unionists although they were both university graduates. Mrs Antokaletz's son was a lawyer who disappeared after defending a number of political prisoners. It is hard to think of any other circumstances which would have brought two such different women into daily contact. Their alliance has been powerful: since the days when they each had to think hard before running the considerable risks of speaking out, and could expect the most brutal treatment from the security forces, the Mothers of the Plaza de Mayo have become one of the most powerful moral forces in Argentina: a continuing reproach to the régime that took their sons and daughters away. And because they stayed the course, in spite of the tear gas and the baton charges, they have outlasted the military; the generals and admirals and brigadiers of those days are mostly behind bars, but the mothers have made the Plaza de Mayo, from which they were once regularly chased away, their own.

The events that brought Mrs Bonafini and Mrs Antokaletz into the same group bear a depressing similarity to the experiences of thousands of other families. On 8 February 1977 a group of men arrived at the house where Mrs Bonafini's elder son, Jorge, lived alone and surrounded it. It was the middle of the day. They broke the door down, and when they found the place was empty they started to ransack it. Jorge Bonafini, who was a physicist, came back from the university half an hour later. He realized what had happened, but it was too late to escape. The neighbours, who were watching, said afterwards that it looked as though he had decided not to run away, but to face up to the men who had broken into his house. It seems that they tortured him before taking him away; Mrs Bonafini, when she went round to see what had happened, found blood and water on the floor of the bathroom, and the house entirely looted. The neighbours saw him being put into the boot of one of the unmarked Falcon cars waiting outside. He was unconscious. Nothing more was ever heard of him.

Fifteen months later, Jorge's wife Elena was arrested at a house where she was having tea with some friends. She too disappeared. Not long afterwards, Mrs Bonafini's other son, Raúl, was attending a meeting of trade unionists who were discussing a strike at the plant where they worked. Several car loads of armed men arrived, and there was shooting. Everyone at the meeting was taken away, and all of them disappeared.

Mrs Antokaletz was divorced from her diplomat husband, and lived an active life in Buenos Aires, where she had settled to be with her son and daughter. In the mornings she would work at the law courts, where her son who was a doctor of law also practised; in the afternoon she would work for various charities. In the evenings she would play cards. She was particularly close to her son, and would go regularly to the cinema or the theatre with him. She would often try to persuade him to give up his work of representing political prisoners in court, or to leave the country. There were a number of warnings – his offices were bombed, and he was beaten up. People would stop him in the streets and warn him that to continue was suicidal. But he would always shrug off the warnings, believing that the government would not want the embarrassment of killing someone as well known as he had become in the field of human rights. When his mother talked to him about it, he would say, 'Yes, yes, yes, I know what you feel, but what would happen to the people I represent, if I go off and leave them?' As an internationally known lawyer, with strong connections with the Organization of American States and the United Nations, and membership of foreign institutes of different kinds, he was convinced that he was moderately safe. But at eight o'clock on the morning of 10 November 1976 he was arrested by a group of six men, who handcuffed him and then hooded him and took him away, as though his foreign links and his membership of foreign institutes and his considerable reputation meant nothing at all. His wife was arrested as well, but for some reason was not maltreated in any way, and was released a week later. They were both held at the Navy Mechanics School. Before his wife was freed a guard who seems to have taken pity on her took her to a bathroom for a few moments, where she was able to see her husband. Long afterwards, she revealed to Mrs Antokaletz that he had obviously been badly tortured. But he said he could bear it, and that she must be patient, because it could take a long time before he was freed. Then the guard took her away, and she never heard anything more of him.

Both Mrs Antokaletz and Mrs Bonafini did what they could,

after the first shock of their sons' disappearance. Mrs Bonafini had little idea of how to go about approaching the authorities, but someone told her that she should get a writ of habeas corpus made out in his name. She had never heard of such a thing before, but she obtained one, and then went the dreary rounds of the police, the armed forces and the prisons, trying to find someone who would take some notice of her case, or give her information. Like everyone else who followed this path, she found that she was seeing the same faces as she waited forlornly on the hard wooden benches in small, inhospitable offices or in echoing corridors: the faces of other mothers who had also lost their children and could get no news of where they were. Eventually someone told her that a group of people like her were planning to go to the Plaza de Mayo, and that she was welcome to come along. Even though at this stage she had lost only her elder son, and her daughter-in-law and second son were still at liberty, Mrs Bonafini had reached the stage where anything was better than going home and forgetting about it all. She asked for the details, and decided to go along. It was to be the second meeting the group had held and there would be 20 mothers taking part.

Mrs Antokaletz had been at the first meeting, not long before. That time there had been 14 of them. Curiously, it was the Ministry of the Interior which had made the founding of the group possible. Mrs Antokaletz had also been the rounds of offices and corridors, and seen the same anxious faces waiting for information, and at the Ministry, where most of them gathered, a small office had been set aside for them so that their cases could be 'processed'. In fact, the processing meant that the cases would be ignored. The officials would make fun of the women who went there, telling them that their sons had run off with someone and didn't want them to know; or that their own terrorist colleagues had executed them. The chaplaincies of the various armed forces, to which many others also applied, were similarly unhelpful; and it was in a moment of anger at the derisory answer she had received that one woman, Mrs Azucena De Vicenti, who was well into her sixties, said to the others, 'It's not here that we ought to be – it's the Plaza de Mayo. And when there's enough of us, we'll go to the Casa Rosada and see the President about our children who are missing.' Mrs De Vicenti later paid heavily for her outburst: she too was kidnapped and presumably murdered. But it was the moment which the Mothers of the Plaza de Mayo could regard as the birth of their organization.

And so on the afternoon of Saturday, 13 April 1977, the first demonstration was held. Each of the 14 women who had decided to turn up knew that it was a dangerous thing to do, and each of them arrived separately, wearing flat shoes and bringing just a few coins for the bus ride home and their identity cards, rather than carry their handbags around. They wanted to be able to run for it if there was trouble. Mrs Antokaletz was nervous, and so were the others. She looked around the Plaza and saw various other women, some of whom she didn't recognize, wandering around by the monument in the middle of the square. But she had already realized, as they had done, that it was a complete anticlimax. In the surge of emotion and determination which had followed Mrs De Vicenti's suggestion, they had settled on a day when they were all likely to be free, and no one had paused to reflect that on a Saturday the Plaza de Mayo, ringed with government offices and banks, would be as quiet and as empty as Wall Street or the City of London. The square and the wide street around it were completely deserted as the women wandered nervously up and down, and the two or three policemen on duty outside the Casa Rosada scarcely took any notice of them. Their gesture of protest went completely unremarked, and later in an atmosphere of relief and a certain amount of embarrassment at their lack of forethought, they decided to meet on a day when someone would see what they were doing. They chose the following Friday.

During the next week, the 14 original members of the new group went around telling the other women they met about the coming demonstration: at the ministries, the courts, the prisons, and the few human rights groups that existed at that time. Among the people they told was Mrs Bonafini, and she, like several others, decided to go along, not caring about the risks they were running. The Plaza de Mayo was perhaps the best guarded public place in Argentina – certainly during the weekdays – and to demonstrate there was not only illegal but a direct challenge to the authority of the state. And yet, at the start, they were relatively untroubled by the authorities. As the bells in the Cathedral at the far end of the square chimed the hour of five o'clock, the women converged on the area around the monument, moving around it in a great circle because to stand around would have been tantamount to holding a meeting, and that was against the law. This happened for two or three Fridays running, the numbers gradually growing and with them the interest of the police. Soon two or three vanloads of police would arrive, and names would be taken and the women forced to leave. After that, one of the original women suggested that Friday was a bad day to hold their protests, because it was unlucky. 'Poor woman,' Mrs Antokaletz says in an aside, 'to us, every day was unlucky.' But she and the others agreed that Thursday was likely to be a busier day, in terms of passers-by, than Friday.

Sometimes, directly they arrived in the Plaza they would be forced out by policemen who used their weapons to threaten them. Sometimes soldiers would be there as well, and men in plain clothes who were more sinister. When the numbers increased, the police would move in and start arresting the women, and some would be held at police stations for up to 24 hours. But it still grew, and other women – not simply the mothers of people who had disappeared, but the grandmothers, and the sisters, and the daughters – would come as well. It ceased to be a movement which was simply concerned with the fate of their own immediate relatives, and became a protest on behalf of everyone who had disappeared. And with the expanding of its purpose there came, for the first time, a name: the Mothers of the Plaza. It came not so much from themselves, as from the people they saw in their daily search for information, the officials and the policemen and the soldiers. But they were also called 'Las Locas de la Plaza' – the mad women. 'It was appropriate enough,' Mrs Antokaletz says. 'We must have been crazy to challenge the government at that time. But our craziness came from our feelings of pain and grief.' Other people got to know them. Sometimes at their meetings in the Plaza people would stop for a second or two and whisper their support. One woman heard about the group from a taxi-driver, who knew that there was some kind of protest about the disappeared in the Plaza, but didn't know what day it took place, so the woman went every day until she found it.

But the only way to find out about it was by word of mouth, or by seeing it for oneself. The newspapers remained silent about the Mothers, with the single exception of the *Buenos Aires Herald* – which, being published in English, was highly restricted in its readership. Jacobo Timerman's *La Opinión* might have been prepared to carry something about them, but Timerman himself was arrested and imprisoned in the month that they began, and after he had gone the paper became as silent on human rights as most of the others. Later, the Jewish magazine *Nueva Presencia* wrote about them, but its readership was very restricted; and very occasionally they were given a mention in *La Prensa*, mostly in hostile terms, though it provided them with something of the publicity they wanted, even so. But it was not enough, and so, after some thought, the Mothers decided to place a paid advertisement in the newspapers, listing the names of a number of men and women who they knew had disappeared. It was an expensive business, and at this stage the Mothers had no formal organization and no money; that had not so far been necessary. They had noticed, indeed, that the demonstrations in the first two or three weeks of the month were always better attended than those at the end, because the women who supported them had often lost a breadwinner from the family, and were not able to afford the fare to the centre of town. But their appeal for funds to pay for the advertisement was highly productive, even if some people had to put off buying a much-needed pair of shoes in order to give something. What was more, the newspapers which were considering running the not inconsiderable risk of publishing the advertisement demanded rates which were a good deal higher than their normal ones. Finally, on 5 October 1977 the advertisement came out in *La Prensa*, in spite of efforts by the armed forces to prevent it. The headline over the advertisement read, 'We do not ask for anything more than the truth', and its text recalled the words of President Videla during his visit to the United States the previous month: 'Nobody who tells the truth will suffer reprisals.' The pictures of some of the 237 people selected for mention were set out in the advertisement, and it was signed by the mother of each of them, together with a demand for a clear statement by the government about the fate of their children. Given the considerable terror that existed at the time, it was an uncharacteristically brave decision by *La Prensa* to publish it, in spite of the high charge the newspaper made for doing so. It gave the Mothers their first opportunity to reach a large section of public opinion in the country as a whole, even though the evidence had always been that most people preferred not to know anything about the disappearances, and unless they had themselves lost a friend or a relative they tended to take refuge in the fact that most of the newspapers and television and radio reported nothing about the people who were disappearing. There was no response to the advertisement, and no details were forthcoming about the people who were featured in it, but the Mothers felt they had made their point.

They continued to face considerable difficulties, and often brutality, but they were also attracting more and more support. Ten days after the advertisement had appeared, several hundred women demonstrated in front of the Congress building, in order to deliver a petition carrying 24,000 signatures. The petition demanded the opening of investigations into the cases of the people who had disappeared. In the police action which followed, two hundred people were arrested, together with a number of Argentine and foreign journalists working for American or French news organizations: CBS, NBC, UPI, AP, *The Wall Street Journal*, and AFP. All of them were freed after a few hours. The following month the BBC correspondent in South America, Derek Wilson, and Al Ortiz, the Voice of America correspondent, were arrested while trying to interview some of the Mothers at one of their regular Thursday demonstrations. The two men were held for seven hours before being released. Up to now, the government appeared to have been prepared to ignore much of what the Mothers were doing. They were harassed and often ill-treated, but the violence which had been used against so many opponents of the military régime had not been turned fully on them. But the growing support, as evidenced by the number of signatures on their petition, and the interest they were arousing among foreign journalists whose news reports could be read or listened to in Argentina itself, seem to have convinced the authorities that they would have to deal with the Mothers more harshly. The crackdown was not long in coming.

People came to the meetings of the Mothers all the time to try to get information about relatives who had disappeared, and many of them, attracted by the determination and the spirit of enthusiasm they found, stayed on to work as collectors of money or of signatures, writers of letters, drafters of petitions. And because the Mothers had always resisted any temptation to become a secret society, everything they did was open, including the meetings at which they discussed their strategy. One of the many people who came during the latter months of 1977 – Mrs Bonafini remembers it as being in August, but others say it was November, about a month after the advertisement in *La Prensa* – was an intelligent and pleasant young man named Gustavo Niño. His brother had disappeared, and the Mothers were able to give him a little information about the case. Although there was nothing more to be done for him, Niño stayed on to help with the organization. He was in his middle twenties, fair-haired and blue-eyed, and he unquestionably appealed to the motherly instincts of many of the women who had themselves lost sons and daughters. Niño became a general favourite, since he was hard-working and generous, and was always sympathetic about the losses other people had suffered.

During the first week in December the organization was planning its next important initiative – a full-page advertisement in *La Nación* to mark International Human Rights Day, and to call for 'A Christmas of Peace'. *La Nación*, like *La Prensa*, wanted a good deal of money for printing the advertisement, and it had to be raised mostly by public collection. A group of workers had spent all afternoon on Thursday, 8 December at the Santa Cruz Church in the centre of Buenos Aires, where the priests supported them, putting the finishing touches to the advertisement and talking about how it should be laid out. They had a little room set aside for them in an annexe beside the church, where the parochial business was usually done. The Mothers felt they were safer there than in a café or at someone's house. Among the people who had gathered there was a French nun, Sister Alicia, who had worked tirelessly for the organization, and had been particularly helpful to Catholics like Mrs Antokaletz, who felt that the Church in Argentina – with some clear exceptions – had refused to support them or give them any comfort.

A number of people dropped by to hand in their contributions towards the cost of the advertisement, including Gustavo Niño, whose pleasant face and friendly manner had already become familiar at such gatherings. He was a particular favourite with Azucena De Vicenti, the originator of the plan to hold their demonstrations in the Plaza de Mayo, who was now the guiding force behind the movement. Niño waited around for a while, talking and helping, in case Mrs De Vicenti came. He seemed disappointed that she did not, and left at around eight o'clock, waving his goodbyes in his usual way.

As it turned out, the others did not stay much longer either. The evening celebration of Mass had come to an end in the church, and people were starting to leave by the main door. The Mothers and their helpers meanwhile slipped out of the annexe by the side door and walked directly into a group of five or six men who were waiting for them outside. One was armed with a sub-machinegun. Sister Alicia and two of the founder-members of the group were arrested and forced into a waiting car. Another man shouted at the rest of the group, 'Give us the money.' Two days later, on 10 December – the day of the advertisement in *La Nación* – Azucena De Vicenti was arrested, together with a young artist who had worked for the organization, and Sister Léonie, another French nun who worked closely with Sister Alicia but had never been connected in any way with the Mothers. In all, nine people were arrested in the street outside the Santa Cruz Church, and a further three on 10 December. All of them disappeared for good.

There was no question about who had organized the affair. Gustavo Niño had presumably left the office in the church annexe with a complete description of what each of the principal workers there was wearing, and the gang waiting outside was able to arrest the ones they most wanted. The Mothers, having decided that their organization should be entirely open, had no method of screening volunteers: they were obliged to take people at face value. As it happened, a man named Niño had disappeared, but he had no brother named Gustavo. It was not for some years that the surviving members of the group discovered that Gustavo Niño's real name was Alfredo Astiz.

The blow to the Mothers' organization was devastating. They, alone of all the human rights groups, had opted to go on to the streets and demonstrate publicly; and as they had managed to survive, and to come out week by week, so their following had grown until they could regularly count on a turnout of two or three hundred every Thursday. Now it was no longer taking a mild risk to identify with the Mothers, it was facing the very real possibility of being kidnapped, tortured and murdered. As for the founder-members, they were badly shaken but felt that there was no real alternative for them but to carry on. And so the next Thursday, a week after the arrests at the Church of Santa Cruz, they headed as usual for the Plaza de Mayo. That day, forty women at most turned up. Some stayed on the far side of the road from the centre of the square, unable to keep away entirely, but lacking the necessary courage to cross the last 20 yards of tarmac and identify themselves fully with an organization which the authorities had plainly decided to smash. Others came, but asked that their names should not appear on the next advertisement because they were afraid for the safety of their family, or perhaps for their husband's job. The worst thing about Astiz's infiltration of their movement was that it had shattered the illusion that many of the Mothers and their supporters had been happy to cherish: that not even a govenment which allowed widespread kidnapping and torture would allow an organization of mothers demanding information about their missing children to be smashed so brutally and so publicly. If, on the contrary, the *patotas* could arrest not simply middle-aged women who possessed a powerful moral case, but also two nuns from an influential country like France, whose links with Argentina were reasonably close, then there was nothing they would not do, and no one who could feel entirely safe.

The military government issued a statement on 16 December, blaming the disappearances of the 12 people connected with the Mothers on 'nihilistic subversion'. The remnants of the Mothers' leadership took the bold step of calling a press conference in the Plaza de Mayo to deny the statement and blame the kidnappings on the government itself. Only four journalists, all of them foreign, turned up; and they and the Mothers were heavily outnumbered by policemen and men in well-cut suits who clearly belonged to the various security services. This time there was no trouble, because of the presence of the foreign journalists, but the atmosphere of menace was maintained.

Buenos Aires is bisected by a grand avenue, several blocks wide, which extends for a mile and a half from north to south down the centre of the city. At the southern end the Avenue of the 9th July turns eventually into a less attractive highway towards the outer suburbs; at the northern end, the boulevard stops short at a pleasant building in grey stone, with a steep slate roof and shutters at the windows. The French Embassy in Buenos Aires looks more Parisian than South American, and the building, although elderly and highly inconvenient, has considerable charm, with its creaking wooden floors and the pleasant, fading frescos on its dingy walls and ceilings. A continuing legend in the city explains the fact that the embassy sticks out into the path of the Avenida 9 de Julio (when it should by rights have been demolished and the embassy housed in more up-to-date premises) by the anger of the French government over the kidnapping of the two nuns. The French had, according to the legend, agreed to move out and make way for the extension of the Avenue when the news of their disappearance came and their attitude hardened. French diplomats nowadays deny the story, but true or not the kidnapping of Sister Alicia and Sister Léonie caused a considerable crisis within the embassy itself.

The ambassador, François de la Gorce, was an old-fashioned diplomat who believed that his task was to maintain as good relations with the host country as was possible. He might not approve of what the Argentine military were doing inside Argentina, but that was a domestic matter in which foreign embassies should not, in his opinion, meddle; he was there to represent French interests, and to inform the Quai d'Orsay in Paris of the political and economic currents in Argentina. He did not see himself as a representative of international moral concerns. So when the news of the disappearance of the two nuns was reported in France, and there was an explosion of outrage and condemnation in almost every newspaper in the country, de la Gorce found himself in a difficult position. He may well have been angry himself at the action of the kidnap gang which had created the trouble in the first place, but he gave his colleagues in the embassy and the French journalists who saw him at this time the strong impression that he was embarrassed by what had happened, more than anything else. It was believed that he regarded the fury of the French press as something which had to be explained away during his visits to the Foreign Ministry in the Plaza San Martín, and that he was lukewarm in passing on the condemnation of his government over the incident. He found himself in conflict, however, with several members of the embassy staff. The first secretary, Edouard de Blanpré, for instance, had been based in Argentina for some years, and argued passionately in favour of a tougher approach to the military authorities. The ambassador overruled him. It was not for two or three days that the embassy requested the Foreign Ministry in Buenos Aires for details of the two cases.

The French consular section, meanwhile, had witnessed various cases of the kind, and knew that it was essential to act fast. The consul and his deputies carried out their own investigation, ignoring the more official approaches of the ambassador which they guessed would lead nowhere, and from talking to eyewitnesses of the kidnappings of the two nuns they soon built up a picture of what had happened. It was clear to them that one or other of the security services had picked them up, and they were even given the licence number of the car, a Renault 12, which had been used to take Sister Alicia away after her arrest outside the Santa Cruz Church.

In France itself, the politicians had become involved in the campaign for the two nuns. Both nuns came from the department of Doubs, near the border with Switzerland, and Doubs was represented in the French National Assembly by Edgar Faure, the Assembly's President. Faure's reaction was to send one of his aides as a special envoy to Argentina, to discover what had happened to them. De la Gorce, as ambassador, was annoyed by the move, regarding it as an intrusion into his own sphere of competence and perhaps believing that it would make relations with Argentina that much worse. When Faure's envoy, an active and tough-minded man in his twenties named François Gadot-Clet, arrived soon afterwards in Buenos Aires, he was cold-shouldered by the ambassador and given little or no official help. But he did not need it. Gadot-Clet was a fixer, not a diplomat, and he had been sent there to speak bluntly to the authorities. He made his own appointments with the Foreign Ministry, and more importantly with the Interior Ministry, headed by General Harguindeguy, and his methods were crude but compelling. He had with him, in a leather briefcase, the details of a number of commercial deals which would be of interest to Argentina, and he told Harguindeguy in so many words that if the two nuns were freed the contracts could be drawn up on terms highly favourable to Argentina. Gadot-Clet told journalists afterwards that the Interior Minister had replied that he did not know where the nuns were, but that his intelligence service was investigating the case and he had hopes of finding out. Harguindeguy had spoken in curious terms of having a dream about the arrest of the nuns, which had ended with their release, and he had concluded by saying he thought the whole matter would be cleared up within a fortnight. Gadot-Clet went back to Paris, confident that his mission would turn out a success. It seemed not unreasonable; he had spoken to the Interior Minister, who might be expected to know what had happened to the two nuns, and the Interior Minister had given him a heavy hint that he knew all about the case and would see that it was ended satisfactorily. But that was to misunderstand the realities of power in Argentina during the Process, which were that each military organization was a law unto itself; the Interior Minister who was an Army man was not in a position to force the Navy to give up its prisoners, and the Navy was not even obliged to acknowledge that it was holding the two nuns. On 17 December, a week after the arrest of Azucena De Vicenti and the second of the two nuns, Sister Léonie, the French news agency AFP received a note which purported to come from Sister Alicia, to say that she had been kidnapped by left-wing guerrillas, and to pass on a number of demands which they were making in exchange for her release. It was clearly a forgery, carried out in an attempt to confuse opinion in France and create doubts about the general assumption that Sister Léonie and Sister Alicia had been abducted by the military. Gadot-Clet waited in

Paris for a message from Argentina to say that the two nuns had been released, but the fortnight which Harguindeguy had suggested as the likely deadline passed, and nothing happened. It was a standard tactic used by the military authorities to confuse and undermine foreign interventions on behalf of people who had disappeared. Gadot-Clet's approach had been based unashamedly on Argentine self-interest, and perhaps on the personal financial interest of the Interior Minister himself, but even that was not enough. The French Government, and the embassy in Buenos Aires never heard anything more about Sister Alicia or Sister Léonie, and their bodies were never found.

The disappearance of several of their leading members was only the start of the worst period of repression that the Mothers had to endure. Throughout 1978 they managed for the most part to keep up a weekly presence in the Plaza, but they were harassed more then ever and frequently arrested. Their numbers were always small. By the start of 1979 they were finding it difficult even to meet at all in the Plaza. In the early days of the movement they had decided that nothing would keep them away from their chosen place of assembly – rain, thunder, heat, or the violence of the police. Now, however, they were reduced to gathering on the far side of the road from the square and dashing across at an agreed time so that for a few minutes at least before the police closed in they could show that they were still indeed the Mothers of the Plaza de Mayo. But soon the violence the police used against them became so great that they were obliged to give up even that. Instead, they met in churches, and those meetings were themselves illegal, so that the few sympathetic priests they could rely on would ask them to turn the lights off, or not to talk. And so anything up to a hundred and fifty of them would sit in church, praying or pretending to pray, and handing round notes which would carry suggestions about when and where they should meet next. It was the lowest and most depressing point in the organization's fortunes.

But right from the start the spirit that had animated them was offensive, rather than defensive. Hebe Bonafini, the powerful-looking President of the movement, says nowadays without any intended irony that they were worried, when they were sitting in church crouched in their pews, passing their pieces of paper backwards and forwards, that they might give the authorities the impression that they could be weakened. In fact the authorities must have been congratulating themselves that they had destroyed them altogether. But in May 1979 the Mothers responded with a characteristic act of defiance. First they held elections, in order to put their organization on a stronger and more formal footing; then, three months later, they constituted themselves a legally registered association. By this time they were getting a good deal of support, financial as well as moral, from groups of sympathizers abroad, particularly in the Netherlands. They could run a bank account, pay out money to cover some at least of the needs of children whose parents had disappeared, and by 1980 they could even afford a headquarters of their own: an upstairs office in Uruguay Street.

But by that time they had taken the single most important decision since the days of the founding: in the last days of 1979, the worst year they had had to endure, they agreed that on the first Thursday of 1980 they would go back to the Plaza de Mayo, and never again give it up to the military even if it meant being killed there. And so on Thursday 3 January at their old time of three-thirty in the afternoon, the Mothers descended on the area around the monument, wearing their flat shoes and their white headscarves, determined that they would leave only when they wanted to. In its way, it was an anti-climax, like that first Saturday in 1977. The police had been so certain that the Mothers had been smashed as an organization that they were too surprised, and too few in number, to do anything to stop them. They duly paraded for forty minutes, circling slowly round the little obelisk with its Grecian figure on the top, their scarves proclaiming the names of the children they had lost, and at the end of it, having ignored the efforts of the police to move them along, they broke up, highly delighted with their success. When they turned up there a week later, the police and the security men were already there, waiting for them, filling the square to such an extent that there were even some up in the branches of the trees. But something had happened: it was as though the authorities themselves could sense that the tide had turned. In future there would be plenty of threats and beatings up, and even one or two disappearances, but the Mothers never again had to cede the Plaza to the authorities. Their offices in Uruguay Street and the one they bought in December 1982, a stone's throw from the square in front of the Congress building, where two hundred of them had been arrested back in October 1977, were never entered by the police or the security organizations.

By 1980, with the Mothers a force again, the tide had indeed turned. The campaign for human rights in Argentina had become much more vocal, and that meant that the political cost of repression was a good deal higher. Hebe Bonafini thinks that she is still alive because of international support; each time the authorities made a move against human rights workers they could expect a chorus of complaint from countries like France, Sweden, the Netherlands, Italy, and the United States (though the United States ceased to take much interest after President Reagan took office, and the British government never took much interest at all, while the Soviet Union and its allies gave positive support to the military dictatorship).

The Mothers had their critics, even in other human rights movements. They were often regarded as the most excitable and least careful of the groups, rushing in to condemn or defend or take up positions when the other groups devoted more time to considering what to do. The Grandmothers of the Plaza de Mayo, by contrast, were usually regarded as being more stable and sensible. But it was the willingness of the Mothers to take action that kept the flame of opposition burning in public view during the worst years; only they had the necessary madness to do it. 'We decided to take to the streets, and it was the streets that taught us,' Adela Antokaletz says. 'That was what gave us our political strength.' They successfully countered the military's calculation that if the terror was absolute enough, no one would dare to complain. They destroyed another of the régime's assumptions too: that parents who did not share their children's political opinions, or reacted strongly against them, would be likely to say nothing when their children were kidnapped and murdered because of those opinions. One of the curiosities of a movement like the Mothers of the Plaza de Mayo is the number of men and women supporting it who would never in their lives before have considered demonstrating in the street against the government on any issue whatsoever. The Process brought radicalization – though it was not necessarily party-political radicalization – to a large number of middle-class people in Argentina, ironically perhaps preparing the way for the big, essentially middle-class rallies that helped to sweep President Alfonsín to power in 1983.

With military government gone, and the No Name graves opened, there is little for the Mothers to campaign for except the punishment of the people who carried out the torture and killing of their children – and not just the generals and admirals who gave the orders. Times, inevitably, are a little tame; not that anyone would want the more exciting ones back. Mrs Bonafini is a widow and Mrs Antokaletz, sitting next to her, is alone too. They devoted seven years of anger and courage to the organization, and now there are few outlets for either quality. Mrs Antokaletz, her energetic frame shifting in her chair, is philosophical about the change: 'Horrible things happened in my life, and because I was free to devote all my time and all my passion to this movement, I did: looking, walking, asking, travelling wherever necessary, conveying the drama of our situation, looking for moral support, trying to get all this uncovered one day; so that those who may be still alive can be found, and the cases of those who are dead can be cleared up. And above all, raising people's awareness, so that what happened here will never happen again. Here or anywhere.'

# 10 THE PROCESS AT PRAYER

*'You must remember that you are a Christian, too.'* – sign in clandestine gaol, Villa Las Rosas in La Salta province.

Monsignor Antonio José Plaza, Archbishop of La Plata, heard no allegations of torture in his archdiocese during the years of the Process of National Reorganization. If such things occurred during those years then, yes, they would constitute a violation of the moral law. But he was Chaplain General to the police force of the province of Buenos Aires, of which La Plata is the capital, and he knew of no excesses carried out by the men under his spiritual care – and, anyway, such questions should more properly be addressed to the penitentiary system, not to him. Yes, he visited the Buenos Aires provincial police at their various headquarters, stations and bases many times, but he never heard of any clandestine gaols which the police might have operated. What did he teach the men to whom he was chaplain? A raised hand is the only answer; the 74-year-old Archbishop gets up heavily, facetiously somehow, and makes his slow way across the dark room to a bookcase that holds mostly encyclopaedias; he picks up several copies of something and hands them out with the observant care of an old man, the facetiousness closer to the surface now. They prove to be little booklets which contain the Catechism, the 'Doctrina Cristiana', published in La Plata by the Archbishop. He looks across at his Vicar-General and the smile is out in the open: the Archbishop taught the men under his care the Catechism of the Catholic religion – what else should he have taught them? The Catechism makes no mention of human rights or torture, being concerned with transcendent things. The whole performance is an elaborate, amusing parable to discomfort visitors who want to pry into things that they have no business with. What about the attitude of the Church in general? 'Each one should mind his own business, each cobbler should mend his own shoes.' The smile is there again. He has a sly expression, his jaw holding his mouth tightly in a half-smile. The Archbishop has a reputation to maintain: he is a card, a slow constructor of traps for the inquisitive, the ill-mannered, the unwary. His Vicar-General laughs deferentially.

Monsignor Plaza has been La Plata's archbishop since 1955. A shrewd, conservative-minded churchman, he is deeply hostile to much of the change which he has observed in Argentina and in the Catholic Church during the years he has ruled the archdiocese. He is profoundly nationalist, too: his office contains no fewer than five Argentine flags of different sizes, on his desk, in among the books on theology, hanging down over the shelves. Clearly in view, and no doubt placed there for a purpose, is a copy of *El Terrorismo en La Argentina*, a vehemently right-wing justification of the policies of the Process and particularly its denial of human rights. It too is decked out in the national colours, and explains in sometimes gory detail why the left-wing violence of the Montoneros needed firm handling. Archbishop Plaza would agree with that proposition wholeheartedly. He sits behind the desk in his black soutane, looking a little like a sexton in a nineteenth-century English cathedral. His hands are curiously young, and the only sign of archiepiscopal magnificence is a heavy amethyst ring on one finger. His voice is ancient and creaky, and the words are distorted by his ill-fitting false teeth. The Videla government, he says, supported Christian values, the values, that is, of Western civilization; the sharp eyes watch for any hint of agreement, and finding none, the Archbishop understands that he is preaching to the unconverted.

'I am not responsible for what President Videla did. Maybe there were some excesses. It is not for me to judge if the Videla government did so many bad things that it undermined its role in supporting those values. I cannot judge Videla, but I can judge what the guerrillas did.'

La Plata is an important provincial city with a major university, and as such it was the centre of considerable Montonero and ERP action. In 1976 alone, 140 policemen – Archbishop Plaza's special charges – were murdered in the city. Military men and their wives and families were shot and blown up and killed or dreadfully injured, and the Archbishop does not forget it. He knows that even if his functions are spiritual ones, he is a lord of the Church, with a powerful political position to uphold. What distinguishes him from most other spiritual lords is that he is not afraid to talk about his views publicly. He expects that his words will be twisted, though the antique voice expresses it in more diplomatic form: 'I've been quoted so many times and people have said I've said so many things – but I don't care.' The Vicar-General lights another cigarette and shifts uncomfortably in his chair, still smiling dutifully; that kind of talk is not for him.

Behind the Archbishop, in between the identically-bound quarto volumes of Patristic writings which have the look of books on civil or criminal law, several cherubs in bronze or wood are set out, and beside a painting of the Virgin a sign bears the English word 'Smile'. It has been alleged very strongly that the Archbishop visited places where the provincial police carried out tortures, and that by doing so he lent his authority to the practice; but since he denies the charge, there is little point in trying to pursue it. The conversation turns instead to an old friend of the Archbishop, General Ramón Camps, the commanding officer of the Buenos Aires provincial police, who has admitted giving the orders that led to several thousand executions; he was proud of it, he once said. Would the Archbishop describe Camps as a man who had done his duty? The smile again. 'I am not going to describe General Camps – he wouldn't describe me. He was a man who carried out his duties, yes. He has accounted for what he did. I can't say whether that is right or wrong; justice alone will say. But if these people had not carried out their duties there would be a Montonero government in Argentina now. The people who are now in the government, what did they do all these years? If they're in power now, it is because the armed forces defeated the guerrillas.'

And the Mothers of the Plaza de Mayo? They say they had precious little help from the Church when they were trying to find out what had happened to their missing children. The Archbishop laughs a silent, shoulder-shaking laugh and shakes his head. In the first place, he says, that is not the case. In the second, he is not certain that they are really all of them mothers. Thirdly, the Archbishop would like to know who is backing them. And finally, everything *was* done to help them when they came to the churches. The Vicar-General, smiling and nodding energetic approval, stubs out his cigarette half-smoked and interjects: there was a special office set up here which he ran himself, he says; the Archbishop looks down at his amethyst ring and turns it on his finger, not wanting to play any part in the proceedings for a minute or two, and aware perhaps of the effect his assistant's words are likely to have. It is one thing not to care about the effect, another thing not to realize it. Hundreds of women came to the centre, the Vicar-

General continues, seeking information. He, the Vicar-General himself, dealt with many of them personally. There was one woman, for instance, who came and told him that her daughter had disappeared. How long was it since she had last seen her? he asked. Eight years, was the answer; it transpired that the daughter had run off with some man and had a child by him and married him. 'So I told her, "You didn't lose your daughter now, you lost her eight years ago."' The Vicar-General smiles triumphantly, looking from face to face for the reward of his sharpness. There is a silence for a while.

Archbishop Plaza has done many things for the people in his care. He has set up particular programmes to give training and employment to young men and women. He is known throughout the city and the area, and people – religious people – come to him with their complaints and their problems and their anxieties, and he sees them all. He may be a prince of the Church, but he is not a proud man; the simple black soutane and the readiness to talk to anyone who wishes to talk to him are clear evidence of that. His principles – the uncomplicated acceptance of the Church's teachings, a love of his country, a hatred of disturbance and of the flouting of law and order – were the principles upon which the government of the Process founded itself, and the Archbishop stayed loyal not just to the principles, but to the men who put them into practice, and perhaps to the way they were put into practice as well. He is on record as having said, 'There are no innocent victims in Argentina' and having called the Mothers of the Plaza 'these Mothers of subversives'. Like his conservatism, such attitudes have ceased to be fashionable and being out of step with the change in the country has also meant the loss of position and some of his privileges. He is no longer police chaplain and his stipend from the provincial government has been stopped. That was worth 26,000 pesos (roughly $500) a month. A decree from the new civilian government of the province also stripped away his two government cars, his metallic grey and his azure blue Ford Falcons. The Archbishop accepts this; he is not interested in what is fashionable or in making public repentances or private confessions.

What, finally, can be done to heal Argentina's wounds? There is another silence, then the hand, with its heavy amethyst ring, points mockingly to the pile of booklets once again, mocking not the booklets but the questioner. 'Teach them the Catechism. Let them comply. Teach them to comply with the law of God.' The creaking voice is quiet. The audience is over. Duty comes before pity, law before reconciliation.

The Church as a whole was noteworthy for its silence during the years of repression – a silence which helped the military régime even while individual priests and members of congregations were being abducted, terrorized and killed. The families of missing people waited in vain for a strong public condemnation of the military's activities, for a public appeal to the government to respect the law and Christian ethics. When concern was expressed, it was in private, or about specific cases which could not be ignored, or it was very late in the day. The Church failed to distance itself from the régime by a formal public denunciation. That was left to a few individuals in the Church, some of whom died for it.

The Catholic Church, admittedly, was in a difficult position; it, like much of the country, shared the military's aims. The hierarchy condemned terrorism and agreed that it should be eradicated. Argentina's was a conservative Church and many of the hierarchy were as strongly nationalistic and anti-communist as many of the military officers. Of course, they did not endorse the methods being used to combat the guerrillas and Marxist ideas, but they were reluctant to break a traditional alliance of Church, powerful landowners and military even when the violence turned against the faithful. Although Roman Catholicism was not a state religion as such, it was in a pre-eminent position in the education system and in politics: the President of the nation had to be Catholic, according to the Constitution, and the military placed Catholic citizens in charge of education, in the Ministry and in universities and secondary schools. The junta and other top officers also explicitly committed themselves to the defence of Christianity and to be devout upholders of the Faith themselves. This made it very difficult for the Church to oppose the State and renounce the military's view of Christianity, as it would have laid them open to charges of unpatriotic, even subversive, behaviour.

There were two other broad tendencies besides the 'Plaza' school of conservatism. There were moderates, who had been sympathetic to the military's anti-Communism and desire to defeat terrorism, but who became increasingly worried by their methods. And there were the progressive priests and bishops, influenced by the Vatican II 'populorum progressio' doctrine of the 1960s, which expressed concern for social justice and encouraged a much more radical approach to social change. Among the moderates were some of the Church grandees who did little about human rights, tacitly supporting the régime by their inaction. The head of the Argentine Church, Cardinal Juan Carlos Aramburu, refused to receive the relatives of people who had disappeared, and was careful to avoid making his opinions known publicly. When the Mothers of the Plaza took refuge in his cathedral, he allowed the federal police to go in and clear them out. Many priests refused to say Mass for those who had been murdered by the military, for fear of being accused of giving succour to subversion. Very few priests took up the cases of people who had disappeared.

And yet the Catholic Church was certainly not without its martyrs and its defenders of human rights. Early one Sunday morning, in the Buenos Aires suburb of Belgrano, three priests, Fathers Kelly, Leacen and Duffau, and two seminarians, Barletti and Berbetto, were in their living quarters beside San Patricio's church, which belonged to an Irish order. Across the road, the building was being kept under surveillance by an unmarked Ford Falcon car. The son of a senior military officer who lived nearby saw the car, and went to the police station in Belgrano to report it; his father's position presumably gave him the confidence to do so. The police took no notice, and sent him home; and as he passed San Patricio's he saw a police car drive up to the Ford Falcon, so that the occupants of the two cars could speak to one another. Then the police car drove off.

The next day a boy from the parish discovered the bodies of the priests and seminarians. Their hands were tied behind their backs and they had been machine-gunned; the priests looked as though they had been struck in the mouth with the butt of a rifle. The murderers had stolen books, cassettes and other items, and had left a number of messages, one of which was spray-painted into the carpet and read, 'To those who poison the virgin minds of our youngsters'. Another, chalked on the door and quickly rubbed out by the police when they arrived, said, 'For our dynamited comrades in Federal Security'. Two days before, the Montoneros had blown up the Federal Police Security headquarters in Buenos Aires, killing twenty-five people. The police commander in overall charge of the investigation into the priests' murder suggested at once that it was the work of subversives, but it was not a particularly convincing theory. As for the accusation that the priests or the seminarians had been linked with the guerrillas, that was denied by members of their congregation.

In the first eight months of military rule, thirty priests were picked up. Of these, four were deported and nine were released; the rest were either held as prisoners or had simply disappeared. The most usual targets among the clergy were the worker priests who lived among the poor in rural areas or in the shanty towns outside the main cities. They were identified with the Third World Movement which had sprung up in response to the Vatican II call for greater social justice. There were similar groups in other Latin American countries, and many of the priests who belonged to them espoused the more or less leftist approach of 'liberation theology'. The Montoneros themselves had their intellectual origins among left-wing as well as some very far right-wing Catholic elements, though the Third World Movement itself did not back violent change. But it had shown sympathy at times for the guerrillas and their demands, and a few priests, like Camilo Torres, were themselves guerrillas. But the rejection of violence was in itself no protection for priests who leaned to the left, and many Church leaders, by no means all supporters of the military like Mgr Plaza, felt that there was a certain truth to the charge that there were 'subversive' elements within the priesthood, given the military's broad definition of subversion.

After the funeral of the five murdered priests and seminarians, a strongly-worded letter was sent to President Videla by Cardinals Primatesta and Aramburu, and by the Archbishop of Sante Fe, Mgr Vicente Zaspe. The President agreed to see them, and promised that there would be an inquiry headed by a federal judge. But both the representations and the reply were made in private, as was to be the pattern in many cases involving churchmen. The Church authorities felt more comfortable in making their views known quietly, and they never went as far at this stage of the Process of National Reorganization as to threaten the withdrawal of chaplains to the military or the police, or the exclusion of leading military figures from official Church functions. As a result, the government was always able to brush aside the complaints and accusations which were occasionally made as the outbursts of individuals.

La Rioja, a province in the north-west of Argentina, near the Andes, is a region of few towns, poor farmers and some powerful landowners. Its bishop, Enrique Carletti Angelelli, was a man of considerable independence of mind and some courage. The day before the 1976 coup he preached a sermon at Chamical Air Force Base against military involvement in politics, and after the takeover, he withdrew religious services from the base. In the wider community, Angelelli worked with poorer farmers, helping to establish co-operatives and improve conditions. His progressiveness created enemies. The ultra-conservative organization, *Tradición, Familia y Propiedad* (Tradition, Family and Property), originally founded in Brazil, had a regional headquarters in Chamical, and as early as 1974 they had branded the bishop as a 'Marxist'. After the coup, the organization denounced the bishop and his clergy in paid advertisements in newspapers. At this time, Angelelli was also denounced to the Pope, probably by this extreme right-wing group, and the Pope himself sent Archbishop Zaspe to the province to examine the situation. Archbishop Zaspe, one of the few senior clergymen deeply concerned with human rights, was satisfied that the bishop was fulfilling his proper duties, but he saw the depth of conservative feelings in the diocese when he and Angelelli were praying in a small church. They were besieged for some time by a crowd headed by the richer members of the community, probably organized by *Tradición, Familia y Propiedad*. Before leaving the province, Archbishop Zaspe expressed his and the Pope's confidence in Bishop Angelelli during a sermon. But feeling in the diocese continued to run high.

Two of the priests who worked in Chamical, Father Gabriel José Longueville, who had come to Argentina under the auspices of the French Episcopal Committee for Latin America, and Father Carlos de Dios Murias, who had studied at the Military College in Córdoba before entering the priesthood, supported their Bishop's actions in the community. The priests were visiting a nunnery in Chamical near the Presbytery when officers came and asked for them. The men showed their police credentials and asked the Fathers if they would accompany them to La Rioja, the capital of the province, to help identify several people being detained. They agreed and departed in the officers' cars, which bore no number plates. Three days later, on 25 July, the bodies of Father Longueville and Father Murias were discovered, wrapped in army blankets and bound and gagged, near the Chamical Air Force Base. Father Murias's body showed signs of torture. They had each been shot a number of times, and a list of names of other priests had been left with the bodies. The official explanation was that the priests' kidnappers had masqueraded as policemen; but it was noticeable that one of the first things done when the bodies arrived at the mortuary was that the army blankets were burned.

The Chamical killings brought a telegram from the Pope, condemning the killings and criticizing the human rights violations going on throughout the country. The letter was relayed to President Videla and parts of it were leaked to the press, but the Argentine Church as a whole said nothing in support of it. Bishop Angelelli of La Rioja was not, however, satisfied with the official explanation of the killings, and protested vigorously about them. He went to Chamical for the funeral, and spoke at length about the priests' work, suggesting that they had been murdered to silence the voice of the Church. Over the next few days he met various other priests in the area, and on 3 August left for La Rioja with Father Arturo Pinto, promising to denounce those who were responsible from the pulpit of his cathedral.

There are different versions of what happened next; in the atmosphere of fear witnesses were not prepared to come forward at the time, and their evidence, sometimes conflicting, either emerged in the form of rumour or was suppressed for several years, until it became safe to speak. The official version was that Bishop Angelelli had died in a car accident on the road to La Rioja. His small Fiat Multicarga van had, it was said, blown a tyre and crashed, throwing him through the windscreeen. He had died instantly of a broken neck. The case was closed quickly, and the autopsy took place only after the bishop's body had been laid out for the funeral.

The official version found little acceptance in Bishop Angelelli's diocese, however. Father Pinto, who had been travelling with him, said he had noticed a white Peugeot following them from Chamical. It had, he said, caught up with them and forced them off the road. Their van had flown fifty feet through the air and landed on its roof. The bishop, he confirmed, had been thrown through the windscreen, but Father Pinto himself had been picked up by a passing motorist and taken to hospital in Chamical.

Another witness, who would not be named, said he saw two cars parked in some thickets at the side of the road. One of them was a white Peugeot. Further up the road, he found the bishop's body lying face upwards, his arms stretched out, but didn't recognize him. The bishop died in his arms. A few minutes later, a lorry driver stopped, and on seeing the body, said, 'It's the bishop – they've killed him.' The other man, very shocked, let go of the bishop and they both got away as fast as they could. The nurse who laid the body out said she had seen none of the cuts which she would have expected on someone who had been thrown through a windscreen, while on the back of his head there were bruises which looked more like the result of blows than a crash. There were also suggestions that the van may have been tampered with; strange noises had been heard outside the place where Angelelli had been staying the night before, near to where the van was parked, and a car with its lights out had been seen driving away from the place.

The van itself was taken to the Air Force Base. The bishop's writing-case, containing reports on the deaths of the two priests, disappeared, and the judge who went to pick up the bishop's body wanted the police to search Angelelli's private rooms, but they were refused permission to enter. The judge pronounced the case closed: it was an accident, he said. The funeral was attended by eighty priests, many bishops and large crowds of local people.

Reports of the death appeared in small-circulation Catholic magazines, and some were reprinted in the liberal newspaper *La Opinión* and the English-language *Buenos Aires Herald*. *La Opinión* also ran an article which cast doubt on the official version of the affair. There was widespread shock abroad, and Israel, West Germany and France all made their feelings known publicly that month, not just about the attacks on the Church but on the human rights situation generally. The United States government made representations to the Argentine junta about the arrest of an American priest from Connecticut, James Weeks, who was being held in Córdoba on suspicion of involvement with subversive groups. After two weeks, he was expelled from the country. But within Argentina, the main expressions of concern came from human rights groups, not from the Catholic Church. The Ecumenical Movement for Human Rights, led by the Bishop of Quilmes, Monsignor Novak, protested at the growing violence. But its position was undermined by lack of support from the Church as a whole, and Monsignor Novak took great personal risks in leading the movement. The Permanent Assembly of Human Rights, founded in 1975 to counter the abuses of both left and right under the Peronist government, was more forthright in its protests. One of its founding members was the Bishop of Neuquén, Jaime de Nevares, a particularly outspoken critic of the repression. The Assembly included other distinguished people from many walks of life: Raúl Alfonsín, of the Radical Party; a leading member of the Jewish faith, Rabbi Marshall Meyer; the head of the teachers' union, Alfredo Bravo, and eminent former civil servants and practising lawyers like Dr Emilio Mignone and Dr Juan José Prado. Many members had lost their own families. The Assembly was protected to some extent by the position of its members and its meticulous approach. Hundreds of cases were taken up together and tested in the courts, in an attempt to force the judiciary to deal with all the habeas corpus writs and accept responsibility for saving the lives of those who had been abducted. But even finding office space for the Permanent Assembly was difficult because no one wanted to rent property to them. They finally raised enough money to buy an office in the centre of the city, though until then they, like the Mothers of the Plaza, were obliged to meet on church premises. In some ways, after they had established their own headquarters, it was easier for the security services to monitor their activities, and they were under constant surveillance. One day one of the Assembly's members found that there was bad interference on a radio set in the office, and when they investigated they discovered a bugging device planted inside a light fixture. After that, the Assembly's staff became so used to finding bugs in the office that they would give them to visiting children to play with. They never discovered how or when the security services managed to plant them. But the military never tried to crush the Permanent Assembly as they had the Mothers.

Bishop Jaime de Nevares spent much of his time commuting between the Assembly's headquarters in the capital and his bishopric in Neuquén, in the eastern Andean foothills. Like La Rioja, it was an isolated diocese, with many poor farmers and, like Bishop Angelelli, Bishop de Nevares worked in near isolation, without the official backing of the Church. The Episcopate adopted a policy of non-co-operation towards both the Ecumenical Movement and the Permanent Assembly, which left de Nevares with little protection. He was outspoken from the beginning of military rule, and inflexibly maintained his position on human rights. After Angelelli's death there were perhaps ten bishops who actively defended human rights; Jaime de Nevares was one of the most uncompromising of them. De Nevares studied theology at Córdoba; of the group he was ordained with, one was shot dead and another was kidnapped and is missing. He knew many other people inside and outside the Church who suffered similar fates. Twenty or more letters a day would arrive at the bishop's residence in Neuquén from families who had lost someone. Many more people came to see him personally, especially after they heard that he was with the Permanent Assembly.

In October 1976 a 31-year-old Irish priest from County Cork was picked up. Father Patrick Rice was the superior of the order of the Little Brothers of the Gospel in the working-class district of

Buenos Aires, Villa Soldati. He was out for a walk with a young woman, Fatima Cabrera, who had come to him for help, when a van drew up and an armed man shouted to them, 'Stop, or I'll shoot.' They were taken to Police Station 36 where Father Rice was told, 'Now you'll find out that the Romans were very civilized towards the early Christians compared with what's going to happen to you.' They placed a yellow hood over his head, warning that if he looked up at the guards, he would be a dead man. He and Fatima were taken to a barracks, where they were both tortured. He was accused of putting up slogans around Villa Soldati, which he denied. He was told, after being beaten and given electric shocks, that he was to say his injuries had been caused by falling downstairs. 'If you say anything else, you'll find yourself in the river,' they said. Through the work of the Irish Ambassador and human rights organizations, Patrick Rice was eventually freed and deported, after more than a month in prison. Fatima Cabrera was not released and he was never told what had happened to her. Several of his friends, including another priest in his order, died or disappeared that year and the next.

The Argentine Church as a whole said almost nothing when, in January 1977, the Protestant theologian and ecumenical leader Mauricio López was abducted from his home in Mendoza. He had been about to move from his position as Professor of Philosophy at the University of Mendoza to go to the Buenos Aires Institute of Theology. The World Council of Churches, in which he had been active, appealed to President Videla to help in obtaining his release. The United Nations General Secretary, Kurt Waldheim, contacted the Argentine authorities on López's behalf, and so did church and government figures in the United States, the Netherlands, France, and other countries, but there was never any satisfactory reply.

Finally, after this succession of attacks on churchmen, the twelve bishops of Argentina met in March 1977 to discuss the problem. The divisions of opinion between them were deep, but they agreed on a common position: that since all men were created equal in the sight of God, all must have equal rights. They agreed, too, that events in the country were causing anguish among different sections of the population. It was, perhaps, something to have managed to get the conservative group among the bishops to admit as much as that, and a letter containing their findings was sent to the President; but at the insistence of the conservatives and the conference of the moderates, the letter remained unpublished.

Later that month, however, one of the twelve was much more outspoken. In his pastoral letter for Lent, one year after the coup, the Bishop of Lomas de Zamora, Mgr Collino, wrote: 'With increasing frequency, afflicted relatives and friends come to us, telling us how armed groups come to their houses, and with the most violent procedures, literally take all their property, taking away one or more members of their family without any explanation, either before or after the operation.' It was a clear-cut statement of what had been happening to thousands over the past twelve months, and followed the disappearance of one of his own social workers. It expressed the frustration of some bishops at the failure of the Church to take a united, public stance on the violence.

Hundreds of people were contacting their priests and bishops, asking for help. Reactions to the pressure to act were diverse among the clergy. Some limited themselves to deploring the violence but took it no further when the authorities gave no answers. Others tried to confront the officials and demand how, why and where people were being detained; they gave public lectures to tell people what they couldn't read in the newspapers or see on television; and they openly sided with the victims of repression.

Two months later, in May 1977, the 35th Episcopal Conference produced a document entitled *Christian Reflections for the Country's People*. It was the first time the Church had taken a position on how far the régime could go in combating its enemies and still follow Christian principles. *Reflections* was also the first political document drawn up by all the Church in Argentina as a group. But the document did not accuse the military authorities directly; rather it stressed the importance of the community of all men, and the need to defend human dignity above collective security. Only implicitly did it criticize the armed forces for allowing notions of security to override the Pope's principle that one must defend human life. The overall tone was one of respect, and the arguments were defensive, but *Reflections* did go on to say that the Church had received information that groups of kidnappers had been identified as belonging to the police and armed forces, and that torture and detention without trial were unacceptable. In the final editing of *Christian Reflections for the Country's People*, further comments about the regular looting of homes and reprisals against families and relatives of people who were apprehended were accidentally left out, but it was still the most forthright document yet produced by the Church. The bishop submitted it to President Videla and suggested that there should be no debate about it until they received an official reply. All the government said, however, was that it was up to the bishops to discuss what they liked; but there was no response to the report itself. Due to military censorship, the document also got very little publicity. By this time, the bishops had returned to their dioceses, and the collective force of their conclusions was lost.

But the document did achieve something, despite the way it was launched. It finally separated the Church as an institution from the régime's official policies because of its human rights record, though many in the hierarchy had been reluctant even to take this step. The Episcopate did not succeed in establishing its independence in the eyes of most people, however, because few knew what it was saying, and because it had taken so long to say it. It also failed to back it up with concrete institutional measures to support human rights groups or to establish their own Episcopal body for victims of repression, as the Church in Chile and Brazil had done, or to make an effort to speak publicly about the situation. It was left to individual bishops and priests to take their own risks.

Nowadays the Bishop of Neuquén, Jaime de Nevares, no longer isolated in his diocese in the foothills of the Andes, is clear in his analysis of the Church's failure: 'If we accused the military of crimes against the people, we should also have broken off relations with them; yet we continued to receive them and co-operate with them.' President Videla was, for instance, invited to say prayers at the Marian Congress of the Church in Mendoza in 1979, though Bishop de Nevares refused to attend, and held a Congress of his own in Neuquén. But that was an exception. When a new bishop was appointed, it was normal for the military leaders in the area to be invited to his enthronement. The supply of chaplains to the armed forces was uninterrupted, and senior churchmen presided over the traditional Te Deum on the country's Independence Day each year without exception during the period of military rule.

But the Church is made up of the faithful, as well as the clergy, and its inactivity was also the inactivity of ordinary Catholics as well as of the priesthood and the hierarchy. Those who had a good idea of what was happening in Argentina preferred to take refuge in the assumption that people who disappeared must have been guilty of something. Others may have thought the sacrifice of human rights worth it, on balance, if terrorism was to be controlled. There was little or no pressure from laymen on the conservative churchmen who believed that the military were fighting to destroy Communism.

And even when the full extent of the military's crimes was revealed and a civilian government had taken office, there were still those who, like Archbishop Plaza, were not prepared to condemn what had been done. Archbishop Carlos Mariano Pérez of Salta province, where a savage war had been waged against the guerrilla forces of the ERP and the Montoneros, opposed the exhumation of bodies from 'NN' graves at the beginning of 1984. It was, he said, a vile attempt to set people against the armed forces. They had, after all, been fighting for Christianity.

# 11 THE PYRAMIDS OF PHARAOH

*'For somebody who kills, robbing is only a minor misdemeanour'* – Buenos Aires civil servant.

The atmosphere in the Bolsa, the stock exchange in Buenos Aires, was buoyant. Crowds gathered, armed with binoculars to watch the proceedings on the floor where clerks chalked up the changing share prices on large elevated blackboards. A cheer went up as some stock made a large gain, more as if the spectators were urging on a favourite horse at the races than observing a speculating extravaganza. The stock market had been undergoing a seemingly unstoppable boom ever since 24 March 1976 and by August the average price of shares had increased by a factor of seventeen, rising from 3 cents to 50 cents a share. The excitement of the crowds flocking to the Bolsa was transmitted to the punters on the floor where they were shouting and jostling to trade ever more shares. Their eagerness was justified; it wasn't unusual to see good stocks rise 30 per cent in a favourable day's trading. Some of those who had invested in the market before the coup saw their stake earn a small fortune several months into the new government, with $10,000 making one American investor $300,000 in the space of seven months. The market itself expanded from a daily volume of $5 million worth of stocks traded a day to $15 million between July and August alone. It seemed that the junta was already working financial wonders for the country.

As the guerrilla casualties mounted during the first year of the Process the armed forces were also succeeding on the first battlefront against 'subversion'; the ERP guerrilla organization had been largely dismembered by the middle of the first year of the coup, with the biggest blow struck on 19 July when the charismatic ERP leader, Mario Roberto Santucho, was killed in a 'confrontation' in an apartment at Villa Martelli on the outskirts of Buenos Aires, after a neighbour had apparently tipped off Army troops and police. As for the Montoneros, within a year of the military's taking power, they had sustained two thousand casualties and their leadership had moved overseas. By the end of 1976, the Minister of the Interior, General Albano Harguindeguy, was able to claim that 'long before the end of next year, subversive delinquency will be reduced to acts requiring only police handling'. The régime was confident that the war was in its closing stages. One general, speaking at the end of 1976, was confident enough to be contemptuous of the calibre of the guerrilla forces facing him, even though those identical forces had, on the military's own admission, threatened the very existence of the State only months earlier. General Domingo Bussi, Governor of the Province of Tucumán, a region which had experienced the longest anti-guerrilla campaign in the country, described the enemy in October 1976 as no longer even deserving the name of guerrillas: 'I've seen the real thing in Vietnam . . . our type here are cowards who run from a fight, attack only treacherously and kill defenceless people. They are not true nationalists: they are abandoned by God and deserve only death.' Under General Bussi's leadership, the Fifth Infantry Brigade had helped wipe out any remaining guerrillas in the jungle and mountains of Tucumán; altogether some 600 ERP 'militants' were killed, including Santucho's brother, Asdrubal. 'The Army has won the war and it is now up to the people, with the Government's support, to win the peace,' Bussi declared, but he added that the resurgence of subversion would have to be prevented by improving the lot of the ordinary worker who 'as a result of many years of official neglect . . . owns nothing, has had no opportunity to educate himself and has suffered from the absence of public health and social welfare.' His solicitude for the impoverished sugar-cane workers of the region was not echoed by his superiors in Buenos Aires; already well down the road towards winning the first war against terrorism, they were increasingly turning their attention to waging the second war against 'economic subversion' and the chaos of the Argentine economy.

In October 1976, the military leaders in Buenos Aires were considering a rather different response to that suggested by General Bussi of Tucumán, to deal with economic problems. They were facing their first major confrontation with organized labour since the coup. Although strikes were outlawed and trade unions taken over by the military, the power workers of the Italo and Segba power plants in the capital had decided on industrial action and were enforcing a go-slow. Some industrial parts of Buenos

Aires had had their electricity supply cut off after several generators were damaged by unknown saboteurs. The power workers were protesting against the laying off of two hundred men, and were particularly angry that many of them were shop stewards or organizers in the Light and Power Workers' Union. The go-slow meant that some of the workers were liable to prosecution under the terms of a new industrial security decree which allowed up to ten years' imprisonment for inciting strikes. The decree had been brought into force a few weeks earlier, following industrial unrest among Ford car workers. The authorities' response to the power workers was first to threaten to use the new laws, and, when the go-slow continued, to arrest hundreds of them. When the threat of a full-scale strike occurred early in the new year, the leader of the Power Workers' Union, Oscar Smith, was abducted, shortly after visiting the Ministry of the Interior to hold talks about calling off the strike. The case of Smith was, almost exactly two years after his disappearance, to establish a major legal breakthrough against the junta, as the courts finally ruled that they could not be expected to assume responsibility for habeas corpus writs for missing persons and that it must rest on the shoulders of the government.

The unions themselves failed to inflict any real blows against the junta's labour policies. The historically powerful Peronist trade unions were weakened by the clampdown on industrial action and, more effectively, by the persecution of labour leaders like Oscar Smith. A third of the victims of the Dirty War were ordinary workers or trade unionists. Trade union leaders were prime targets for victimization, dismissal, and legal and illegal detention; 27 of the country's most prominent union leaders were detained, abducted or found dead within the first four years of military rule. The military government also had to fight a war in purely economic terms, and the man it chose to be its general was Dr José Martínez de Hoz, a member of one of Argentina's leading patrician land-owning families which had settled in the country at the time of its independence. His ancestors had founded the Sociedad Rural, the powerful association of estancia owners, as well as the Jockey Club in Buenos Aires. But the Martínez de Hoz fortune came mostly from industry. He himself was chairman of the country's largest private steel company, Acíndar, and was president of the Argentine Entrepreneurs' Council. He seemed an ideal candidate to represent the country's manufacturing and land-owing interests, but he was also widely respected in the international banking community, which proved highly receptive to his requests for loans and credits for Argentina.

Martínez de Hoz studied economics at Harvard and the Massachusetts Institute of Technology after leaving Eton, and had already been Economics Minister in one previous government before 1976. A lean, intense man, his most startling and heavily caricatured feature was a pair of outsized, alarmingly pointed ears, which cartoonists would one day (when he was discredited and it was safer to do so) use to depict him as Dracula. Martínez de Hoz agreed wholeheartedly with the Friedmanite school of monetarism, and viewed inflation as his country's gravest economic problem. In Isabel Perón's last three months in office it was heading for 500 per cent, and there were projections that it would reach 1,000 per cent by the end of 1976. When Martínez de Hoz took over, in March of that year, Argentina owed 12 billion dollars in foreign debts, there was a balance of payments deficit of nearly 2 billion dollars, a negative growth rate, heavily depleted reserves of foreign exchange, and a currency which fluctuated alarmingly.

It was an open secret in the business community in the months before the 1976 coup that Martínez de Hoz would be brought into any government that took over from the Peronists. He would hold meetings over lunch and dinner at the London Grill Room in Reconquista Street in Buenos Aires as early as 1974, working out his strategy with senior financiers and bankers. When he became Economics Minister, he was unequivocal about the economic regulation which must take place to clear up the gross mismanagement of the economy and to clear out the corruption. Martínez de Hoz wanted to encourage a free and competitive economy unhampered by state intervention and open to the international market, in contrast to the protectionist and regulatory policies of the Peronists. During the last three years of Peronism, employees on the State payroll had grown by a quarter; the new economic team was determined to reduce that. Argentine manufacturers had also been well cushioned from outside competition under previous governments because high tariffs either kept foreign goods from entering the country or made them very expensive. The Peronists and past military governments had also pursued economic policies which left a great number of industries in the hands of the State; companies in difficulty were often bailed out by being taken over by the government and 50 per cent of industry was nationalized by 1976. Martínez de Hoz was determined to sell off as many of these concerns as possible, leaving the state as a guiding force rather than a prime mover in economic matters. But unlike in Chile, reducing the public sector was not to be accomplished at the cost of 20 per cent unemployment. The new government in Argentina was aware that a huge increase in numbers out of work could be playing into the hands of the Montoneros and the radical Peronists, providing a source for their support – 'one more jobless equals one more guerrilla' was the equation in military men's eyes. Instead Martínez de Hoz would squeeze living standards and increase the productivity of industry, thus pushing down inflation while keeping most people in work. That was the theory.

But the free economy model also meant letting prices rise to their natural market levels, and so petrol prices shot up immediately by 30 per cent, and cigarettes doubled in price overnight when the long-standing controls were lifted. Most goods rose rapidly in cost, and price increases often averaged 50 per cent each month. In July of 1976, the Economics Minister went on television and radio to explain his policies to the public. Reading in a dry monotone, he assured everyone that profiteering would be dealt with, although he did not specify how. He simply said that a government supported by the people 'has the moral authority to influence productive enterprises to avoid uncontrolled price rises.' And, he added, 'the Argentine economy has no basic or irremediable flaws.' Meanwhile, to combat inflation, wages were frozen. Within six months, real wages had plummeted to half their 1974 value and the buying power of most people had shrunk to half of what it had been prior to the coup.

Argentines were used to living with inflation, bribes and the black market dollar, which was so much a part of daily economic life that its rate was quoted in the daily newspapers. They were used to not paying tax. State-salaried workers were the only regular source of personal income tax, as it was an accepted practice for those not tied to government salaries not to offer to pay it; often bribes to income tax officials proved to be the cheapest safeguard of all. Companies, too, were notoriously corrupt and half-hearted when it came to paying taxes. It was not too difficult to live on a salary if it were dispensed wisely; if only a small portion of a monthly pay cheque were drawn in cash, and the rest spent on the stock market or government bonds, with their 5 or 6 per cent daily rise in value, then it was possible to sidestep the worst effects of inflation. Bonds could be cashed as needed, to pay for living expenses. For people less well-paid, savings came in the form of big items like a car which, if kept in good condition, would be a kind of insurance policy, while anything which had to be purchased was bought as soon as the money was available, and before prices went up again. Houses were often sold for cash and preferably in dollars, because the time it would take to process a cheque or bankers' order might mean the loss of perhaps 5 per cent of the deal.

The great hope, as far as the new Economics Minister was concerned, lay in the riches of the rolling pampas and in oil. Argentina was nearing a 90 per cent self-sufficiency in oil, and this could provide a valuable export. But the traditional grain crops and Argentine beef were at the heart of Martínez de Hoz's plan to get rid of the enormous budget deficit and balance of payments crisis. Some 80 per cent of the country's exports came from the land and it was back to the land that Argentina should go, to its natural role as the world's food supplier and away from dreams of rapid industrialization. Incentives were to be given to agricultural producers while the manufacturer was to be forced to become more competitive. That this strategy masked what was, in effect, the de-industrialization of the country and an asset-stripping exercise at that, as foreign capital was allowed into the country and foreign goods were allowed to replace locally-produced ones, was not obvious for several years.

To attract foreign investment and to stabilize the currency, Martínez de Hoz freed interest rates, which were allowed to keep on rising, while import tariffs were gradually reduced. Some exchange controls were lifted, so that exporters would be able to exchange a third of their earnings on the 'free' (unofficial) market, where the peso had improved its value from 340 to 230 to the dollar. The official value of the peso was still grossly overvalued at 140 to the dollar, but this was a deliberate effort to get inflation under control. In August, foreign companies were allowed to operate on similar terms to Argentine ones. The non-interventionist policy of the new government also meant that there was no capital gains tax, and in an early reform, Martínez de Hoz abolished death duties. His father had died some ten days before, leaving him with a large estate and one of the biggest fortunes in the country.

The problems with credit abroad were greatly improved by the minister's good contacts with the international banking community. His overseas trips to Washington and London in the first years of the junta were highly successful in raising loans from private international banks and in renegotiating with the International Monetary Fund. The country was treated as if it were creditworthy again. When Martínez de Hoz sat down for lunch with the Labour Chancellor Denis Healey in July 1976, some eyebrows were raised about the wisdom of doing business with the régime, but the trip was a success, both in the City and with the British Government. 'Joe', as he was known to many in the banking world, managed in several foreign trips in his first year as minister to raise $500 million from a consortium of American banks, sign a new memorandum of understanding with the IMF allowing Argentina to receive more help in repaying foreign banks, and get finance worth several hundreds more millions from British and European banks. Fourteen months later, he was back in London to open the European branch of the Argentine Banco de la Nación in the City, going on to deliver a seminar on the prospects of the Argentine economy to a high-level group from the CBI. By 1977 the Western press was dubbing him a 'miracle worker' who had returned the country to creditworthiness, having raised over $870 million in loans, including more than $60 million from Britain and another $300 million in credit from the IMF. Only the Americans were beginning to be difficult, as Jimmy Carter's human rights policy began to bite.

At home, the fruits of the new economic policies were also being warmly praised. The wages freeze and the fall in living standards had contributed to a huge drop in the rate of inflation, from 444 per cent in 1976 to a modest, (by recent Argentine standards) 178 per cent. Cheaper imports had helped to keep domestic prices down and perhaps the competition encouraged productivity, because, for the first time in two years, there was a positive rate of growth of nearly 5 per cent. An excellent grain harvest helped ensure that foreign reserves and the balance of payments were finally in the black at about 2,500 million dollars each. The Bolsa was behaving bullishly and foreign investment appeared to be pouring in. Argentina had its own 'Wizard de Hoz'.

The country's greatest living writer, Jorge Luis Borges, once decribed the Argentines as people who look upon the land as something to be exploited rather than developed. The over-easy conquest of a country enriched with great natural resources, sparsely populated by educated immigrants from Europe and administered by a series of crisis-ridden governments might all have contributed to such an attitude. But the military control over the country after 1976 made it into a doctrine. As one officer later put it: 'We turned it into a feudal system. It was going back to the Dark Ages in which feudal lords owned people and properties and decided who was to be killed and who was to be spared. It was a vast moral degradation in which the whole structure was corrupted from those who checked the meat to the running of the biggest company. It was absolute.' When the junta divided up the country between the three branches of the armed forces, it also split up the spoils of the economy. And while Martínez de Hoz wanted to sell off the industries and businesses owned by the State and return them to private enterprise and thus offload a large portion of public spending, he met with opposition from the feudal lords who had only just been given access to huge chunks of the Argentine economy. After two years of the Process, it was obvious that Martínez de Hoz was failing in his efforts to divest the State of either its ownership of industry or its intervention in the economy. The number of public employees stayed roughly the same; those made redundant were soon replaced by others and the State's share in overall spending actually rose.

The first problem was the vast and secret budget. While in Paris on business, Martínez de Hoz confessed to a colleague, 'There is one figure that I will never know; and that is how much the military are spending on themselves.' At least 7 per cent of the national budget was spent by naval and military engineers alone on financing their own industries – steel and chemical factories and shipbuilding. But an even greater and unknown sum was being spent on military projects in the state-owned Fabricaciónes Militares which manufactured weapons and military equipment. Yet more was being spent abroad on West German tank parts, submarines and destroyers: on American Skyhawk fighter planes, French Super Etendards, and Israeli Dagger fighter planes; and on British radar, destroyers, Lynx helicopters and Sea Dart missiles.

But the military did not just spend *qua* military men. They were now also responsible for huge enterprises like the State oil company, the airlines, the Atomic Energy Commission and countless other companies. The military had a traditional interest in the running of the Argentine economy; Kennedy's Alliance for Progress and the civic programmes run by the military in Latin America had only reinforced a propensity for tinkering with economic development which had already been practised by military rulers earlier in the century. By the 1970s Argentina's armed forces had a much more corporatist attitude towards managing the State, and once in power, could indulge their enthusiasm for big, impressive and unproductive public works projects, and big, complicated business deals. While Martínez de Hoz claimed to be an economic liberal who decried public spending as the 'motor of inflation' the military men actually running the State enterprises were all too keen to spend. A few companies were sold, such as printing presses and even some small banks. But much was spent, too. Aerolíneas Argentinas, the State-owned airline, purchased six passenger planes in 1980, costing $240 million. The four 727s and two 747s were to be used on new routes to Japan and Australia, according to the management, but somehow the flights never materialized. In the same year, the private airline Austral, which operated on domestic routes, was taken over by the government, even though Austral was going bankrupt, with $5 million in debts. It seemed that the interventionist habit of the Peronists, of bailing out bankrupt companies, was hard to shake off. The nationalization of Austral was handled by Martínez de Hoz, the Planning Secretary, Walter J. Klein, and Videla himself. The transaction led the civilian government to charge all three men with questionable dealings over Austral four years later. The shares of Austral and its two smaller subsidiaries, Sol Jet and Lagos del Sur, were offered for sale to the government by the firm's chairman and chief shareholder, Williams J. Reynal, before any bankruptcy proceedings were entered into. This was allegedly done with the exclusive purpose of saving the owners' assets and to relieve them of any criminal liability which might have been faced if bankruptcy proceedings had been started, according to the civilian investigators. The Austral company had owed almost all of its $5 million debt to the government.

Another large purchase was of the private company, Italo, which supplied electricity for Buenos Aires. It was valued at around $60 million, but the junta paid $300 million for it. Such exercises were not purely for the sake of nationalization. There was a great deal of money to be made on any number of deals, and the opportunities weren't lost. Most of the money was sent abroad, or used for expensive new foreign cars now stocking the capital's showrooms, or for Rolex watches, furs and property. Many people bought houses in the beautiful resort of Punta del Este in Uruguay, which was becoming so much an annexe of Argentina for the wealthy that it was referred to as 'that little country in the corner with the nice view of the sea'.

Much of the money was made, at a lesser level, through bribes, backhanders, and 'commissions' on transactions, often laundered through bogus companies, or just received as straight payments for helping to secure contracts or for accepting tenders put in for work. One businessman estimated that, under the military, 3 to 5 per cent of any deal was paid in some form of bribe.

Even private companies were brought into the military's grip. Most firms felt it essential to hire a retired military officer to work as a 'consultant' or senior board member, to smooth the way with the military. The officer would help secure contracts, put in tenders and lobby in high places. It was commonplace to be beckoned to a backroom to be told what percentage would have to be paid to have an order renewed. The system didn't make the management of the economy any easier.

The new mayor of Buenos Aires looked out over the city that was now his. It could have been mistaken for an old European capital, with its high-rise apartments and grand residences, the bright office building and landscaped parks and boulevards. The smart shops on Florida with the leather goods, jewellery and its own Harrods department store were filled with elegantly-dressed women and men. The mayor was proud of the sophisticated city he had inherited. He liked going to the opera at the Colón Theatre, then dining at one of the French restaurants nearby. He took an interest in the fashions and the press, even the advertising posters in his city. He was also concerned to improve the quality of life for its 11 million inhabitants. He was particularly annoyed by the disfiguring sight of the *villas de emergencia* that were ringing the city. These shantytowns, also known as *villas de miseria*, were not on the scale of Chile's or Brazil's but they were surprisingly large for a country as relatively wealthy as Argentina.

'After me, Buenos Aires will be a different city,' Air Force Brigadier Osvaldo Cacciatore decided. And he was to be proved right. He didn't have any experience of running a large metropolis, but he was under no illusions about its importance. Forty per cent of the country's population lived in Buenos Aires, and the headquarters of the armed forces were all based there. Even the marine regiment had moved its base from Puerto Belgrano down the southern coast, to the land-locked city of La Plata, just in order to be near the centre of power-broking and coup-making.

Mayor Cacciatore, out of his Air Force uniform, looked the part of the jolly burgermeister; in his early fifties, with his black hair going a distinguished silver, he always seemed to be smiling: a slightly insincere, foxy smile. His nickname in the Air Force had been *el cazador*, from the Italian for 'hunter', and his career had demonstrated an appetite for power and influence, now at its height. Cacciatore's career had been promoted for nearly two decades by his friend, General Benjamín Menéndez, (whose son, Mario, was to lead the forces on the Falklands). They met at the School of Military Aviation in the 1940s. The two of them had been involved in a failed coup attempt against Juan Perón in 1951 led by Menéndez himself and executed by Air Force officers including Cacciatore who set off from El Palomar Air Base to force the surrender of the President from the Casa Rosada. The plot was discovered and Cacciatore had to flee to Uruguay along with a number of other officers, to bide his time until it was safe to return. Meanwhile, in Uruguay Cacciatore played football professionally for 'Liverpool de Montevideo' as a full back. *El cazador* gained the reputation of being someone who was never left doing nothing; he either kicked the ball or one of his rivals.

Cacciatore was able to return to Argentina in 1955 after the 'liberating revolution' which ousted Perón, and was promoted to rank of Air Force Captain, thanks partly to his role in the earlier coup attempt. By 1970 he was a Brigadier and although during the three years of Peronist government he was once again in the political wilderness, in 1976 his patience was rewarded by Videla, who made him mayor.

Cacciatore declared that he would make Buenos Aires 'the best city in the world', but first he had to make sure that his own personal style was going to be reflected within City Hall. He appointed his own men to a personal staff of 47, only 6 of whom were given full-time duties. The rest were there as political scouts, taking salaries for acting as the mayor's supporters. Like many State enterprises, including the largest one, YPF, and like most government ministries, the mayor also set up his own intelligence and security service. In the basement of City Hall he stockpiled a large cache of machine-guns, rifles, handguns and other munitions. He hired or assigned mainly Air Force officers as a paramilitary, plain-clothes secret service. Their work was not just aimed at outside enemies; they had equipment useful for internal espionage as well, including tape recorders, cameras and video equipment. The operation was deemed necessary in order to check on doubtful employees. But the force would have been of use in picking up others in wider operations under the State intelligence agency, SIDE. By far the greatest number of abductions was in Buenos Aires or nearby towns in the province.

But Mayor Cacciatore was to gain fame not for the way he used his mini-security service, but as the creator of 'projectos faraónicos' – his Pharaonic plans. The building of the Pyramids by the Pharaohs of Egypt was the only just comparison that the people of the city could make with what the mayor had in mind for them. It was an apt description of the mayor's visions. The Pharaoh of Buenos Aires prided himself on his independence of mind. 'I plan things to such an extent that there is no doubt how they are going to come about,' he said in December 1979. 'They're going to come about as I want them to. It's necessary to have very concrete plans and to make very firm decisions . . . At first, in making the plans, you've got to have a lot of plans and you mustn't stop. As for the decisions, you must exercise your capacity for making them. For me, it's indispensable to be absolutely immoveable. It's always been that way.'

The biggest and most costly of his concrete plans was the brainchild of Guillermo Witta, who had written a book called *The Arterial City* in 1970. This book captured Cacciatore's imagination: broad motorways which would speed the traffic out of the city centre, linking it with airports and other cities. The author became Municipal Secretary for Public Works. But there was immediate hostility. The Society of Architects and the Centre for Engineering questioned the value of a motorway building programme when there was a world energy crisis. But opposition was summarily dealt with: the city's director of transport was dismissed and the Office of Architecture and Urban Development dismantled. With an urgency unusual in Argentina, work on the first motorway started in early 1977 and was completed before Christmas 1978. But the work was so expensive that money for it had to be raised on the international market. The first of the Pharaonic projects was also costly in human terms; more than two thousand houses were pulled down to make way for the airport motorway, and many attractive nineteenth century buildings were demolished so that the central avenue through Buenos Aires could be widened to eight lanes.

There was a similar grandeur about projects undertaken by the Navy in nuclear energy and hydro-electricity. But since Argentina's gross national product was only the size of Denmark's, all this spending had to be financed by printing more million peso notes. Martínez de Hoz, the Friedmanite in the economics ministry, understood that perfectly well; but the military were in the saddle, and spending money on a grand scale was more congenial to them than the restraint he was preaching.

The road-building programme used 183,000 tonnes of asphalt,

640,000 cubic metres of concrete, and over 3,000 steel and concrete supports. Although the total cost was never disclosed to the public, the mayor's road-building programme was estimated at $1,000 million, without having been completed. His next project was much cheaper. As the motorways went in, the shanty towns were to come out. Cacciatore wanted to sweep away all 32 of them overnight, claiming that the 270,000 people living in them could easily find alternative accommodation. 'It's not just a matter of moving them on,' he said, 'We know that a lot of these people living in these places have their own piece of land, a house, a dwelling. There's no logical reason why they should be living in these places.' Many people were forcibly removed and shipped out of the settlements in lorries and just left somewhere in the country. The expulsions did little more than push the slums further into the outskirts of Buenos Aires, and a number of them sprang up again in the same place, to the mayor's consternation.

The greatest scheme was yet to come, however. Cacciatore wanted to create a swathe of parkland around the capital, comprising an ecological belt with a giant amusement park. To be named Hollywood Park, it was to be one of the world's largest; under the original plan, it would have nearly ninety attractions, most of them available only by being imported from abroad, and a cinema, aquarium and scenic tower. The 600-foot high tower would have a bar in the middle, a revolving restaurant, and lookout levels further up so that visitors could see the whole panorama from the fake 'Russian mountains', roller coaster, fountains and the dancefloor for 13,000 people, to the huge ferris wheel. Hollywood Park would be the third largest in the world, out-doing Tivoli Gardens or Coney Island. And beyond this a zoological and nature park would be established, covering another 70 hectares. The mayor identified himself most closely with it all; but this particular Pharaonic project turned into a monumental folly, draining the city's coffers, bankrupting companies and increasing many overseas bank accounts.

In theory, Hollywood Park and the rest of the 'ecobelt' around Buenos Aires was to be paid for at no extra cost to public funds. The lucrative contracts which were first put out to tender in 1978 were supposed to attract competing bids, with the lowest winning. The intention was also to make the initial investors liable for losses if the park didn't make a profit. Early on, within a few months, something started going wrong with this plan; the municipality was anxious to get the park under way, and to attract investors more quickly, offered financial help and public money to anyone who got the contract. Whoever put in the lowest tender in open competition would be given credit worth $40 million or 80 per cent of the value of the work in public funds. At the time, there were three companies in the running for contracts, but two of them dropped out at this point, despite the generous credit terms being offered. Rumours in financial circles suggested that the two were never informed about the extra funds and that only the last remaining company, a consortium which included one general among its ranks and an Air Force brigadier, was told. This company, not surprisingly, won the contract for the park. Hollywood Park would bear the name of the company unofficially from then on. It would be known as 'Interama'.

As soon as Interama was chosen, the council issued orders allowing yet more finance to be made available, although it was under no obligation to do so; Cacciatore himself approved credit for Interama worth $20 million through the National Savings Bank and borrowed more money for the city's own funds in order to raise yet more credit. Interama undertook to complete the park no later than 30 November 1980. If they failed, they would be liable for fines of $30,000 for each day they left Interama unfinished. The contract was agreed in mid-1978.

The construction work started on the amusements park. The zoological park, which was supposed to be the primary land improvement scheme, was ignored while funds were poured into Interama. It seemed that the consortium, despite the credit and aid being given them by the mayor, was slipping ever behind in their schedule. The City Hall came to be known as the bottomless barrel, as the motorways, underground car parks, Interama and other municipal projects sprang up. The city was fast draining its own funds away and had to start closing hospitals, such as the Rawson Hospital and postpone plans for a new children's hospital.

Stories began circulating in Buenos Aires that large container shipments for Interama were coming into the country without clearing customs. Most of the rides and amusements equipment came from Germany or the United States and appeared to be entering the country as official contraband. Some of the containers had nothing remotely connected to an amusements park inside; shipments were later found to contain toothbrushes, thousands of rolls of toilet paper and a consignment of Argentine flags. Enormous containers would arrive at the huge Interama work site, just a short drive from the centre of the city, but they would not have certificates or documents stating that they were legal imports and many of them were not, the contracts being made informally and the payments laundered through various channels. The investigation into what was causing such an increase in costs was delayed for several years, after the big 'Skydiver' ferris wheel had already been erected and paid for and the whirlygig ride was in operation and the refreshment trolleys had arrived in the country. It was later that invoices came to light that showed that the little trolleys, painted bright red and yellow with shiny lacquer selling 'Fresh hot popcorn' had been bought for $35,000 plus a 30 per cent surcharge. The popcorn trolleys, sold by a Kansas company, should have cost a tenth of that price. The figures for the various rides were staggering: the 'Hidrovertigo' $2,800,000, the Vertigorama $5,300,000, the speedway and bumper cars each $500,000, 'Aerogondola' nearly $3 million, the 'Wild-cat' $1 million, the great revolving tower and restaurant $10 million. While the park should have cost something like $40 million to equip and fit out with amusements, the real cost was nearing $200 million. And no effort to start the zoological area had even been made; that was abandoned as wasteland and work only slowly progressed on the Interama scheme.

When the deadline of 1980 arrived, the Interama consortium was nowhere near completing the work on the park and the project was getting into deeper and deeper trouble. The consortium seemed to be failing to invest its funds in the park, relying on money from the City Hall to keep the building work afloat. The money paid to cover the inflated invoices was probably going straight from the city's coffers into fixed interest accounts overseas which were then credited to the shareholders of Interama. The city council soon dropped its demand that the work be completed on time, and ignored the $30,000 a day penalty clause; instead Interama was given a 180 day extension. Then $20 million of public money backing the project was forfeited, as the city accountants realized that they had no hope of getting their investment back, because Interama was now in serious financial difficulties itself. Early in 1981 an accountant was appointed to look into the consortium's affairs, and by March of that year his report was in Cacciatore's hands. Its main finding was that the public funds for the park, provided by the city and raised through bank loans, had gone mostly to deposit accounts in Switzerland and Luxembourg.

The details were kept secret, but Interama was beginning to founder. Its interests were handed over to its main creditor, the

Banco Sidesa, but that too began to collapse, and the Central Bank had to take Interama over and oversee its liquidation. The debts fell to the bank, and to the Municipality of Buenos Aires, to service and maintain; and although the park itself was eventually opened to the public, the income from the turnstiles could never match the enormous cost of paying for the project or its interest payments. The pyramids of Buenos Aires crumbled before they were properly built, and the Pharaoh who had them built would one day make his escape to Uruguay, carrying a briefcase which was said to be packed with hundred-dollar bills.

By 1980, the scenes in the Bolsa had been replaced by a new spectator sport: watching the fluctuations of the currency on the boards in the windows of the foreign exchanges. After the brief spell of a more stable peso and lower inflation, the peso had taken off again. People would stand in the street gazing at the latest figures, deciding whether to convert pesos into dollars or not, or whether to put their money into one of the new bank accounts for a short time to make a speculative gain. Inside the ministry, Dr Martínez de Hoz had watched the signs of an economic recovery slip away into an ever-worsening crisis. The over-valued peso which had been in theory supposed to prevent inflation from rising too fast, was sucking in foreign imports and killing domestic industry. By mid-1980, the peso was being valued at 1,870 to the dollar. It wasn't until late in 1980 that the Economics Minister gave in to the desperate pleas of industrialists and allowed a creeping devaluation of the peso, but by then the damage was done, and the recession was biting hard. The new 'open market' economy, combined with an overvalued peso, had created the climate for de-industrialization, hot money and speculation.

One of the biggest psychological blows to industry came towards the end of 1980, when the once healthy tractor industry died almost wholesale. Four companies, Fiat, Massey Ferguson, Deutz and John Deere had been at the centre of the economic recovery at the start of the military's rule, but the strength of the peso and the lowering of tariffs meant that they could not compete with imports from abroad, which included tractors from the firms' own overseas factories. Farmers, too, had been given incentives to buy foreign machinery. Banks such as the Banco de la Nación Argentina were offering them 80 per cent credit on the cost of imported goods. The steam-engine of the recovery was supposed to be agriculture, but the farmers, too, were hit by the unfavourable exchange rates and the high cost of loans for investment. Argentines were used to decades of negative interest rates, which were always less than inflation itself. Now, because Martínez de Hoz had freed interest rates in order to stop speculation on the dollar, they were actually higher in real terms than inflation, by as much as 37 per cent. Suddenly, traditionally heavy borrowers like farmers were left with impossible debts. Positive interest rates had made it unprofitable to reinvest money in long-term projects; it was better to put the money into 30-day interest-bearing deposit accounts. And as demand for local goods declined, it was often better to go into liquidation and attempt to sell off fixed assets and speculate on the financial markets instead.

By 1980, the promising export record of the agricultural sector had been reversed and the largest grain and food processing group in the country, Sasetru, had collapsed with unpaid debts of $600 million, largely in short-term debt, and was taken over by the creditor banks who were owed the money. This failure was quickly followed by that of the huge paper company, Cellulosap, which stopped payment on its loans. The great bread-basket and meat-market of the world actually saw a decrease in the number of acres being sown by 12 per cent between 1977 and 1980. The number of cattle being reared also declined, from 61 million head to 58 million in just three years – the first time in that decade that there had been a fall in the size of Argentine herds. The tractor workers of the Deutz factory appealed to the Vatican for some sort of intervention, but there was nothing the Pope could do, and besides, it wasn't just agriculture which was collapsing by 1980: big multinationals established in Argentina, such as Fiat, Renault and Citroën were in severe difficulty while foreign cars were now taking some 15 per cent of the market.

The old system of dealing with inflation had been to buy black-market dollars. Then in 1976, Martínez de Hoz had introduced government bonds which were pegged against the dollar or the retail index. When he switched to a system of positive interest rates, most people abandoned bonds and dollars and rushed to put their pesos into fixed interest deposit accounts where there was no risk and 30 to 40 per cent profit on one month's investment. The system blatantly favoured the speculator, the wealthy, and the foreign investor, and worked against the farmer and industrialist, both of whom might be better off if they had sold up and put their money, too, in short-term accounts. The positive interest rates attracted enormous quantities of overseas captital from July 1980 onwards, when the country's capital markets were thrown wide open to unlimited inflows of foreign money. Martínez de Hoz took the decision in order to keep interest rates from rising and to avoid an economic recession, but the result was that about $500 million arrived in the country in one month alone, and then left again, increasing the foreign debt because the Central Bank had to pour money into this easy money system to keep it afloat. Ninety per cent of the money which came into Argentina was going into short-term deposits and almost none went into fixed investment. The high interest rates policy, introduced in the year after the coup, also created a race for the highest deposit accounts and frantic competition for deposits from finance houses. Speculators, who ranged from housewives to multinationals, would shop around to find the best rates; often people would sell their cars or houses because it was much more profitable to get real interest on cash than to just keep up with inflation. That was, of course, assuming that one was affluent enough to be able to risk selling a car or a house. But for those with cash, it was too tempting to ignore the possibility of actually beating inflation.

The cut-throat competition among banks soon took its toll. In April 1980, Argentina's two largest private banks collapsed and the Central Bank was forced to pour over $2 billion into supporting the banking system whose reserves had fallen very low. Towards the end of the year, the Banco de los Andes also failed with debts of $25 million. It became more and more difficult to call in loans which had been given out to farms and factories, because, if the chain of credit was broken it would mean the bank would take over control of bankrupt concerns which had no prospect of making a profit.

While industry floundered, affluent Argentines were able to take advantage of the strong peso and cheap dollar, and went on wild spending sprees abroad. Two to five million Argentines travelled overseas in 1980, taking $1,000 million with them in spending money. Over 1980 and the next year, $10,700 million left the country and by the end of military rule, some $30,000 million had gone abroad, much of it into United States bank accounts, once the quick money had been made on Argentina's short-term deposits. And money inside the country could be spent on new electronic toys from abroad, as long as the peso remained so overvalued. Imports rose by 55 per cent in 1980, as the new speculating class took advantage of the free-trade environment. Even in the first year of the coup, sales of Argentine household appliances dropped 65 per cent as a result of the squeeze on wages and the arrival of foreign goods.

Martínez de Hoz saw some success in two areas: inflation, until the Falklands War, stayed below 200 per cent and Argentina was turned back into a grain and meat exporter, and away from a mixed economy. But the State controlled a huge portion of the economy with some 40 per cent of industry still nationalized. Martínez de Hoz failed to keep the spending of the brigadiers and generals under control as their industrial and military empires fiercely protected their own budgets. The main foreign investment attracted into Argentina went into quick speculation which created foreign debt and ruined banks. By 1980, Martínez de Hoz had been transformed in the public's mind from the 'Wizard de Hoz' to the 'Ministro del hambre', or hunger. The government was forced to ban a spate of cartoon caricatures of him which showed fiendishly long, pointed ears and an evil, messianic glow about the eyes. His days in the cabinet appeared to be numbered as Videla's term of office approached its end.

The economic war had ended in utter defeat. As the *Herald* put it in its measured tones, the Martínez de Hoz experiment had 'fired the imagination of so many and disappointed them all'. The incoming civilian government was unable to put a final figure on the massive government deficit it inherited, because it could not find out what was actually spent during the years of the military. But there were statistics which calculated the effects of the management of Martínex de Hoz. Of all credit and currency 89.6 per cent had ended up in the hands of the State, with only 10.4 per cent with private individuals or companies. The standard of living was lower than it had been in 1975 and so was the level of manufacturing. The foreign debt was up from $8 billion to $40 billion by 1982, and inflation was running at 200 per cent. By 1983 it was 381.8 per cent. As the incoming Economics Minister admitted, 'All we get left with is cigarette kiosks, grocery stores and butcher shops.'

Martínez de Hoz was probably the first Argentine Economics Minister to abolish his own unit of currency, having got rid of the single peso note as inflation mounted. Perhaps it was fitting that the currency, under him, had become only a multiple of a purely fictional unit of account; after all, the economy had started operating in a realm of fantasy, too.

One of Brigadier Osvaldo Cacciatore's long-standing critics, the writer Ernesto Sábato, commented on the man's ambitions and concluding achievements, 'although Brigadier Cacciatore had the talent of Aristotle, even Aristotle made mistakes. Absolute power is creating in government the illusion that these people are perfect.'

On 11 January 1984 ex-Mayor Cacciatore was asked to appear before the Argentine courts to be questioned about the Interama case. He faced grave charges of corruption and fraudulent administration, particularly on the matter of where the municipal funds for Hollywood Park had gone. The case being drawn up against Cacciatore covered a range of activities: exempting Interama from the 30,000-dollar fine due when they failed to complete the park at the end of November 1980; the loss of 200 million dollars provided as collateral for Interama; and the serious irregularities in the way contracts had been originally given out for Hollywood Park. City Hall itself had run up massive debts of 2.5 billion dollars, 1 billion of which was owed to contractors. But the Mayor had taken some precautions to escape legal action; before the elections, municipal lawyers had prepared a major contract with the date deliberately omitted, with instructions that they were 'to find a legal way out, before the change of government'. But by the time the court met in January to charge Cacciatore, he had gone into hiding; according to the rumours, he fled to Uruguay, accompanied by his black briefcase stuffed with hundred-dollar bills. He stayed on the run, an official fugitive from the law, for a week; then, apparently taking advice from his lawyer that he should fight the charges, the former Mayor decided to return to Argentina. On 18 January, he flew back, was placed under 'preventative arrest' and was imprisoned in El Palomar Air Force base, the very base from which he had first made his name as one of the daring pilots who had tried to overthrow the government of the day.

But there were many reminders of Pharaoh's rule over the city. Many of the motorways remained unfinished, their steel and concrete structures jutting out raggedly over existing roads and houses; few people could afford the toll charges on the motorway to Ezeiza Airport and the lanes were often empty of cars. The zoological park reverted to wasteland and weeds; and the hospitals remained closed for a time. Interama, as everyone called the amusements park, was open, however; the big wheel, fountains and towers provided a spectacular and diverting monument to the years of fantastic and unreal spending when the junta had attempted to act as a board of directors over an increasingly uncontrollable economy. Those who walked along Interama's brightly coloured walkways and looked at the rides whirling around them or down at the bankrupt city from the lookout point on the big tower may have been reminded of the old joke about Argentina, one which Argentines tell at their own expense: after God created the Earth, he discovered that Argentina had received riches far greater than those he had given to other countries. He had given it the pampas, oil, the cattle, the Andes and the River Plate and then, for the sake of balance, he had given the country Argentines.

# 12 THE WAR AGAINST IDEAS

*'Up to now, only the tip of the iceberg has been affected by our war against subversion . . . It is necessary to destroy the sources which feed, form and indoctrinate the subversive delinquent, and this source is the universities and the secondary schools themselves.'* – General Adel Vilas, Fifth Army Corps, 1977.

In November 1975, four months before the coup in Argentina, the publishers Ediciones de la Flor produced for young children a book called *Cinco Dedos* (*Five Fingers*). Its purpose was to teach children how to count, and also perhaps to instil in them the rudiments of social behaviour. At the beginning of the book there was a picture of a hand with the fingers closed into a fist, and subsequent pages showed the fingers being extended, one by one, as the readers were taught how to count up to five. The text informed them that the whole hand worked best together, in unity, even though each individual finger was capable of acting independently of the others. Given the near-anarchy in Argentina at the time when the book was written, the message was well-meaning and didactic, even if a little obvious. But when the military government of General Videla took over, the author, Daniel Divinsky, hardly knew what hit him. Within a few months, in February 1977, *Cinco Dedos* had been banned under special government decree number 269, and when Divinsky appealed against the decision, arguing that the book was not intended in any way to be subversive, he and his wife were placed under arrest, held at police headquarters for nine weeks, and then transferred to a state prison for a further three months. The premises of the publishing house that had produced the book mysteriously caught fire. Directly the Divinskys were released, they left the country. The book was banned for preaching Communism and subversion: the clenched fist was, the military censors felt, a symbol of international communist solidarity, while the idea that the unity of the five fingers together represented strength was, they maintained, intended to indoctrinate innocent children. No doubt the fact that the Divinskys had a Jewish name influenced the decision as well. The military's campaign of censorship by violence – what one professor was later to describe as 'cultural cretinism' – had begun.

Argentina had been through periods of censorship and control before: Isabelita Perón, especially, had borne down harshly. But the controls had never been particularly effective, and there had never been anything akin to the cultural repression in the Soviet Union, for instance. Argentina was highly sophisticated, with a large and wealthy middle class which supported the arts enthusiastically and had a lively tradition in music, the theatre, and in particular the cinema. But cultural life after the coup was different. The military sought to create an approved, orthodox culture, which would be based on the fight against Communism, on simple patriotic values, and on the family and Christianity. The persecution of journalists, the use of terror to silence writers, musicians and teachers, and the widespread black-listing of people all bore an unpleasant similarity to what happened in Nazi Germany in the Thirties. The comparison is an overworked one, but in the case of Argentina under the Process of National Reorganization there was a clear decision to tolerate the circulation of Nazi concepts on a large scale by the use of Nazi and neo-Nazi literature. Bookstands in Buenos Aires carried publications with titles like *The SS in Action* and *Maybe Hitler Was Right*, and *The Protocols of the Elders of Zion* went into print again, in an attractive format and binding. And there was an organized burning of books. In April 1976, the commander of the Fourteenth Paratroop Regiment in Córdoba staged a mass public burning of left-wing literature gathered up in raids on bookstores and private houses, in front of reporters. The books included writings by Mao, Lenin, Che Guevara, left-wing magazines and some early letters of Perón in his radical days. The example, reported widely, was regarded by ordinary citizens as a warning; fires were lit at home and people burnt their own books to destroy anything which could get them into trouble.

In July 1976, the proofs of the first novel of one writer went up in flames at the publisher's because it was considered subversive, and the author fled to Mexico. That same month, the Education and Cultural Minister ordered all school inspectors to check secondary school libraries 'because many dangerous books have entered the schools'.

The cruel evidence. EDUARDO FRIAS

In the weeks that followed Argentina's return to democracy in December 1983, local government officials and human rights workers uncovered the mass graves of the military's victims in cemeteries in every city and in many towns. But the human remains they found represented only a small proportion of the eleven thousand or so who were murdered. The majority were dropped from planes and helicopters over the River Plate estuary or out at sea

SPOONER/GERRETSEN

General and Isabelita Perón, 8 October 1973 – his 78th birthday. On Perón's left is José López Rega, who set up the death squads which prepared the way for the military's campaign against political opposition

The first junta: (from left) Admiral Emilio Massera (Navy), General Jorge Videla (Army), Brigadier Orlando Agosti (Air Force)

GUILLERMO LOIACANO

CAMERA PRESS

General Roberto Viola,
leader of the second junta

SOURCE: ANON

The body of a man executed
by a military task force.
The photograph is believed
to have been taken by the man
who shot him

ESMA – the Navy Mechanics School in Buenos Aires

Mrs Nelva Falcone

Dagmar Hagelin

RAGNAR HAGELIN

El Banco – the clandestine gaol where Dr and Mrs Falcone were held

Astiz – Mar del Plata, January 1984

SPOONER/GAMMA

Archbishop Plaza of La Plata

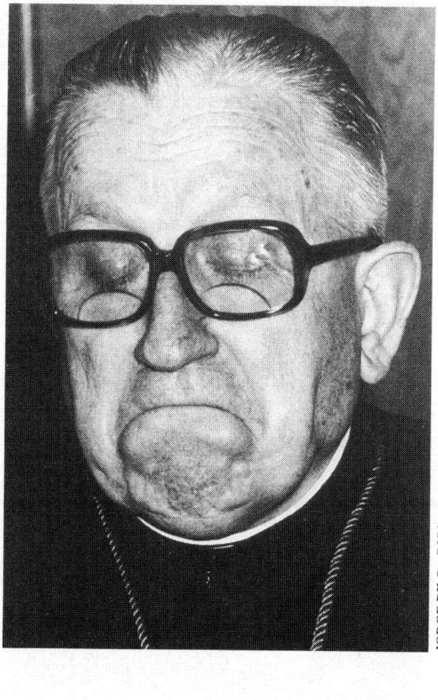

JORGE RILO – DYN

General Ramón Camps

DANI YAKO – DYN

Raúl Vilariño

DANI YAKO – DYN

BLAWA/GAMMA

Galtieri salutes an ecstatic crowd
in the Plaza de Mayo after the invasion of the Falklands,
3 April 1982

The Mothers
of the Plaza de Mayo

SPOONER/VILLALOBOS

The triumph of democracy:
Raúl Alfonsín acknowledges the applause of the crowd on the day of his inauguration as President of Argentina, 10 December 1983

A less drastic form of censorship was used through Law 20.216: books like *Das Kapital* and writings on dialectical materialism or the methodology of labour could be banned for their ideological content; children's books like *Ultrabomba* and *Cinco Dedos* for their ideological indoctrination. And in the case of *Un Elefante Ocupa Mucho Espacio* (*Elephants Take Up a Lot of Space*), the fact that the prestigious Cuban cultural institute La Casa de las Americas had given it an award was enough to make it undesirable. But the junta had also pledged itself to eradicate 'the vices which afflict the nation, once and for all', and to reintroduce ethical and moral principles into Argentine life. And so the mayor of Buenos Aires, Air Force Brigadier Osvaldo Cacciatore banned from 38 stores in the city posters advertising blue jeans because they featured a woman's bare bottom. 'Racy' novels and sex-education books came indiscriminately under similar bans. Theatre, music, radio, television, newspapers, books and the cinema – all suffered the restrictions of a dual censorship, political and moral, which was imposed by the new guardians of the nation.

Previous military régimes in Argentina had tried to control civilian society, but none had actually tried to replace it with a form of militarized society which would obey the values laid out in advance by the junta. Before, the objective had been to enforce change from the top by making sure that civilian administrators followed the military's orders, but the Process of National Reorganization set out to saturate governmental and non-governmental systems alike with military thinking – and staff them with military officers. Videla had indicated this in his first presidential address, when he had said they could not accept the role of 'a mere spectator' in the life of the nation; and one of the objectives the military set themselves was to create 'a new national being' – not unlike the 'new Soviet man' or the Aryan man of other totalitarian régimes. In a way, the idea was derived from the doctrine of national security, as taught in military schools like Fort Gulick in Panama: the role of the military, the precepts of the doctrine taught, should be regarded as unlimited, and one Brazilian theoretician wrote that 'national security includes everything that in one way or another affects the life of the nation'. But it was only in Argentina that this aspect of the doctrine was put into such all-encompassing effect.

Following the original principle on which the Videla régime came to power, control of the arts, of education and of communication was shared out on the basis of a third to each of the armed forces – the 33⅓ per cent principle. In the Press Information Secretariat, for example, the posts were divided up as follows: the director of communications was an Army Colonel, the press director was a Naval captain and the man in charge of radio and television was a wing commander in the Air Force. Serving officers were installed in almost every public organization or institution. Military officers were put in charge of departments at universities (though the rectors themselves were usually right-wing, pro-military civilians); the much-respected medical school at the National University of Buenos Aires, for instance, was headed by Captain Edmundo Said of the Navy; a man not known for his medical knowledge, he was to distinguish himself by his repressiveness. Medical and other research was greatly favoured by the military, because of the opportunities for handing out lucrative contracts for supplying and equipping laboratories, though the emphasis tended to be on securing deals with big foreign companies, while the research element itself was disregarded and often wound down deliberately.

Throughout the educational system, sackings became wholesale. Order 572, one of the first measures introduced by the junta, permitted the dismissal of 'dangerous' members of staff, and amounted to an instruction to purge the schools and universities of left-wing teaching staff. At the University of Buenos Aires alone, more than fifteen hundred lecturers were dismissed, while in their place came right-wing supporters of the new régime. Within the secondary school system, three thousand teachers and administrators were dismissed within the first five months of military rule. In a way, though, the military were merely redressing the balance which had earlier been tipped to the left under the presidency of Héctor Cámpora, shortly after Perón returned in 1973. The National University of Buenos Aires, for instance, had been renamed 'The National and Popular University' under its new left-wing rector, Rodolfo Puiggrós; within two years he had thrown the university open to almost anyone, increasing its student body almost three-fold to 237,000 students, and encouraging courses in subjects such as 'The Emancipation of the People'. Student politics became dominated by left-wing Peronist movements which tended to support the Montoneros.

Directly the military were in power, they tightened up entrance requirements greatly, rounded up student activists and dismissed left-wing staff members. Special intelligence units were given the task of hunting down alleged subversives in the universities. One of those to suffer most heavily was the University of the South at Bahía Blanca, in the area of the Fifth Army Corps whose deputy commander was General Adel Vilas, a dedicated anti-terrorist. In August 1976 he announced the arrest of 17 professors and issued a list of 31 others who were wanted on charges of 'organizing subversion'. 'Until we can cleanse the area of teaching', the general declared, 'and until the professors are all followers of Christian thought and ideology, we will not achieve the triumph we seek in our struggle against the revolutionary left.' The university had to be closed down altogether for a time in order that the cleansing operation could be carried out. People disappeared and the bodies piled up on the outskirts of the city, and it proved almost impossible to find a lawyer who would draw up a writ of habeas corpus, or a priest who was willing to say Mass for a dead left-winger.

The staff who lost their jobs had little chance of recourse to the existing procedure of appeals, since being 'potentially subversive' constituted a sackable offence, and university administrators were under orders not to review dismissal cases, even if there seemed to be good grounds for doing so. A secret directive from the Education Ministry, although expressed in opaque language, made this clear: 'This authority [i.e. the university administration] will not adopt any measures concerning such cases of dismissal, thereby implicitly denying any further consequences of it.' A memorandum headed 'Consideration of Cases' states that administrators who were military officers could use the military code rather than university rules to deal with any complaints, if they so chose: 'It is considered that the authority which gave rise to the case – the Dean or Rector – represents military authority as such.' Few university teachers, not surprisingly, chose to take on the full authority of the State by entering a complaint, especially as the State showed itself more than ready to murder its opponents.

In the war against ideas, the social sciences came under the fiercest attack. Curricula were altered and books withdrawn. Political science, sociology, psychology and even architecture were all suspect, because they were heavily dependent on foreign influences, and had been much favoured by left-wing students and academics in the past. The Faculty of Architecture at Buenos Aires University was described by one observer as being 'emptied of contents, little more than a brass nameplate on a door with a pile of useless papers inside an empty office'. The teaching staff were afraid of initiating new projects or teaching modern texts because they dealt with sensitive issues like urban deprivation, social change and problems of development. Textbooks were examined with obsessive and sometimes ludicrous care; Darwin's *The Origin of Species* and the theory behind it were condemned because they were considered unchristian; the book *Medicina de Trabajadores* (*Workers' Medicine*) was banned because it encouraged the notion of trade unionism; a serious history of the men who tamed the pampas, *Montoneros y Caudillos*, was prohibited because its title contained a forbidden word - the word the left-wing Peronists had taken over to use as a name for their movement from roughriders who had fought the big ranchers in the nineteenth century. *Salvat Encyclopaedia* was banned because its wording was held to be Marxist, and the *Encyclopaedia Britannica* was banned because it referred to the Malvinas as the Falkland Islands.

Psychology, with its links to Jewish theorists including Freud, and its emphasis on sex, was especially suspect. The Dean of Buenos Aires University School of Psychology, Dr Mario Peña, who was also a judge, was imposed on the department by the military in order to ensure that it taught only 'safe' psychology: little more than a careful study of behaviour, with as little emphasis on clinical disorders as possible. Dr Peña, in his capacity as a judge, demonstrated his reliability by allowing some six hundred and fifty bodies to be buried as 'NNs' (*nihil nomen*) even though many of them were riddled with bullets. Later, he was appointed head of the Ethics Commission of Lawyers, a body which demonstrated *its* reliability by disbanding itself. Peña also served as Argentina's delegate to the UN Commission on Human Rights, and drafted the Amnesty Law of 1983 which attempted to free the military from the consequences of any abuses that had been committed while they were in office. Like many of the imposed academics, he kept his university job when the civilians took over government because his contract, like those of twelve thousand other academics, was renewed by the military for another 18 months, only days before they relinquished office.

Secret portfolios were handed out to every mayor and provincial governor which prohibited 'the use and publications of texts, bibliographies, teaching, cultural and scientific aids whose contents are imbued with extreme ideological connotations', and in order to deal with the threat of 'external and internal Marxist aggression' the portfolios recommended that people as well as published materials should be neutralized. There were a number of gradations in this process: people were of course physically neutralized in large numbers, but in lesser cases they could be classified as simply being 'no longer necessary', the broadest definition of redundancy. This too carried a considerable penalty; if someone tried to get another job after being dismissed under the redundancy laws (number 21260 and 21274) their prospective employers could check with SIDE, the state information secretariat, and get a report on the reasons for the applicant's previous dismissal. This happened throughout the professions: law, teaching, psychiatry, public administration, journalism. It was a major reason for people's decisions to leave the country; and it meant that the news stands, cigarette kiosks and taxis of Argentina's cities were operated by a small army of former professionals who were unable to get any better employment.

On 31 August 1976 the military government urged on by the right-wing Catholics in the Education Ministry, issued Decree 1867 in an effort to impose their view of Christian orthodoxy on the country more rigidly. The decree prohibited the Jehovah's Witnesses from practising their religion in public and members of the sect were accused of offending against 'the public order, national security, morals and good customs' of Argentina. The Jehovah's Witnesses were not officially recognized as a religion although for the past thirty years they had attempted to explain their Christian position to various governments; but there was a prejudice against them backed up by the Constitution itself, which gives a favoured position to Roman Catholicism. But under the Process, discrimination against the Jehovah's Witnesses went much further than the simple refusal to accept their existence officially; on the day Decree 1867 was enacted, the Army deployed troops and lorries to close the Jehovah's Witnesses' central Buenos Aires offices, shut down their print shops and six hundred meeting rooms throughout the country. The religion's 60,000 members had nowhere to worship but their homes; 300,000 books including Bibles and teaching manuals were confiscated over the next three years; according to evidence received by the OAS Commission 225,700 books were taken in one single action. Jehovah's Witnesses found peacefully reading the Bible in their own homes by the armed forces were arrested in their hundreds, their books destroyed and their property ransacked. Arrests and imprisonments could last for several months, yet not a single case of offences against 'public order, national security, morals or good customs' was proved against any of them.

The Jehovah's Witnesses were equally badly treated in the

school system; at least one thousand children were expelled for refusing to salute the national flag or for failing to sing the national anthem, as the teachings of their religion required. Several hundred of them were not allowed to return to school, even after a 1979 ruling by the Supreme Court determined that no disrespect had been shown by these actions. The final catch came when youngsters were old enough to be called up for national service. Because Jehovah's Witnesses were not recognized as a religion, they could not be granted the legal exemption granted to other conscientious objectors; more than 250 Jehovah's Witnesses were sent to prison as deserters or common law-breakers.

The campaign to stamp out dangerous thought was, however, as carelessly implemented as many of the military's other operations. In February 1977, for instance, an Army detachment arrived at the offices of the Buenos Aires University's publishers, Eudeba, and sealed off the approaches to them with lorries. The purpose of the raid was to destroy 150,000 books which had been published by the company in 1973. Eudeba, however, came under the jurisdiction of the Navy, and the naval officer in charge refused to let the Army officer supervise the operation at the publishers, arguing that if anyone was going to burn the books in question, it would be his men. Eventually, after a good deal of haggling, they arrived at a compromise: the Army could have the books, but the officer would have to sign a document accepting full responsibility for the affair. The books were duly destroyed – but the document survived, with the signatures of the two men involved clearly marked on it; it later featured in a case brought under the civilian government in 1984 for maladministration at the university. Since the military managed, for the most part, to destroy the evidence for what they had done, the case was unusual. The lawyer who gathered the evidence for it commented, 'We were lucky. It just goes to show that there is no such thing as a perfect crime.'

The Teatro Colón, the opera house in Buenos Aires, is an impressive neo-classical structure built along the lines of the Albert Hall in London or La Scala in Milan. On its imposing front steps, well-dressed opera goers gather to show off their evening wear and meet their friends before performances. The auditorium is furbished in red velvet, and obscure allegorical paintings about Art and History cluster on the domed ceiling. Backstage, it is as grubby and untidy as most theatres: left-over props bulk absurdly large as they lean against the wall in passage-ways and alcoves, and little dusty offices open off the corridor which runs in a circle around the perimeter of the building. Behind the stage, giant flats, three storeys high, wait to be painted for the next production. The only part of the area backstage that is neat and tidy is the director's freshly-painted suite of offices. Suddenly the rooms are carpeted, and furnished with chairs and tables in chrome and leather, while in the director's own room there is a sizeable leather couch and a vast mahogany desk. The walls are covered with photographs of past productions, and of guest opera stars from abroad. The Teatro Colón was once the most famous opera house in South America; but by the end of military rule it was so deep in debt that there was no money to pay foreign artists with, and the invitations no longer went out to Italy and the United States. Productions were cut down, and staff made redundant. The Teatro Colón had been managed by the Air Force, and Air Commodore Gallagher had been the arbiter of music and opera.

After the change to democratic government the Teatro Colón, like the rest of Argentina, was swept by a sense of enthusiasm about its new freedom. Amid the chrome and leather of his office, the theatre's new director, Cecilio Madanes, in an open-necked shirt, sat with his feet on the impressive desk and reflected. 'When I took over here, there was something new in the theatre. We were free of repression and the fear of informers and being told what to think. Everyone feels that way: technicians, musicians, administrators. No one's afraid now of saying what they think.'

Madanes was never blacklisted, but he spent much of the Process of National Reorganization in France. He had been director of Channel 7 television, in the 1950s, and started a famous little theatre in the poor Italian quarter of Buenos Aires, La Boca, which managed to escape closure by the military. Madanes was an energetic exponent of community theatre, and when he took over the Colón he began staging shows for children, beginning with *Hansel and Gretel*. He did away with the convention that required people to wear dinner jackets and black tie at the opera, and even allowed the orchestra to give up formal wear. There were cheap tickets and workshops in stage design, and the theatre's musicians began giving open air concerts in the poorer parts of Buenos Aires. It was all very different from what went before.

Air Commodore Gallagher would come in to work at eleven, and by one he would have gone to lunch. Returning at four, he would stay until the early evening and then be taken home in his official car. 'He knew about as much about opera as I know about the maintenance of aircraft engines,' Cecilio Madanes says. But he did know how to spend public money. He ran up immense losses, and under him the opera house cost six and a half million dollars to run, only 7 per cent of which was covered by box-office takings. Part of the problem was the immense over-staffing. The Colón employed at least a thousand people more than comparable opera houses in Europe or North America.

The Colón stagnated. Its staff continued to keep standards as high as they could, and the artistic director managed to maintain a certain control over the productions that were staged. But there was a strong tendency to play it safe, in case the puritanical sensibilities of the military should be offended. The mayor of Buenos Aires, Brigadier Cacciatore, attended the opening night of a Béjart ballet, and was scandalized when the dancers came on in costumes so scanty that the stage seemed full of naked people; and when a male dancer arrived on stage as a motorcyclist, wearing the briefest of briefs, it was too much for the Mayor. He stormed out, shouting to the hapless air commodore, 'That's the last time you do something like this to me.' Gallagher was appalled at what had happened, and never allowed his staff to put on a Béjart ballet, or anything remotely resembling it, again.

The notion of controlling the arts by imposing on them people who had no understanding or aptitude to fit them for the job was to have a serious effect on the Argentine cinema – potentially one of the most creative in Latin America. In July 1976 the director Octavio Gelina announced that he was going abroad because he was no longer able to work in safety in Argentina. Two months before, another director, Raimundo Gleyser, had been picked up by the military as he was about to leave for the United States, and all his equipment had been stolen. Gleyser was considered dangerous because he had made films about trades unions and the Mexican revolution. He disappeared, and was presumably murdered. Octavio Gelina had been in charge of the National Film Censorship Board in the liberal days of President Cámpora, three years before, but he had been replaced while Isabelita Perón was still President by a Scrooge-like figure, bad-tempered, spiteful, and in his late seventies, who came to dominate the Argentine cinema in all its aspects. Miguel Paulino Tato had once been a film critic, but he took his duties as censor with such seriousness, relishing the business of striking out unacceptable political ideas or anything indecent or corrupting – and his definition of such terms was a wide one – that the military decided to keep him on when they staged their coup. As he sat in the darkness of the small viewing theatre at the Censorship Board's headquarters, he knew what he wanted and his judgements were completely consistent. His ideal was something along the lines of *South Pacific*: sentimental, safe, and with a touch of patriotic humour. John Wayne's films invariably received his approval too: right always triumphed, and the action was clean. Seven hundred films were banned over a period of 18 years by the Censorship Board, but in the first two years of the Process, with Tato as chief censor, no fewer than 180 films were banned. Foreign films did especially badly, though sometimes Tato was doing Argentine audiences something of a favour. Among the British films which failed to pass his critical eye, for instance, were *The Amorous Milkman*, *Percy's Progress*, *Keep It Up Jack* and *The Bawdy Adventures of Tom Jones*. The mid-Seventies were years of particular violence in films from the United States, and many were cut or banned altogether by Tato for that reason, especially if (unlike in John Wayne's films) the outlaws were shown in an admirable or heroic light. Films like *Vigilante Force*, *Ode to Billy Joe*, *Breaking Point* and *Posse* with Kirk Douglas, were prohibited because they set a bad example to society, though Tato and his military supporters may also have been aware that the shoot-outs and ambushes in films like this bore a considerable resemblance to what was going on in the streets of Argentine cities, and that it was by no means the terrorists alone who were behaving like that. There was little doubt, either, why a Spanish film called *Mujeres Desesperadas – Women Without Hope* – should have been banned in 1977: its title was a little too close to the bone, and so was that of an Italian film banned at the same time: *Silence the Witness*.

Films which dealt with sexual or social themes were Tato's natural targets. *An Unmarried Woman*, which dealt with divorce in the United States, was banned for its undermining effect on Christian society. Films by Bertolucci, Fassbinder and Wajda, together with *The Marriage of Maria Braun* and *The Night Porter* were all banned for decadence. Fewer Argentine films were being produced by this time, because of the enforced flight or disappearance of directors and actors; but those which were made, and which passed Tato's rigorous inspection, tended to avoid any subject which could be regarded as 'social'. Tato liked middle-brow films, especially situation comedies, and that was what the cinema-going public was given.

Tato's office, housed in a narrow, anonymous concrete building just off one of the biggest boulevards in Buenos Aires, became more and more powerful in controlling the destinies of directors and actors. The blacklists which he, together with the authorities in television, radio and the theatre drew up, could have a profound effect. The existence of a blacklist was never admitted officially, but once an actor was banned, all the films he had ever appeared in could be affected. One such actor was Héctor Alterio. Blacklisted by Tato, he left Argentina and went to Spain, where he made a film. The film arrived in Argentina and was given a certificate – but only after Tato had insisted that Alterio should be cut out of it completely. Cutting out one of the stars made the film entirely incomprehensible, with plot, continuity and the lop-sided dialogue left hanging in the air at each appearance (or non-appearance) of Alterio. Blacklisting made actors, directors, journalists and musicians into non-persons in all other areas of communication. Once it became known that someone was banned, producers would be reluctant to take them on for fear of jeopardizing the film as a whole. The distributors, for their part, offered little resistance to the banning of films, and accepted the cuts made by Tato and his assistants without complaint; ten films only were the subject of appeals against a banning order. And yet in several of those cases the courts overturned Tato's judgement and permitted the films to be shown, so that if the distributors had been less timid they might well have avoided the damage done to many actors and directors, as well as to the Argentine film industry as a whole.

Towards the end of 1978, Tato finally retired, and the military allowed a slightly more liberal atmosphere in the cinema. *An American Gigolo*, *Pink Floyd: The Wall* and *Equus* were examples of films that were banned under the new censor as well, but in general there were fewer outright bans and less of Tato's puritanism. Some actors were allowed back to Argentina to work, like Héctor Alterio, Tato's invisible man. But for the majority on the blacklists, there was no reprieve until military rule itself ended, in 1983.

The resort city of Mar del Plata is Argentina's Riviera, with room both for the better-off and for the masses. The beaches are not quite as good as those of the more expensive Uruguayan resort,

Punta del Este, which attracts the fashionable and the really wealthy of Argentina, but it was opened up with the encouragement of Evita Perón, who persuaded the trades unions to provide annual holidays for their members in the late 1940s. The unions bought up or built large hotels there, and over the years the numbers of people who go there to spend their summer holidays by the sea have increased steadily: by Christmas 1983 (Christmas being the beginning of the summer season) more than a million people have poured into the city. The carparks just behind the beaches stretch for miles, creating the most intense glare as the hot sun reflects off acres of windscreens, chrome and paint. The seashore itself is packed with bodies and edged with thousands of little beach huts, the roofs of which are brightly painted and shimmer in the intense heat-haze. To the south, away from the city, are the more exclusive resorts and private beaches, and there are yacht clubs around the large naval base, just visible in the haze, some miles further on. Mar del Plata is the summer capital of Argentina, and the nation's nightlife, like the holiday-makers, migrates the 450 kilometres south-east from the capital. New films are launched there, and new plays receive their première performances.

In the first summer holiday after the ending of military rule, a youngish woman in a sheer negligée, black stockings and high heels parades about on the stage of the Atlas Theatre. Her stage boyfriend, Papi, encourages her, and when a footballer friend of his arrives he tells her to flaunt herself in front of him, and she agrees. *Papi*, which takes its name from the male lead, is a bedroom farce, at least on the surface, and in the new atmosphere the audience loves the constant play of innuendo; it makes a refreshing change from the military-approved theatre. But there is a more serious undercurrent running through the stock action of the farce. The woman, Tatiana, who is persuaded to go to bed with the footballer in order to improve his performance in the next match, is a hooker, and Papi is her pimp. All the characters in the play are either being bought or sold, and each is corrupted by money, sex, greed, or vanity. It is, intentionally, a commentary on the moral disintegration of a country which has lived too long under dictatorship, and although the audience is there to be entertained, the message is not lost on it. Everyone in the theatre is aware, too, that it represents a special occasion; it is not only the humour that has been liberated. The playwright, Carlos Gorostiza, has recently been appointed Secretary of Culture in the new civilian government after years in which the plays he wrote had been blacklisted. The director, David Stivel, was blacklisted too, and so was the leading actor, Luis Brandoni, one of Argentina's best-known theatre, cinema and television actors, and his wife, Marta Bianchi, who plays Tatiana. The play is a kind of celebration for all these people, a return to the theatre and to public life. Not surprisingly, the play is a smash hit in Mar del Plata.

The last time Carlos Gorostiza saw a play of his being performed on the Argentine stage was in October 1981. It was about the life of a group of exiles, and it was put on by a new group, the Teatro Abierto, at the Picadero theatre in Buenos Aires. One night, the theatre was badly burned by a group of arsonists, and it remained closed after that, its gates chained, its façade attacked by vandals, with warnings spray-painted on its walls advising people to keep away. The theatre group managed to keep working, but it was plain that the military found it easier to do their work by intimidation rather than by the use of decrees and formal orders. Luis Brandoni had been an active member of an actors' trade union and an outspoken critic of the military. He was threatened by the Triple A before the coup, and left the country for ten months, but returned before the coup in March 1976. Two days after it, Brandoni was due at the studios of Channel 9 TV to record a drama series called 'La aventura de vivir' ('The Adventure of Living') which took place mostly in a medical clinic. Brandoni's scene was being recorded after another between two doctors at the clinic, in which they discussed the character he was playing and talked about an unexpected trip he would have to make to Japan. Brandoni then arrived, knowing nothing of the previous action, and recorded his scene; afterwards, as he was having a cup of coffee with the leading actress, he heard for the first time about the trip to Japan. It was a hackneyed soap-opera ploy to write an unwanted character out of the script. Brandoni, furious, tried to see the military officer who had just been put in charge of the television station, but the man refused to see him. Later, he was told that he would continue to receive his salary for the duration of his contract, because it was cheaper than settling the matter in court. Brandoni knew that it was his popularity as an actor which had protected him from something worse, and he was never able to get an explanation for what had happened to him. It was repeatedly denied, too, that he was on a blacklist, but he once saw a list of names which was being passed around to advertising agencies and radio and television stations, with the suggestion that it might be 'inconvenient' to employ the people named on it: Brandoni was one of them. His wife, Marta Bianchi, received much the same treatment: a play by Jean Genêt, *The Battle of the Angels*, in which she was one of the stars, was taken out of the schedules by Channel 13 TV directly after the coup.

A blacklist drawn up as late as April 1981 contains 348 names of actors and actresses (including Brandoni and Bianchi), painters, directors, journalists, script-writers, professors of art, musicians, singers – the whole spectrum of art and communications. The list does not, however, take into account the hundreds of artists who had fled the country; it was a guide to the large group of 'internal exiles' who were to be cut off from their professions and from the chance of earning a living. Nevertheless, in the close and loyal world of acting, Brandoni did manage to get jobs with a number of small, independent theatres, though it was often a risky undertaking. Once, not long after the coup, he and his wife were leaving a theatre where they had been performing in a play written by someone who was banned, when they were picked up by a gang of a dozen or so men, taken away, and interrogated. They were released after some hours. Later, when Brandoni was acting in a play called *Convivencia* (Living Together), the theatre management discovered some fumigation tablets in the auditorium; the following night two men in the audience started to light them when they were caught. At another attempt to stage *Convivencia*, this time in Mar del Plata, someone telephoned the theatre with a bomb threat. The theatre was evacuated, and as they stood outside on the pavement, some four hundred or so of them, it began to rain heavily. But when the theatre was pronounced safe, all but a half-dozen or so trooped back in to watch the rest of the play. In these circumstances, at least, Argentine audiences were not as timid as many of the people who ran the entertainment industry. The Actors' Association in Argentina, braver than many of the managements they worked with, made repeated inquiries about the prohibition of actors after 1976, but were never given official confirmation that a blacklist actually existed, although there was regular proof, in the non-employment of well-known actors and actresses, that it did. In some ways, though, the fact that the blacklist's existence was denied made it easier for people like Brandoni to get employment in the theatre: it was a risk to hire him, but it did not involve the certainty of prosecution or worse. Being taken off the blacklist was just as unofficial, and although

Marta Bianchi, Brandoni's wife, heard that she was no longer on it some time in 1980, it was still very difficult to get jobs in television. Brandoni remained blacklisted throughout, banned, he believes because he was a man who understood that the world of entertainment was something more than just a way of making a living. *Papi*, the first stage play he appeared in after the end of military rule, was a suitable vehicle for that understanding: in spite of its surface humour it was a bitter play, in some ways, in which no one is entirely blameless, the innocent suffer for being stupid, and the cunning are caught in traps of their own making.

The climate in radio and television was a good deal worse than in the theatre, because they were much more closely monitored by the military and not just the state-run channels, which were run directly by senior officers, but also the various privately-owned radio stations and the four private television stations. Programmes were censored after they had been recorded, which made the various production departments all the more careful; an unwary reference could spell the end for an entire expensive programme. A chat show, for instance, had to be scrapped altogether because someone taking part in one edition of it had criticized the spread of Fascist literature in Argentine bookstalls. News programmes were particularly subject to scrutiny, and were watered down to the point where they rarely conveyed much real information about the state of affairs inside the country – about the security situation, or the economy, or the manoeuvrings of the military leaders which had taken the place of real politics. The American television network CBS tried to transmit by satellite pictures of a shooting outside the offices of the Communist Party's newspaper *Nuestra Palabra*, in which a number of the paper's employees were killed or injured by a group presumably composed of military men, to New York via Channel 9 TV in Buenos Aires. But the censors insisted that the pictures should be transmitted without sound or commentary, which made them of little value, and Channel 9 were warned not to accept such material again for broadcast abroad. As for material broadcast to the domestic audience, that was rarely of good quality, and the better programmes tended to be screened later at night or dropped altogether from the stations' output. There was a much heavier emphasis on imported programmes, American game shows and soap operas in particular.

Television was used by the military as the battleground for their efforts to compete for public favour. Advertisements issued by several of the main ministries would extol their successes – the

Economics Ministry would proclaim its achievement (usually illusory) in controlling inflation, or the Ministry of Social Welfare would boast of the various ways in which life was improving for the poor and elderly. The Army was usually portrayed, not simply in these advertisements but also in the news programmes of radio and television, as playing the major role in putting the country back on its feet, though in the matter of air time the other two services were given almost the same amount of opportunity to promote their own causes. A good deal of care was lavished on providing each new President with an attractive persona – not always an easy task. Videla was shown as a responsible, moderate man, taking his decisions with thoughtfulness and care. Viola's image was that of a chessplayer, making clever and methodical moves. Galtieri, described in Washington by a senior US official as being 'endowed with a majestic personality', allowed the adjective 'majestic' to become his trade mark. After the disaster in the Falklands, though, the majesty left him and he was more often portrayed (in graffiti and in the more daring humorous magazines) as a heavy boozer of Scotch whisky, sometimes drinking it, red-nosed, from a baby's bottle. As for the grey men who succeeded Galtieri, no one so much as bothered to think of a way of making them attractive to the public. Military rule, after Galtieri, was too discredited for that.

Radio, like television, opted for safety in its choice of programmes. Political commentaries were abandoned altogether, since even pro-government views contained a dangerous element of personal opinion, and the broadcasters might unwittingly find themselves giving offence to one section of the military while trying to please another. Some political programmes were continued, though references to political events had to be made with the utmost care. One man who managed to continue to make his voice heard was a Peronist intellectual, José Miguens. As a Professor of Sociology he was barred from teaching at a university, and he was unable to get anything published in mainstream magazines. But he was given space in a lively, slightly scandal-mongering publication called *Tal Cual* late on in the military's period in power, and was able to get an article about the misgovernment of the country printed – though even so he was very guarded in what he wrote. As a result, he was offered a job with a news programme broadcast by a private station, and wrote five-minute talks for it which he himself thought were bland and inoffensive. But when he met one of the Mothers of the Plaza de Mayo, he was astonished to find that she and her friends felt he had been speaking out on their behalf. He assured her that she must be mistaken, and that he was obliged to be very careful, but she assured him that they could read between the lines and understood what he was trying to say. 'We listen for your words,' she said. Soon, however, he lost his job. The military, too, could read between the lines.

Most radio stations preferred a solid diet of pop music, dominated by safe, middle-of-the-road bands from Britain and the United States or else home-grown 'national rock', which was the Argentine equivalent. They shied away from the more politically-minded folk singers. The upper echelons of the military may have found the music they broadcast distasteful, but they could appreciate the reasons for it. Bob Dylan and Joan Baez were strictly forbidden, and so – for less obvious reasons – were the Beatles. Songs from the musical *Evita* were also banned, on the assumption that it was favourable to the Peronists, though in fact it was deeply unpopular with many of them, too. Television or radio stations which dared to play music associated with Latin American guerrilla movements faced temporary closure, and on several occasions the broadcasters were arrested and never reappeared. Mercedes Sosa, an Indian from the Andes who had achieved an international reputation as a singer of folk songs, and was an avowed communist, emigrated to Spain. Other left-wing singers, like Victor Heredia or the group Los Trovadores, were unable to appear on radio or television, though they could sometimes give concerts in small private clubs. Slowly, some singers worked out how to circumvent the absolute ban on songs about politics, and by 1980 there were a few songs being sung in bars or clubs which dealt with the appalling events of the previous four years. They were heavily coded, but the message got through to those who wanted to hear it. Victor Heredia, for instance, recorded a song called 'Informe de la Situación', which was ostensibly about a manager of an estancia who writes a report on the state of property for its owner, who lives in Buenos Aires, far away. The title was also the same as the OAS commission's report of the previous year. A song of haunting sadness, it records how the property has become broken down, and the young crops destroyed. The code, after so many deaths and the near-collapse of the national economy, was scarcely very hard to break, but for one reason or another the authorities decided not to ban the song, and it achieved great success among the young who had themselves survived so much destruction.

The military repression had a deadening effect on almost every aspect of social and artistic life. There was even a kind of 'Process Art', a painting style which became sought after and traded in: the artists who became suddenly fashionable by it covered their canvases with inoffensive geometrical and op art patterns, carefully avoiding any kind of imitation of reality, as they turned their backs on what they saw about them and plumped for safety and lack of precision. No one could accuse the aimless paintings which were produced like this of being politically dangerous or of revealing unhealthy tendencies. In much the same way, the habits of everyday life were muted and dulled. In the early Seventies, as in the past, Argentines would go out to eat as late as three in the morning after seeing a film or a play. After the coup, it was too dangerous to be on the streets; you could be stopped by a police patrol and be arrested, perhaps to disappear for good, simply for being young or for having an appearance which displeased them. Women were particular targets, and an unknown number were picked up to be tortured and raped. And anyway it was often not worth going out; the cinemas which had once shown more interesting films were mostly closed down, and the films themselves banned. There was the fear of speaking about important things to anyone who was not a close personal friend; and even then there was always the possibility that he or she would be arrested in a random operation, taken in for questioning and torture, and would give your name in order to have something to tell the questioners. A magazine editor who is still in his early thirties, Gabriel Levinas, describes how he once came back to his parked car to find a man waiting there to accuse him of having damaged another car, next to his; there was a mark on the car, but it was over the windscreen. However, the man was a policeman, and Levinas was taken down to the police station. He was held there for 24 hours, sometimes listening to a woman being tortured in the next room, before he was finally allowed to buy his way out by agreeing to pay the policeman for the damage he had not caused. Even then the police had not finished with him: he tried to leave three times, and on each occasion the guard on the gate would deny that anyone had told him to let Levinas out. Eventually, on the fourth attempt, they let him go, contemptuously. Anyone who was young during those years was liable to find similar treatment. It was a war in which the young were a particular enemy, and one of the main weapons in the armoury of the military was to close down or deaden every form of social existence. Levinas, a Jew, is pessimistic about the after-effects of such an experience on an entire generation: 'I think it's like when Moses left Egypt: God decided that because the Children of Israel had been a generation of slaves, they would have to wander around in the desert until that generation had died out and a new one arose that would not remember having been slaves. That is what's going to have to happen here, to erase this experience from Argentina.'

# 13 THE SILENCED PRESS

> *'It is far from our desire and spirit to want a press that is complacent and not objective'* – President Jorge Videla, speaking to Argentine journalists, May 1976.

Left to their own devices, newspapers always mirror the kind of society that produces them: whether they are excitable and competitive, or narrowly parochial, or sombre and heavily responsible, they depend on the general habits of mind of the people who read them as well as of those who write for them. The press in Argentina is effervescent and fickle in its moods, not always concerned with accuracy above all things, but never, in normal times, failing to be readable and stimulating. At the same time it shares the Latin and European Continental tradition, in which journalism is classed as a profession for intellectuals, and therefore newspapers in Argentina, as elsewhere in South and Central America, are seen as performing an important function in moulding opinion. When it is free, then the Argentine press has two powerful currents, directing its course: the requirement to be lively, and the consciousness of its own significance.

And so, because Argentine journalists believed that they were performing an important national function, the majority of them behaved rather well during the dangerous years of the early 1970s, when kidnapping and murder were commonplace and journalists themselves were often a target. They carried on writing in spite of the threat. And the threat was not always from anonymous groups of armed men only. In February 1974 an outspoken left-wing journalist, Ana María Guzzetti, of *El Mundo* newspaper, asked President Juan Perón a particularly pointed question at a news conference in his residence of Olivos. The transcript reads as follows.

*Journalist*: Señor President, when you held your first press conference [on 20 December 1973] I asked you about steps to be taken by the Government to stop the escalating Fascist attacks on popular activists. Since [then] . . . that Fascist escalation has grown. Within two weeks twenty-five offices of political parties have been blown up, and they do not belong to the extreme left; twelve party workers have been killed, and yesterday we learned of the murder of a press photographer. It is obvious that this is being done by extreme right-wing para-police groups.

*Señor President*: Are you going to stand by what you say? That bit about para-police has to be proved. (*To his aides*) Please take the necessary details so that the Justice Ministry can start proceedings against this lady.

Fourteen months later Ana María Guzzetti was crossing Las Heras Avenue in the centre of Buenos Aires when a car shot forward and two men bundled her into it. She managed to shout out her name, and her friends did what they could to find out what had happened to her. A week later she was found alive, but tortured and drugged, beside a highway on the outskirts of the city. The incident had been a warning not just to her but to Argentine journalists in general.

During the chaotic government of Mrs Perón the press was often threatened but never controlled outright. Newspapers could say what they wanted, and most of them did; the penalty they ran was that of losing government advertising. In a country where 70 per cent of the economy was controlled or owned by the government, the threat was a serious one; though since the government agency involved was chronically slow in paying what it owed, one or two newspapers felt they were better off without it anyway. There remained, of course, the more immediate threat presented by the 'para-police groups' – but most Argentine journalists felt they could live with that, uncomfortable and occasionally dangerous though it was. Abductions became so common that if a journalist were freed alive and unhurt, as sometimes happened, no one thought it worthy of being reported.

There is another factor in the editorial policy of many Argentine newspapers: the desire to be on the winning side. As the rumours of a military coup grew stronger, in the last few months of 1975 and the start of 1976, more and more newspapers began trying to get on to good terms with the military. Mrs Perón's government stepped up its pressure on the press to try to swing it round, but it was plain that some newspapers at least had had assurances from the military that they would be protected against murder and intimidation if they continued to criticize Mrs Perón. On the eve of the coup a Peronist organization complained that all the main newspapers, as well as radio and television, were actively encouraging the end of 'institutional order'. It was true. And when the military took over the government every main Buenos Aires newspaper that was not linked with Peronism welcomed the coup as a necessary intervention to get the country back on its feet. The only newspapers that would later dare to take a stand against the military government's gross abuse of human rights, the *Buenos Aires Herald* and *La Opinión*, both welcomed the coup in strong terms. The *Herald* said: 'So far, so good', and spoke of the new government's 'laudable moderation in language and actions'. It had already set out its hope, and that of every other newspaper: 'that the new government will be able to guarantee the basic requirements of a civilized society – honesty, decency, concern for human life, and the will to uphold the law and justice – that will make it possible to rebuild democracy once again, this time on firmer foundations.'

Instead the government that had just installed itself had decided that its overriding purpose was to wipe out terrorism, subversion and opposition of every kind, and that the newspapers which had welcomed its arrival in power would play their part in the process. The previous November the Radical leader, Ricardo Balbín, had told a newspaper interviewer, 'Between a press that is under political pressure and a press that makes mistakes, I choose the press that makes mistakes.' From now on nothing that seemed to the new government remotely like a mistake would be allowed.

For the first 24 hours after the coup there was a form of prior censorship, which means that every galley proof containing political reporting had to be submitted to the armed forces command before it could be printed. That was followed by a system of self-censorship which was based on a sketchy and moralistic set of guidelines. They were known as 'The Principles and Procedures To Be Followed by Mass Communications Media', and were drafted by the new junta's press director, Captain Alberto Corti. Written in a kind of military-speak, they are worth quoting at some length:

PRINCIPLES

1. Foster the restitution of fundamental values which contribute to the integrity of society, such as: order – labour – hierarchy – responsibility – identity – honesty, etc, within the context of Christian morals.
2. Preserve the defence of the family institution.
3. Tend towards the informative and formative elements which contribute towards the Nation's cultural enrichment in its widest spectrum.
4. Offer and promote, for youth, social models which answer to the values mentioned in (1.) to replace and eradicate the present ones.
5. Strictly respect the dignity, private life, honour, fame and reputation of the people.
6. Work towards the eradication of stimulants based on sexualism and criminal violence.
7. Take firm and consistent action against vice in all its manifestations.

PROCEDURES

8. Publish information checked at source and never of a sensationalist character.
9. Do not enter fields which are not for public debate because of their effect on audiences which are not prepared (educated) or because they are unsuitable for their physical and mental age.
10. Eliminate all obscene words and images that are vulgar, shocking or have double meanings.
11. Eradicate sources which seek effect or are truculent in the use of word or image.
12. Tend towards the correct use of the national language.
13. Eliminate all mass propagation of the opinion of persons not qualified or without specific authority to give opinions on subjects of public interest. This includes interviews and/or street polls.

It was an authoritarian blueprint of a kind that is not unfamiliar in many other countries; with certain exceptions, for instance, *Pravda* or *Rude Pravo* or *Neues Deutschland* must have a set of house-rules which are much the same. The South African government, with much less success, has tried to enforce a code that contains a number of similar provisions; and there is no shortage of people in Britain and other Western countries who would like to see some at least of the ideas in Captain Corti's list imposed on the press. What was different in Argentina was the suddenness of the change. The various Peronist governments of 1973-6 had been brutal and threatening in many ways, but they had not sought to control every word the newspapers printed, and every thought they expressed. And from now on, Corti's principles and procedures would have the sanction, not just of law, but of terror behind them; a newspaper which failed to follow the guidelines would be in trouble, but its journalists could be killed.

Some newspapers and magazines buckled immediately. The magazine *Gente*, for instance, which was owned by a big right-wing family and made a habit of supporting the government of the day, celebrated the coup by giving over its cover to the words 'We Were Wrong!': wrong, because prior to the take over by the military *Gente* had supported the government of Mrs Perón. On 2 April President Videla received a number of newspaper proprietors at the Casa Rosada, and thanked them for their co-operation and for their objective reporting of the military coup; the next day a newspaper from the town of Santa Rosa was closed for 72 hours for 'casting doubt on the actions of the armed and security forces', and a member of its staff was arrested. In another provincial town, La Rioja, the newspaper *El Independiente* was closed for 24 hours, because of its 'tendentious character', and its deputy editor, news editor, legal adviser and one of its photographers were all arrested. All of them were tortured. At the same time a former reporter on the paper was arrested and tortured by being hung by the feet for nine days, and the wife of another former reporter was also arrested and tortured. The two of them 'confessed' to an elaborately invented plot in which three of the four members of *El Independiente*'s current staff who had been arrested were supposed to have carried out a kidnapping. The paper's deputy editor, Mario Paoletti, held out against the torture and the accusations, and refused to accept that he was guilty, but the others gave in and 'confessed' in their turn. One of them later tried to commit suicide.

By the early part of April, there were reports in the newspaper every day of bodies turning up, riddled with bullets and usually bearing the marks of torture. They were found by the sides of roads, or on rubbish dumps, usually on the outskirts of Buenos Aires. But by 19 April the reports were noticeable by their absence, although the bodies were turning up in numbers no less large than before. The newspaper *Clarín*, which had previously been much respected and would one day become so again, was strong in its support for the military from the day of the coup onwards. On 22 April it carried a report that there were no longer any restrictions on the press. Later that day a piece of paper was handed out to correspondents at the Casa Rosada; it carried no name at the top and no signature. It read simply:

> As from today, 22/4/76, it is forbidden to inform, comment or make reference to subjects related to subversive incidents, the appearance of bodies and the death of subversive elements and/or of members of the armed and security forces in these incidents, unless they are reported by a responsible official source. This includes victims of kidnappings and missing persons.

Torn between the desire to report accurately and the instincts of self-preservation, the newspapers found themselves printing what they knew to be the absurdities. When the Montoneros placed a bomb on a suburban railway line in Sarmiento on 4 May, for instance, *Crónica* reported that there had been a breakdown, while *La Nación*, after waiting a day, blamed a failure of the electricity supply. It would be at least five years before most newspapers dared to print anything that the military authorities might take exception to. Journalists who themselves wanted a greater freedom to tell the truth were weeded out, or arrested. The newspapers became bland purveyors of things that both they and their readers, if they were honest with themselves, knew to be untrue. But to proprietors and editors who were used to sudden switches of their political policy in order to ingratiate themselves with a new government, the idea of falsifying the news in order to protect their papers and their lives was not by any means completely unthinkable. There were only two newspapers which stood out against the general tendency to run for cover: *La Opinión*, the foremost liberal newspaper in Argentina, and the English-language *Buenos Aires Herald*.

The *Herald* is a mildly unlikely institution to have acted in complete defiance of a government which was prepared to murder its opponents. In its pleasant, ochre-painted building not far from the Casa Rosada and the headquarters of the three services, it gives the impression of being a house magazine for the country's small

English-speaking population. The editorial staff, many of them people from Britain, the United States or Australia who are doing little more than passing through Argentina, sit intently over their copy as it appears on visual display units in the newsroom. The ancillary workers – secretaries, clerks and librarians – are mostly Argentines with strong British or English-speaking links. The news content of the paper is small – a front and back page which usually contain more foreign news than news about Argentina, another foreign page inside, and only one page which is always devoted to Argentine affairs alone. For the rest, there is business news and classified ads and the kind of notice-board material about the doings of the 'Anglo' community which is no doubt the major reason for the newspaper's existence. Much of the material printed in the *Herald* is translated from Spanish, and sometimes it shows. There are several dozen such papers around the world, catering for small communities of people who speak English as a first or second language: useful, pleasant, but rarely distinguished for the quality of their journalism. The *Herald*, in the years of the Process, was to prove a notable exception.

The position of the Anglo-Argentine community meant that, right from the start, the *Herald* was likely to disagree with the Peronist government and feel relieved when the military took over. The British influence in Argentina has always been exerted on behalf of big business and the great landowning interests: the precise areas which Perón and Evita once defined as 'oligarchic'. What the readers of the *Herald* wanted in March 1976 was stability for the economy and an end to the guerrilla war, and they wanted it if anything more than most other Argentines. Over the following months and years the *Herald* was to follow a curious, almost contradictory line towards the military régime: praise and support for its economic policies, and a criticism of its destruction of human rights which was far more outspoken even than that of *La Opinión*. There are reasons for the *Herald's* survival: because it was an English-language paper, it reached only a small readership – perhaps forty thousand people in total would see each day's editions. And because it was an English-language paper, it had much stronger links with countries like the United States and Britain which the Argentine junta did not altogether want to alienate. Then again, there was its defence of the junta's economic policies: and that appeared all the more to be based on conviction because the *Herald* was obviously not willing to bow to self-interest and self-protection on the issue of human rights.

Nowadays it has become usual for Argentine journalists who did not themselves speak out to regard the *Herald*'s position and that of its editorial staff as impregnable, but it did not seem like that at the time. Andrew Graham-Yooll, its news editor, was obliged to leave Argentina in September 1976; its editor, Robert Cox, finally left in December 1979 after his ten-year-old son received a death threat which seemed even more serious than the ones Cox himself had received; and its present editor, James Neilson, as well as receiving a number of death threats, was once challenged to a duel by three Argentine generals and an admiral whom he had publicly accused of supporting anti-Semitism. In retrospect that seems almost amusing, but in Argentina during the Process no one lightly offended senior military men, whether they were in or out of the government.

After the return of democratic government, Neilson became a figure of respectability and honour in Argentine journalism. The big human rights organizations, and in particular the Mothers of the Plaza de Mayo, had given public testimony about the help which he, the *Herald*, and Robert Cox had given them during the worst times of repression. But when people like Uruguayan senators and Bolivian ex-presidents and former Argentine Presidents like Lanusse could be arrested with impunity, the people who worked on the *Herald* felt extremely isolated. 'In 1977 I was a very small fish indeed,' Neilson says. 'Who knew or cared about me? I could have been just another British drifter, dragged off to gaol and never heard of again. No one would have made much of a fuss about it.' Some years later, in 1980, there were signs that Neilson, who was by now the *Herald*'s editor, was the subject of a carefully-laid plot by the security forces. Advertisements were placed in the *Herald* which could have been interpreted as referring to bombs, while another in *Clarín* said that someone called 'Jimmy' was selling unmarked guns. Some days later Neilson was at home when a group of armed men came to the door. He refused to open it to them, telling them to put their identity cards under it so that he could see who they were. And because he had no telephone at the time, he was reduced to lowering a message on a piece of string to his neighbour downstairs. The policeman who had been given the task of guarding Neilson's flat had by this time melted away. But the refusal to open the door seems to have discouraged the men in plain clothes, and there were too many witnesses around for them to act freely. They went away, and later Neilson reported the incident to the local police. A senior officer at the station, who was friendly, told Neilson he thought the men would have killed him if he had opened the door. After that he was followed around from time to time, and in July 1980 Neilson's Argentine wife received a letter signed 'Susana' which said that she was having an affair with Neilson and loved it so much when he lay down with her. Neilson's wife was half-inclined to believe it, until he pointed out to her that 'Susana' was the name the torturers gave to the bed on which people were chained for electric shocks with the *picana*. There were also various phone calls in which the speaker with a brass band blaring military tunes in the background would name Neilson's children and say that it would be a pity if anything happened to them. When that happened, Neilson went to see the Secretary-General of the President's office and said angrily that the only way he would leave Argentina was of his own free will or in a coffin. It became a front-page story in the Argentine papers, which were allowing themselves a little more freedom by this stage; and then President Videla himself, approached by the British ambassador, promised that Neilson would get complete protection. That was in July 1980, and was to prove something of a turning point, not only for Neilson himself but also in the whole question of threats and attacks. They did not come to an end by any means, but the issue had finally been aired in public and the President had come out against the men who were making the threats and carrying out the attacks.

In the 1950s and 1960s the *Buenos Aires Herald* was little more than a small community newspaper, which only occasionally essayed a little circumspect criticism of the government of the day. There was a mild controversy over whether Argentina should be called 'our country'. But none of the senior editorial people who worked on the paper at the time of the 1976 coup felt that they could possibly ignore the fact that murder and torture had now become an established part of the political culture of the country. It was, one of them later said, 'barricades stuff' that they started writing; even though at first no one seemed to take any notice of what they said. But slowly the *Herald*'s editorials were read and quoted by newspapers abroad, and then quoted back to Argentina – though they were not reprinted. And because it had been the custom for some time to print the day's editorial in Spanish underneath the English version, it was passed around among people who opposed what the government was doing like a kind of *samizdat*.

The *Herald* began printing indications of what was starting to happen under the new government within days of the coup, even though at first it was done obliquely – by reprinting the comments of the London *Observer*, for instance, which warned that Argentina might become a wasteland. By mid-April it had reported a number of kidnappings and murders (as indeed had several other Buenos Aires newspapers at this stage) and mentioned the use of unmarked Ford Falcon cars in these incidents. But the *Herald* began to be outspoken only after the government prohibition of 22 April on publishing details of abductions, murders or the discovery of bodies unless they were mentioned in an official statement. An editorial said, 'We should all be on our guard against any attempt to slant the news. But it can be argued that even slanted news is better than no news at all. If issues are purposely ignored, they tend to swim, like sharks, to the depths – only to surface later and cause endless trouble.'

The government prohibition seems to have made things easier for Cox, Neilson and Graham-Yooll in a way, by showing them that they could not continue reporting the situation in Argentina and keep to the official guidelines. It was no doubt frightening, but they felt now that they had a duty to perform. On 7 May they published the first account of someone who had been kidnapped, in clear breach of the prohibition. No other paper, including *La Opinión*, carried details of the case, though it was a particularly important one: that of the left-wing novelist Haroldo Conti, who had disappeared from his home in Chacarita two days before. He had been returning from the cinema with his wife when he found five armed men in his flat. Eleven days later, when the two Uruguayan ex-politicians, Senator Zelmar Michelini and Héctor Gutiérrez Ruiz, the last a former chairman of the House of Representatives, were kidnapped, *La Opinión* reported the case, and gave almost a full page to a detailed account of it – Michelini had been working for *La Opinión* at the time he disappeared. The *Herald* reported the case, but not at such length. Again, no other newspaper even mentioned it. A *Herald* editorial said, 'Let us stop behaving as if we are still afraid that in addition to the terrorists (whom we have been fighting for a long time) we have to continue to ponder the possibility of those Ford Falcons without number-plates drawing up outside our doors.' There were disagreements within the *Herald* at this stage about the precise editorial line which should be taken. Robert Cox was concerned with the future of the paper and the security of its staff; James Neilson, as the main political writer, concentrated on the need to tell people the precise nature of the new government. Soon after the Michelini-

Ruiz case he wrote an article which drew the parallels between the Videla régime and the Nazis. Cox refused to print it. 'It'll get us all killed,' he said, and he was probably right. But there was never any dispute about how the *Herald* should report cases of human rights violations.

Nevertheless, it was necessary to be careful. The military allowed details of fake operations to leak out, precisely in order to trap journalists into reporting them – and then the newspaper involved could be accused of printing false information. It was a risk which almost no one was prepared to run by the end of 1976, but the *Herald* did. Among the articles about economic prospects and the latest cattle prices would appear paragraphs like the following:

> *Kidnapping in Martínez*
> A group of armed men broke into the home of Monica Graciela Scolsy and Daniel Chijo on Monday September 5th and took them both away, according to a report filed in Martínez police station. Abraham Scolsy, who filed the report, says he has had no news of his daughter and his son-in-law since they were abducted from their Martínez home.

It makes about a column inch. But the fact that the kidnapping was reported at all broke through the careful construction of secrecy which the authorities had erected around what they were doing. People whose children had disappeared would go to the offices of the *Herald*, not so much for information as for the relief of being able to talk with someone who would take them seriously and not turn them away with an insult. Sometimes twenty or thirty people a day would come to the office. Someone on the staff would see each one, though often they had to be told that nothing much could be done for them. The *Herald* required to see a writ of habeas corpus before they would print the details of a case, and they did not print the details of every one that was brought to their attention. But they did print as many as they felt were justified on the basis of public interest.

Other subjects had to be dealt with more carefully. On 22 April 1977, for instance, Robert Cox was arrested at the newspaper office by two men in plain clothes and held for 25 hours before being released over the *Herald*'s reporting of a press conference which the Montonero leader Mario Firmenich had given in Rome two days before. At the press conference Firmenich had announced the creation of the Peronist Montonero Movement which was intended to bring all the various open and clandestine groups still operating into one organization. The arrest of Cox was said to have been carried out without the authority of President Videla, who was frequently praised in the pages of the *Herald* as a moderate and intelligent man, and was attributed to 'freelance' activity by a group of Army officers. When the case came to court, in September, all charges against Cox were dismissed. The judge said that to read the intention of apologizing for subversion into the articles the *Herald* had printed on the news would be to rob journalism of its educative function. No doubt the judgement had been carefully cleared beforehand, but it gave considerable support to the *Herald*'s policy of publishing what it felt to be right.

Being edited by a British team (if owned by an American one) had its advantages; in the fantasy world of many Argentine army officers, it meant that the *Herald* must have the protection of the British government and perhaps the British secret service. On the other hand it was sometimes regarded as a national insult that the *Herald* should be criticizing Argentina in the English language: one Radical politician complained to the *Herald* at the time, 'How dare you criticize our President?' Readers, too, did not always appreciate what they found in the *Herald*'s columns. 'You may argue that it is your duty to publish news, but your readers know that spreading information about evil can also convey dismal views for present and future prospects', one reader's letter of 1978 says. Because even civilized people did not want to be reminded of what was happening around them, they were angry at the newspaper which carried the reminders. The *Herald* itself sometimes felt obliged to bow to opinion of this kind, though not in its editorial or news columns. It printed occasional pieces from outsiders who burned to defend the country against the allegations being made against it abroad. In April 1978, for instance, Maria S. de Gosztonyi wrote an article which said, in part:

> It is impossible to eradicate violence from one day to the next . . . If you put out a raging fire, the embers smoulder on for quite a while . . . You can't stop disappearances and killings. But instead of getting help from the developed countries, they only cause us more trouble . . . We need good will – and I just cannot understand why highly-developed, cultured nations are helping to further the cause of the subversives (left or right) with their senseless meddling in our affairs.

The *Herald* pressed ahead with its accounts of disappearances without taking much notice of the complaints. It provided the only detailed account of the kidnapping of Professor Alfredo Bravo, right down to giving the names and numbers of the men who had kidnapped him: the other newspapers, including *La Opinión*, only did so many days later, and mostly only after it seemed safe to do so because the government itself was involved in the controversy. By 1978 the *Herald* was printing reminders about people who had disappeared:

> *Student Missing for Two Years*
> Today is the second anniversary of the disappearance of Margarita Erlich, a young student of fine arts. Her parents say that a group of armed men took her from the family apartment in this city around 1.30 a.m. on April 6th 1976, and they have been unable to learn anything of her fate or whereabouts since then. The parents, Mariano and Genoveva Erlich, have applied to public authorities and to the public to help them in their two-year search for Margarita.

There was little news value in such items; the *Herald*'s staff felt obliged to print them because it demonstrated the state of the nation at the time. In the files of the newspaper such paragraphs seem slight and unobtrusive, but during the time of the Process they provided the only public mention that had ever been made of Margarita Erlich or any of the other thousands of people who had disappeared. Merely by printing the name, the *Herald* helped the parents and relatives of such people to break out of the sense of utter helplessness and silence. The *Buenos Aires Herald* was not a particularly exciting paper then or later; it was capable of leading on, say, the result of the Norwegian general election at a time when most other newspapers elsewhere in the world found more important subjects to headline. Its writing style and layout leave a certain amount to be desired, but it nevertheless has a delicate air, which has never reached print in even the most oblique form, of having done its duty. And although James Neilson, for one, would sometimes worry that they had treated the hundreds of people who came to the office a little callously, in giving them only a few minutes and not being able to help them much with information, those who went there have a different story to tell. 'I never bothered with the British embassy,' said one woman whose husband and kidnapped son held British nationality. 'The *Herald* was our embassy – the embassy of everyone who had lost a son.'

* * *

At the end of December 1977, *Le Monde* in Paris reported the arrest of a freelance journalist and translator, Susana Lugones. She was the fortieth journalist to have disappeared since the coup, 21 months before. Seventy others were in prison, and four hundred in exile. Many of those who were imprisoned had been cleared of the charges against them in civil courts, but had nevertheless not been released. Three months later, on 31 March 1978, ADEPA, the Argentine Newspapers Publishers' Association, which had campaigned bravely against the arrest of journalists, reported that the number and intensity of violations of press freedom had decreased over the previous six months, and although there were occasional arrests and kidnappings after that, the pressures were never as strong again. Not surprisingly: with the solitary exception of the *Herald*, there was no fight left in the Argentine press at all. *La Opinión*, which had been the only outspoken Spanish-language newspaper, and had done as much as its staff dared, was now run by an Army officer. Jacobo Timerman, its publisher and editor, had been arrested a year before.

Timerman, the son of Jewish immigrants to Argentina from the Ukraine, was born in 1923. The newspaper he founded and edited had become the foremost liberal newspaper in the country, respected and moderate. Throughout the troubles of the early 1970s it had condemned extremism and the resort to violence, and Timerman himself received countless threats.

Timerman has many critics and not a few enemies in Argentina who are not by any means extremists. He has been accused of being a self-publicist, and of having had too friendly a link with some sections of the military. It is true that his paper did not come out against the coup of March 1976; like most people, Timerman seems to have believed that there was no real alternative to a period of military rule. Nevertheless as the repression grew, *La Opinión*'s approval turned to muted disapproval, though it was always careful not to show outright hostility to the Videla régime. It may be that by not antagonizing the more 'moderate' members of the military government, Jacobo Timerman saved his own life in the long run.

Looked at objectively after the terror has abated, *La Opinión* seems to have been timid in its reporting, especially in comparison with the *Buenos Aires Herald*, which would not otherwise be worthy of comparison in terms of intellectual content or presentation. *La Opinión* failed to report some of the more significant and disturbing arrests when they happened, sometimes mentioning them days after the news had been carried in the *Herald* first; and *La Opinión* never tried to match the *Herald*'s steady coverage of cases of missing people who were largely unknown outside their own circle of friends and relatives. Nevertheless, if *La Opinión* felt unable to say much, the rest of the Argentine press said almost nothing at all. Those who had lost a son or daughter knew that Timerman was someone they should go to see, and he usually received them courteously and took an interest in their story – which, as the same sort of people found at the offices of the *Herald*, was an important act of support at a time when they most needed it. Often Timerman would have to explain that if *La Opinión* carried a news item about someone who had been arrested, it would be likely to lead to his or her death. Given the far greater influence and circulation of *La Opinión* compared with the *Herald*, this was almost certainly true.

The newspaper was often in trouble. In July 1976 it reproduced an editorial from the *Buenos Aires Herald* which accused the police of carrying out vengeance murders – something the press as a whole had hitherto been silent about. The press director at the Casa Rosada was furious, and wanted both *La Opinión* and the *Herald* closed down for five days, but this was vetoed by the Interior Minister, General Harguindeguy. In January 1977 *La Opinión* was closed for two days, for reprinting an article by a Jesuit priest about human rights. The newspaper's staff was also in some danger. Three of them were kidnapped in the first year of the new régime; one of them, the former Uruguayan senator Zelmar Michelini, was found dead within hours of a statement by the Press Information Secretariat which said that the government shared the deep concern felt about the disappearances of journalists. In its reporting of the case, *La Opinión* took the considerable risk of mentioning that Michelini's abductors had looted his apartment.

The line between careful reporting and offending the authorities was a very fine one. The police, for instance, seized copies of a book containing the collected articles of a *La Opinión* columnist. As individual pieces in the paper, they had not caused sufficient offence for the authorities to take action; collected, they were too much. Timerman himself regarded it as one of his main functions to encourage the 'moderates' among the military leadership – Videla himself and Viola – against the out-and-out fanatics. 'The moderates', he writes 'in my opinion had to be supported by way of public pressure rather than patience.' The moderates, in their turn, repaid the favour: 'If *La Opinión* succeeded in surviving between March 1976 and April 1977, the first year of military government, it was because army moderates decided that this journal, critical but not antagonistic, opposed to terrorism but supportive of human rights, ought to survive.' The fact that the public pressure which Timerman and *La Opinión* managed to exert on the moderates does not appear particularly strong nowadays, does not for an instant mean that it was not plain at the time. *La Opinión*'s reputation was perhaps stronger than its practice, but the fact that its offices were one of the obligatory stops on the weary journey around Buenos Aires that the relatives of each new victim of the disappearances would make shows that its reputation was solidly based.

Writing from Israel, after his experiences in clandestine gaols in Argentina, Timerman allowed himself to go a little further in his view of *La Opinión*'s function: 'The Argentine rulers wanted to be viewed like Dorian Gray, but *La Opinión* was the mirror hidden above, which appeared daily on the streets, presenting Dorian Gray's true face.' That, certainly, is over-statement. Broadly speaking, *La Opinión* supported much of the military government's disastrous economic policy, and it rarely spoke out in unambiguous terms about the government's total disregard for human rights, or the continuing practice of torture and murder. What it did was to highlight some of the cases that came to light, and that was itself dangerous enough. Given that there were divisions of opinion between the military men who were running the country, there was also the risk that it might provide ammunition which could be used by one faction or another to force its views through.

At dawn on 15 April 1977 however, Timerman's careful balancing act was brought to an end, when twenty men claiming to belong to the Tenth Infantry Brigade of the First Army Corps, arrived at his flat. They ripped out the telephone, covered Timerman's head with a blanket and handcuffed him. They forced him to go with them down to the basement garage and took off the blanket for a short while so that he could point out to them which was his car. Opening it with his keys, they threw him into the back, put the blanket over him once more, and drove off without saying anything. Jacobo Timerman had ceased to be the best-known campaigning journalist in Argentina. He had become the prisoner of men who modelled themselves on the German SS; and he was a Jew.

# 14 PRISONERS WITHOUT NUMBERS

*'To you who carry on your backs the weight of a grief that comes from long ago. To you in whom history repeats the tenacious resurrection of tragedy, almost as a perverse miracle of cruelty. To you who arrived in this land seeking to satisfy the hunger and the thirst for justice, and found the protection of a people who do not know hate. To you, who are no worse than others, but have certainly wept more than others. To you, on this religious and transcendent day, we men of the Navy say "Peace".'* – Message from Admiral Emilio Massera to the Jewish community on the occasion of the Jewish New Year, Rosh Hashana, September 1977.

The journey to the first clandestine prison was to be repeated many times over the coming months as Timerman was transferred from one secret interrogation centre to another. He was kept bundled down on to the floor at the back of the car, a blanket thrown over him, with the feet of his captors resting on his body. It was difficult to make out where they were taking him, but the noises he heard helped to give him a sense of how far out of the city he was being driven, as he heard the sound of heavy traffic along one stretch giving way to quieter surburban streets, then the distant whine of an airplane passed overhead as they went along what seemed to be a road heading out towards the airport. As the car slowed down on that first trip, Timerman could hear the barking of a dog nearby, then gates creaking open, and the passenger and his abductors from the Tenth Infantry Brigade of the First Army Corps had arrived.

The torture he was to receive repeatedly for four months was conducted in the most ordinary of surroundings; often it was a simple room with a bed where he would be given the *picana*, the electric shocks intensified by drenching him with water. In other clandestine centres, the torturing might be done in the kitchen and the *picana* would be rigged up above the kitchen table, where the guards would later eat their meals. Sessions on the 'machine', as the prisoners referred to the electric cattle prod, were supplemented by beatings and by being tied up or chained to the foot of a ladder for several days.

Timerman described the simplicity of the methods used by the Argentine Army in his bestselling book, *Prisoner Without a Name, Cell Without a Number*:

> When the electric shocks are applied, all that a man feels is that they're ripping apart his flesh. And he howls. Afterwards, he doesn't feel the blows. Nor does he feel them the next day, when there's no electricity but only blows. The man spends days confined in a cell without windows, without light, either seated or lying down . . . The man spends a month not being allowed to wash himself, transported on the floor of an automobile to various places for interrogation, fed badly, smelling bad. The man is left enclosed in a small cell for forty-eight hours, his eyes blindfolded, his hands tied behind him, hearing no voice, seeing no sign of life, having to perform his bodily functions upon himself.
>
> And there is not much more. Objectively, nothing more.

But it wasn't the torture so much as the verbal abuse which distinguished Timerman's treatment from that of gentile prisoners; being a Jew exposed him to a peculiar type of sadistic pleasure and emotional hatred from guards and torturers. Although most of those abducted were tortured and badly treated, the torture was a way of breaking prisoners down, getting them to co-operate with the other side, or punishing the prisoner before his 'transfer' from the jail. But for Jews, there was the added aspect of being hated for their race. This Timerman sensed was a desire to eradicate: 'Interrogating enemies was a job; but interrogating Jews was a pleasure or a curse.'

The many sessions of questioning, with and without torture, went over and over the same ground: was he a Jew? Did he support Zionism? Was he a Zionist? Did his newspaper, *La Opinión*, support the Zionist cause? Did he have any contacts with Israel? Did he know why there was an international conspiracy to take over part of Argentina by the forces of Zionism? Apart from the last line of interrogation, the answers were always 'yes', but it didn't seem to stop the First Army Corps from asking them again, at a later date, at another interrogation centre.

Jacobo Timerman was being held by the Army and that put him into the hands of two of the most notorious proponents of the 'Dirty War': the chief of the Buenos Aires provincial police, Colonel (later General) Ramón Camps, and General Guillermo Suárez Mason, head of the Tenth Infantry Brigade. Camps was responsible for overseeing Puesto Vasco, now the site of the Fourteenth Police Investigative Brigade, and one of the three clandestine gaols Timerman was held in from the time of his abduction on 15 April 1977 until August of that year. Suárez Mason supervised the running of another centre, known as Coti Martínez, about twenty kilometres outside of Buenos Aires. Timerman himself classified these two men as part of a group of 'extremists' in the Army who may have been acting on their own without the authorization of the junta; it certainly wasn't uncommon for the commanders in a particular province to decide on whom they should be picking up and only later inform other branches of the military or the Ministry of the Interior of whom they were holding or who had already been 'transferred'. If Camps and Suárez Mason had wanted to kill Timerman, it would have been possible for them to do so, according to Timerman, because the 'moderates' in the junta were not always able to restrain the extremists and dictate what should be done with him.

Early on in his captivity, he was brought before Colonel Camps, a tall, bony man, whose deep-set eyes had a frightening, even messianic intensity about them. After allowing Timerman's wrists to be freed from the handcuffs which bound them behind his back and ordering him a glass of water, Camps informed his prisoner that his life depended upon how he answered the questions. When Timerman asked whether this was to be done without a preliminary trial, Camps just repeated that his life lay in his answers. The fact that the answers he gave confirmed that he was a Jew and an avowed Zionist may have been responsible for his survival, because they kept alive the theory of a Zionist conspiracy against Argentina, according to Timerman.

It was true that the military arrested Timerman with the explanation that they were investigating a possible conspiracy which involved some leading Argentine Jews, but the action against Timerman wasn't simply the work of anti-Semitic extremists pursuing crazy theories. Although Timerman does not mention it in his account, he was initially picked up as part of an investigation into a financial scandal. His arrest came shortly after the 'Graiver group' was detained by the army for 'serious subversive activities' and economic crimes linked to the reported death of David

Graiver, a 35-year-old banker, whose private plane had crashed on a mountainside in Mexico on 7 August 1976. David Graiver was presumed to have been on board travelling from New York to Acapulco, and with his death a fortune was lost. The junta discovered that he had been handling $17 million, mainly raised through robberies and ransom demands by the Montonero guerrillas. Graiver had been putting the money into investments in property and businesses and was thought to have been transferring funds through the American Bank and Trust Company of New York not long before the accident. The $130,000 raised in interest each month went to the Montoneros based in Havana, to support their activities. Rumours at the time of the arrests suggested that Graiver may have been forced to become involved with the Montoneros' finances as the price for the release of his wife, who had been kidnapped two years before. Graiver's disappearance was followed by the collapse of several of the banks used by him, in Belgium, Switzerland and the United States. After the arrests of Graiver's widow, his father and brother, and three others, the junta informed the press that 'economic delinquency must be dealt with with the same rigour as armed subversion. The health of the republic needs such examples.' The authorities promised that details of an 'important investigation which will startle public opinion' would be revealed in a few days time by the President himself. Before President Videla made his public statement, Jacobo Timerman was detained. At first, his arrest was a disappearance, but the junta was forced to admit that it was, in fact, holding him within one day, because of the protests of his family and diplomats. The Argentine Press Information Secretariat said he was being detained because of his connections with the Graiver affair, not because of *La Opinión's* activities or the fact that he was a Jew. Graiver had been Timerman's business partner on *La Opinión*, and had owned a 45 per cent share in the newspaper, so the junta was not altogether unjustified in questioning Timerman about Graiver's role as guerrilla financier. Timerman's arrest and detention were also a convenient way of killing at least two birds with one stone: Timerman's paper would be controlled and the rumours about Graiver could be attached to his partner, the editor.

The week after Timerman was taken by the First Army Corps, Videla made his statement about the Graiver banking group and their associations with the Montoneros and announced that the family of the financier would be dealt with under an 'Act of

Institutional Responsibility' in June that year to combat activities 'harmful to the nation'. This meant that Graiver's father, a Polish-Jewish immigrant, and five others of the group would remain imprisoned at the disposal of the executive branch and they would lose all political and civil rights. The Act also stripped them of their property and wealth, until they could prove that it was gained legally. A month later, four enterprises belonging to the Graivers were taken over by the military, including *La Opinión*. A colonel was installed as the paper's editor. Although the military did not explicitly accuse Timerman of involvement in Graiver's underground business dealings, the effect of the timing of the arrests and statements by the military was to insinuate that *La Opinión's* editor (and publisher) was involved in subversive activities and that *La Opinión* might even have been entangled in Montonero money. Other rumours were also circulated at the same time: there were stories about massive flights of capital leaving Buenos Aires for Montevideo in Uruguay because of the Graiver affair, with sums as high as $20 million being mentioned. Several members of an Argentine currency exchange enterprise were arrested for illegal currency transactions, allegedly sparked off by a panic over official investigations into the Graiver group. There was even an implied link between the arrest and subsequent disappearance of Timerman's new business partner and *La Opinión* printing manager, Edgardo Sajón, on the first of April 1977 and another corruption investigation, this time into a former President of Argentina, General Alejandro Lanusse. Lanusse was arrested and charged in May 1977 for corrupt dealings over the granting of contracts back in 1971 for Argentina's first aluminium plant, and Sajón had been Lanusse's press secretary during his time as President. There was even an attempt to spread the Graiver investigation as far up as the former Minister for the Economy, José Ber Gelbard, who was Jewish. Gelbard also happened to have been a personal enemy of the powerful López Rega, who was a well-known anti-Semite.

The Graiver affair deepened the atmosphere of anti-Semitism already prevalent within the armed forces and police, by seeming to provide grounds for a connection between the war against subversion and the presence of influential Jews in the press, the financial world and other professions. The co-ordinated series of arrests also indicated that Timerman's arrest may not have been just the work of an 'extremist' faction in the Army, but was part of a wider upsurge: the culmination of a campaign rather than an exceptional case. The campaign had elements that could be described as fascist; it wasn't that more Jews were detained or abducted than other groups in the country – according to the Organization of American States, 204 Jews were known to have disappeared in the first three years of the Process and 16 officially detained – but their treatment was generally harsher and more humiliating than that received by other prisoners.

There were over a quarter of a million Jews living in Argentina in the 1970s; some put the figure as high as 400,000, making it the world's seventh largest Jewish community. Mena Nehemias Reznizky was their representative as President of DAIA, the Delegation of Argentine Jewish Associations, an organization which had been founded in the 1930s to defend the Jewish culture and community. Reznizky had been DAIA's President since 1973 and had witnessed an upsurge in anti-Semitism under López Rega's guidance. Reznizky's family had been one of the first Jewish families to settle on the Argentine pampas and begin farming, having emigrated from Russia in 1895. He was in his early fifties and had been a lawyer before becoming DAIA's leader. Under López Rega, he and his family had received death threats at night from the Triple A, who wanted him to leave Argentina. He had had a meeting with López Rega, to complain about the upsurgence of neo-Nazi publications and harassment of members of the Jewish community. He had told López Rega that Nazi propaganda was being produced, paid for by taxes from Jews, at which the minister grew red and very angry at being spoken to in such a way. But now, under the military, the stakes were higher as the anti-subversion campaign drew in more and more victims from different walks of life, and, therefore, more Jews. Although in the past when the military had taken power there had been a clampdown on anti-Semitic literature, under this régime it was on the increase. Soon after the coup, publications which were blatantly Nazi or neo-Nazi were being openly sold in kiosks on the streets. Two of the most offensive were *Militia* and *Odal* but there were others which proclaimed 'Four million Jews didn't die', or 'Why Hitler was right'. The extreme right wing which had carried out acts of violence against Jewish synagogues and community centres before the military took power, continued their activities under the Process; bombs were planted in synagogues, and in January 1977, a cinema in Córdoba which was showing the film *Victory at Entebbe*, about the successful Israeli rescue of Jewish hostages being held in Uganda, was destroyed by a bomb. On top of this, people were coming to Reznizky with stories of abductions and disappearances among their families.

The Jewish community was beginning to feel afraid, although it was still mostly a case of being fearful of what was happening to the neighbours. In Argentine society at large, Jews had not been subject to overt discrimination. During the 1930s many Jews had found a refuge there from Nazi persecution in Germany. They joined many other Russian and European Jews who had settled in Argentina earlier that century and in the 1800s. There were many prominent families who had established themselves in banking, universities and other professions as well as in government circles. There were well-known scientists, film-makers, artists and architects who had not found their being Jewish an obstacle. But it was an uncomfortable integration in Argentine society in some ways; Argentina's neutrality during the Second World War and the welcome given to Nazis like Eichmann in its aftermath, betrayed a racism which was felt by Jews in many subtle ways. In addition, the Constitution of the country barred non-Catholics from becoming President and the Roman Catholic hierarchy ensured that education was controlled by the Church, which led to the creation of a separate, and excellent, private school system for Jewish children. There were unwritten rules against any Jew's being appointed to the judiciary or being given a post in the Foreign Ministry, but even more exclusively non-Jewish was the military officer corps. No Jews were made admirals, generals or brigadiers and the police academies, too, discouraged the promotion of Jews in their ranks. The military schools were well-known for their often blatant anti-Semitism and showed signs of official Nazism, perhaps because of their tradition of employing German instructors. The military academies had a highly-structured, well-planned training in political theory, and soldiers passing through the system confirmed that some parts of Nazi ideology had been incorporated into the teaching, which equated Catholicism with the idea of the Fatherland and the Family, a formula not calculated to encourage religious tolerance or the promotion of Jews.

Despite the poor reputation of the armed forces, many Jews looked upon civilian rule with more apprehension than military rule. Most periods of overt anti-Semitism had occurred under democratic governments; both Frondizi's and Illia's time in office had been marked by racist incidents, and by the increased circulation of anti-Semitic literature, as had Isabel Perón's; no doubt it was easier for right-wing extremists to operate in a free society than under military rule. But the military, under Videla, did show occasional signs that they were disturbed by the anti-Semitism in their ranks, realizing that it gave the country a bad name abroad.

This gave Reznizky a certain amount of leverage, and at his first meeting with the Interior Minister, General Harguindeguy, he raised the subject of the Nazi literature which was on sale in the streets of Buenos Aires. Harguindeguy joined him in condemning it, though he refused to condemn anti-Zionist tracts. Eventually, by protesting regularly, Reznizky managed to get both *Militia* and *Obal* banned, while a major publishing house which put out neo-Nazi material was closed down. In 1979 DAIA scored another notable victory, when the Education Ministry backed down over a compulsory civics course it had been planning to introduce, which had a blatantly anti-Semitic text book. When Harguindeguy asked Reznizky why he was so concerned about such things, he answered that it was better to be aggressive in defence of the Jewish people than silent and passive.

Shortly after eight o'clock on the evening of 27 May 1976 a group of unidentified trouble-makers smashed the window of an office on the Avenida Díaz Vélez in Buenos Aires. They hurled a bottle filled with petrol at it, followed by packets of pamphlets about the popular uprising in Córdoba several years before: the Cordobazo. They then ran off. A young Jewish boy, Horacio Oscar Sargovi, had been standing in front of the building, trying to go to a Jewish club, but was held up, waiting for a taxi to arrive. He left as soon as he saw that there was a disturbance, as did everyone else in the immediate area, but he was stopped and arrested at the next block because a policeman saw him coming from the direction of the incident. Of the three people arrested that night, seventeen-year-old Horacio was the only one brought to trial and convicted by a military tribunal for 'breaching public order' and 'violence against members of the police force', although he had not made any disturbance and had been arrested without resisting. He came before the tribunal even though he was under-age. The policeman who had picked him up had somehow dug up a witness willing to testify against Horacio and the policeman invented a story against the boy. As the judge on the military tribunal looked down at Horacio, before the trial got underway, he disparaged him for being a Jew, and the secretary and the prosecuting attorney made anti-Semitic comments about his club, and his religion. His own defence attorney wasn't even a lawyer and, once the trial started, stayed completely out of the proceedings, aside from participating in the formalities of the military court. Horacio had only been asked to give a statement that day; he had been given nothing to eat for 48 hours and had not been allowed to sleep or relieve himself. His defence at the tribunal was not the strongest that could have been put up since the young man had to prepare it himself, even though the only actual eyewitness said that he didn't recognize him as having been present when the window was smashed. Sargovi was given a sentence of six years.

Sargovi's case was eventually reopened and the judgement overturned by the Supreme Tribunal of the military but because it referred the case back to the original Tribunal for review, the young man was again found guilty and given the same sentence. And since a military judgement could not be declared null and void twice, the case was closed.

Reznizky heard about such cases; he also heard that in the prisons and during interrogations, Jews were being treated worse than others. Jewish girls were raped more often; men were given more beatings and were put on the *picana* for longer periods; they were humiliated by the guards, some of whom had pictures of Hitler or Nazi insignia hanging on the walls of the interrogation rooms. DAIA began drawing up lists of Jews who had disappeared to hand to the government. Reznizky estimated that he visited the Ministry of the Interior offices once every month or fortnight with lists of detained and missing people; he was asked by one high-ranking military officer, 'Why are you Jews the only community which comes here with lists?' But the lists had no more success than the ones put in by other groups such as the Mothers of the Plaza or the Permanent Assembly; the replies, when they came, said nothing was known about those said to be missing. He also kept in touch with the ambassador at the Israeli Embassy, Ram Nigrad, and together they managed to get the Minister of the Interior to accept that anti-Semitic and anti-Zionist literature were one and the same thing, which tipped the balance against the racist publications being sold. The Jewish community, through DAIA, also appointed a member to the Permanent Assembly for Human Rights to represent them. Roberto 'Bobby' Graetz was one of the Assembly's most vocal members. Graetz eventually had to move to Brazil because of two attempts on his life. Reznizky, too, was vocal, he claims, in denouncing the ill-treatment of Jews when he heard of it or when there was evidence which showed what was happening, although sometimes it was more difficult to present the junta with accusations, when the actual facts were hard to discover.

Reznizky had considered himself a close friend of Timerman's in the past, but they had increasingly disagreed about what tactics should be adopted in the face of the military's excesses during 1976 and early 1977. Timerman himself was in a somewhat ambiguous position because he had been one of the more influential journalists who had questioned Mrs Perón's capacity to govern and was widely seen as having encouraged the coup against her. During previous civilian governments he had contributed to coup-making through the papers he owned, by bolstering those who he judged to be 'intelligent generals'. His papers *Primera Plana* and the more populist *Confirmado*, had been very critical of President Illia, and had provided platforms for the promotion of the careers of several military officers, including that of General Juan Carlos Onganía, who toppled Illia. Timerman's importance as an opinion-former gave him good contacts with the military and made him many personal friends; Videla and Viola were to be counted among them. Timerman himself tells of meeting senior military officers in the wood-panelled bar of the Plaza Hotel in the centre of Buenos Aires before the coup, advising, cajoling, discussing. Yet these same men were now detaining him in secret prisons, holding out against enormous international and domestic pressures to release or charge him. Timerman's hope lay with his personal contacts, the 'moderates', Videla and Viola, and the fact that they wanted to retain the image of civilized, rational military leaders.

Reznizky could use this to advantage, but the Graiver affair complicated the handling of Timerman's case. It wasn't simply that Timerman was a Jew, nor that the independence of *La Opinión* was annoying to the junta because it openly flouted the new censorship rules; Timerman also had a reputation as a king-maker and wheeler-dealer which made the human rights side of his case more difficult to get across.

On the third day of Timerman's detention, the DAIA leader went to see General Viola, who as head of the Army, was at least nominally in charge of the activities of the First Army Corps and responsible for the actions of Camps and Suárez Mason. He told Viola that the international Jewish community would not be silent about Timerman's case, and that Argentina's reputation abroad would suffer if he were not released. No doubt Viola took the point, but the feudal divisions within the military limited what he could do for Timerman in the short term. The most that proved possible, Timerman later said, was to try to convert his disappearance into an arrest in order to save his life. A month after Timerman's detention, Reznizky criticized 'forces in the country which were waging a campaign against the Jewish community' in a statement published by DAIA, some of which was reprinted in the *Herald* on 18 May 1977, under the headline 'Pogromist forces at work'. The wording showed a certain amount of caution, because of the Graiver case. 'We do not know what the charges against him are. Obviously we will respect what the court finds out. But his case is different' (i.e. from that of the Graiver group). 'Since he was a young man, Timerman belonged to the organized Zionist movement and from the pages of *La Opinión* maintained a constant and courageous struggle against Nazism and anti-Semitism.'

Two months after Timerman's arrest, Reznizky travelled to the United States to lobby on behalf of the Jewish community and spoke to the head of the Latin American section of the B'nai B'rith, the powerful Anti-Defamation League, one of the most important international Jewish pressure groups. The leader of the ADL, Rabbi Morton Rosenthal, was apparently reluctant, at first, to take up the case. He told Reznizky, 'Don't get involved in the Timerman case; he's said to be mixed up with Graiver.' That at any rate, is how the DAIA leader remembered the meeting. It was with great difficulty that Rosenthal was persuaded to campaign on Timerman's behalf.

But Reznizky was under great pressure not to attack the régime abroad, on the grounds that, if he encouraged an anti-Argentine campaign things could get much worse for the Jewish community as a whole. The Zionist political parties, for instance, which were still allowed to function, could be prohibited if DAIA was stirring things up too much, and the condition of ordinary Jews might get worse. Reznizky's response was that he was not part of Argentina's Foreign Office, and that he would continue to tell people both the good and the bad things about the country. Nevertheless, he himself admits that the general approach was to work behind the scenes where possible. 'There are two ways – one open and one silent. To save lives, you have to act silently,' he said, when it was all over. 'There are two ways of fighting a fascist dictatorship; one is open confrontation, the other way is to keep up your contacts, like Raoul Wallenberg during the Second World War. He would shake hands with Himmler because it was necessary to do it. My tactic was to take a middle way, denouncing inside the country on the one hand and on the other, saving people's lives by acting silently, with a certain pragmatism.'

But those in human rights organizations such as the Mothers of the Plaza de Mayo were later to express their disappointment with the reaction of the Jewish community, accusing it of failing to denounce the disappearances of young Jews vigorously enough.

On 28 July 1977, Nehemias Reznizky's son Marcos was taken from his home in the middle of the night. A squad of twelve men ransacked the house, looking for incriminating material, but three months before, Reznizky had gone through the house, getting rid of 'leftist' publications, so that nothing was found. Reznizky went to Harguindeguy and told him he was not willing to let his son pay for his own activities, and friends in the Catholic Church exerted pressure on his behalf. Harguindeguy decided to help Reznizky and his son, and after four days' disappearance, Marcos was released. He had been tortured and interrogated about Israel, Zionism, the American Embassy, and terrorism. After that, Reznizky sent all three of his children to live in Israel to keep them safe. But the fact that the leader of DAIA saved his own son's life while others who disappeared remained unaccounted for, fuelled rumours in Buenos Aires that a deal had been done with the junta. Certain members of the Mothers who travelled abroad to publicize the situation were told by some human rights organizations that DAIA had let them know that it opposed outside intervention, even from Jewish organizations. One Argentine woman, who was sent on an Amnesty International – sponsored trip to Europe met a French-Jewish official who confirmed that organizations had been asked not to interfere by DAIA. It seemed that an effort was made to avoid any suggestion that what was happening in Argentina was part of an anti-Semitic campaign. Jewish mothers would speak later of being received politely enough at DAIA's offices and receiving assurances that their missing children's names would be handed in to the office of the President and the Ministry of the Interior, but they would hear little more after that. Another critic, more accustomed to be strident in his views, went so far as to say that Jewish community leaders failed to denounce what was happening to Jews in detention, and that some, in his words, 'acquiesced calmly in the torturing of Jews'. The critic was Jacobo Timerman.

At the clandestine prisons of Coti Martínez and Puesto Vasco, Timerman was usually held near the rooms where prisoners were tortured. Once he heard a man in his seventies being beaten by the guards for being a Jew, even though he was a convert to Catholicism and wore round his neck a medallion given him by the Pope. Timerman was angered by the passivity of some Jewish prisoners, and by the way Gentiles would plead with their guards, telling them they were making a mistake in thinking that they were Jewish, in order to avoid punishment.

During the fourth month of his detention, Timerman was taken by car to a military gaol, Magdalena, where he became an 'official' prisoner, permitted to receive visits from his family at weekends and to walk round the prison yard – in silence, but nevertheless in the company of other prisoners. There would be no more torture, even though his conditions remained harsh.

At the Beth El Synagogue, in the suburb of Belgrano, there was no equivocation, no suggestion that it would be better if everyone kept quiet in face of the disappearances. Week after week there were powerful sermons, denouncing the use of violence and terror on all sides. Some members of the congregation were nervous that this would draw unwelcome attention to the synagogue. But their rabbi took the view that as a foreigner he was better protected than an Argentine, and could speak out with greater freedom. The accent in which he spoke out was a strident New York one.

Rabbi Marshall Meyer had arrived in Argentina in 1959, a rabbinical student of twenty-eight who was still working on his doctoral thesis and had nowhere definite to settle. He came from a prominent philanthropic family, whose members had founded the Jewish Conservative Movement, as well as the Meyer Brothers' Pants Factory, one of the leading clothing companies in the United States before the First World War. Marshall Meyer had been tempted to go on the stage after leaving Dartmouth College, but he had always been interested in religion and decided eventually to train as a rabbi through the influence of the Jewish scholar Abraham Joshua Herschel. After the sudden death of his parents, Meyer asked the World Council of Synagogues if they could arrange a posting for him with a Jewish community abroad. As Meyer tells the story, they tried Singapore first, but the line was busy. Next they tried São Paulo in Brazil, but nobody answered. Thirdly they called Buenos Aires, and this time they got through; his future was decided.

He and his wife taught themselves Spanish on the boat trip to Argentina, and with the same energy and enthusiasm he helped set up a Jewish camping movement directly he arrived. Within three years he had established his own seminary in a mansion in Belgrano, where for the first time rabbinical students could be trained without having to go abroad. About half a mile away, Meyer and thirty other families founded the Beth El Synagogue, which by the time of the 1976 coup had grown to a thousand families. He was accepted by the Jewish community, though his brash New York way of doing things grated a little on the conservative Jews of old European stock who had settled in Argentina.

Right from the start, Meyer showed he was not afraid to raise the subject of the disappearances in his sermons, and he kept in close contact with the Mothers of the Plaza de Mayo as well as the Israeli and United States Embassies. He was also Timerman's friend, and acted as his rabbi, visiting him in prison when he could. Seeing him was not a pleasant or an easy task, however. Meyer would undergo humiliating body searches, being forced to stand naked in the cold while Catholic priests who were visiting prisoners were allowed in without being searched at all. But the ordeal was worth it: once an individual had been identified, the authorities could no longer deny his existence.

Rabbi Meyer's activities brought a regular flow of hate mail, and the papers sometimes printed suggestions from readers that he should be 'annihilated'. But, as he himself believed, his American citizenship was a powerful protection, and it helped him keep in contact with a number of foreign embassies. Sometimes he was able to warn people about the possibility of arrests; if he were told that psychiatrists were being picked up, for instance, he would get on the telephone at once and ring every psychiatrist he knew to warn them. Once, one of his students at the seminary brought him a copy of a document called 'Counter-subversion' which was being handed out at the Air Force academy where he was being trained as a cadet. The document, crudely produced and mimeographed, showed a 'family tree' of subversion, which linked Zionism with Marxism, Masonic lodges and the trades unions. From these roots, it said, flowed direct subversion and its branches – Protestantism, Jehovah's Witnesses, Lion's Clubs, Rotarians (though not, it seems, boy scouts), all human rights groups, Third World church movements, hippies, and so on. The pamphlet explained that there was an international Zionist conspiracy to take over

Patagonia, the southernmost part of the country, in order to create a second Jewish State there, which would be called Andinia. The secret document comfirmed that the plan had now been revised: Jacobo Timerman was revealed as one of its prime movers. He represented, it said, Soviet financial interests while Marxists in Buenos Aires and Montevideo were promoting the interests of American contractors. It was almost certainly the product of a crazed mind: possibly that of a well-known anti-Semite in the Law Faculty of the University of Buenos Aires, who had once warned that he would never permit a Jew to pass one of his courses.

Crazed or not, the scheme formed part of Timerman's questioning in prison. He was asked how many troops Israel would send to take over Patagonia; and no matter how he tried to explain to his interrogators the stupidity of the idea, they returned to it again and again. They assured him, too, that President Carter was a Jew, who had changed his name from Braunschweig, and that an American plot existed to take over Brazil, Argentina and Chile.

In September 1977, Timerman went before a military tribunal. He was asked if he was a Jew, a Zionist, a contact for terrorists. The members of the Special War Council asked him to explain why he had been a member of Jewish or Zionist organizations when he was a youth, and why he had been opposed to Argentina's neutrality during the Second World War. The hearing lasted 14 hours and covered his whole life as a political journalist, a Jew and a Zionist. Timerman was taken away to prison to await the outcome.

On 13 October 1977, he was informed that no case had been found against him and that he was not being charged, but he was not released from prison. A month later, the 'Act of Institutional Responsibility' was used against him, stripping Timerman of his property, including his newspaper, which was worth well over $5 million. The Act also deprived him of his Argentine citizenship and all his civil rights, effectively making him a social vegetable. In December, Videla told a group of visiting British journalists that Timerman was still being investigated in connection with the Graiver case. Finally, on 17 April 1978, just over a year after his arrest, Timerman was removed from prison and placed under house arrest. The 'moderates' of the junta had triumphed over the 'extremists', if only in a small way.

For the next two years, Timerman remained under house arrest. In the middle of 1978, the Argentine Supreme Court ruled that he should be released, because there were no grounds for indicting him on any charges, but the order for his detention was not lifted. By this time, there was a well-organized international campaign pressing for Timerman's release, but it wasn't until September 1979 when the Supreme Court met again and ordered his release that the case came to a head. Although the court ordered that Timerman be freed, the generals decided to ignore their decision. The members of the Supreme Court said they would resign *en masse* if they weren't obeyed and for a time it looked as if the Court itself would be placed under arrest. Then Videla tipped the balance in Timerman's favour, saying that if the Supreme Court resigned he would resign as well.

On the morning of 24 September 1979, Rabbi Meyer drove out to the airport to meet the editor of the *Jewish Chronicle*, who had flown in from London to lobby on Timerman's behalf. After dropping the journalist off at his hotel, Meyer passed Timerman's apartment building, and noticing an unusual amount of police activity there, stopped and went in. He was not allowed to go upstairs, but one of the policemen told him that Timerman had been released and was no longer there. Meyer, disliking the sound of that, ran to the Israeli Embassy to find out what was happening and he telephoned the American Ambassador, Raul Castro, who was just about to see President Videla. It turned out, however, that Timerman had just been told that he was being expelled from Argentina, and was about to be put on an Aerolíneas Argentinas flight for Rome with a passport valid for two days. The Israeli chargé d'affairs stayed with him the whole time; and later it turned out that their fears were not altogether groundless: a quarter of an hour after Timerman had been taken from his flat, another group of armed men had arrived, apparently in order to prevent his going.

Soon after the election of Raúl Alfonsín to the presidency, Rabbi Meyer received a phone call. 'On behalf of the President,' the voice at the other end said, 'I would like to invite you to join the President's Commission on the Disappeared.' Meyer had to be persuaded that the call was not a practical joke, but when he was, he pointed out that he was still an American citizen, and not an Argentine. The aide, taken aback, said that the decree setting up the Commission had already been drawn up, specifying that it would consist of 'outstanding citizens'. Meyer said he understood the situation, and the aide rang off. Two days later, the aide rang again: the President had decided to redraft the bill, changing the wording to 'outstanding persons'. Meyer was duly made a member of the commission.

One of its first witnesses was Jacobo Timerman, who gave evidence against Generals Camps and Suárez Mason, and pressed charges against Videla as well. Courted by newspapers, magazine and television, but no more greatly loved than he had been in the days when he was a leading journalist, Timerman went back to several of the clandestine gaols where he had been held, searching them out and examining them for the sake of the cameras. Nevertheless, it was clearly a moving experience for him, and the presence of the cameras became irksome as the memories flooded back. 'This was a terrible place; you can have no idea how terrible,' he said. And yet, in the bright sunlight of a hot summer's day, the place where he was standing seemed fresh and attractive, its outside painted white with new wooden shutters over the windows and a group of workmen decorating the inside as well. It was almost impossible to believe that it had once been a place of torture – that the officer in charge had slept on the bed where the *picana* was used on his prisoners, or that the guards had eaten on the table where, a few minutes before, their victims had been stretched out and shocked or beaten. It seemed exactly like a suburban police station, clean and bright, and the cellars where the worst-treated of all the prisoners had been held were closed up and cemented over. And yet not everything had changed: barbed wire still ringed the courtyard, and the loudspeakers which had blared out pop music all day and night to drown the noise of torture were still mounted on their wooden frames, overlooking the little prison, Coti Martínez. Timerman, noticing the loudspeakers and the surrounding houses, said, 'I wonder what the neighbours were thinking all the time they were hearing us inside? What kind of country can allow this to happen?'

The years of the Process divided Jew from Jew, as well as Argentine from Argentine. The Jewish community in Buenos Aires had its factions and tendencies before 1976, and there were often arguments between those who wanted to stress their Jewishness and those who felt it hindered their acceptance as Argentines. But the divisions were violently exacerbated by what happened after the military came to power. Rabbi Meyer and Jacobo Timerman represent one side of the argument: the side that said it was always necessary to come out into the open and take risks for the sake of Jewish freedom in general and of Jewish prisoners in particular. Nehemias Reznizky, by his own account, took the other side of the argument – even though he himself courted considerable risks at times in raising the cases of Jews who had disappeared. The argument has been decided, as it has turned out, in favour of Meyer's more public, flamboyant approach: the Jewish community survived, and has been able to draw a little vicarious pride from Meyer's boldness. In his dark, book-lined office, from which he conducts his legal practice, Reznizky, the former head of DAIA, continues to fight the battle, unwilling to accept that he was wrong. The *Jewish Chronicle*, Marshall Meyer, Jacobo Timerman: he takes them all on, rebutting their arguments one by one with letters from long-discredited generals who once held the power of life and death over the community Reznizky represented, testimonials from Jews who had been released through Reznizky's intercession, cuttings from newspapers that showed how Reznizky had been libelled by his opponents. It gets darker inside the office, even though the sun outside is shining. Timerman has his own battles to fight now; having been taken up the world over when he was first released, his account of what happened has been increasingly criticized as selective. Rabbi Meyer has moved on to the business of building up his synagogue and serving on the President's Commission, dealing not just with Jews but with every Argentine who disappeared. Only Reznizky is left to fight over the old ground, with the obsession of a man who knows himself to be right even if much of the rest of his world believe him to be wrong. 'Things are not only done by confrontation and shouting,' he says, holding out a sheaf of closely-typed documents fan-wise, and gesturing to them with his other hand as though they can speak up and give evidence on his behalf. 'Things are also done by quiet work, so that Jewish life must go on.' He looks sharply across at his visitor in the dark room, watching for a hint of disagreement. 'So that Jewish life must go on,' he repeats.

# 15 THE TURNING POINT

*'The Americans were wonderful. When you went round there, they really made you feel they were interested. You couldn't say that of some of the other embassies.'* – Mrs E Walker, mother of the 'disappeared' journalist, Enrique Walker.

'It was,' Tex Harris says, 'like a fast dentist's.' Every afternoon he set aside several hours to talk to people whose relatives had disappeared as a result of the military repression; he had the use of two offices in the United States Embassy, and his assistant, an Argentine woman named Bianca Vollenweider, would be sitting in the first room and would take each person's name and basic biographical details, together with those of the person who had disappeared. Then he or she would be ushered into the second room, where Tex Harris, his bulky 240-pound frame overflowing his chair, sat behind a standard, utility foreign service desk. His training, before he joined the State Department, had been as a lawyer. 'I would counsel them through the empty avenues of the Argentinian legal system,' he says, the Texas accent moderating a little the direct, punchy style. In a New Yorker it might sound brittle and self-regarding; coming from him, there is a kind of heavy rightness about his phrases.

Tex Harris saw thousands of people in his dentist's surgery, and he and his assistant recorded the details of fifteen thousand in all during his two years' service in Buenos Aires. He was there as a first secretary in the political section, but instead of reporting to his ambassador on the brutal simplicities of Argentine politics, which in the absence of political parties were, in effect, nothing more than the manoeuvrings of senior military officers, his task was to be the eyes and the ears of President Carter's foreign policy in Argentina, which was to treat the country favourably or unfavourably according to its record on human rights. It was, in many ways, a simplistic and therefore an unsuccessful way of approaching international affairs, but in Argentina, where human rights were being trampled on in a blatant and wholesale manner, the policy was to succeed, and succeed admirably. Tex Harris, with his immense files and with the pattern which they helped him to piece together, played an important part in the achievement.

When he arrived at the embassy, in June 1977, the repression was still at its height. Very few people were prepared to say publicly that they had lost their sons or daughters, and aside from the *Buenos Aires Herald* and to a much lesser extent Timerman's *La Opinión*, there was scarcely anyone worth telling; and so the scale of what was happening and the responsibility for it was very difficult to gauge. Tex Harris's new colleagues in the embassy told him what they genuinely believed – that a vigilante operation was being conducted by right-wing elements who had the silent encouragement of the authorities – in other words, that left-wing thugs and right-wing thugs were battling it out on the streets. At that stage, to be in charge of examining the human rights position at the US Embassy was hardly a full-time job, since there were fewer than twenty cases on the embassy's books, all of them those of people with US nationality. The majority of those also had Argentine nationality, and were therefore regarded by the authorities as Argentines. No one at the embassy, before Tex Harris came, had thought of interviewing people to find out the facts of each case; when someone was missing, the embassy would approach the Interior Ministry or the Foreign Ministry, would request information about him or her, and would be told that there was no information. After that there was nothing more to be done. Perhaps it went contrary to Harris's legal background to accept that; or perhaps he was ambitious to make his name with an Administration which set a high value on human rights. Either way, he decided to ask a few questions himself when the next complainant came in.

In a country where the relatives of the disappeared were starved of support and comfort, as well as of information, the news that someone at the US Embassy was willing to listen to them was passed around as quickly as news of bread passes round a hungry town. Literally hundreds of people showed up at the embassy to see him immediately and he and his assistant, Miss Vollenweider, had to call in someone from the commercial section at the embassy to give them some help. By recording the details of all the cases that were presented to them, and not just those where there was an American interest, they began to pick up trends, to see the common elements in what they now realized was a widespread campaign. The pattern was a frightening one: during one weekend, say, there would be 13 members of a political group who all disappeared at once, in different parts of the country; or 32 young people who belonged to some Third World church group. It was unpleasantly clear that there was nothing of a random vigilante nature about all this: it was being planned, and presumably at a high level.

For the majority of the people who came to him, the help that Tex Harris could give was very limited. He explained the complexities of applying for a writ of habeas corpus, but he felt obliged too to tell them that their chances of getting anywhere with that were almost nil; these were the 'empty avenues' of the system. All the same, many of the people who were coming to him were from the provinces, and many of them had no idea at all of what they should do or what the empty avenues were; and in a large proportion of all the cases he was asked about, there was nothing much to be done anyway. Applying for a writ of habeas corpus was a ritual which made people feel that they were not entirely helpless, even though they expected little or nothing from it. Harris, for his part, was coming to be known as the human rights attaché: and his bulk, and the practical interest he took in each of the people who came to him, gave them something of the comfort they craved. But in a number of cases he wasn't without some hope, right from the start.

Argentina, like the United States, is a nation built up virtually entirely by immigration, from much the same countries of origin, and both have a large population of Jews who came, or whose parents came, from Russia and from Poland. Very many Italians and Germans, too, had settled in Argentina, just as they had settled in the USA, and in a sizeable number of cases, immigrants in one country had relatives in the other. Once Tex Harris and his assistant had established that a particular complainant had relatives in the USA they knew that here at least was a case in which they might achieve something. A case that they could present to the Argentine government as being one of interest to the United States did have some chance of being solved, especially when it was accompanied by the implicit threat of Washington's disapproval.

The Deutsch family, of Austrian origin, was a case in point. One branch lived in California, while the other lived in Córdoba, the beautiful colonial city halfway between Buenos Aires and the Andes. The son of the Argentine branch had been active in the

Radical Party while he was at high school – the equivalent, perhaps, of belonging to the British Young Liberals, or to some youth branch of the Democratic Party in the United States. He could not, on that basis, be remotely accused of involvement in left-wing or subversive activities. But, as Tex Harris's pattern showed, it was part of a much wider campaign against the Radicals as a political force. A group of armed men raided the Deutsch family's house, at a time when the son happened to be out. They found a number of Radical pamphlets in his room, and on the strength of that arrested everyone else in the house – his father, mother, brother and two sisters, though they were soon released. For no very clear reason the men put a charge of plastic explosive around the door and blew it up, then, having obtained the telephone number of the place Deutsch himself was visiting, rang him to say what they had done. It was never clear why they did not go to arrest him themselves; perhaps they thought they would catch him by getting him to come home to see the damage for himself. Either way, he had the presence of mind to head straight for Buenos Aires, where, in the near-anonymity afforded by a big city, he was able to ring his uncle in California and ask for help. The uncle had connections with a powerful figure in Washington, DC – Senator Alan Cranston, who had run for the Democratic nomination against Jimmy Carter and was the majority whip in the Senate. Soon after he had made his call, Deutsch was picked up. Often, not even the fact of having influential friends was enough to help someone who had disappeared without witnesses, but, by chance, Deutsch's arrest had been seen by someone who was prepared to come forward and speak about it – a Jewish air-conditioning salesman. With his practical evidence that Deutsch had not simply vanished or escaped abroad – a familiar counter employed by the authorities – and with the pressure Cranston was able to summon up in Washington, Tex Harris had the elements he needed. It took him two weeks to get Deutsch freed, and the young man had been badly beaten up in the meantime, but it was a valuable and encouraging success.

The pressure which the United States could exert on Argentina was not a direct one. Despite the problems with its economy, Argentina was not a poor country, dependent on American hand-outs. Its military did not require US hardware for their forces: France and West Germany were, as the Falklands War showed, suppliers of effective matériel. But Argentina's leaders were anxious for the world to think well of them; and since they were claiming to be defending the Western world, and Christian civilization, from the influence of godless Communism, it was more than a little disconcerting for them to find that the West's premier power, the acknowledged opponent of Communism, disapproved of what they were doing. The month after the Carter Administration had come into office, the new Secretary of State, Cyrus Vance, told the Senate Foreign Relations Committee that the amount of military aid to Argentina, and to Ethiopia and Uruguay, was to be cut because of the record of human rights abuses in the three countries. In Argentina's case the cut was to be from 36 million dollars to 15 million. The Argentines, not expecting the decision, were stung by it and by the fact that they were being linked with a Third World country in Africa which had recently turned to Communism, and a Foreign Ministry spokesman in Buenos Aires countered swiftly by accusing the United States of interfering in its internal affairs. It had been a calculated attack by the new administration, carried out with a certain amount of misgivings by Cyrus Vance himself, though his commitment in general to the principle of rewarding or penalizing countries according to their human rights record was strong. What appears to have decided him in the end was the argument from the new President himself that the policy would not be credible unless the worst offender in the hemisphere was rebuked right at the start. The following year the State Department blocked a loan of 270 million dollars from the US Export-Import Bank for the sale of hydro-electrical equipment to Argentina which was intended for a vast power project on the Paraná River, between Argentina and Paraguay.

The argument against this kind of pressure was easy to make, and was frequently put forward by Republicans and by senior figures in the business and banking communities. At its simplest, it was that Argentina might be fighting subversion in a way the Carter Administration found distasteful, but that if the junta were to lose the war, the United States itself would suffer; and that it was more likely to lose it if the United States ranged itself on the side of its enemies. A refinement of the argument was to the effect that there were two wings to the Argentine junta, an extreme wing and a moderate wing, and that by attacking Argentina so publicly, the United States was simply strengthening the hand of the extremists – with the result that the Dirty War would become dirtier than ever. With the benefit of hindsight, this argument proved to be untrue: largely because of US pressure, the 'moderates' like

Videla were gradually able to push the wilder men out of power, and the deaths and disappearances (though they had perhaps run their course anyway) gradually declined.

If anything, indeed, it is fair to assume that efforts to undermine the Carter Administration's seriousness and authority had the effect of strengthening the hand of the extremists. In June 1978, the former US Secretary of State Dr Henry Kissinger paid a five-day visit to Buenos Aires as an official guest of the régime, during which time he lost no opportunity to describe Carter as a one-term President whose approach to human rights in Argentina would vanish with him. At a meeting with Argentine officials, businessmen and journalists, each one of whom was a close supporter of the military junta, Kissinger criticized the Carter Administration for failing to recognize that it was sometimes necessary for a government to suspend civil liberties in order to overcome organized terrorism. Those countries which had not experienced terrorism might not always understand, he said, what it could do to a society and how difficult it might be to fight. 'I would say that the United States owes you some understanding of the tragedies of your recent history,' Dr Kissinger said, and was applauded to the echo. Argentina, which was acutely conscious of its status and appearance in the world, spent a good deal of money in trying to attract what it called 'opinion-makers' to come to Argentina and be convinced by its arguments, and it employed the services of a New York public relations company, Burson Marsteller, to try to combat some of the damage done by the outspoken attacks of the US government.

But the maladroit timing of some of the arrests countered many of the efforts of the junta's friends: the telegram from the Permanent Assembly for Human Rights announcing the disappearance of Alfredo Bravo, one of its leading members, arrived just as President Carter was about to meet General Videla in Washington. Bravo himself believes that Carter's action in tossing it across the table for Videla to read was the one thing that saved his life. And even the less significant kidnappings had a powerful effect on the State Department, when they were presented by Tex Harris from the embassy in Buenos Aires in such a way as to show the underlying pattern behind them. The State Department soon came to depend on Harris's breakdowns of the human rights situation there for its guidance on handling the Argentine government. Statistics had become the litmus-test of Argentina's behaviour, and Tex Harris was continuing to provide hundreds of statistics each month.

But it caused problems, even within the embassy. Harris himself is unwilling to talk about this phase of his work, but it is clear that the ambassador, Raul Castro, was disturbed by the importance which Harris's reports were assuming in Washington. Castro himself was sympathetic to the State Department's campaign against Argentina, and gave Harris his full support in setting up his reporting centre; he was, after all, Jimmy Carter's personal appointee to the post of ambassador. But it tended to undermine his role as the chief interpreter of Argentine affairs to the State Department if one of his first secretaries was producing the real material on which it was taking its decisions. If the Export-Import Bank decision was taken on the basis of a statistical deterioration in the human rights situation in Argentina, for instance, then Castro, as ambassador, was losing his element of control over US policy. Unquestionably, Harris's career suffered as a result; he came by his reputation of being a poor team player at that time, and it has stayed with him ever since. Not that Castro tried to get rid of him; on the contrary, when General Viola, as Commander-in-Chief of the Army, asked Castro to have him withdrawn, Castro talked him out of the idea by saying that his removal would show that Argentina was bothered by Harris's reports. But within the State Department the view is that Castro sometimes tried to reduce the importance of those reports by deliberately delaying them at moments when there was an important decision to be taken in Washington. If, for instance, a trade agreement of some kind was coming up for renewal, Castro would ask Harris to rewrite a section of his report in order to ensure that it would arrive too late to affect the decision. As a result, Harris apparently found other channels for sending his statistics to Washington, but Castro easily found out about it, and it did no good to Harris's already damaged reputation.

He decided early on that there was no chance that a man who weighed 240 pounds could avoid attracting attention, and so he made a virtue out of his visibility, driving around in an equally eye-catching station-wagon. Some of the intelligence people at the embassy, while appreciating what he was doing, were shocked by his methods; their training and instincts led them to hide themselves in the crowd, and they found it hard to accept that he should be conducting such overt operations against the covert activities of the murder gangs. Occasionally Harris ran into trouble: once his station-wagon was stopped by a group of men who advanced on him waving guns; another time he was threatened by armed men as he was leaving his house with a guest. But the purpose was to intimidate rather than to injure him, and the habit was for men to hang around his house and his office, making it obvious that they were armed. For the most part, he believes, they were Navy men. He was watched continually – if he met someone from the Argentine Communist Party, for instance, there would be a call later to the ambassador or to some other senior diplomat asking why Harris was meeting subversives. But it soon became clear to him that several people who had been helping him with snippets of information they had picked up were disappearing, and it became more difficult for him to keep in contact with ordinary people who had not themselves lost relatives.

Curiously, Tex Harris's influence on the Argentine situation was probably greater at the level of national policy than in terms of the number of people he was able to help individually. Of the thousands of cases which he presented to the authorities as being of some interest to the United States, only a small number were released outright, while a larger number were transferred from the 'missing' list to the list of those whom the authorities acknowledged as being prisoners. That was not enough, necessarily, to protect them from ill-treatment or even torture, but it did ensure that almost all of them survived the Dirty War when the merely disappeared almost always died. To be on an official list in Argentina was to receive a kind of official protection. But Harris's real achievement was much greater than that; it was to provide the Carter Administration with the necessary ammunition which would penetrate the official defences and strike home at the heart of the campaign of repression. By the middle of 1978 the junta was beginning to understand how widespread the distaste for its methods and policies had become. Admiral Massera, for instance, paid a visit to Italy, and came back appalled. 'They hate us there,' he told his senior colleagues, and they believed him as they had not believed the diplomats and journalists who had indicated the same thing as tactfully as they could.

The following month, Videla himself went to Rome for the funeral of Pope John Paul I, and Vice-President Mondale was there to represent the United States. Another Export-Import Bank decision was due in Washington, and the Argentines, after the humiliation of earlier decisions, were particularly anxious about it. Mondale went to a meeting with Videla immediately after the funeral, armed with Tex Harris's latest figures on disappearances, which were high, and prepared to threaten a lower credit rating for Argentina in the terms of the Export-Import loan.

Videla, faced with the figures, felt obliged to accept that the human rights position was not improving, as he had maintained, and in return for an agreement by the Carter Administration not to press for the lower credit rating, which would have cost Argentina much more in terms of interest, Videla agreed to accept that the Organization of American States could send a fact-finding team to Buenos Aires to investigate the human rights position. That, in turn, enabled Videla to put pressure on his own hard-liners, since every member of the junta and each one of the commanders-in-chief agreed that it would be in Argentina's interests for a group as important as the OAS to give a favourable finding. From the time Videla returned from Rome, extremists like General Ramón Camps, the Buenos Aires police chief, and General Luciano Menéndez found themselves being eased out. It was indeed the turning-point. Not many months afterwards, Tex Harris and his family were recalled to Washington, leaving the faithful Bianca Vollenweider and the packed filing-cabinets and the well-armed thugs behind them. Tex was scarcely going back to a promotion. Within days of settling down at Foggy Bottom, he found himself buried in the complexities of one particular aspect of the SALT II nuclear arms negotiations. The man who was not a team player had become a member of a very large and – by his standards – less exciting team.

On 9 August 1978 a very different American campaigner for human rights in Argentina began to testify publicly before the House Inter-American Affairs sub-committee. Under questioning by the chairman, Gus Yatron of Pennsylvania, Assistant Secretary of State Patricia Derian gave perhaps the most effective and accurate assessment of events in Argentina that had yet been made public. A soft-spoken, rather birdlike woman in her forties, she was married to the State Department spokesman, Hodding Carter III. Asked why her human rights office had recommended against agreeing an Export-Import loan to Argentina, she replied, 'The reason for our advice was the continuing violation of basic human rights by Argentina. The systematic use of torture, summary execution of political dissidents, the disappearance and imprisonment of thousands of individuals without charge, including mothers, churchmen, nuns, labour leaders, journalists, professors, and members of human rights organizations.' In her strong Mississippi accent, Patricia Derian recounted, in round terms, the figures that Tex Harris had supplied to the State Department:

three thousand people 'executed' by the junta since 1976, and at least another five thousand missing.

The reaction began as soon as she had stopped talking. State Department officials from the Inter-American Bureau – notably less keen on the idea of linking relations with Argentina to the human rights issue than other sections of the State Department – tried to cross out Miss Derian's words from the transcript, but it was too late: the hearing was public, and word was already on its way to the news organizations of Buenos Aires. Ambassador Castro was called in by the Argentine Foreign Ministry, and the Argentine ambassador in Washington was brought home. The strongest anti-US statement in anyone's memory was issued in Buenos Aires, calling Derian's remarks 'false and tendentious, an offence to the Argentine people and harmful to ties between the two states'. *Siete Días*, one of Argentina's leading magazines, came out later that week with a cover showing President Carter and pictures of policemen kicking the heads of blacks in Philadelphia and troops shooting at rioters elsewhere in the USA. 'Mr President,' it asked, 'is this the bulwark of human rights?' A leading women's magazine, *Para Ti*, urged its readers to send postcards with Argentine flags on them to the country's foreign critics, as a symbol that the war against terrorism had been won. Reaction in the United States was scarcely less angry. The accusations Patricia Derian had made were called 'unsubstantiated', 'undiplomatic', 'naïve'. A syndicated column by Rowland Evans and Robert Novak said that her figures came from private sources of dubious reliability. 'US government bureaus with vastly more experience than Miss Derian's say the figures cannot be verified and seem inflated . . . Moreover, objective observers agree that Argentina's human rights record has improved markedly the past year.'

Patricia Derian's figures, far from being unsubstantiated or inflated, were in fact accurate, even perhaps a little of an underestimate. Each of her other accusations was true and verifiable at the time. Some of the opposition to what she had said was overtly political – a part of the generalized accusation of naïveté and clumsy betrayal of Washington's friends which was levelled with great effectiveness at President Carter himself. But it was also part and parcel of the sense of controversy which Patricia Derian seemed to carry around with her wherever she went. Her sharpness and tendency to angularity offended the macho tastes of Argentine military men almost as much as the things she said about them – but with great courage she continued to travel backwards and forwards between Washington and Buenos Aries, keeping contact with human rights activists there and giving them confidence that the United States was keeping its eye on their safety. Rabbi Marshall Meyer, the outspoken Jewish activist, speaks of her as a bastion of fortitude, sympathy and effective diplomacy, and describes how she would switch cabs several times when she came to see him, in order to avoid being followed. Since she was alone, there was a considerable danger that she might be kidnapped herself, not on the orders of the 'moderate' military leaders, but at the behest of one of the extremists.

When she paid official calls on senior government ministers, Patricia Derian would be kept waiting in the rudest way, sometimes being forced to stand up for an hour or more. Once she was jostled and spat on. In a sense, the accusations in Washington that she was conducting a personal campaign against the Argentine junta were right: she went farther than others in her position might have gone, simply because she knew many of the people involved, and because – armed with Tex Harris's statistics – she was confident that she knew just how bad the situation in Argentina was.

But her influence declined in Washington as the effect of the tough line she had espoused became more and more obvious in Argentina. President Carter and his National Security Adviser, Zbigniew Brzezinski, began to wonder whether some of the criticisms levelled at Derian's Argentine policy might not be accurate, after all – in particular the suggestion that the Soviet Union might be encouraged to move into the place of influence which the US had vacated. At first sight such a possibility might seem highly unlikely: the Argentine junta had, after all, believed it was fighting the Third World War against Communism on Argentine soil. But relations between Buenos Aires and Moscow were more complex than that: the Russians were always a potential market for Argentine beef and Argentine grain, and that meant that neither side wanted to annoy the other too much. And so the Soviet Union, instead of attacking the far-right-wing ideology of the Argentine junta in 1976 in something of the terms it had used to attack the no less far-right-wing régime of General Pinochet in Chile, ordered the small Argentine Communist Party to praise the military coup as being in the interests of the working class, and the junta reciprocated by allowing the Communist Party to exist more or less openly. There were, indeed, attacks on Party offices, but they always seem to have taken place on the initiative of local commanders, rather than on the orders of Buenos Aires. It is notable that despite the holocaust which overtook so many more moderate left-wingers, very few members of the Communist Party disappeared during the entire period of military rule.

The Soviet Union, which invariably claims to have a 'principled' foreign policy, returned the favour in the international sphere. In the August 1977 session of the United Nations Sub-Commission on the Prevention of Discrimination and the Protection of Minorities, for instance, the Soviet delegate voted with the representative of President Somoza's Nicaragua to avoid a discussion of Argentina's human rights violations, and they carried the day. Not long before, the Soviet Union had offered to buy Argentina's grain surpluses for the next ten years, and had apparently been accepted. From each side's point of view the arrangement paid off with great neatness after President Carter's decision to cut supplies of US grain to the Soviet Union as a result of the invasion of Afghanistan in December 1979. The Russians needed grain, and Argentina's economy was desperate for foreign currency: the deal was done.

In the light of this kind of arrangement, Carter agreed early in 1980 to a gradual improvement in relations with Argentina, to counterbalance the Soviet relationship. Within the Administration, three powerful voices joined together: the Defense Department, anxious about the possibility of a military link-up between the Russians and the Argentines, the National Security Council, and the State Department's Bureau of Inter-American Affairs, worried as always about the declining influence of Washington in Buenos Aires. Ranged against them was the lone voice of Patricia Derian, who for a time threatened resignation. Even she admitted, however, that the position was no longer clear-cut. There were occasional kidnappings and murders, but by and large the improvement which she and some of her colleagues had helped to bring about was being maintained. Reluctantly, Patricia Derian looked on as the Carter Administration, which four years before had begun its human rights campaign by attacking Argentina, slowly began the business of opening a new dialogue.

If it was Walter Mondale's meeting with Videla in Rome that marked the precise turning-point in Argentina, it was the visit by the Organization of American States Commission on Human Rights, agreed to at the Rome meeting, which made the change obvious. The Commission, consisting of six men, arrived in Buenos Aires on 6 September 1979 and stayed there for two weeks. During that time they saw everyone of importance in the country, from the generals and admirals who ran it to the human rights groups composed of relatives and friends of those who had disappeared. Directly they arrived in Argentina they announced that they wanted to hear from anyone who had a complaint to make, and thousands of people lined up patiently outside OAS offices in Buenos Aires, the line usually stretching down the street and around the corner. The report which the Commission produced was the most effective counter to the argument that the repression in Argentina had been exaggerated; in 266 concisely written and unemotional pages it listed dozens of cases and called on the Argentine Government to bring to trial those responsible for the deaths of those known to have been killed by men working for the government, to compile a register of those who had disappeared, and to make significant changes in the way in which the emergency powers were being used. The military authorities ignored the recommendations, but were not able to ignore the report itself. The fact that it had been compiled by a group of men whose credentials were impeccable meant that it was no longer possible for the Argentine authorities to pretend that gross violations of human rights had not occurred. Instead, there was a return to the earlier justifications for what had happened – the campaign of terrorism by left-wing guerrillas and the widespread threat to the security of the state. Now, though, they sounded increasingly hollow.

In the following year, 1980, there was a public condemnation of the Videla régime which was, in its way, just as damaging. The government-run television news announced it as simply and uninformatively as it could: 'An Argentine architect has won the Nobel Prize.' It did not say who the winner was, or which Nobel Prize he had won. A radio station gave a little more detail, but swallowed it as best it could: 'The Argentine architect Adolfo Pérez Esquivel today was awarded the Nobel Prize for Peace. And speaking of peace, there are serious problems between Iran and Iraq . . .' The official reaction was that it was an insult to Argentina, though few people had any idea who Pérez Esquivel actually was. Even the Norwegian news agency which announced that he was the winner of the prize described him as a Brazilian. As sometimes happens with the Nobel Committee, it wanted to give its accolade to a campaign, and had to search around for an individual to sum up that campaign; Pérez Esquivel was not the obvious choice among human rights activists. A man given to sudden excitements, he is nevertheless a sincere advocate of non-violence, who condemned the murders of Army officers by the Montoneros in terms as strong as those he used afterwards to condemn the repression. He was one of the founding members of the Permanent Assembly for Human Rights and of the Service for Peace and Justice, which is a mixture of influences which include Christianity, socialism, and the teachings of Gandhi. (Gandhi's photograph, together with that of Martin Luther King and of a Brazilian bishop who preaches to the poor, hangs on the wall of the Service's barren little office in the Calle Mexico, in one of the poorer parts of central Buenos Aires.) No longer a practising architect, nor even a professor of sculpture, for which he was better known, he now works full-time for peace and for human rights. In 1977 he was arrested when he went to a police station to renew his passport, and was held for 14 months without being tried or even interrogated. He was, he says, tortured, but he refuses to go into details and it is possible that his torture was mostly mental rather than physical. 'I found out that the man who was torturing me was also a child of God,' he said once. 'It may not have much to do with liberation, but it does mean something for non-violence.' 'Nobel Peace Prize for an Agent of Subversion' ran the headline in one magazine, but when Pérez Esquivel returned to Buenos Aires from Norway with his cheque, which he immediately put towards the business of fighting poverty and repression, he found that some people at least knew who he was and were glad about what had happened. 'We went to a restaurant,' he says, 'and when we entered, everybody got up and began to applaud. It was full of workers. And on the streets, many taxis stop, or buses, or cars, and people give a thumbs up sign, to say "Good!" or "We're with you".' The storm in Argentina was at last receding.

# 16 THE CRACKS IN THE SYSTEM

*'We are now entering a new stage in the Process of National Reorganization. In this new stage we will make all the corrections and all the changes of personnel which may be necessary.'* – General Videla, in a radio broadcast, 1 August 1978.

The winter sun glanced obliquely down into the River Plate soccer stadium and, in shining through the fog of Argentine flags and favours, turned the steep terraces a delicate shade of azure. Seventy-seven thousand people were crammed in there, and the concrete beneath their feet was thick with abandoned paper cups, greasy wrappings, empty bottles and cans. The great majority of the crowd had been waiting for hours for the big match to begin. There were relatively few foreigners among them; the tens of thousands of football enthusiasts from abroad who had been expected for the finals of the World Cup had not materialized, and without them there was no real hope of recouping the immense cost of staging the competition. Four months earlier, in February 1978, the Finance Secretary in the Videla government, Juan Alemann, had revealed that the expected bill would be 700 million US dollars, as against the original estimate of between 70 and 100 million. If they had known how expensive staging the competition would turn out to be, Alemann said, they would never have agreed to act as hosts.

Still, everybody agreed that the money had been well spent. The River Plate Stadium itself, where the crowd was now waiting for the two teams to come out on to the field and begin the *Mundial*, the final of the World Cup, was constructed on the most up-to-date principles: there were elaborate defensive works and a moat to keep the enthusiasts off the pitch, and yet the view from the terraces was completely unrestricted. Other stadiums as good, or almost as good, had been built for the World Cup elsewhere in Buenos Aires, and in most of the main cities of provincial

Argentina: Mendoza, Córdoba, Rosario, Mar del Plata. Corruption, too, had been on an outstanding scale, and without it the final cost of staging the World Cup would have been a great deal closer to the amount the government had expected to pay. But the organization, after a shaky start, proved to be meticulous, and the small army of foreign journalists who had come to Argentina was swiftly won over and began praising the arrangements. A government advertising campaign in the newspapers and on radio and television urged people to be helpful and courteous to foreigners, and it worked.

All of this was something of a relief for those football enthusiasts and sports journalists – and they were probably in a small minority – who were aware of Argentina's unenviable political reputation and had been worried about whether they should come to Buenos Aires at all. They had, however, already been reassured by a skilful campaign devised by Amnesty International, from its headquarters in London. Early on, Amnesty had decided that it would be pointless to try to dissuade people from going to Argentina: that would simply create a form of counter-sympathy for the régime. Instead Amnesty launched a campaign to tell the foreign journalists who were going to cover the World Cup, and the audiences who would be watching the matches on television, what kind of government was staging the competition. And Amnesty's advice was intended to enlist the aid of even the most entrenched supporters of the ideal that politics should play no part in sport: by all means go, but keep your eyes open. Sports journalists are not always noted for their political acuity, but the Amnesty campaign flattered them and encouraged them to look beyond the confines of the football field a little, and the result was that a great many of the background articles written in the Western European press about the World Cup betrayed some awareness somewhere of the overall political atmosphere in which the finals were being played.

But for those who had read and heard stories about the savage guerrilla warfare in Argentina's towns and cities, and had been nervously expecting to see some evidence of it, there was a surprising air of peace and acquiescence everywhere they went. Predictions that the World Cup of 1978 would come to rank in violence with the 1968 Mexico City Olympics or the Munich games of 1972 were completely unfounded. In part, the surprise arose from the natural slowness of foreigners to keep up with the changing situation in Argentina. The violence there had made a deep impression on the outside world; Graham Greene's novel about a kidnapped British consul had sold by the hundred thousand in the Western world by the time of the 1978 finals. What was not so clear, in the absence of regular, sustained news coverage from Argentina, was how effective the military's campaign against the guerrillas had been. By the middle of 1977 the Montoneros had been reduced to about 20 per cent of their membership figure of two years earlier, and as the numbers dwindled, so did the number of operations carried out by the survivors. But the Montonero leadership recognized that the World Cup would offer them a superb opportunity to show the world that the movement had not, after all, been defeated. In January 1978 a member of the leadership, Juan Gelman, told *Le Monde* in Paris that the *Mundial* would be 'a festival of the people, a gigantic press conference which would inform the world of the tragedy which our people are enduring'. Later, Gelman and several other Montonero leaders held a series of secret news conferences in Buenos Aires itself, urging opponents of the military régime not to let slip the opportunity before them. People who were going to see the matches were asked to chant 'Argentina for the Cup – Videla to the wall'.

But the Montoneros' tactics were poorly thought out. Later, there were allegations that the self-seeking and politically ambitious naval member of the junta, Admiral Massera, had paid a million dollars to the Montonero leader Mario Firmenich, in return for an undertaking that there would be no attacks on the *Mundial*. There is little question that Massera was perfectly capable of conceiving and making an offer of this kind, and he certainly travelled to Paris at a time when Firmenich could have been there; but it is doubtful whether another million dollars would have made any difference to an organization which already had almost as many millions as it had active members working in Argentina itself. And indeed the Montoneros did carry out a number of remarkably bold attacks while the World Cup was on, though the foreign journalists in Buenos Aires scarcely reported them, and details leaked out only days or even weeks later. During the 25 days the competition lasted, the Montoneros staged no fewer than 18 attacks, each one a success in its own terms and yet a complete failure from the point of view of the international publicity the movement was hoping for. Most of the attacks were carried out with a new weapon, the RPG-7 rocket, manufactured in the Soviet Union and supplied in the early 1970s to terrorist movements by Libya, Czechoslovakia and other Moscow-oriented countries. Some of the Montoneros' objectives were 'softer' than others (the homes of senior Army officers, for instance), but included in the list were a number of police stations in Buenos Aires and elsewhere which were being used as torture centres and clandestine gaols, and some genuinely spectacular targets: the Casa Rosada, where President Videla worked, the offices of the Army High Command close by, and the headquarters of the Army's intelligence service. And as a particular gesture against the torture and murder of their comrades the Montoneros even fired their rockets at the buildings of the Navy Mechanics School, ESMA.

For the few who did hear about the campaign, it provided formidable evidence that the Montoneros were still, in spite of everything, a force to be reckoned with. Their tactics, however, got in the way of their strategic aims. The intention had been to provide a 'gigantic press conference', but the Montoneros were so meticulous about avoiding civilian casualties (in order not to antagonize world opinion) and so swift in carrying out the attacks, that it was relatively simple for the authorities to keep the details quiet. The Argentine press carried next to nothing about the Montoneros' campaign, and most of the foreign journalists who were covering the World Cup never found out about it, lacking the necessary contacts. Afterwards the Montoneros were to blame themselves for having wasted their opportunity, and there was a brief return to the kind of massive explosion which brought enough loss of life to ensure that it could not be ignored – but by that time the World Cup was over.

In the River Plate Stadium the crowd was starting to get impatient. The noise, reverberating among the steep terraces, was already deafening. The Dutch, who were about to contest the final with the host side, Argentina, had their supporters in the crowd, but they took cover under the violent chanting and the wall of azure and white favours, and drew as little attention to themselves as possible. The entire Argentine nation had been given the day off to watch the match on television, though only ticket-holders were allowed within several blocks of the ground where the match was to be played. The biggest team of security men ever assembled in one place in Argentina guarded the stadium, and remote-action cameras watched every section of the crowd. Their job was not only to protect players and spectators from the kind of bomb attack that would have demonstrated the Montoneros' continued struggle but also to watch out for any sign of the more passive shows of resistance which the Montoneros' leadership had called for. Senior policemen scanned the thousands of blue and white banners for any sign of subversion, but saw nothing; and if there were indeed any chants of 'Videla to the wall', then they were swallowed up in the immense barrage of purely patriotic noise.

The game was not a particularly impressive one. The Dutch, angry at the Argentine efforts to upstage them, carried out a number of savage fouls early on in the first half, and the Italian referee let several of them go unpunished – much to the fury of the crowd. In the second half, the run of play turned against the Argentine team and it began to look as though the Dutch would win, but by the end of time they had been unable to capitalize on their opportunities and the score remained level – one goal all. Half an hour's extra time followed, and in it the ecstatic crowds on the terraces saw Kempes of Argentina score his second goal, while Bertoni, with five minutes remaining, took a pass from Kempes and scored from it. The final score was three goals to one. Even the habitually mournful face of the Argentine team manager, Cesar Luis Menotti, took on a faint smile, and he laid aside at last his cigarettes – he had chain-smoked throughout the competition. President Videla, who had antagonized an unknown number of the people he ruled by admitting beforehand that he was not particularly interested in football, was now visibly delighted by the result. And yet, as Videla waited to present the trophy to the winners, the only sign of widespread public irritation showed itself. The long-winded concluding speeches, relayed throughout the stadium by loudspeaker, delayed the presentation of the World Cup for so long that loud whistles and shouts of impatience broke out, and the television cameras showed the 23 million viewers in Argentina, and an estimated 1,000 million in the rest of the world, how nervous and agitated Videla became when he saw the restlessness of the crowd.

But the success of the national football team was also the success of the junta, and no passing moment of public annoyance could detract from that – not, at any rate, for the time being. The towns and cities of Argentina went wild with joy and national pride. Traffic policemen ignored the violations which hundreds of thousands of carloads of frantically delighted people committed each night in the towns and cities of Argentina, and they blew their whistles deafeningly in time to the incessant hooting of car horns.

The next day was a national holiday, and the enthusiasm and excitement continued unabated. 'This is the first time Left and Right have embraced,' one foreign journalist was told again and again. For the first time in years there seemed to be something genuinely worth celebrating.

A windfall such as this naturally makes people think better of themselves, and therefore of their country. Winning the World Cup in 1978 had much the same effect in Argentina. Not that there had been much in the way of general discontent in the months beforehand. Most people were prepared as ever to overlook the kidnappings and disappearances, and assume that the authorities had better information than they about the subversive activities of their neighbours or their neighbours' children. Nor did the restrictions on information cause any great anxiety, as the letter to the embattled *Buenos Aires Herald* quoted on page 224 made apparent. The economy was the touchstone of people's attitudes to the military government, and that appeared to be performing well by the middle of 1978. Foreign banks were queuing up to lend money to Argentina, and it was possible for the government to claim that living standards were rising.

But behind the reasonably successful façade, the ruling junta was developing some serious divisions, and the World Cup victory helped to widen them. The decision to bring all three of the armed forces into government two years earlier had by now created a confirmed propensity to dispute and manoeuvre within the upper ranks of the administration, and it was more like a coalition between divergent political parties than a unified government. And yet the armed forces were not in any sense political parties, but elaborate structures based on the principles of obedience and loyalty. In other words, the men at the top of the military structure were free to pursue their own ambitions with little check from below, and with only the hostility of the other armed forces to keep them in bounds.

Admiral Massera, who may or may not have demonstrated his undoubted lack of scruple by doing a deal with the Montonero leadership before the World Cup Finals, appears to have regarded Argentina's sporting success as a useful opportunity to win a popular power-base for the military government, and more especially for himself. He found no similar interest in the colourless Brigadier Agosti, the Air Force representative on the junta, and President Videla himself was too fastidious and too patrician to be interested in popular power, just as he had little interest in the wilder views of the military ideologues who believed that the Jews, the Communists and the Freemasons were at the root of Argentina's ills. Videla was, in this one limited sense, a moderate, but he had no hidden yearnings to be a democrat as well.

Emilio Eduardo Massera was different. He had always been an outsider, not just among his fellows in the other armed forces, but in the snobbish world of the Argentine navy as well. He was of Sicilian ancestry (which has led to some suspicions about a connexion with the Mafia), and was known as 'El Negro' because of his dark complexion. In a country where light skin and fair hair are regarded as indications of good breeding, that did not help. Nor did his evident ambition, though it eventually took him to the top of the service. He was for a time close to Perón, during *El Líder's* last years in power; it was, perhaps, the outsider in Massera that Perón noticed and took a liking to. Always a shrewd judge of other people's motives, Perón told him sardonically not long before his death, 'You've got all the right qualities to take my place. What a pity you're in the wrong service.' But it was not just Admiral Massera's choice of service that told against him: for all his efforts to imitate the early Perón in his range of political contacts and allies, he could never arouse anything approaching the devotion that Perón was able to call upon in others. Massera was all too clearly working for Massera, and no one else.

From the day of the coup in 1976 he proved a difficult member of the triumvirate. Men under his command had, with his full knowledge, been involved in the Triple A's murder campaign under López Rega and Mrs Perón, but Massera, though he sometimes expressed himself in strangely apocalyptic fashion, was never a fanatic like Luciano Menéndez, Suárez Mason or Ramón Camps. There was a cynicism in his nature which left little space for their wilder enthusiasms. On the other hand, he had none of Videla's aristocratic distaste for the crimes that were being committed in the name of Christianity; Massera controlled the death squads because that brought him greater influence with López Rega and Mrs Perón. Once they had disappeared and he was in a position of political power, he was primarily concerned with increasing that power. The example of Perón had always been important to him. Perón was not a social outsider, as Massera himself was, but he had aligned himself with outsiders and had demonstrated the potential political rewards of doing so. And since Perón had clearly been right when he pointed out that Massera belonged to the wrong service to become President as the result of a military coup, Massera set himself to create a less conventional basis of support. In this case, his cynicism proved to be quite breathtaking.

As early as July 1976, four months after the coup, some of the higher-ranking Montonero prisoners being held at the Navy Mechanics School in Buenos Aires began to notice with intense relief that their conditions were becoming slightly better. Many, perhaps most, of them were already co-operating with their questioners, giving information and sometimes going out with members of the task groups to spot or capture other Montoneros who were still at liberty. In the dreadful conditions of the Mechanics School, co-operation did not necessarily buy anyone their freedom, nor even relief from torture. But in the course of 1977, for about a hundred of the leading prisoners, the torture sessions inexplicably came to an end. The men and women who were selected were given better food and allowed to read some newspapers and magazines. They were moved to new cells, away from the torture chambers and their attendant noise; they were even permitted to meet each other for a few hours each day. At first they were too relieved to ask questions, but it soon became clear that they were being set aside for some special reason.

The reason lay in the complex politicking within the military junta. At first, when the military took over, the relative standing of the three armed forces had depended on their success in the war against subversion. The Navy, under Massera, soon began to achieve some remarkable successes thanks to the efficiency and ruthlessness of Task Force 3 3/2, which operated out of the Navy Mechanics School. Under the command of Captain Jorge Acosta, a man in his late thirties with a deceptively vacant expression and a receding hairline, 3 3/2 started its run of successes by arresting Norma Esther Arrostito in December 1976. Soon other leading Montoneros were captured, several of them through betrayal, and these arrests led to others. The Navy's standing within the military government grew accordingly, and so did Captain Acosta's within the Navy. Soon, indeed, he was in the position of being Massera's chief advisor, with the right of access to him at any time. Acosta was allowed to walk into Massera's office at the Edificio Libertad building in Buenos Aires, regardless of the more senior officers who might be waiting outside. He built up Task Force 3 3/2 to the point where it had its own intelligence service, and that permitted him to bypass the Naval Service of Information, SIN, which was hostile to Massera. In return for serving his master's purposes, he was allowed to serve his own: for a period of two years he accumulated a private fortune by selling the property of people who were detained.

By the middle of 1977, though, Acosta's very success began to tell against him. The war against subversion waned, because there had been so many arrests, and the balance of power within the military government began to be determined by other factors. The business of government became more important than the business of carrying out arrests, and Massera turned his attention to that instead. At first he met with little success. There was a lengthy battle within the armed forces about whether there should be a so-called Fourth Man in the junta, a President who would be separate from the three service representatives. Massera put up a powerful fight to be the Fourth Man, and failed; the Navy, in spite of his and Acosta's efforts, still did not have the necessary strength. Further, Massera's position within the existing junta was coming to an end: he would reach retirement age in 1979, and after that would have to disappear into civilian life. His only chance was to create, as Perón had done before him, the structure of a political party, and it seemed reasonable to him that, since the Peronist Party was itself without a proper leader after the toppling and imprisonment of Isabelita Perón, there was no reason why he should not take it over.

There was no room in his plans for Captain Acosta, and Massera began to gather round himself a group of political advisers to enable him to turn into a political, rather than a military, leader. From his office at the Navy Mechanics School, Acosta, shut off from access to Massera, cast around for a method by which he could regain his influence – and realized that the materials lay to hand in the cells and cages of the prison block. Clearly Acosta's project appealed to Massera's Peronist ambitions: what better method than to convert the Montonero Soldiers of Perón into Soldiers of Massera? Perhaps, too, it appealed to his unscrupulousness, his pleasure in the outrageous. Massera accepted the plan, apparently at once, and it was left to Acosta to begin *Operación Recuperación*.

Prisoners who were already being better treated found themselves being turned into a kind of brains trust, with access to a library containing thirty thousand books, and to a short-wave radio, and being given the status of advisors rather than prisoners.

'If you agree to co-operate with us,' Acosta told each of his candidates, 'one day you will be able to leave here alive, and we will allow you to get back to a normal, everyday life.' Few if any of the people he approached rejected the offer. The Montoneros' own history of this difficult period, published in Geneva in 1979, gives the impression that the prisoners themselves thought up the scheme and proposed it to Acosta and through him to Massera, in order to obtain for themselves the opportunity for rejoining the struggle for revolutionary Peronism. In fact, all the evidence is that they accepted the chance of better treatment for its own sake, and left the justifications until later. There are signs, however, that they put forward suggestions constantly which would draw in other prisoners and free them, too, from torture, and Acosta's curious ideas factory grew and expanded. Some prisoners were sent to Europe in order to spy on their exiled colleagues – and once there, promptly sought asylum. Others, such as Nelson Latorre who had once been one of the Montoneros' leading 'military' figures, collaborated with Task Force 3 3/2 from an early stage and became important members of the team of political advisors. Marta Bazan de Lebenson, another senior Montonero, informed on her former colleagues and allegedly became the mistress of Admiral Rúben Chamorro, the overall commander of the Navy Mechanics School. Once Massera's political team was established, she joined it, and was used to pass on ideas to the press and to the Ministry of External Affairs.

Massera seems to have been delighted with his new advisers. They suggested, first, that he should change his whole appearance, in order to give himself a greater popular appeal; he took their advice wholeheartedly. He stopped wearing his uniform, and affected expensive sports shirts by Lacoste, the more readily because Perón, too, had worn similar clothes. They advised him to emphasize what Argentines called his *gardeliano* look, after the popular singer Carlos Gardel, who was, like Massera, dark-haired and dark-skinned. They persuaded him to be photographed regularly with the Argentine football team, and when it won the World Cup his identification with the team brought him nothing but good. The overall purpose was to present Massera to the public as the one man who could provide the necessary link between the military government and civilian politics, and as a part of that the Navy began a public relations campaign to try to distance itself from the repression of the military government, in spite of the fact that the Navy had been the most effective service in carrying out the repression.

Military dictatorships tend to present themselves as providing a necessary period of respite from the quarrels of weak politicians, but what almost always happens is that a new form of politics emerges within the ruling élite: a politics based on the manoeuvrings of members of the inner circles of power, who come to resemble courtiers around an emperor. When the government is in the hands of a triumvirate, each member of which has his own and his followers' interests to consider first, the manoeuvring is hugely intensified. Admiral Massera, with the Montoneros to advise him, the death squads to carry out his wishes, and his own political ambitions to spur him on, added the element of gangsterism to the pattern of intrigue. At first Massera's new think tank suggested that José Alfredo Martínez de Hoz, the languid, British-educated Finance Minister whose Friedmanite politics were inflicting immense damage on the Argentine economy, should be the admiral's chief target. Hostility to Martínez de Hoz was present in the Argentine business community from the moment of the first bankruptcies directly attributable to him, and Massera's efforts to present himself as a bluff, straightforward man of the people made the Finance Minister a natural target for him. But Martínez de Hoz had powerful support: not simply the President, but the international finance community, who took the view that his policies were having the required effect on the disastrous state of the Argentine economy. In an article on the Argentine economy printed as late as April 1979, the *Financial Times* of London could write: 'As a result of Sr. Martínez de Hoz's good luck and good management, the days of bankruptcy are over.' The Finance Minister was armour-plated: nothing Massera could do against him would have any effect.

Soon, however, Massera was faced, not with targets he could choose at random, but with the kind of rivals that Argentina's court politics was beginning to produce. The resolution of the long-drawn-out crisis over the 'Fourth Man' meant that General Viola seemed certain to take over at some stage; and with him, it was strongly rumoured, he would bring a man who was currently Argentina's ambassador to Venezuela, Héctor Hidalgo Solá, as Minister of the Interior. In July 1977 Hidalgo Solá paid a visit to Buenos Aires and was kidnapped. At the time it seemed possible, though not very likely, that the Montoneros were responsible. Their strength might have been seriously depleted, but it fitted in better with the proprieties than the suspicion that the military rulers of the country might be turning against one another's favourites. Most people were content to allow Hidalgo Solá's disappearance to remain a mystery.

The following year another diplomat, this time a woman, disappeared while on home leave in Buenos Aires. Elena Holmberg was forty-seven and a middle-ranking officer at the Argentine Embassy in Paris. She was kidnapped in the centre of the city by three men in a blue Chevrolet on 20 December 1978, and her body was found three weeks later in the River Lujan. Once again, it was easiest to assume that the Montoneros had murdered her, though by this time the idea was distinctly less credible, and the circumstances of her seizure were so much those associated with the disappearances arranged by the military, particularly those of the Navy, that there was a good deal of quiet suspicion that she had in some way offended someone in a position of power. Her embassy was the base for the Argentine government's so-called 'Pilot Centre', which was intended to counter anti-Argentine propaganda in Western Europe. Some of its activities were indeed purely in the area of information, but since it came under the auspices of the Argentine Navy, and Massera was trying from 1977 onwards to get away from the association with repression and kidnapping, the Pilot Centre was regarded as a useful place to send Navy officers who were a little too closely linked with the Dirty War. Among those who were based there was Alfredo Astiz. It was clear that their primary task was to keep watch on the *émigré* community in Paris and elsewhere, rather than to turn out counter-propaganda in an unknown tongue. Elena Holmberg seems to have fallen foul of some of the officers at the Pilot Centre. She may have felt that her influential connections protected her in some way; after all, her uncle was the former Argentine President Alejandro Lanusse and her immediate family was wealthy and respected. But while at the embassy in Paris, she apparently made the mistake of hinting about knowing something of great importance; what it was emerged only three years later, in the pages of the *Buenos Aires Herald*. In its edition of 22 September 1982, the *Herald* printed a story under the headline 'Holmberg Knew of Massera Terrorism Link', and it quoted a former Argentine diplomat who had been friendly with Elena Holmberg as saying that she had told him two days before her disappearance that she had clear proof of Massera's meetings with leading Montoneros in Paris. The former diplomat was Gregorio Dupont, who had been sacked from the Foreign Ministry in 1977, perhaps at Massera's instigation. A cautious ten days after the *Herald* had published the story, *La Nación* reported it too – and almost next to it ran an article about Dupont's brother Marcelo, whose body had been discovered ten days after the *Herald* story, having disappeared in central Buenos Aires – he had apparently fallen from a building under construction. Gregorio Dupont had, it seems, stumbled across the suggestion that Massera had met the Montoneros. When he went to tell *La Nación* about Elena Holmberg's account of that meeting, it may have led to his brother Marcelo being killed in revenge. Dupont later told the magazine *La Semana* that Elena Holmberg had had documentary evidence of cash transactions between Massera and the Montoneros which were so damning that they would have caused his political downfall. This was the origin of later suggestions that Massera had met Mario Firmenich, the Montonero leader, and paid him a million dollars not to stage any attacks at the World Cup finals, and whatever the reasons for doubting the accuracy of that, there are no grounds for assuming that a man who could use Montonero prisoners as his political advisers was incapable of meeting their leaders abroad. Indeed, Massera did meet the Superior Council of the Peronist movement – to which the Montoneros were loosely linked – in Paris, in April 1978. Gregorio Dupont named two well-known figures as the source of his claim that Massera's meeting with the Montoneros took place: one man saw them together at a brasserie on the Rue Wilson in Paris, and the other came across them in the bar of a leading hotel in Madrid. These allegations were made while the military were still in power, though the fiasco of the Falklands invasion meant that people were no longer quite so afraid to speak out. Massera had by this time retired from the Navy and had left the junta in 1979; but he had not given up his political ambitions. He set up what was, given his views, an absurdly named political party – the Social Democratic Party, PDS – directly the decision was taken by the post-Falklands junta to hold elections, and established its headquarters in an expensive block of flats close to the offices of the Supreme Council of the Armed Forces. The offices were expensively but particularly tastefully furnished, there was a great deal in the way of security equipment, and the staff was mostly composed of crew-cut middle-aged naval men. Massera himself, a neat but bulky figure who had by now exchanged the *gardeliano* look for conservative, well-cut suits, rarely made himself available for interviews and had little to say about his political intentions, though the extent to which he deceived himself about his likely popularity in a free election was extraordinary. The expense of his political operation, indeed, revived rumours that he had arrested the chief treasurer of the Montonero movement and held his family hostage while his men cleaned out the numbered accounts the movement held in Switzerland. But this was only rumour, and perhaps all it does is illustrate the general lawlessness of the time. Massera himself strongly denied that he had had any connection, financial or otherwise, with the Montoneros, and when Gregorio Dupont's allegations were printed in *La Nación* Massera issued a writ of slander against him. Over the following months, however, the case was allowed to drop, and not long afterwards Massera's enemies in the leadership of the armed forces struck back at him. He was arrested – the only senior officer to be detained while the military were still in power – and in August 1983 he was indicted after an investigation into murders carried out by the Triple A movement in the last days of Isabel Perón. For four hours Massera answered questions about the disappearance of a number of other people, including Dagmar Hagelin. Massera denied any personal involvement, and said he had had arguments with Isabel Perón's close advisor López Rega about the Triple A. But he did accept both personal and moral responsibility for any errors which the Navy might have committed. He told the judge, 'Whatever action was carried out during the battle against subversion is none of this court's business. It can only be judged by those who were responsible for it.'

The evidence used to charge Massera was provided partly by Army officers who were eager to wreck his political career, and it implicated him in the kidnapping and presumed murder of a well-known businessman, Fernando Branca. Branca disappeared in 1978, after leaving for a meeting with Massera, with whom he was involved in various business deals of a dubious nature. Branca's wife, a beautiful society woman, Marta Rodriguez McCormack, had left him some time before to live with Massera, who was her lover. The affair was notorious in Buenos Aires: after Massera's arrest, popular satirical magazines used the incident to ridicule Massera's political ambitions. One mock election poster, for instance, showed him with his arms round a bosomy young woman, declaring that his Social Democratic Party protected mothers. In another, sitting up in bed between a man and his wife, Massera presented his ideas for a divorce law. Even a nation starved of democratic alternatives found Massera's career as a politician impossible to take seriously.

During the first half of 1978, people in Argentina could scarcely speak about the future without using the expression 'after the World Cup'. It represented, not simply a marker-point around which time could turn, but a future when things would be indefinably different. It was not that people wanted a civilian government back immediately – not even the Peronist and Radical Parties themselves wanted that, realizing that it was still too close to the disasters of 1975 and 1976 for a civilian government to be able to govern. But the characteristic Argentine liking for change was stimulated by the sense that things would soon be different, even though no one quite knew how. The World Cup provided a useful symbolism for the government in other ways, and leading figures in the junta and the administration quickly latched on to it. 'Are we able,' Admiral Massera asked an audience in the seaside town of Mar del Plata, in the days after the World Cup had been won, 'to give the country at other levels what we have given it in sport? We must set realistic targets. The feeling of solidarity we have enjoyed in recent days must be prolonged indefinitely.' The Finance Minister, Dr Martínez de Hoz, educated at Eton and rarely given to thinking or working in the common man's idiom, nevertheless employed the footballing imagery also. 'The day that twenty-five million Argentines aim for the same goal, Argentina will be a winner not once, but a thousand times over,' he told an enthusiastic luncheon for meat-packing executives. As for General Videla, he too borrowed the phrases of the game he had shown little liking for, and told the nation in a televised speech, 'Let us start moving in pursuit of permanent goals . . . May this collective experience we have lived through show us how to build an Argentina which is truly fraternal.'

In each case, it is possible to detect a mild note of anxiety creeping in. The fact is that the World Cup was a useful victory for the government, but it bore no relationship to anything else that was happening in Argentina at the time. Indeed, with hindsight it is possible to see that by 1978 the economic and political disaster which would eventually bring the military dictatorship down had already established itself. The remarkable turnaround in the economy between 1976 and 1977 would not be followed by any comparable success in the years that were to follow. Inflation, which had run at an annual rate of 444 per cent in 1976 had been cut back to 178 per cent in 1977; but in 1978 it was only 3 per cent lower, and although it dropped to 100 per cent in 1980, it rose again after that, until by 1982 it was up to 165 per cent.

Argentina's Gross National Product followed something of the same pattern: in 1976 the index was −0.2, while in 1977 it had risen to 6.0. But in 1978 it was down to −3.9, and although there was another increase in 1979 the curve was downwards after that, until by 1982 it was −5.7. The other main economic indicators followed the same line. Between 1978 and 1980 the dollar value of companies going bankrupt was $1.39 billion; 58 per cent of that was in manufacturing industries, the worst-hit sectors being textiles, foodstuffs and metallurgy – some of the main areas where the government had tried to replace imports with domestic production.

In other ways, too, the steam had gone out of the dictatorship. Having won its battle against the forces of subversion, the junta had no clear idea what it should do next. As Massera tried to turn himself into 'the Man of Transition' who could lead the way to government with civilian involvement, President Videla, for his part, could only ineffectually attempt to rein in the more extreme ideologues in his government who were calling for a permanent structure of repression. In May 1978 his ally, the Interior Minister General Albano Harguindeguy, made the first public condemnation by a senior government figure of what had been going on when he told a conference of senior police officers that some policemen had disgraced themselves by using terrorist tactics in the war against the guerrillas, and that the abuses must stop. It had no serious effect; the habit of violence had established itself too deeply for that, and Videla and his supporters were never in a position then or later to bring the killings and the torture to an end. But it did serve to distance Videla a little from what was happening, and it helped to give the outside world a feeling that something was being done about the Dirty War. As for his own position, that was at one and the same time more secure and more vague. A number of changes and reshuffles, carried out against a background of unceasing political in-fighting, took place at various points during 1978. In May 1978, after at least four months of political argument and manoeuvring behind the scenes, Videla finally won the so-called 'Fourth Man' battle, becoming President and at the same time relinquishing his post as commander of the Army. That was taken, however, by his friend and supporter, General Viola. Videla's term of office was set at three years, ending in 1981, but there were conflicting statements from senior officials and military men about how long the military régime would last. But if there was disappointment that there would be no elections until at least 1981, there was general relief that Videla had won the battle of the 'Fourth Man'. The crisis within the military régime had gone on for so long that there had been serious fears that the Videla administration would fall, and be replaced by something even worse. Videla went out of his way to court the backing of civilian politicians, and when, in November 1978, he sacked five cabinet ministers (though retaining the unpopular Martínez de Hoz and General Harguindeguy) he dropped some careful hints about having wanted to replace them with civilians who would have been acceptable to Peronist and Radical opinion, but had been prevented by opposition from some of his more hardline colleagues. At the beginning of December he announced, to widespread astonishment, that he would turn up at two annual dinners, one given by top civil servants in the previous, civilian, government, and the second by members of the Congress which he and his colleagues had closed down in their coup of 1976. As a result, senior Peronists and Radicals (under their elderly leader, Ricardo Balbín) stood and applauded the man who had brought civilian politics to an end and presided over the kidnapping and murder of thousands. Whether or not they believed that the President was a late convert to the values of democracy, they and the many others who had boycotted the dinner or observed it from a distance had the clear impression that Videla recognized that the military's hold on power was weakening, and that he was looking around for friends – even civilian ones.

As Britain found to its cost three years later, a government which is accustomed to act strongly and then finds itself weak can be dangerous. As early as February 1978, Admiral Massera was making angry declarations about the Beagle Channel dispute with Argentina's neighbour Chile, and he ended with the ominous warning, 'The time for words is running out.' It was, in part, a challenge to General Videla, who only two days before had signed an agreement with President Augusto Pinochet of Chile which was intended to defuse the long-running dispute over the Channel. In the second half of the year the war fever was increased. The armed forces spent anything up to four billion dollars on weapons to fight a war with Chile, and General Luciano Menéndez, the leading Argentine hawk, boasted publicly that he would drink champagne in La Moneda – the palace of the Chilean president, in the centre of Santiago – by Christmas. There were air raid precautions in the two capitals, and at one stage Chilean bombers actually took off for a raid on Argentine cities before being recalled. It required the intervention of the Pope to calm the situation and prepare the way for an arbitrated settlement. When the arbitration finally came, in 1984, the civilian government of President Alfonsín was able to accept it without difficulty – as were the citizens of Argentina, in a popular referendum. In 1979 Menéndez, however, continued to be a problem for General Videla, and that October he staged an abortive rebellion from his base in the city of Córdoba. It was put down without bloodshed by a superior force under General Viola, and Menéndez was sentenced to three months' imprisonment – even though the Argentine military code decrees death by firing squad as the penalty for mutiny. Menéndez had been restive for months about the government's 'soft' handling of its left-wing opponents, and he came out in rebellion as a result of Videla's decision to abide by the decision of the Argentine Supreme Court and free the journalist and newspaper proprieter Jacobo Timerman. As Menéndez was led to an aircraft which would carry him to his place of imprisonment he called out to the reporters who gathered to watch: 'I am convinced that a military government ought to exercise power in a military fashion.'

But Videla had not been exercising power in that way at all. Uncertain as he was about the future of military government, he was unwilling to go back to the methods of 1976 and 1977 in repressing opposition to his policies. At the same time, the austerity measures imposed by the policies of Martínez de Hoz, the Finance Minister, were having a greater effect on ordinary people by the beginning of 1979 than they had in previous years. Strikes, although officially outlawed, became commonplace, and in spite of occasional outbreaks of brutality by the police and Army most of the strikers not only escaped punishment, they managed to obtain something of what they were demanding. In 1977 the wages indicator had stood at −12.0 (with 1974 as 0). In the following year, 1978, it went up a little to −7.5; and by 1979 the barriers were broken, at least for the time being, and the indicator rose to 13.0.

The justification for military intervention in political life, frequently put forward in Argentina since the coup of 1930, is that civilian government, owing to its lack of consensus, can get itself into such a state of paralysis that only an institution which does not depend in any way on the vagaries of public opinion can be relied upon to take the required decisions. In practice, the Argentine military had also found itself in a dead end, most notably in 1973, when the only alternative was a return to civilian government under the Peronists. But that lesson had been forgotten in the dreadful conditions which applied under Perón and Isabelita from 1973 to 1976, and the system which was introduced after the 1976 coup, with the intention of ruling out inter-service rivalries, in fact reproduced the worst features of weak democratic government while lacking the legitimacy of an election. By governing through a junta which represented the three armed forces, the military ensured that every decision taken would be haggled over in the interests of each of the services. Far from providing swift, clean-cut decision-making, disputes could take months to settle: the 'Fourth Man' crisis, for instance, lasted for almost six months in all. And although the service leaders were prepared, by and large, to abide by the convention that they should leave public life on their scheduled retirement date – even Massera was willing to accept that – the spite and intrigue that went on behind the scenes was as bad as, if not worse than, the kind of in-fighting that the military had so despised among civilian politicians. Videla duly left office as President in 1981, and was succeeded by General Viola, who had been the Army representative on the junta.

Videla's last full year in power had been marked by an increasing sense of drift, and by the middle of 1980 yet another financial crisis, accompanied by a frightening flight of capital and further increase in the external debt, proved conclusively that Martínez de Hoz and his team had lost all control of the economy. The National Bank began to contemplate the need for a one million peso note (though it was not in fact put into circulation until 1981) and the immense scale of corruption, coupled with a lack of any serious control over military expenditure, made any kind of control over government spending impossible. The economic failure provided businessmen and civilian politicians with the opportunity to start attacking the whole record of the military government, though even now it had to be done carefully. Eventually, however, the five main political parties – the Peronists, Radicals, Intransigents, Christian Democrats and the Movement for Integration and Development – came together to form the multi-party alliance, the *Multipartidaria*, which would negotiate an eventual return to civilian government with the military. By the middle of 1981, even the Catholic Church, whose bishops had mostly supported the aims and even the methods of the military dictatorship to the extent of blessing the weapons with which the armed forces fought the Dirty War, began to inch away from the régime. The Episcopal Conference of the Roman

Catholic Church criticized the excesses which had taken place, and pointed to the evils of usury – by which they meant, in part, the growing problem of external debt. By June 1981 the country's car workers staged a strike, during which up to four thousand people were arrested, and the following month the biggest of the union groupings, the CGT called a general strike which attracted more than a million supporters.

General Roberto Viola, the faithful ally of Videla, and the bloodless conqueror of the rebellious General Menéndez, proved to be completely incapable of dealing with the problems he inherited when Videla retired in March 1981. He came to power in a blaze of public relations, sacking Martínez de Hoz and promising to restore constitutional rule by 1984; but his hold on power lasted only eight months, and he was continually undermined by his personal enemy, General Leopoldo Fortunato Galtieri, who replaced him as commander of the Army. Videla tried to whip up support for Viola, but failed, and by the end of November, when Viola suffered a mild heart attack, it became clear that this would be Galtieri's opportunity to bring him down. Like everything else the junta found itself divided on, though, Galtieri's coup took an inordinate amount of time. On 1 December, Viola's allies in government were saying that his health had improved and that he would be able to return to work soon. Galtieri, for his part, was allowing it to become known that he would slacken the rigid restrictions of military rule and restore constitutional government, this time by 1985. No one pointed out in the Buenos Aires newspapers that this was a full year later than Viola's promise. Viola resisted all attempts to persuade him to resign, until 11 December – 32 days after the heart attack which had precipitated it. Even then, it required six visits by four generals on the 11th to resolve the problem. Admiral Anaya, the commander of the Navy, read out a statement which said that the junta had run out of ways and time for resolving the current situation. Galtieri formally took office as President on 22 December 1981, at the age of fifty-five. His public relations advisers made certain everyone was aware of his most famous utterance up to that point: 'We do not want just a country, but a great country; not just a nation, but a great nation.'

# 17 THE GAMBLER'S LAST THROW

*'The only thing that can save this government is a war'*. – 'La Prensa', February 1982.

The bell for the end of the eleven o'clock break has just rung, and thirty children, each dressed in a purple blazer and grey shorts, or a purple dress, are taking their seats noisily, their heavy shoes scuffing the tubular steel of the desks. They are well-to-do children, since this is an expensive school, and when they speak to each other it is in a mixture of Spanish and English with a Home Counties accent. That, indeed, is one of the few indications that distinguish this from a mixed preparatory school in Britain; the weather is another. Tomorrow morning these children will be learning about Queen Elizabeth I and the Spanish Armada, and they will be taught in English. Today, though, the medium is Spanish, and the lesson is Argentine history. Few of the thirty children have Anglo-Argentine parents; the great majority are no different from the mass of Argentines, in that they have Spanish or Basque or Italian surnames, and they are attending an English school in order to give them a certain social and linguistic advantage later in life. The teacher unrolls a map and pins it down on the blackboard: on it are a cluster of untidy islands, as ragged as a Rorschach test. The wording, in thick italic letters, says 'Islas Malvinas', and a little azure-and-white Argentine flag floats on either side of the name. The teacher who tomorrow will be describing the triumph of Protestant England over Catholic Spain begins to explain to the children in front of her how the English acted as pirates in 1833 and took from Argentina what rightfully belonged to her. Another generation is about to have instilled into it a deep and abiding sense of historical wrong.

Until 1982, everybody in Argentina, apart from a few eccentric exceptions such as the extravagantly pro-British writer, Jorge Luis Borges, accepted without question the proposition that the Falkland Islands belonged to Argentina and should one day be returned to her. It was regarded, not as matter of opinion, but as a matter of objective reality. And yet, because it was so clearly established in the national mind, almost nobody felt obliged to do anything about it. There were occasional gestures from absurd ultra-nationalists, who might land a chartered plane on the islands and plant a flag there, or commit some act of symbolic damage to British property, but for the most part an active interest in seizing control of the Falklands was the mark of extremists only. Until 1982 and the invasion of the islands, there was never a single public demonstration of any size, anywhere in Argentina, calling for the islands' recovery. Argentine Governments, from 1964 onwards, often made strenuous efforts to get control of the islands from Britain by negotiation, but even then it was not because there was a public demand for it; it was simply that ministers and officials knew it would be popular if they succeeded. There was certainly no intention in the inner counsels of any Argentine Government until Galtieri's to use force to reclaim the Falklands, and although various invasion plans were worked out by the armed forces from time to time, they were nothing more than academic exercises. Argentine foreign policy has invariably been cautious and conservative, no matter who is in power in Buenos Aires; and it was not until the fabric of the nation began to split that there was even a suggestion that Argentina should take some sort of warlike action against Britain – partly because, from the viewpoint of the South Atlantic, the decline in British power after the Second World War was not always fully obvious. The first time, as far as is known, that any Argentine Government considered the use of force was in 1976, a few weeks before the coup, when Mrs Perón's military advisors urged her to give orders for the British survey ship *Shackleton* to be fired on, in the mistaken impression that she was carrying Lord Shackleton to South Georgia as part of his mission to investigate the economic prospects of the Falklands and their dependencies. An Argentine ship fired a shot across *Shackleton's* bows, but Isabelita, more careful than her advisers, refused to go any further.

The 1982 invasion was not, therefore, the culmination of a gradual build-up of anger and resentment; there was no public pressure of any kind on the Galtieri régime to do anything. Not even when it became abundantly clear in the months before the invasion took place that the British Government had no plans for satisfying Argentina's demands over the islands, was there any sign of public anger on the part of ordinary people. If there had been demonstrations then, the invasion itself might not have come as such a surprise to the British Government a few weeks later. One of the major factors, though, was the mutual incomprehension between the two countries about the significance of a claim like Argentina's to the Falkland Islands. There are said to be 300 territorial disputes between nations in Latin America, and some of them are contested angrily. Guatemala claims Belize, and Venezuela claims the Esequivo region of Guyana, and there is an underlying bitterness about the two disputes; both Guatemala and Venezuela have a sense of national grievance as a result of them, and each feels somehow diminished in its own eyes and in the eyes of the world. For decades, Argentina was a moderately successful country, which had no sense of being diminished, and during that time the claim on the Falklands was little more than a *pro forma* one. The subject started to take on an importance only when Argentina's self-image began to crumble.

It was hard, too, for Britain to grasp that something as remote and lacking in intrinsic value as the Falklands could stir up so much emotion. Having owned so many pin-points of rock in different parts of the world, to Britain one particular set of pin-points in the South Atlantic scarcely seemed of particular importance. And the language in which some Argentines expressed themselves sounded simply absurd in British ears. 'After a century and a half of shame and dishonour', one Buenos Aires editorial thundered, after the capture of the islands by Argentina, 'each one of us must be prepared to shed his heart's blood to retain what belongs by glorious right to the Fatherland.' By contrast, the Anglo-Saxon view was neatly expressed by the US Secretary of State, Alexander Haig: the Falklands, he said, had been a pimple on the ass of progress for two hundred years. And although Argentines talked optimistically of the oil that might be found off the shores of the group, and Lord Shackleton and other British enthusiasts believed that a fortune could be made from harvesting the krill (small organisms which swam in the waters around the islands), the fact was that with a population of 1,800 and 500,000 sheep, the Falklands had provided less than two million pounds in total tax revenue to the British exchequer in the 22 years from 1951 to 1973: the year when Perón returned to Argentina and the downward spiral in Argentina's economic and political fortunes began in earnest.

Even before the Argentine ship *Almirante Storni* fired across the bows of the *Shackleton*, in Isabelita's last months, the Foreign

Office in London had been mildly nervous that the growing disasters at home might lead her to undertake some kind of adventure connected with the islands. When the incident happened, angry messages were exchanged and the British ambassador in Buenos Aires was withdrawn, though diplomatic relations were otherwise unaffected. But the British were mistaken. Mrs Perón, for all her unsuitability for office, was in fact much too cautious to become involved with Britain, and it was the military dictatorship, welcomed by Britain as likely to have a stabilizing effect on Argentina, which began almost immediately to plan a probing operation against the islands – the first time a government in Buenos Aires had done any such thing. A secret naval expedition established a base on the farthermost island of the South Sandwich group, Southern Thule. When its existence came to light, two years later, the Argentines described it as a scientific station: another indication that they thought it necessary to tread carefully with Britain. In reality it was nothing less than a distant outpost of the Argentine Navy, manned by fifty men and maintained there in order to create the groundwork of an eventual claim to sovereignty. Naturally, the Argentines kept a prudent silence about the Southern Thule base; but what intrigued them was that the British had said nothing about it either. Its existence was discovered by a ham radio operator on the Falklands, but when the Royal Navy's Antarctic survey ship *Endurance* went to investigate her captain was given orders to say nothing about what he found there. The orders came from the Foreign Office in London, via the Ministry of Defence, in order to prevent any outcry in Britain about the existence of the base, and any demand for its removal. It was not until the summer of 1978 that the House of Commons was told that the Argentines had established themselves on Southern Thule, and even then there was no clear demand from London for its removal. The judgment in Whitehall was that any such demand would goad the Argentines into doing something worse, but the lack of a strong reaction by the British Government had in fact already convinced even the more cautious members of the Argentine junta that it would be safe to go further. In November 1977 the Argentine Navy had plans for establishing a larger base on another island in the South Sandwich group, but this time British naval intelligence got word of it, and the Callaghan government acted with more determination. Two frigates and a submarine were sent down from the Caribbean, and although officials at the Foreign Office in London have maintained that the Argentines were not informed that this small predecessor of the 1982 Task Force was on its way (James Callaghan himself says they were told, but indirectly) the plan to repeat the Southern Thule operation lapsed.

The links between the Royal Navy and the Argentine Navy have always been strong, and many senior Argentine officers have been trained in Britain. It is highly likely, therefore, that one or other of the organizations that make up British intelligence had reasonably good information from Argentina. If so, it is probable that London had long known about the Argentine Navy's plan for the invasion of the Falklands, drawn up in the 1950s and revised in or around 1968 by a senior officer of the naval staff, Captain Jorge Anaya. The plan demonstrated that it would be possible to occupy the islands with a minimum of bloodshed; and when Admiral Emilio Massera took over the most senior post in the Navy, at the insistence of the newly returned Perón in 1973, he soon consulted Anaya about the plan and added a gloss of his own: the invasion should be bloodless, the inhabitants of the islands should be transported to neutral territory – either Brazil or Uruguay – and their places taken by carefully selected Argentine settlers. The model would be India's takeover of Goa in 1961; the most that Argentina would have to endure from Britain would be a serious complaint at the United Nations: the sole course of action which had been left to the Portuguese after the *fait accompli* in their former colony on the Indian sub-continent. Portugal, however, lacked the means as well as the will to resist the takeover; the ebullient, cynically persuasive Massera convinced Anaya, a much quieter, more thoughtful and more puritanical man, that Britain would never have the will to recover the islands, even if she had the means, but it would be necessary to wait until the means no longer existed either.

Anaya, almost alone of the senior figures in the military governments of 1976 to 1983, was never to be accused of corruption. A small, saturnine figure with dark, almost black eyes, he was a quintessential Argentine patriot who believed that the Falklands should be recovered, not as an act of political expediency, but as a matter of principle. He was profoundly anti-British, and while based in Britain refused on principle to learn English. He also took a hawkish line on the Beagle Channel dispute with Chile and on Argentina's claim to Antarctic territory, but he was passionate on the subject of the Falklands and on the likely success of the strategy he and Massera had between them worked out. He regarded it as an article of faith that Argentina should repossess the islands before the hundred and fiftieth anniversary of their takeover by Britain, which would fall in January 1983. And now, a little over a year before the anniversary, he was a member of the military junta governing Argentina, and he was a personal friend and close ally of the junta's leader, General Leopoldo Fortunato Galtieri. The timing was perfect.

The Galtieri family had emigrated from Italy to Argentina just before the turn of the century, and its history could be that of hundreds of thousands of other Argentine families. Galtieri's grandmother came from the slums of Genoa, but she had married a peasant from a small village in Calabria who had gone to Genoa to find work. When they made the long journey to Argentina and settled in Buenos Aires they found that conditions were scarcely better than they had been at home; though the difference was that Argentina was, if anything, under-populated compared with Italy, and there were virtually no class distinctions to hold back a Calabrian peasant, if he were quick-minded and intelligent. But the first generation Argentine Galtieris were not to make their fortune in the new country, and it was left to the second to establish themselves and build a more comfortable basis for the family. The sons found their natural element in the Argentine Army, and in small business concerns, and though the shopkeepers prospered a little, it was Galtieri's father, a non-commissioned officer in the Army, who was in the best position to ensure that the next generation could achieve the kind of success that the original immigrants from Genoa can scarcely even have dreamed of. Leopoldo, at the age of thirteen, managed to get a place at a secondary school run by the Army. It was a good education, and did not automatically lead to an Army career – indeed, by an extraordinary coincidence, two other thirteen-year-olds who were cadets in Galtieri's class were to have a profound effect on the country's future, but neither of them went on to join the Army. One was the future Admiral Jorge Anaya, whose obsession with reclaiming the Falklands led Galtieri into the absurd gamble of April 1982; the other, who was to become a lawyer after cadet school, was Raúl Alfonsín – the man elected with a sweeping mandate in October 1983 to restore civilian government after the years of destruction caused by Galtieri and his colleagues in the military leadership.

Leopoldo Galtieri was a competent rather than a clever cadet, but he had great confidence in himself and his ability to make his way in the world; his parents seem to have foreseen this by giving him the middle name of Fortunato, which was not a family name, and Galtieri himself is said to have believed strongly in his good luck. His openness and friendly character stood him in good stead when he began to rise in the ranks of the Army, and he was able to call on a wide circle of influence in a service which was always the most open to talent of the three Argentine armed forces. His friends found him generous and given to rather Italianate gestures of kindness, but he was also capable of occasional brutality, and seems to have had no compunction about ordering the arrest and torture of suspects during the Dirty War. There were stories during the period of his presidency that he had personally taken part in the torture of political prisoners, but such stories were told about a number of senior military men, and few of them have been substantiated. In general, people like Galtieri wanted to rid the country of political extremism, but preferred not to know how it was done.

His handsome, fleshy face, the crinkly white hair, the sympathetic network of wrinkles round the eyes, all helped to make Galtieri appear reliable and friendly, and his occasionally generous impulses provided him with a wider range of friends inside and outside the Army than most senior officers could call on. At some point during the early Seventies, when he and the quiet, intense Admiral Anaya sat together on a number of inter-service boards, the two of them renewed their boyhood friendship, and for once the institutional mistrust which was usually present between the upper echelons of the Army and the Navy could be set aside. There is no record, up to this stage, that Galtieri had shown anything other than a conventional interest in Argentina's disputes with Britain over the Falklands, or with Chile over the Beagle Channel. But from the moment when Anaya became the Navy's representative in the ruling junta, and therefore the second most powerful man in Argentina, it became certain that at one point or another he would demand a commitment to the recovery of the islands as the price for giving Galtieri his full political support. The issue arose almost immediately. Galtieri, confident of his powers and certain that he was the man to rescue Argentina from the atmosphere of decline and decay which had enshrouded the last days of Videla and the brief reign of Viola, wanted a change in the political structure to give himself greater personal scope.The 'Fourth Man' structure, forced upon General Videla by Admiral

Massera in the days when he still believed in a political future for himself, did not suit Galtieri at all; he wanted to be the President of the Republic as well as the Army commander. But the Navy, having created the structure in the person of Massera, had to agree to its dismantling in the person of Admiral Anaya. Galtieri can have had few doubts about paying Anaya's price. His public relations men had already presented him to the Argentine press as a man of decision, a bluff no-nonsense soldier who would take whatever steps were necessary to give Argentina its rightful place in the world as a major power, and it was probably clear to him even before he took over as President that this might well require him to involve the country in a foreign war. The economic and political situation inside Argentina was worsening, and for all Galtieri's self-confidence and his belief in his good fortune, he must have been aware of the need to break out of the narrowing circle of failure in which the military government found itself. The economy, in particular, was in serious trouble, and although Martínez de Hoz, the Finance Minister under Videla, had been sacked by Viola, his replacement was a man whose doctrinaire enthusiasm for the free market and its forces was even greater. The watchwords with which Dr Roberto Alemann introduced his first budget in January 1982 were 'deflate, deregulate, denationalize'. Taxation was increased savagely, public sector wages were frozen. Against a background of increasing public hostility, it was a risky thing to do; for the first time since the 1976 coup there were starting to be demonstrations against the military government itself, and on 7 November 1981 there had been a march of fifty thousand workers, white-collar as well as blue-collar, which the unions had organized under the slogan 'Peace, Bread and Work'. Not long before, such a demonstration would have been impossible, but now the lid was starting to come off Argentine society with a vengeance and Galtieri and his colleagues knew it would be almost impossible to clamp it on again: the necessary will-power could not be summoned up in the armed forces after five years of failure in government. To the ruling junta, the idea of staging some spectacular diversion seemed very attractive indeed.

And yet as late as January 1982 there was no certainty in Galtieri's circle where this spectacular should be staged. No doubt the necessary assurances had been given to Anaya that something would be done about the Falklands before the hundred and fiftieth anniversary , but at that stage it was still a year away. Chile and the Beagle Channel provided a quarrel nearer to hand, and to some extent more pressing. There had already been trouble between the two countries the previous April, when two Argentine officers were arrested in Chile on spying charges. Ignoring the fact that several Chilean officers were in Argentine gaols on precisely similar charges, the junta closed the border with Chile in retaliation for what it called an intolerable provocation. For a time the dispute died down, but now that Galtieri was President, replacing the more cautious Viola, and the efforts by Brigadier Lami Dozo, the Air Force representative on the junta, to negotiate a diplomatic solution had broken down, the dangerous step was taken of repudiating the ten-year-old treaty between Chile and Argentina, which provided for the arbitration of border disputes through the International Court of Justice. That was on 21 January 1982; war was averted only because the Chilean leader, General Pinochet, was a great deal too wary to become embroiled in a fight he could not be certain of winning, especially when the United States was using all its influence to stop it happening. There can be no better evidence, however, of the haphazard nature of Galtieri's aggressive instincts than this incident – and no clearer proof that an attack on the Falklands was far from being the junta's one central purpose. As it was, Galtieri despatched some of Argentina's best trained professional soldiers, from the Third Army Corps and the Eighth Mountain Infantry Brigade, to guard the mountain passes that connect Chile with Argentina. As troops, they were far superior to the conscripts who were sent later to the Falklands, but they were obliged to remain in their positions in the Andes throughout the war with Britain, guarding against a possibility even more dangerous than the recapture of the Falklands: a surprise invasion of Argentina itself by Chile.

Galtieri would never have taken any action, either against Chile or against the Falklands, if he had not been certain of being highly regarded in Washington. From the moment he became Argentina's President, in December 1981, the American Embassy in Buenos Aires and the new administration of Ronald Reagan in Washington had regarded him as a useful ally. The embassy found him more down to earth, more inclined to backslapping humour, than the dull Viola or the restrained, fastidious, aristocratic Videla. But the real change had come a year before in November 1980, and not so much because of the character of Argentina's military leaders as of a complete turnabout in US policy towards Latin America and Argentina in particular. The incoming administration had no time for what its leading figures saw as Jimmy Carter's self-defeating obsession with human rights. The real battle, President Reagan's advisers believed, was against Communism in the southern hemisphere, and in order to ensure that the United States had strong allies in that battle it was prepared to overlook, as Carter's administration had not been, what one State Department official described as 'a more robust approach' to internal security. The new doctrine, enthusiastically adopted by Mrs Jeane Kirkpatrick, the United Nations ambassador appointed by the Reagan administration, was based on a definition set out as far back as 1949 by Francis Adams Truslow, chairman of the New York Council on Foreign Relations, who was justifying United States support for the Nicaraguan dictator, Anastasio Somoza. Truslow distinguished between dictatorships which involved autocratic rule, and totalitarianism, which he defined as 'autocratic rule, plus total, absolute control of economic life as, for example, communism'. He went on to say, 'Totalitarianism we refuse to co-operate with, but with dictatorships we will.' There might have been a case for arguing that the deliberate militarization of every aspect of the Argentine economy after 1976 had brought the dictatorship there much closer to the definition of totalitarianism than run-of-the-mill right-wing autocracies of the kind the Reagan Administration was supporting elsewhere in Latin America; but that was scarcely the purpose of the doctrine, which was intended simply as a formula to explain why the United States backed régimes that treated their populations no whit less badly than ones on the Marxist model did.

Directly the Reagan Administration moved into the White House, in January 1981, the atmosphere was transformed, as far as Argentina's military régime was concerned. Human rights as a matter of United States concern in Argentina was scarcely mentioned again. The Carter Administration's arms embargo was brought to an end, and the Argentine armed forces were encouraged to regard the United States once again as a major supplier. In exchange, Washington got exactly what it wanted from Buenos Aires: an active, anti-Communist stance and a willingness to send advisors, and possibly even combat troops, to El Salvador, Guatemala, Honduras and Bolivia in order to help the fight against left-wing subversion. The Americans were particularly impressed by Galtieri. When he visited Washington in November 1981, as commander of the Army but not yet President, Reagan's national security adviser Richard Allen described him publicly, in the phrase that echoed around Argentina for months, as being 'possessed of a majestic personality'.

The following month, almost certainly with Washington's foreknowledge, Galtieri elbowed the sickly Viola aside and took over the presidency. For the Americans, he was ideally suited to the job. Apart from an ability to intrigue his way through the upper levels of the military hierarchy, he had absolutely no political experience and would be unlikely to succeed in outmanoeuvring Washington. Secondly, he represented a new beginning; the crimes of the Videla years were fading, and he quickly replaced most of the leading figures who had served during those years with new men of his own. In his conversations with senior officials in the Reagan Administration Galtieri seems to have offered to withdraw from the Non-Aligned Movement, and in the week of his takeover there were strong reports that the Argentine military attaché in Washington, General Miguel Mallea Gil, had begun negotiating with the Pentagon about the price Argentina would be paid in return for allowing the United States access to a base in Patagonia. Whether or not the subject of the Falklands was raised during this heady period is uncertain; Argentine officials have hinted that it was, United States officials have denied it. What no doubt happened is that, in the welter of subjects on which there was general agreement, the Argentines made general points about possessing rightful sovereignty over the islands, while the Americans, though not specifically agreeing, gave the impression that they understood and sympathized.

The newspaper columnist Jesus Iglesias Rouco, a small narrow-faced man with white hair and long expressive hands, was one of the stars of the newspaper *La Prensa*. Rouco had excellent contacts which included the Foreign Minister, Nicanor Costa Méndez, and may have extended to the President himself. On 17 January 1982, he wrote in his column, 'Everything indicates that in the opinion of people at the topmost level of power, the solution of the Malvinas question depends on that of the Beagle Channel. Or vice versa. I repeat: or vice versa.' The message was none too clear, but that was more likely the fault of the minds who had thought it up, than of Rouco himself. Shorn of its gnomic quality, the meaning seemed to be that once the necessary steps had been taken to sort out one of the two problems in Argentina's favour, the other would automatically be settled in the same year. Clearly Rouco had received a hint of what had already been decided: that by the end of the southern hemisphere's winter, about September of 1982, when the Navy's pilots would have been trained in the use of their new batch of French Super-Etendards and air-to-ground Exocet missiles, and the British survey vessel *Endurance* would have been withdrawn as part of Whitehall's planned defence cuts, Argentina would be free to move into the Falkland Islands and take them without firing a shot and without spilling any blood – exactly as India, twenty years before, had taken Goa from the Portuguese. There would be no military response from Britain, any more than there had been from Portugal over Goa. What was more, Washington would not permit one of its close allies to fight another – and Galtieri and his colleagues, after the kind words of Mrs Kirkpatrick and Richard Allen, believed themselves to be just as close an ally to the United States as Britain was. A week later, Rouco's column was a great deal more specific: Buenos Aires would demand firm negotiations with Britain within a short time scale on the future of the islands, and Washington would give its support in advance for any action that might be required, including military action, to get the islands back. If the negotiations broke down, Buenos Aires would take the islands by force this year – 1982 – though it was determined not to shed any blood unless it was necessary to do so.

The problem was, Argentina was not the Soviet Union. If such an article had appeared in *Pravda*, or if it had come out on TASS prefaced by the words 'TASS is authorized to state . . .', then everyone would have known that it was indeed firm government policy. But journalism in Argentina is a free-range affair. Reporters pick up stories in competition with other reporters, and often get them wrong, even at times of great military repression. As a result, even though Rouco had picked up the signals with absolute correctness, and his article expressed precisely what Galtieri and Costa Méndez were thinking, it was impossible for outsiders to be certain. The US Embassy did not feel, on the strength of a column in *La Prensa*, that it should jeopardize its interests with so useful and friendly a government by warning that it would not give its backing for some hypothetical operation, and so the question was never raised in the embassy's dealings with the Argentine junta. The British Embassy noted the column too, but interpreted it as being an attempt to warn the Foreign Office that the long-drawn-out negotiations between the two countries about the islands' future would have to achieve something concrete soon. Rouco's prophecies were mentioned in a telegram to London, but not given any great weight. The Foreign Office desk dealing with Argentina agreed.

At the very beginning of the nineteenth century, after two British expeditions had captured Buenos Aires in 1806 and 1807 and had both been expelled by the city's inhabitants, the government in London decided that its relations with South America were better conducted through business than through colonization. It was Italian peasants who colonized Argentina – people like General Galtieri's grandparents – but Britain dominated the economy. The railways, in particular, were founded and built by British capital: the Central Argentine, the Buenos Aires and Pacific, the Buenos Aires Great Southern. British engineers drove the trains and oversaw the stations. British companies dominated the meat-packing trade, shipping, insurance, banking – Lloyds Bank International is the direct descendant of the London and River Plate Bank, founded in 1862. In 1900 Britain provided 90 per cent of all the foreign investment in Argentina. But the twentieth century, which has seen the gradual shrinking of Britain in matters of trade as well as political power, saw the British involvement in Argentina shrink too. By 1923, the British share of investment was 66 per cent and by 1939 it was 50 per cent. But Argentina still saw itself as an honorary member of the British Commonwealth, despite the gradual pressure from countries like Canada and Australia, which really were members of the Empire, for Britain to give them preferential access to the valuable British market for beef. In 1933 Argentina's first military government signed the humiliating Roca-Runciman Treaty with Great Britain, which gave (sometimes at the Argentine negotiators' own suggestion) such concessions as an end to the independent bus and tram operators' lines in Buenos Aires, and their replacement by British-owned companies. But the Second World War, which made Britain's decline all the faster, also cut the links with Argentina. The wartime military governments in Buenos Aires looked to Hitler and Mussolini, not the Allies, and Perón's brand of populism after the war led him to undermine the big British business interests, which supported the aristocracy of Argentina.

As trade dwindled, so did the mutual interest and awareness. The figure for British investment in Argentina from 1977 to 1981 was precisely 0.8 per cent and no fewer than eleven countries invested more. For Argentina, and especially for military governments there, which based themselves on ideas of discipline and

Christianity, Britain had become irreversibly decadent, sinking into poverty and socialism. It may be, too, that many senior military men, with the experience of Mrs Perón behind them, believed that no country governed by a woman could act strongly or decisively. As for Britain, there was little or no understanding of the origins of the crisis in the South Atlantic which arose suddenly in the last days of March 1982. Few of the speeches made in the House of Commons during the emergency debate on the day after the invasion showed any serious awareness of the nature of the country, and it was noticeable that almost none of the MPs who made accusations about the fascist nature of the Argentine junta had spoken out or taken any interest on the few brief occasions in the past when the Commons had briefly touched on the repression in Argentina. Indeed, the only times the repression had been mentioned, it was always in the context of the future of the Falkland Islands, and there is evidence that successive British Governments, Labour and Conservative, preferred to bring the subject up in the Commons as little as possible, in order to prevent relations with Argentina from becoming more difficult.

If each side had been a little more aware of the other, it might at least have ensured that the signals which Britain and Argentina were making in the run-up to the invasion were not so disastrously misread. Nevertheless, the problem was not that the signals were ignored; it was that the Argentines, in particular, thought they read them with great clarity. The British decision to say nothing for two years about the probing expedition to Southern Thule, for instance, or the way in which the government of James Callaghan made it abundantly clear that it had no interest in putting into effect the recommendations in the Shackleton Report on methods of making the Falkland Islands more productive, and thus strengthening its links with the British Crown. By the time Mrs Thatcher replaced Mr Callaghan as Prime Minister, the signals were already clear as far as the Argentines were concerned: Britain had no interest in keeping the islands, and was looking for a way to get rid of them. The new Conservative Government, elected on a platform of cutting public expenditure and (among other things) tightening up on immigration, only reinforced the Argentine view. A far-reaching series of changes in the nature of British nationality ensured that the Falkland Islanders, like citizens of other British colonial territories around the world, were deprived of full citizenship rights; while the 1982 round of spending cuts not only envisaged a serious reduction in the Royal

Navy's ability to fight a war at long distance, but also specifically included the withdrawal of the research ship *Endurance*, which was in fact 'stuffed' (to use the expression of one of her senior officers) with electronic listening equipment and acted partly as an early-warning system to guard against an Argentine attack on the Falklands. The Argentine Foreign Ministry, keen to find evidence for what it believed it knew anyway, was convinced that its analysis of British intentions was accurate. But there was another, more personal reason for the judgment. The new Foreign Minister in Buenos Aires, whom Galtieri and Anaya between them had appointed, had served in the post before, and in 1967, when he had opened negotiations on new links between the islands and the mainland with the British Foreign Secretary, George Brown, he received the very strong impression that Mr Brown and his Foreign Office advisers knew the damage that possession of the islands was doing to Britain's relations both with Argentina and the rest of South America, and wanted nothing better than to hand them over. The Foreign Minister in question was Dr Nicanor Costa Méndez.

Suitably enough, Dr Costa Méndez's office is situated next door to the Ministry of Defence, and overlooks the headquarters of the armed forces. It is an expensive office, panelled with light-coloured wood and thickly carpeted. Costa Méndez himself sits behind a vast desk, and smiles. It is a familiar smile, seen on hundreds of millions of television screens throughout the world during the Falklands crisis and the war which followed it. It is also slightly misleading. Nicanor Costa Méndez is a witty man, and the way his secretaries look after him is an indication that his attractiveness to women, for which he was once famous, is not altogether a thing of the past. But he is a tough and in some ways rather bitter man, who happens to smile easily. He bears no responsibility whatever, though, for the events of the Dirty War; he may well have sympathized with the attempt to crack down on subversion, but he was not a part of the government which carried out the real excesses, and he has not sought to justify them, at least publicly. He is, in fact, a survivor of a slightly older breed of Argentine conservative. Socially, he has little in common with people like Leopoldo Galtieri, who has never quite thrown off the air of the third-generation Italian immigrant. The Army which Costa Méndez supports is the Army of the 1930s and 1940s, the polo-playing officers in British-tailored sports clothes, who moved in the same social circles as the Anglo-Argentines who owned and operated the railways and the big cattle ranches. Sitting at his desk, wearing a well-cut suit of grey English wool, an airmail copy of *The Economist* in front of him, there is something almost mocking about his English, and when he asks if this expression or that is a correct one, it is as though he is saying ironically, 'I know that I am only a benighted foreigner, but I am trying my best.' In the 1970s he was a visiting lecturer at St Anthony's College, Oxford. Even the stick he uses to walk with – he was a victim of the Argentine polio epidemic of 1956 – is carved in an expensively English style.

Nowadays, he supports the civilian government of Raúl Alfonsín wholeheartedly, and has little, either good or bad, to say about the military government in which he served as civilian Foreign Minister. But he is frank about the judgement which he contributed so much to – the judgement that Britain would not react militarily to an invasion of the Falklands. It was a mistake, he says, a complete misreading of the importance Britain attached, not to the islands – which he is still convinced that consecutive British governments have wanted to hand over to Argentina – but to the fact of seeing territory it occupied being forcibly taken over. It had never occurred to any of them that a Western European government would react in that way in the last quarter of the twentieth century; they had supposed that the days when Europe fought wars for colonial possessions were over. It was also a grave mistake – and he makes it sound as though, in his judgement, the mistake was more serious than his misreading of British reactions – to assume that the United States would regard its relationship with Argentina as being just as important as its relationship with Britain. 'We learned some lessons,' he says. But he must realize that the main responsibility was his. Galtieri and Anaya were men with very little understanding of the outside world, and depended heavily on his judgement. Costa Méndez was regarded as one of the country's foremost experts on foreign affairs; if he told them that Britain would limit itself to complaining about the invasion at the United Nations, and that Washington would step in to prevent the British from taking military action, then Galtieri and Anaya would believe him implicitly. The problem was that Costa Méndez was, despite his enthusiasm for things British, an extreme right-wing patriot who believed passionately in the return of the islands to Argentine control, and had founded the Institute and National Museum of the Malvinas Islands and their Dependencies as long before as 1966. And he, like so many other Argentines, subscribed to the macro-political view about the strategic importance of the South Atlantic in the world-wide struggle against Soviet Communism, a struggle in which his own observations told him that Britain had already fallen. In Nietzsche's phrase, Costa Méndez's undoubted intellect had become the servant of blind will.

At the beginning of 1982, though, there was no intention whatever of forcing the issue. The Navy's idea was to build up slowly to an all-out operation which would take place in about October. In the meantime, another probing operation of the kind that had proved successful on Southern Thule in 1976 (the 'scientific station' established there was still in place) would be launched, this time against the main island in the Dependencies, South Georgia itself. The operation would be led by the notorious commander of one of the kidnap gangs from the Navy Mechanics School in Buenos Aires, Lt-Cdr Alfredo Astiz, apparently with the idea of wiping the slate clean in the eyes of the public by associating him with a major patriotic triumph. The Navy's first plan had been to send Astiz and a group of men from ESMA to South Georgia in December, but for some reason – perhaps connected with the possibility of war with Chile – the operation was cancelled at the last minute. A new opportunity soon arose, in the unlikely person of Constantino Davidoff. Davidoff was a well-to-do businessman, whose interests varied from used cars to dealing in scrap metal. He has always denied any connections with the military, especially over the South Georgia affair, but his timing, from the Navy's point of view, was superb. In December, not long after the cancellation of Astiz's assignment, Davidoff visited the harbour at Leith, on South Georgia, to inspect the remains of a whaling station, abandoned 16 years earlier. From a scrap metal merchant's point of view the profits must have been doubtful. Most of the whaling station was built of wood, and the only source of scrap metal was the corrugated iron roofs of most of the buildings, the remains of a short railway, and the rusting mechanisms for hoisting the whaling boats out of the water and rendering down the bodies of the whales. Nevertheless, Davidoff returned to Buenos Aires having decided to go ahead with the scheme, and a week or so later he visited naval headquarters. Whether he or the Navy had initiated the idea is impossible to establish; what is certain is that, even if Davidoff had dreamed up the idea on his own, prudence would have caused him to inform the Navy of his plans, and sound out its willingness to give him support if the need should arise. The Navy made it abundantly clear that it would back him to the hilt, and offered to let him charter Navy transport to do the job. The decision was taken to begin the recovery of the scrap metal at Leith in March.

Costa Méndez, however, seems to have known nothing of the Navy's plans. His deadline remained October – the target date for the takeover of the main islands – and he began the diplomatic ground-work. The aim was to prove to the world at large that Britain had no intention of satisfying Argentina's demands for possession of the islands, but no serious alternative plans either. His judgement, on this at least, was precisely accurate. In December 1980 the junior Foreign Office minister Nicholas Ridley reported to the House of Commons on the plan he had been negotiating with Argentina and the Falkland Islanders for giving the Argentines long-term sovereignty over the islands, while allowing for their continued administration until such time as the lease agreed with Buenos Aires should run out. It was a copy-book Foreign Office solution. But MPs from all sides of the House, aware of the hostility of the islanders, attacked Ridley savagely over the plan to such an extent that the Conservative Whips, who controlled government business in the Commons, warned Mrs Thatcher that they could not ensure a majority for Ridley's proposals, if it came to a vote. The Prime Minister herself decided hastily that the idea should be dropped. With its passing, British ideas for solving the problem positively had run out, and there was nothing left to do except to play for time. Costa Méndez, understanding this, refused to allow the British any time to play for.

In January 1982, Costa Méndez was one of fewer than a dozen people who knew of the invasion plan; not even his deputy, Enrique Ros, was told; and so Ros began a round of negotiations which were to prove crucial to the unfolding of the crisis, without himself understanding their basic purpose. Nevertheless, when the talks began in New York the following month, Ros was under strict orders from Costa Méndez to negotiate toughly. On 26 and 27 February, at a series of meetings in the British and Argentine diplomatic missions in the city, and over lunch in one extremely expensive French restaurant as well, Ros demanded a permanent British-Argentine commission to examine the question, with monthly meetings and an alternating chairmanship. He also demanded that the commission should report its findings by the end of the year. Much to the Argentines' surprise, the British minister at the talks, Richard Luce, agreed to the idea of the commission, and Enrique Ros, who had a considerable affection for Britain and often found his military masters boorish and objectionable, was delighted. As far as he knew, his mission was to reach agreement with the British; and he and Luce worked out a joint statement which spoke of the 'cordial and positive atmosphere' of the talks. When Costa Méndez read the text, back in Buenos Aires, he was furious. The purpose of the talks had been to push Britain into a corner, not to create a cordial atmosphere, and so, instead of issuing the statement from the Foreign Ministry, as had been agreed, Costa Méndez put out a version of his own, saying that unless Argentina were given sovereignty over the Falklands in the near future, it would use other means to get them back. At that stage, though, Costa Méndez himself did not realize that the other means were only 33 days from being employed.

Small wars have small causes. In the case of the Falklands War, the immediate cause came in the cold early morning of 19 March, when the elderly Argentine naval transport, *Bahía Buen Suceso*, off-loaded a group of 39 workmen at Port Leith. They were working for a hastily-founded company called Georgias del Sur SA, headed by Constantino Davidoff, who had applied two weeks before to the British Embassy in Buenos Aires for permission to go to South Georgia to dismantle the whaling station. The embassy, noting that Davidoff had negotiated a contract with the British shipping firm Christian Salvesen, which owned the whaling station, agreed. Once ashore, two men – the foreman, Antonio Patané, and a doctor attached to the expedition, Rúben Pereira – located the flagstaff which was already in place there, and ran up the Argentine flag while the rest of the group sang the national anthem. In the chilly desolation of South Georgia, it did not occur to anyone that they might be under observation – but they were. A British scientist, Peter Hutchinson, had been taking observations in the hills above Leith when he saw the *Bahía Buen Suceso* come inshore, and he swiftly reported back to base at Grytviken about the arrival of the Argentine party and the raising of the flag. The news passed by radio to Port Stanley, in the Falklands, and from there it was relayed to the Foreign Office in London. The following morning, Saturday 20 March, *Endurance* was ordered to leave Port Stanley and make for South Georgia, taking with her a detachment of marines, who were to be landed on the island, and two Whirlwind helicopters.

From the moment *Endurance* received her orders, the entire

Argentine timetable for the recovery of the Falklands was wrecked. It was no longer a matter of waiting until *Endurance* herself had been withdrawn from the South Atlantic, and Argentine pilots had been fully trained in the use of their new French fighters; it was a matter of reinforcing a position already established. On 23 March an Argentine naval survey ship, *Bahía Paraiso*, passed *Endurance* at the entrance to Leith harbour, and headed inshore. On board was Lt-Cdr Astiz, together with his group from ESMA and one or two other naval murder gangs. What neither they nor the men in Buenos Aires who had sent them knew was that the commander of *Endurance*, Captain Nicholas Barker, was under orders not to disturb the men of Davidoff's scrap metal company, but simply to put pressure on them to get the necessary authorization from the British Antarctic Survey base at Grytviken for their presence on the island (one of the stipulations the British Embassy in Buenos Aires had made when it gave Davidoff permission to dismantle the whaling station). Costa Méndez, having assured his masters that Britain would not intervene militarily to stop an invasion of the Falklands, now agreed with them in interpreting what was in fact a warning action as the beginnings of a military response. Britain, on the other hand, was anxious not to make the situation worse, and yet had done so. On the evening of 26 March, Costa Méndez attended a meeting at the Libertador building with Galtieri, Anaya and Lami Dozo, together with the chiefs of staff of the three services. It was decided to send two corvettes, *Granville* and *Drummond* – both of which took their names from British officers attached to the Argentine Navy early in the nineteenth century – from their position off the Uruguayan coast where they were taking part in manoeuvres, and down to South Georgia. It is believed that information reached London from intelligence sources the same evening that an invasion of the islands was now imminent.

The members of the junta had been in almost continuous session for several days, discussing the situation in South Georgia and the question of when *Operación Rosario*, their code name for the invasion, should take place. On 28 March another *La Prensa* journalist with excellent military contacts wrote a story which apparently contained accurate information from the meetings Galtieri and the others were holding. Published in the paper the following day, it said, 'It is in the South that the historical destiny of the Argentine Republic will be played out.' But the military leadership had signally failed to work up a warlike atmosphere in

Argentina during the period of the crisis in South Georgia. On Tuesday 30th, the big Perónist union grouping, the CGT, called a massive demonstration in the centre of Buenos Aires, calling for 'Peace, bread and work', and the tens of thousands of people who supported the strike headed for the Plaza de Mayo for the first open confrontation with the authorities since the coup of 1976. A new chant was heard: 'Se va a acabar, se va a acabar, la dictadura militar' – 'The military dictatorship is going to fall, it's going to fall'. The timing of the demonstration was purely fortuitous; the CGT organizers had planned it well before the South Georgia crisis blew up. The police responded savagely, using tear gas and water cannon, and four hundred arrests were made. In other cities there were demonstrations as well, and in Mendoza ten people were seriously injured. There is no question that the junta, still in session in the Libertador building, within earshot of the demonstration, were unnerved by it. That night, or possibly in the early hours of the next morning, Galtieri and others took the final decision to launch Operación Rosario. The naval base at Puerto Belgrano is the biggest centre for the ships of the Argentine Navy, and on Sunday 28 the most powerful ship in the fleet, the aircraft carrier *Veinticinco de Mayo*, the destroyers *Hercules* and *Santísima Trinidad*, the submarine *Santa Fe* and the tank transport *Cabo San Antonio*, together with lesser ships, were all grouped together in the harbour, ready to sail for what were described as 'routine manoeuvres'. Together, they composed the 'Flota de Mar' commanded by Rear Admiral Guálter Allara. For the first time in a century, Argentine soldiers and sailors were about to face foreign troops in battle. The *Cabo San Antonio* was weighed down by the landing-craft, lorries, jeeps, ambulances and so on that she carried. One man on board said later that there was scarcely any room even in their bunks, since the eight hundred soldiers and marines had to be fitted in somewhere, and you had to be careful when you walked along the deck because there were so many guns and so much equipment everywhere. Not long after they set sail, they hit bad weather, and many of the soldiers, in particular, became seasick. Sleep became impossible; large objects which had not been properly lashed down broke loose and crashed into others, and knocked them loose as well. The soldiers were forbidden to go out on deck, or even to smoke.

On the morning of Thursday 1 April, the senior officers of the expedition were summoned to a meeting on board the *Santísima Trinidad*, several of them being brought over from the other ships by helicopter. There, they were finally let into the secret of the expedition's purpose. Admiral Allara briefed them on the disposition of British forces on the islands, and warned that if at all possible no British soldier and no islander should be injured. 'You should be firm with the enemy, but courteous,' he said, and he ended, 'Destiny requires that it should be we who have the task of undoing almost a century and a half of usurpation.' He was cheered to the echo.

The atmosphere within the Casa Rosada was not nearly so cheerful. President Reagan tried for nearly two hours to contact Galtieri by telephone that evening, to persuade him at the last moment to order the invasion fleet to turn back. Costa Méndez continued to assure Galtieri that Washington would stay neutral in the dispute, but Galtieri was nervous of speaking to President Reagan, unwilling perhaps to provoke him by an outright refusal. When he finally agreed to take the telephone, Reagan warned him of Mrs Thatcher's firmness of character, and the likely consequences of taking Britain on. 'You don't know her,' Reagan was reported later as having said: 'she's a very difficult woman.' Galtieri's reply sounded firm, but it masked a growing uncertainty: 'Mr President, it isn't possible to turn the fleet back. At the moment the initial phases of the military operation have begun, and they cannot be countermanded.'

Within hours, it all seemed so right. At nine-twenty in the morning, Buenos Aires time, a communiqué was issued to the press which said that there would shortly be a public announcement about the progress of the conflict with Britain over the islands. Reports of the intended invasion had been going the rounds in Buenos Aires since the previous evening and this seemed to confirm everything. Rex Hunt, the Governor of the Falklands, had in fact surrendered only fifty minutes before. The second communiqué was issued in Buenos Aires almost immediately afterwards, and confirmed that the islands had been 'recovered'. A special edition of the pro-government newspaper *La Razón* ran no fewer than four headlines across its front page: the first three, in successively bolder type, read: 'Today Is A Glorious Day For The Fatherland', 'After A Captivity Of A Century And A Half A Sister Is Incorporated Into The National Territory', and 'THE MALVINAS IN ARGENTINE HANDS'. Galtieri gave an address on radio and television at two-thirty that afternoon, in which he said, in his customarily tortuous style, 'We have recovered, thereby safeguarding the national honour, without rancour but with the firmness which circumstances required, the southern islands which belong by legitimate right to the national heritage.' It was to be several more hours before the British Government was able to get independent confirmation that the islands had indeed been invaded and that Rex Hunt had surrendered.

By that time, the crowds were gathering once again in the Plaza de Mayo, but in a very different mood from three days before. This time there were no riot police on duty, and no need for any, as Galtieri appeared on the balcony to the raptures of the crowd, and announced that the junta had simply interpreted the feelings of the Argentine people in staging the invasion. There must have been many thousands in the crowd who had no great love for the military government, and some who had suffered personally from its policies, but even those who doubted the wisdom of a military takeover of the Falklands rejoiced that the Argentine flag should be flying there 149 years after the British had taken possession of the islands. 'Somehow, it made up for all the disappointments,' someone who was there said later, 'even my own personal disappointments. It never occurred to me that the British might come and get the islands back, but even if it had I don't suppose I would have cared. I felt liberated that night, for the first time in years.'

Several weeks later, with British troops back on the Falklands and advancing towards Port Stanley, the formidable Italian journalist Oriana Fallaci sought an interview with Galtieri, and perhaps to her surprise was accepted. Galtieri's advisers may not have been fully aware of her reputation in savaging right-wing leaders; they seem to have believed that she would give them the kind of worldwide publicity which they believed Argentina's case required. Her questions were lengthy, longer often than Galtieri's answers. She attacked him for his *machismo*, blamed him for underestimating Mrs Thatcher because she was a woman, and virtually accused him of imitating Mussolini, but she did manage to get him to admit that he had never expected, either, that Britain would send a task force to recapture the islands. 'Why should a country situated in the heart of Europe,' he asked, 'have so much regard for a few islands so far away in the South Atlantic, which couldn't possibly be of any use to them? It seems to me to be completely devoid of sense.'

Nicanor Costa Méndez has had longer to think about the whole thing, and he is less concerned to put the blame on others. His mistake was to see Britain in stock terms as a power that had declined to the point of paralysis, and not, he says, to have understood the effect that one person could have on its reactions and its attitudes. 'I should have realized, of course,' he says, and he looks away to the rows of neat law books, bound in blue leather. 'But you see, I didn't understand the woman then.' Another pause. 'I have only the greatest respect for Mrs Thatcher,' he says, and the pleasant, attractive smile breaks out again.

# 18 THE CASUALTIES OF WAR

*'All we see is military and economic and ethical defeat. One concludes that any change would be for the better.'* – Jorge Luis Borges.

The temperature in the crowded room is so high that even on a hot evening the windows are steamed up. One person has already come close to fainting, and everyone, men and women alike, have great patches of sweat on their backs and under their arms. The voices drone on, cataloguing injustices and grievances with an obsessive care for detail. Others nod, too taken up with the subject in hand to notice the heat. The average age of the audience is around twenty-two, and they have been drawn there because someone, for once, is prepared to talk about their problems at a time when no one else will. Nevertheless, the group which has called the meeting is an extraordinary mixture of left and right, a kind of socialist Fascism, which uses the language of the left to articulate its views about the duty of everyone to defend the Fatherland; and its complaint is that those who have fought for the Fatherland and suffered for it (one or two of the young men in the audience bear the scars of war) are being ignored or despised by their ungrateful fellow-citizens. Probably only a few of the audience realized that they were coming to a meeting organized by a political party – tiny and irrelevant though the party may be, the fact that someone was prepared to take their problems seriously was enough to bring them along.

The ex-combatants of the Falklands War often compare themselves with Vietnam veterans in the United States, and there is a good deal of accuracy in the comparison. But there is one major difference: the Argentine people took less than three months to turn from near-hysterical support for the invasion of the islands to an outright contempt for the leaders who lost the war with Britain and the soldiers who followed them to defeat. Now, most people ignore the war altogether; there is virtually no sign in Buenos Aires or the other cities and towns of Argentina to show that it ever took place – just an occasional poster, which no one has bothered to take down, almost defensive: 'The Malvinas were, are, and will be Argentine.' Previously, it was the Dirty War which most people preferred to know nothing about; now they have been forcibly made aware of that, it is the war that they have decided to forget. Argentina is a country which is unable to come to terms with all of its history all of the time; there always has to be a blind spot somewhere of one sort or another.

There is a remarkable uniformity about the complaints of the ex-combatants. They rarely so much as mention the British soldiers who defeated them, since for the most part they mostly saw them only when they surrendered. The great majority of Argentine soldiers on the Falklands saw no action of any kind. There is a good deal of self-pity in what they have to say about their experiences; they were all conscripts, and they had had only a basic training, which was insufficient for the circumstances in which they found themselves on the islands. What was more, their officers and NCOs, all of them regular soldiers, despised them and systematically abused them and maltreated them. There was little comradeship, given the fear, and the cold, and the sense of injustice. And the hunger. Almost every ex-combatant speaks of that, and for many of them it was their one, all-encompassing sensation while they were on the Falklands. Oscar David López, who comes from the town of Mercedes, and served in the Sixth Mechanized Infantry Regiment, for instance:

> One minute I was with a whole group of people in the Plaza de Mayo, yelling and shouting that if the British came we were going to break their fucking necks, and there was someone who thought he was Napoleon standing up there on the balcony, sounding off about everything we were going to do; and then the next minute, there I was in the Malvinas. I knew we'd been conned, from the start. There were thirty-six of us, and thirty-four were going to have to fight the war with only 9mm pistols. They punched you, they pushed you around, they hit you with their sticks, standing there with their stripes on their arms, kicking you and calling you cowards. I won't ever forget it. We were stuck nineteen kilometres out of town, and all we had to eat were wild berries, red ones that were bitter and white ones that tasted better. The day before, they'd given us something they called stew, and we were supposed to make do with that in temperatures of twenty below. You could see soldiers fighting

for the officers' left-overs. Hunger can make you go mad. They'd threaten to use their guns, just to get more of the dishwater which was all we got to eat. We were so hungry, we were like savages. Once, when the sergeant shouted at us to take cover in the trenches because they were firing shells at us, we just laughed and carried on heating up some milk we had. We were so hungry and so tired, it nearly drove us out of our minds. Once I saw a mate of mine, from the same stake-out, being hit over the head by them. He died after that.

López, like many of the other ex-combatants, rarely bothers to say who 'they' were; they were the officers, the sergeants and the corporals: men who had a certain *esprit de corps* themselves, but who regarded the conscripts as useless rabble, and the cause of their impending defeat. And yet, in the minds of men like López, society itself treated them in much the same way when they were repatriated by the British:

> We were sorry and pleased at the same time when we got back. We'd hated the Malvinas, and yet when we left them we'd learned almost to love them because of all the sacrifices we'd had to make there, and the sweat, and our mates who'd died there. And when we landed at El Palomar and went through San Miguel, it was a Sunday, and there were plenty of young people out and about, but no one took any notice of us. We yelled out, 'We've come back from the war,' but they didn't say anything to us or speak to us. I was so angry, that day, I could have grabbed the NCOs and killed the lot of them. We may have been defeated, but we gave everything we could.

There is a violent note in López's voice now, a note that has made many Argentine ex-combatants turn to alcohol, or drugs, or suicide:

> When they say on TV that they're going to give us all jobs, they're just making fun of us. Why, otherwise, do they turn you down for stupid reasons, like you've got flat feet or something, when you go after a job, say with the telephone company? How come you're good enough to go into the army, but you can't get a job back here? [And then the self-pity comes back.] I'm not crazy or anything, so I'm not going to any psychiatrist. It's just that my nerves were affected by the bombing and the things I

saw, that's all. A psychiatrist might feel sorry for me, but he couldn't help me. Sometimes I think, what do they expect us to do? Do they just think we're going to go crazy, like the Vietnam veterans, and start loosing off against society? I wonder.

The ex-combatants are an embarrassment, and they are punished as such. If they were wounded, they can expect little or nothing in the way of a pension. If they were killed, their parents sometimes – but not always – received a lump sum in the way of compensation. In the case of Mrs Marta Vassallo, whose son Angel went down in the cruiser *General Belgrano*, it amounted to about US$2,800. 'My son wasn't brought up to fight in wars', she says. 'He wasn't very brave, and I was sorry at the time when he started his military service. I didn't agree with the war, I don't think any war is right.' When Admiral Franco gave her a medal to commemorate her son's death, at a ceremony a year after the *Belgrano* went down, she refused to speak to him. Unable to restrain the tears now, she says: 'Nothing will bring my son back. But I feel so unhappy, and so powerless to do anything. And I feel bitter, too, against the people who killed him – the Americans and the English. He wasn't a hero, he was a martyr. He couldn't defend himself.'

The sinking of the *Belgrano* came as the most savage shock to Argentina. The euphoria which had swept the country in the early days after Argentine troops had landed on the Falklands and the small contingent of British marines had been led humiliatingly away had subsided a little, but almost nobody thought the British naval task force, sailing for the South Atlantic against all the expectations of Nicanor Costa Méndez and President Galtieri, would actually be called upon to fight. There would, everybody assumed, be a negotiated peace before that occurred. And then, at around three o'clock on the afternoon of 2 May with the *Belgrano* in his sights, Captain Chris Wreford-Brown of the British nuclear submarine *Conqueror* gave the order to fire two torpedoes from a range of five thousand yards. The *Belgrano* was 35 miles away from the Total Exclusion Zone imposed around the Falklands by the British, and was heading north-west towards the Argentine coast, away from the islands. The first torpedo struck her towards the stern, below the engine compartments; three seconds later, the second one hit her near the bows. But the damage, both structural and in human terms, had already been done. The official *Gaceta Marinera*, published ten days later, reported that the force of the first explosion had been upwards, and had gone through four decks, completely destroying two of the crew's main sleeping-quarters, the canteen, and the ship's galley. All power went instantly, and the survivors had to fight their way through the darkness and the thick smoke which was rapidly filling the entire ship. Within twenty minutes of the first explosion, the *Belgrano* was listing to port – the side on which both torpedoes had struck – at an angle of 21 degrees. Five minutes later her captain, Héctor Bonzo, saw that there was no point any longer in trying to fight the fires that were raging, and gave the order to abandon ship. Miguel Angel Alvárez was one of the hundreds of men who had to make their way through the dense fumes and the heat. He had been asleep at the time of the impact, and threw himself out of his bunk wearing only shorts and a sweater. He ran for the escape hatch in the darkness, with the roar of the flames and the screaming of injured and frightened men all round him. But the hatch was small, only large enough to take one man at a time, and he had to wait some time with a panicking group until it was his turn. Once he got in, he found that fuel oil had leaked into it, and had filled it almost to the top. But there was no alternative; he had to plunge in, holding his breath, and eventually he emerged on deck, covered with oil. Once there, he saw hundreds of men in every stage of fear and pain, some clutching their personal belongings – a photograph or a radio – others fearfully burned by the lethal mixture of petrol and diesel oil which had fuelled the ship. In spite of the flames, some members of the crew who were uninjured went back to the areas of worst damage to see if they could find any survivors; but there were very few. More than two hundred men had died in the first impact.

The order to abandon ship was carried out for the most part with order and discipline, and once the survivors were in their life-rafts there were further dangers: a storm blew up, and waves twelve feet or more high caught the rafts and threatened to overturn them. By the time the *Belgrano* went down, however, the storm had died away. Tipping over to port, the ship which as USS *Phoenix* had survived the Japanese attack on Pearl Harbour 41 years earlier slowly sank. A number of life-rafts with men on board were sucked under with her. There was now no hope that the two Argentine destroyers escorting the *Belgrano* would rescue the survivors; they had dropped depth-charges at random in the hope of catching the *Conqueror*, and had then escaped as their orders required. Huddled together for warmth in their hermetically sealed rafts, the survivors watched as the sun went down and the temperature dropped; at times during the night it went as low as 20 degrees below zero. 'You couldn't sleep,' said one survivor. 'If you dropped off, you'd die. You had to do something to mop up the water that was leaking in, otherwise you ran the risk of freezing, and your legs would be completely paralysed with the cold. We prayed, and we chatted as best we could, and we gave thanks to God that we were still alive: that's how we passed the time.' The shortest period any of the life-rafts stayed in the water was 28 hours; the last ones were picked up 48 hours after the order to abandon ship. When the *Belgrano* was attacked, there had been 1,042 men aboard her. The number rescued was 674.

Mrs Vassallo, whose son Angel was among the 368 who died, is one of the few Argentines who still feels bitterness for the sinking of the ship. There was anger, later on, when photographs were published showing *Conqueror* flying the skull and crossbones as she returned to her home port of Faslane from the South Atlantic, but on the whole the shock which the *Belgrano*'s sinking caused was succeeded by so many other emotions that the effect slowly passed away. Two days after the *Belgrano* went down, the Argentines sank the *Sheffield*, and there were more Argentine successes to come. Few of the accusations made in Britain about the supposed reason for the *Belgrano*'s sinking – that it also torpedoed the chance of peace talks on the instigation of President Belaúnde Terry of Peru – have found an echo in Argentina. The assumption there was that the *Belgrano* had been sunk because she was one of the most important ships in the Argentine Navy, and that her loss could be expected to cripple the Navy's participation in the war. That, indeed, was the result. Admiral Anaya, having been a driving force behind the decision to invade the Falklands, withdrew his ships to port after 2 May and played little part in the conduct of the war thereafter. As for the Peruvian peace plan, no one close to the junta at the time appears to believe that Galtieri would have been in a position to accept it, or any other peace proposal; the loss of prestige would have been too great. As for the great majority of people, the loss of the *Belgrano* was just another episode in a war they have chosen to forget.

By the time the war began, the repression and the disappearances were starting to be things of the past. It was still unwise to be too outspoken, and the murder gangs were still in existence, but the fact that thousands of people could turn out on the streets and scream insults at the government showed that the balance had already turned. Most people probably accepted that things were getting a little easier – though not in economic terms – and in the first few weeks of the war there was almost total support for Galtieri. The government fostered this carefully. Millions of stickers were printed with the slogan 'United, it's much easier', and in a country which had long become sick of divisions and disputes, the idea caught on. Newspapers and television were swamped with an advertising campaign which featured the rallying-cry 'Ganemos la batalla en todos los frentes' – 'Let's win the battle on all fronts.' The five advertisements showed people in everyday civilian life – a car mechanic, a motorist, a teacher, and so on – each giving a thumbs-up sign to the camera and pointing out some useful moral: 'My combat position is my place of work. At a time like this, learning to change a wheel is as important as learning to pull the trigger.' 'While these pupils are with me, I'm their mother. Looking after them and giving them confidence is my way of doing my duty.' 'If I charge customers more than is necessary, that only helps the speculators. Even my store can help to create a more peaceful atmosphere.' Underneath the pictures, which demonstrate clearly enough the problems the military government felt it was facing, there was another hand giving the thumbs-up sign and a more warlike slogan: 'Argentines, on to victory – each in his own way defending what is ours!' It was a successful campaign, and for a little the thumbs-up, repeated at regular intervals every evening on television – which many more people than usual were watching – was taken up as a sign of patriotic support for the war. People listened obsessively to the radio for the latest news of the war, carrying transistor sets around with them in the streets, pressed close to their ears, or switching from station to station with one hand as they gripped the steering-wheel with the other.

But the eagerness for news and the implicit confidence which people had in those who provided it was soon to be changed into bitter cynicism: a cynicism which eventually drove the military out of office altogether. The official version had said that *Hermes*, *Invincible* and *Canberra*, the three main ships in the British task force, had each been sunk at one point or another during the fighting, and every time people had come out on to the streets in Buenos Aires and elsewhere to dance and sing and shout at the success of their forces. The newspapers assured them that the British would never be able to stage a landing on the Falklands, and people believed them with the ardour of those who wanted to be convinced. The pro-military newspaper *La Razón*, for instance, carried a huge headline on the front of its editions of 5 May quoting international news agency reports from London which, with a little discreet doctoring by the sub-editors of *La Razón*, said precisely that: 'Great Britain will not be able to stage a large-scale landing on the Islands.' The article quoted military experts as saying that an all-out invasion would need a three-to-one superiority for the attackers over the defenders, and was therefore out of the question. Like so much of the armchair speculation in Britain and elsewhere at the time, it proved to be completely inaccurate; and so, on 21 May, sixteen days later, *La Razón* was obliged to report, in letters just as large, that the impossible had in fact happened: 'A British landing is being resisted in the Malvinas.' At first, the government's propaganda machine dismissed the landing at San Carlos as being a small-scale affair, carried out by no more than two hundred men, and there was an immediate sense of relief throughout the country. Then, within hours, and with no preparation whatever, the radio stations were suddenly announcing that two thousand men had been landed. Television and the afternoon newspapers followed suit. It was, perhaps, the worst blow to confidence of the entire war; and nothing the official spokesmen said afterwards achieved the kind of acceptance that people had enthusiastically accorded the junta's pronouncements in the past. When the tabloid *Clarín*, for instance, carried two banner headlines on its front page of 30 May, the one reading 'Contact lost with the defenders of Darwin' and the other, clearly inserted to raise people's spirits, reading 'Galtieri does not discount military aid from abroad', it was the first one that people paid attention to.

After the battle at Goose Green, the whole thrust of Argentine propaganda was to encourage people to believe that the real struggle for the islands would take place in front of Port Stanley, and that it was still possible for Argentina to win. General Benjamín Menéndez, the Argentine military governor, was presented as a patient, cunning man, and his message to his troops on the eve of the British assault of the town was given huge prominence. But he was still using the kind of bombast that Galtieri and the others had used at the start of the Falklands invasion, and people in Argentina had begun to see through it: 'The moment for the final battle has begun. All our endeavours, the cold, the weariness, the long vigils, have reached their end . . . If each man with his rifle, his mortar, his machine gun, his field gun, fights with the valour and the heroism which has always distinguished us, success is certain.' Menéndez had already promised to defend the islands with his last drop of blood, and so when Port Stanley duly fell, with very little extra bloodshed, and indeed very little evidence of effort on the part of Menéndez, the claims on television and in the press about the heroic resistance he had put up were almost entirely ignored. The natural pessimism which had been fostered by years of national failure, political and economic, took hold again more intensely than ever. The flags came down, and so did the slogans about being united.

The distinguished Argentine journalist Hugo Gambini blames much of this feeling of betrayal on the fact that scarcely any genuine correspondents were allowed on to the islands by the Argentine authorities, and therefore the absurdly optimistic picture which the propagandists presented was allowed to go unchallenged. It is hard to believe that a military dictatorship could have acted any differently; but with hindsight, as Gambini maintains, it was the realization that they had been duped which created the strongest backlash of feeling against the authorities. His conclusion, reached at a time when Argentina was once more a democracy, is undoubtedly true, but says little about the state of surrealism in which Argentina found itself by the end of the war: 'If you trust a free and independent press, even at times of war, then you are trusting in democracy. Ignore it, and you deny the existence of public opinion, which will sooner or later show itself, as we have seen, in all its magnitude.'

Nevertheless, Argentine public opinion continued to be curiously difficult to forecast. Feelings ran very high against the United States, for siding with Britain and – as almost everybody believed – providing the British with detailed information from spy satellites of the movements of Argentine ships; which explains why Mrs Vassallo, whose son died in the sinking of the *Belgrano*, included the Americans in her catalogue of bitterness. And yet there were few signs of hostility to Britain as such. Mrs Thatcher was often treated in the newspapers and magazines as a strident figure of fun, something akin to a difficult mother-in-law. People regularly accused the British of piracy – the standard allegation ever since the British takeover of the Falklands in 1833, and perhaps before: the attacks by Sir Francis Drake and almost every other English privateer in Latin American waters over the centuries made it a natural complaint. There were occasional large demonstrations outside British premises, and a regular series of attacks against the clock-tower in the centre of Buenos Aires which had been the gift of British residents in the city at the start of the century, and which chimed like Big Ben. But no Anglo-Argentines reported any hostility, Jorge Luis Borges was able to condemn the military authorities for the invasion, and the large number of British foreign correspondents who gathered in Argentina to cover the war were left in peace for the most part. The veteran BBC correspondent Harold Briley, who was based in the city, was given a police guard, and people went regularly to the Sheraton Hotel, which overlooks the English Tower, to speak to the British press and give them stories. One Uruguayan cameraman was kidnapped and beaten up, apparently because he worked for British television, but there were no other serious incidents. Outside the sophistication of Buenos Aires, journalists sometimes encountered problems in making observations of military installations; a Canadian television team was arrested at Puerto Belgrano and brought to trial after several weeks on a charge of espionage, but the charge was dismissed when they appeared in court. Three journalists from British Sunday newspapers – including Simon Winchester of the *Sunday Times* and Ian Mather of the *Observer* – were gaoled in Ushuaia, the southernmost port in Argentina, but the officer in charge of the naval base, Admiral Zaratiegui, was intensely pro-British, and made a point of allowing other European and North American journalists to remain in the town, so that British public opinion could be reassured that no harm had come to the three men; though their conditions were often harsh. It was, in its way, all part of the unreality of the war. Perhaps it was that, after a century of peace, Argentina could not come to terms with the fact that its soldiers were trading shots with an enemy, and so in some way there was less hostility to the physical foe, Britain, than to the supposed ally, the United States, which had turned its face away from Argentina. Disloyalty, as most people saw it, was something that was easier to grasp than outright battle.

On the night of 15 June, 24 hours after General Menéndez had surrendered the islands in their entirety to the British forces, the crowds gathered once again outside the Casa Rosada. The previous great demonstration there had been on 10 April, at the beginning of the war, when Galtieri – 'someone who thought he was Napoleon', according to the conscript Oscar López – had acknowledged the near-hysteria of the patriotic crowds. Now he stayed inside, working on his speech of resignation, a bottle of Chivas Regal whiskey beside him. He had staked the entire future of the country on a blind gamble, and had lost. When he appeared on television, at nine-thirty that evening, he looked a broken man. He rarely raised his eyes to the camera, reading his words dully and with little sense of their meaning. At times, his voice was slurred. The phrases were full of the windy rhetoric he had used from the beginning of the war, but this time his audience recognized them as such. 'The battle of Puerto Argentino is over,' he began. 'Our soldiers have fought to their utmost endeavour for the dignity of the Nation. Those who fell will live for ever in the heart and the great history of the Argentine people . . . They were fighting against incomprehension, scorn, and arrogance. They faced with great courage the overwhelming superiority of a power supported by the military technology of the United States, which was, surprisingly, the enemy of Argentina and its people . . . Dignity and the future are ours, and they will give us peace and victory.'

Outside, the crowd swelled and grew more angry. Few of the people who had gathered there seemed to know what they wanted, or what they thought would happen. Some demanded revenge, and for the first time turned in earnest on the foreign cameramen who were filming them; crews from the American television networks suffered particularly.

Others were content to scream insults at the balcony of the Casa Rosada, hoping that Galtieri would make an appearance and would see their hatred and contempt for himself. In the dispirited atmosphere of the press room inside the Casa Rosada, a presidential aide slipped in and handed out a statement, unsigned and on unheaded paper, which declared that groups of political hotheads had gathered outside, chanting obscene slogans and lighting bonfires, and that the police had been obliged to disperse large numbers of ordinary people who had assembled there in order to hear the President's speech. 'All is now returning to normal,' the statement said, as though in those circumstances normality had any meaning.

When the soldiers returned to Argentina from the Falklands, as disarmed and newly released prisoners of war, stories began to circulate with great intensity and suddenness about the appalling conditions and gross inefficiency which they had had to endure:

living on one issue of cold rations once a day in temperatures well below freezing; no wood to make fires with, no drinking water, no change of clothing in two months; boots that split and let in water, uniforms that tore and wore out after a few weeks. Journalists began reporting that food-parcels which had been sent to the soldiers by well-wishers in Argentina were usually opened long before they reached the islands, and the best contents pilfered. Special packages and gifts assembled by schoolchildren were found being sold on the streets of Buenos Aires. Soon, everyone knew what had gone on in the Falklands: since the troops were mostly conscripts, and returned to their families without completing their military service, it quickly became common knowledge. As the wartime censorship relaxed, and the sense of general aimlessness grew, the newspapers which had up to now stayed quiet on this aspect of the war were emboldened to print a certain amount of the detail which was now available. The magazine *Gente* printed an interview with Major-General Sir Jeremy Moore, who had commanded the British land forces on the Falklands. He was dismissive of the tactics used by the Argentine defenders, and incredulous about the decision to pull them all back into Port Stanley for the final battle. In reply, General Benjamín Menéndez, whose tactics they were, issued a six-page statement which was presumably intended as a rebuttal of Moore's criticisms; it was almost the first comment he had made in public since promising to fight to the last drop of his blood. But his statement turned out to be rambling and vague, mostly praising the courage of his officers (and never mentioning the conscripts). Since the officers had, in point of fact, rarely fought well, and had often not fought at all, it was not only bombastic but tactless. Nowhere in the statement did Menéndez explain how he had come to surrender what had once been called 'his sacred charge'.

In the absence of clear official explanations, people invented their own. In particular the families of men who were missing often believed with passionate intensity that they were still alive somewhere. There were stories about Soviet and Polish trawlers picking up survivors from the *Belgrano* and taking them back to imprisonment behind the Iron Curtain. The parents of men who were missing in the war were in much the same condition, therefore, as the parents of men and women who had disappeared in the Dirty War; and because of the absence of official information, and even of interest on the part of the authorities, the missing servicemen's families turned their hatred on the military government much as the families of the political casualties had. As for the armed forces, they continued to maintain that the war in the Falklands was not over, and that it was only the first battle that had been lost. It was another part of the general refusal to come to terms with reality. Graffiti on the walls of Buenos Aires in the weeks after the defeat at Port Stanley caught the mood exactly. Parodying the 1973 election slogan, 'Neither Yankee nor Marxist – Peronist', the anonymous humorists wrote: 'Neither Yankee nor Marxist – surrealist.'

# 19 BRITISH DILEMMAS

*'Britain does not appease dictators'* – Daily Express editorial, 8 April 1982.

A pleasant-looking man in his early thirties relaxes in the sunshine on a private beach in Mar del Plata, in the first summer after the military have left office. The resort is back to normal, the hot sun beats down on the hundreds of thousands who, like him, are improving their tans and showing themselves off to the sunbathers around them. On one side of this particular private beach lies the city, where Luis Brandoni and the rest of the cast of *Papi* will be appearing in a few hours' time, to the delight of theatre-goers who have been starved of that particular type of pointed, risqué humour for seven years. On the other side of the beach lies the naval base, with the grey shapes of a couple of frigates clearly visible through the heat haze. The pleasant-looking man smiles, and chats to an older man beside him. Both are from the naval base, and both belong to the Yacht Club which owns this particular beach. The younger man has light-brown hair, cut boyishly so that it falls across his forehead rather in the style of John F. Kennedy. He is a little on the paunchy side now, and has the beginnings of a double chin, but otherwise he is fit and active. He has left his clothes, and a book or two, on a wicker-work table in his beach hut, a few yards away. Each member of the Yacht Club has a hut allocated to him or her, and the name of the member is painted on the white crossbar of the flimsy wood and canvas construction. The name over this particular beach hut reads 'ASTIZ, Alfredo B.'

Astiz stays in his deckchair as he sees the journalist and photographer approaching, the waistband of his blue bathing-shorts a little tight across the self-indulgent stomach, the smile still in place. He allows the photographer to take several shots of him as he sits there, but refuses to answer questions. A few days later, when other journalists look for him in row 3 at the Yacht Club, the beach hut is empty, the wicker chairs inside are piled up, and

Astiz's place on the beach is empty. An angry group of members gathers round to tell them to look for subversives instead, and leave decent people alone. Opinion in the rest of Argentina may have changed, but most of the Yacht Club members are from the naval base and their views are strictly unreconstructed.

Plenty of men in the armed forces played a part in both the catastrophic wars which the military governments of 1976-83 planned and fought: the Dirty War and the battle for the Falklands. But no one played as conspicuous a part in the two of them as Alfredo Astiz. In part, it was because of his boyish attractive appearance; he had the kind of looks that senior officers must have liked and found trustworthy, and in his time as an undercover agent he traded on the same reaction among the Mothers of the Plaza de Mayo and the various exile communities abroad. But in a structured, inward-looking service like the Argentine Navy, his family background was the prime reason for his rapid promotion and his secondment to difficult, confidential duties. He was born on 17 November 1950 in the provincial town of Azul, about three hundred kilometres south-east of Buenos Aires and the same distance inland from Mar del Plata, the eldest son of a serving naval officer. Alfredo Edgardo Astiz (the father) rose to the rank of Vice-Admiral before retiring, and in 1962 he commanded the elderly, fated cruiser *General Belgrano* when it was sent by the Argentine Government of the day to participate in President Kennedy's blockade of Cuba during the missile crisis. Six years later, at the age of eighteen, his son entered Argentina's Naval Academy. He had always wanted to enter the service, and his nickname at school, possibly bestowed as a form of mockery, was 'the handsome sailor'. After graduating in 1971 and being posted first to Mar del Plata and then to Puerto Belgrano, Astiz was sent to the United States in 1975 for a year's course in countering subversion; he seems to have been an excellent pupil. His return was admirably timed: the military had just seized power and the war against Argentina's own form of subversion was under way. In the United States he had passed with flying colours a rigorous endurance test, during which he had been exposed to a series of severe physical hardships, carefully controlled, and his father was annoyed when Astiz was ordered to return to Argentina, because he felt his son's career would have benefited from a longer stay. Vice-Admiral Astiz later told the magazine *La Semana* that he thought the Navy had pulled back people like his son because of the political plans which the Commander-in-Chief,

Admiral Massera, harboured for himself. Massera was determined that the Navy should play a conspicuous part in the rooting out of subversion. Later, Massera was to force Vice-Admiral Astiz into early retirement, but the son's career was unaffected, and he rose fast through the ranks. Within two months of the coup he was given command of an anti-terrorist task force, GT 3.3/2, based at the Navy Mechanics School ESMA.

The details of his activities there have formed a significant part of this book: the capture of Dagmar Hagelin, the infiltration of the Mothers of the Plaza de Mayo, the disappearance of the two French nuns, and so on. Astiz was one of a small group of officers known as 'grey wolves', who were permitted to act autonomously and were not obliged to report to a senior officer in their day-to-day activities. Under him, GT 3.3/2 was probably the most active of all the task forces, and was responsible for the arrest certainly of hundreds, and perhaps as many as two thousand, people, almost none of whom survived. He must also have made himself a rich man, from the goods he looted and from the sale of orphaned children to childless couples. The names he used were various: 'Rubio' ('Blond'), 'Angel' ('Angel'), 'Cuervo' ('Raven'), 'Gonzalo', 'Eduardo Escudero', 'Gustavo Niño', and he was soon employed in other kinds of undercover missions, possibly as a result of his success as 'Gustavo Niño' among the Mothers of the Plaza. At one stage he was sent to Spain, to infiltrate a group of Montoneros in Barcelona. By the beginning of 1978, however, the work of the task forces at ESMA and elsewhere was being wound down; people were still disappearing, but not in anything like the same numbers, and the main activity that year seems to have been the systematic murder of people who were already held captive. That was unskilled work; men like Astiz were of more use elsewhere. In August 1977 the so-called 'Pilot Centre' had been established at the Argentine Embassy in Paris, to co-ordinate the military régime's propaganda in Europe. Based in a large office on the first floor at 83 Avenue Henri Martin, in the 16th arrondissement, the Centre was supposedly a part of the embasssy but was in fact completely autonomous, and was run by Navy officers, most of whom could not even speak French; it was their ostensible mission to counter hostile views of Argentina abroad, but the men who worked there had the task of spying on the various groups of exiles who had settled in Paris, and on occasion infiltrating them.

Part of the work at the Pilot Centre was to issue black propaganda in the guise of communications from the three main Argentine human rights groups in Paris, COSPA, CAIS and MADE, as well as sending letters to the newspapers under the signatures of various people, asking for information or providing a false picture of events in Argentina. In March 1978 there was a change of command at the Pilot Centre, and a man known by the code-names 'Martin', 'Rata' ('Rat') and 'Trueno' ('Thunder') took over. At about the same time, Astiz appeared in Paris too. He entered France on the passport made out in the name of Eduardo Escudero, who may well have existed; Astiz's other main alias, Gustavo Niño, certainly did – he was, as we have seen, the young brother of some one who had genuinely disappeared, and who was listed as missing by the Mothers of the Plaza de Mayo. But it is noticeable that the two surnames have a faintly similar meaning: *niño* means 'little boy', and *escudero* means a page or a squire. Perhaps Astiz felt that such names enhanced his boyish quality, and made it easier for people to trust him and take him into their confidence; or perhaps that was, in some way, how the son of the Vice-Admiral saw himself in his relationship to his superior officers: the handsome young sailor of his school nickname.

But Astiz, despite his false identities, did not last long in Paris. He tried to infiltrate the group of organizers who ran CAIS, the Argentine Centre for Information and Solidarity, and was unlucky enough to come up against a woman who had been interrogated by him the previous year in Buenos Aires. She immediately told the others in CAIS, and they decided to lodge a formal complaint about Astiz and the Pilot Centre with the Quai d'Orsay. As a result, the French Foreign Minister called in the Argentine ambassador and demanded an explanation for the activities of Astiz and the Centre. Soon afterwards, Astiz left for Buenos Aires.

Some months later, in June 1979, he surfaced in South Africa as an assistant to the naval attaché under his real name. This time the post was a legitimate one: it had clearly been decided that his value as an undercover agent had evaporated as a result of the incident in Paris. A posting to South Africa was therefore something of a reward for a man who, though still only twenty-eight, had served his masters well. The naval attaché was his old superior officer at ESMA, Admiral Chamorro, but there were no Argentine exiles for them to keep an eye on: the two governments were too friendly for that, and no one who left Argentina on suspicion of being a leftist would have gone to South Africa to take refuge. The two right-wing nations guarding the southern entrances to the Atlantic each felt they were misunderstood by the rest of the world, and were each naval powers in their own right; but they were regional powers, and scarcely obtruded upon each other. Astiz's official duties were few and far between, therefore, and he spent a good deal of time on the beaches of Cape Town and Durban, receiving from time to time the customary honours the South African Government pays to diplomats of particularly friendly governments. He drove around in an expensive (though tax-free) BMW, but his friends and associates found him subject to considerable emotional instability, and he seemed unable to form permanent relationships with anyone. Eventually his past caught up with him. On 18 October 1981, when he had been in South Africa for two years and four months, the Durban-based newspaper *The Sunday Tribune*, which has a strong reputation for liberal crusading (even though it is a little inclined to sensationalize) came out with an almost entirely accurate account of Astiz's activities as a kidnapper and torturer at ESMA during the Dirty War. The South African Government, which might have had its private sympathies with the Argentine junta's general approach, nevertheless disliked being linked with obvious examples of foreign illegality and repression, and it advised the Argentine ambassador that Astiz should be recalled. Two months later, after much harrying by South African journalists, he left. Once again, the timing seemed useful: plans were already being laid for the invasion of the Falklands, and Astiz's name was brought before the attention of the naval authorities at the precise moment when they were casting round for some deserving officer to send on a probing mission to establish a base on the island of South Georgia. In the event, as we have said, the operation was postponed, but Astiz was earmarked to lead it whenever it should take place. It was, perhaps, the best way that the Argentine military could find of laundering the soiled reputations of men who had been involved in the Dirty War: by associating them with some notable patriotic achievement.

In the final days before the invasion of the Falklands, South Georgia – still the focus of attention as the crisis worsened – contained a very mixed bag of inhabitants. They were, in order of arrival, the British scientists at Grytviken who had given the warning about the raising of the Argentine flag; the men from Constantino Davidoff's scrap-metal company, based at Leith; the small force of Royal Marines, who landed at Grytviken to put pressure on them to apply for proper accreditation; and a larger force of Argentine naval men, most of them from the anti-subversion task forces, based at ESMA and elsewhere and commanded by Lt-Cdr Astiz. And there was another group as well, smaller than all the rest, and the only one that was there by accident rather than design: the crew of a 12.5 metre yacht, captained by a French journalist and cameraman, Serge Briez. Briez had been making a film for the French television Channel Antenne 2, when a storm overturned them. They were lucky enough to make it to South Georgia, and arrived not long after the scrap-metal men, who welcomed them. Shortly after midnight, on 25 March, as they were celebrating the birthday of one of the crew members, there was a violent blow on the boat's hull, and they found themselves face to face with a party of Argentine sailors with blackened faces and guns in their hands, who warned them not to make a noise, send any messages by radio, or take any pictures. But Serge Briez, realizing that he was watching the start of something important, got his camera out anyway; he wasn't going to miss a chance like that. As he filmed, the Argentines unloaded a large amount of equipment.

The next day he had his first meeting with Astiz, who was called by his men 'El Rubio', the blond. He was neatly dressed in civilian clothes, and – like Briez – spoke English. Briez, who is an intelligent and sympathetic man, liked Astiz at once. He was, he said, cultivated, well-travelled, and liked art, music and literature, and Briez and he had several pleasant conversations in the course of the next few days. Then, on the morning of 2 April, Astiz asked Briez to film the raising of the Argentine flag, and soon afterwards he headed off to attack the much smaller British garrison of Royal Marines, under the command of Lieutenant Keith Mills. Astiz's tactics were scarcely subtle: he radioed the Marines to tell them to surrender and having thus given them two hours' warning to dig themselves in, he arrived off-shore with a corvette, two Alouette helicopters and a larger Puma helicopter carrying troops. The Marines fought them off for two hours, killing four of them and damaging both the corvette and the Puma, and Mills decided to surrender only when one of the Marines was badly injured and night was beginning to fall. Astiz was shaken by the incident, but when Briez later said to him that he was shocked by the bloodshed, Astiz replied, 'It's your job to take pictures, it's mine to fight. I'm prepared to die for my country.' Not long afterwards,

Briez left to resume his voyage, and Astiz wrote in the logbook of his boat, 'From the world's end, my best wishes – Alfredo Astiz'.

One of Davidoff's men, Carlos Patané, a biochemist who was there to supervise part of the dismantling work, saw a much more sombre side to Astiz's character. Astiz spent many evenings with them, and one night he turned to Patané and said, 'Here you are with Astiz, and yet I can assure you that I know a very different Astiz.' When it came to making decisions, Patané said, Astiz became cold and distant; an interesting psychological case, was his verdict.

When it came to it, however, the interesting psychological case was not, after all, prepared to die for his country. On 25 April, about a month after his arrival on South Georgia, a British naval force arrived off Grytviken where Astiz's garrison now numbered 180. After attacking the Argentine submarine *Santa Fe*, which had brought in reinforcements, and crippling her, the British, unwilling to wait for a larger force, put together an attacking party of 75, composed of Royal Marines and men from the SAS and SBS. While the ships laid down a heavy bombardment, the British troops made their way ashore and – after mistaking a group of seals for Argentine defenders – charged towards the genuine Argentine positions under covering fire from machine-guns and missiles. As they came closer, they saw white sheets hanging from several of the windows: Astiz, apparently without ordering his men to open fire in the first place, had surrendered, though he outnumbered them by more than two to one. Later, a mine-clearance officer on board *Endurance*, one of the ships taking part in the recapture of South Georgia, said he thought Astiz had wanted to take some of his men and make a stand at Leith, where he had first landed. The positions at Leith were surrounded with mines and the officer suspected Astiz of trying to lure the British into the minefield. A landing-pad for helicopters was also, they found, booby-trapped.

And yet Astiz himself was charming to his captors, and, like Serge Briez, they found him likeable and good company. 'I was expecting a swarthy, scruffy person, but he was tidy and smart,' said Lieutenant-Commander Norman Wood, who was in charge of him on board the fishery protection vessel *Dumbarton Castle*. 'He was no trouble at all. He was very friendly, very amenable, very intelligent and highly professional.' In the presence of Captain Nicholas Barker, the independent-minded officer who commanded HMS *Endurance*, and who warned the British Government that an Argentine invasion of the Falklands was likely, Astiz signed a document of surrender. Under the careful penmanship of one of the Royal Naval officers, who had set out the details of the surrender, Astiz added the words, 'Owing to the superiority of the enemy's forces, I surrender to the British forces': but he had written another word too, and when Captain David Pentreath of HMS *Plymouth* asked to look at the piece of paper, worried that Astiz might be putting in some reference to British 'invading' forces, Astiz crossed out the extra word. Pentreath thought it was 'Great' in front of 'British', and that Astiz obliterated it out of spite.

But he had, by all accounts, behaved well to the Royal Marines he had captured a month before, and in return the Royal Navy treated him well. For the first couple of days they knew him only as a rather ineffectual commander whose willingness to surrender had given the British task force its first success of the Falklands War. In Argentina, however, a sizeable number of people knew of his activities at the Navy Mechanics School, the GTs, and the undercover missions that had become public; and when, in the newspapers of 27 April, he received massive publicity in Argentina as the commander who had surrendered South Georgia, the accusations started to flood in. A Madrid newspaper quickly made the link between Astiz and the case of Dagmar Hagelin, and within three days of the signing of the surrender document the Swedish Foreign Ministry had delivered a formal application to the British Government to be allowed to question Astiz before he could be moved from South Georgia; and a few days after that the Quai d'Orsay in Paris made a similar application over the cases of the two French nuns. At first, opinion within the Foreign Office in London was in favour of the idea, and Astiz was held back when the remaining Argentine prisoners from the island were released through Montevideo. A personal intervention by Claude Cheysson, the French Foreign Minister, strengthened the case for allowing some form of interrogation. But the Ministry of Defence in London, less concerned with the niceties of international etiquette or the question of what human rights offences Astiz might have committed, pointed out that the government had promised before the fighting started to abide by the Geneva Convention, even though war had not been declared on Argentina. Article 12 of the Third Geneva Convention, the Ministry of Defence recalled, laid down strict criteria for transferring prisoners of war to third countries, while Article 17 of the same Convention made it clear that prisoners were obliged to give, in the familiar phrase, only their name, rank and number. The Foreign Office was placed in an embarrassing position, since it had already allowed the Swedish ambassador to understand that Astiz would be made available for questioning by a Swedish official about the Hagelin case.

The decision was a complex one, and there was little help from the outside world. The International Committee of the Red Cross, for instance, made it clear that it was a matter for the British Government to deal with, as it saw fit. The Foreign Office began to backtrack, suggesting to the Swedes that they should compile written questions, which could be put to Astiz on Ascension Island, where he was now being held. After two further weeks, with the position still not clarified, the Ministry of Defence decided that Astiz should be brought to Britain; it was suggested that he might be witnessing transfers of military equipment on Ascension which could provide the Argentines with valuable information when he was released. During his long journey to Britain by sea, the pressure built up for some action to be taken in the case. There was no question of sending him either to Sweden or to France for interrogation, and the issue was becoming complicated by a range of emotions and misunderstandings: hostility to Argentina, a desire to score propaganda points with world opinion, mistakes in interpreting what was a highly complicated legal question.

And yet it soon became clear that the real reason for the British delaying tactics was uncertainty about the fate of a British Harrier pilot who was missing after an operation over Port Stanley on May 24: clearly, the British Government was going to play the case of Astiz by the book, in order to encourage the Argentines to do the same with any British prisoners of war who might be taken. From the time when the Harrier pilot was reported missing, the outlook for Astiz improved markedly. When he arrived at Portsmouth on a fleet auxiliary ship, looking, it was reported, tired and dishevelled, he was flown by Navy helicopter to Chichester, where he was to be held at the Rousillon Barracks. The barracks are not in themselves a particularly pleasant place to live, having been built to take French prisoners during the Napoleonic Wars, but the Ministry of Defence whose prisoner he was, went out of its way to publish details of the conditions in which he was to be held, and since the Ministry was notorious for its tight hold on information during the Falklands War, it can be assumed that the intention was to broadcast them to Argentine ears. A statement said that the barracks were set in pleasant surroundings on the outskirts of Chichester, and that Astiz would occupy what it called 'a three-room accommodation comprising a lounge, bedroom and bath-room'. 'The rooms', it continued, 'are furnished to officers' mess standards, and meals will be supplied from the officers' mess kitchens.' He was to be given access to the barracks library, and any requests for books or magazines would be considered. Exercise space was being made available for him. His gaoler, Colonel Wilfred Wood of the Military Police, went even further: 'He is a soldier and an officer, and we are treating him as such. He is being treated according to the standards of human decency. What we don't want, is the chap being tried by public hysteria.' And then Colonel Wood announced the decision which the Foreign Office had been havering over for six weeks: 'I want to make it quite clear that Lt-Cdr Astiz is not being interrogated, according to the rules of the Geneva Convention. And I understand that no access will be given to him for the French or the Swedes or whoever else wants to question him.'

It was, however, purely academic whether the Swedes should or should not be allowed to put the ten questions they had carefully compiled about the death of Dagmar Hagelin, or whether the French should ask the rather longer list of questions about the two nuns; Astiz was within his rights under the Geneva Convention to answer nothing except questions about his name, rank and number. A Detective Chief Superintendant of the Sussex Constabulary was eventually brought in to Rousillon Barracks on 8 June and, in the presence of a number of other people, put the kind of questions to him that the Swedish and French Foreign Ministries had compiled. Astiz shook his head at each one, and smiled apologetically from time to time, but said nothing. Seven days after he had arrived in Britain, he was taken to Gatwick Airport by helicopter and put on a British Caledonian flight to Rio de Janeiro, at a cost to the British taxpayer, it was later announced in Parliament, of £726. The flight was probably the worst part of the entire experience for him, since a number of Fleet Street reporters were also on board, and questioned him closely and photographed him; but they obtained as little in the way of information about his activities at ESMA as the Sussex Chief Superintendant had. At Rio he was taken off the plane by a different exit from the other passengers, and disappeared from sight.

The Swedish Goverment was privately furious about the way Britain had handled the affair, and went as far as deploring in public the decision to release Astiz so quickly. The French, for their part, said they considered the case to be still open. Swedish officials stressed afterwards that they had never asked for Astiz to be sent to Sweden, nor for him to be put on trial; but they were offended that the British should have stuck so closely to the letter of the law and had never made the gesture of inviting Swedish and French officials to put their questions to him, or even to be present while he was examined. As for the idea of putting him on trial, opinion was divided. A study by the International Commission of Jurists said that the case had shown that there was a loophole in the international legal system, but decided that Britain had no alternative but to free him. Other authorities pointed out that the Third Geneva Convention, signed in 1949 by 138 countries including Britain and Argentina, made it a crime to torture people in an internal armed conflict, and that prosecutions were open to any country under the terms of the Convention, regardless of where the crime was committed. Furthermore, it was said, Britain, like the other signatories, had given its solemn undertaking to uphold all the provisions of the Convention, so that Britain was, in a sense, under a binding obligation to take action in the case of Astiz.

But the argument was a purely academic one, and the decision had already been made on purely practical grounds. The chief priority, as far as the British Government was concerned, was to get back, safe and sound, any British servicemen who might fall into Argentine hands. This laudable objective did not, it seems, extend to all British citizens, by any manner of means. The Foreign Office made it clear very quickly that there would be no intention of using the Astiz case as a lever with the Argentines to help the three British journalists who were languishing under considerably less comfortable circumstances than Astiz, in gaol in Ushuaia. Despite complaints from MPs and groups of journalists, the Foreign Office stressed that the legal processes of Argentina, however imperfect they might appear to be in British eyes, would have to be allowed to take their course. Quite clearly, then, the British Government was determined to resist all demands and appeals which related to anything other than the matter in hand: the conditions and safe return of prisoners of war. As for discussions about a wider moral duty, they were, in the British view, strictly irrelevant. And so Alfredo Astiz was sent back as quickly as possible to Argentina, having been kept in the best conditions that his captors could devise, in the hope that the Argentines would reciprocate; which to some extent they did. In Buenos Aires, 18 months after the end of the war, Ragnar Hagelin, the father of Astiz's best-known victim, listens to a detailed explanation of the British approach and shakes his head. 'You can't blame us here for thinking that there was always something more important to the British than justice,' he says.

Richard Whitecross would probably agree with that. He is a British subject who nowadays lives in Oxford with his Argentine wife and works for a big auctioneering firm. In November 1975 he had been living in Argentina for several years as representative for the Oxford University Press. He and his wife had a number of friends from Chile – exiles from the right-wing dictatorship, but not particularly radical ones; they were, however, rather more active than Whitecross or his wife had thought, and one of them had brought back several thousand dollars from Europe as the proceeds of the fund-raising trip on behalf of prisoners and their families in Chile.

Whitecross assumes, now, that DINA, the Chilean secret police, knew all about his friends and their money, and tipped off the Argentines. They, in turn, seemed to have had little interest in the people they came to arrest, and were probably more concerned with getting the money. Nevertheless Whitecross and his wife were picked up, together with the Chileans, and taken to the main police station in Buenos Aires. The newspapers later carried stories that they had all been part of a resistance network, and that Whitecross was the courier. As it turned out, perhaps because they were British, or because the evidence against them was plainly cooked up, neither he nor his wife were particularly badly treated, though he was hooded and kicked and threatened and told she would be killed. But their Chilean friends were in a much worse state, and were badly beaten up right from the start.

The ramshackle government of Mrs Perón still had four months to run at this stage, and the large-scale disappearances which the military introduced when they staged their coup were still a thing of the future; nevertheless, the system was hit and miss, and people could disappear without trace. The British Embassy in Buenos Aires, when the arrest of the Whitecrosses was brought to its notice, contacted the Foreign Ministry, but received the kind of answer that was to become standard over the next few years – that there was no information about them – and allowed the matter to remain there. If anything, the Whitecrosses found out later, the embassy seemed rather embarrassed by the whole affair.

Whitecross's father-in-law, who lived in the city of Rosario, was not prepared to let the matter rest, and came up to Buenos Aires to go through the unpleasant and dreary and sometimes frightening routine that thousands would go through over the following years: he visited each police station in central Buenos Aires in turn, and as he was walking down the street having got nowhere, he bumped into a friend of his who was a well-connected lawyer. He explained what had happened, and the lawyer agreed to help him. Not long afterwards, the father was told that the Whitecrosses were in fact in one of the police stations where he had already been, and he took along a parcel of food and handed it in for them. At first the police still denied they were there, but eventually and grudgingly they accepted the parcel and so declared, in effect, that the Whitecrosses were prisoners there. It was the start of the process of freeing them – and in some ways the most important part. The father-in-law went off to inform the British Embassy.

A senior member of the embassy staff visited them the next day. Whitecross was particularly worried because two of his Chilean friends had been taken out earlier and were tortured; he could hear their screams. And so when the British Embassy man arrived he was very relieved, and asked him to get in touch urgently with the United Nations High Commission for Refugees in Buenos Aires, with whom both of the Chileans were registered. The British official did not seem particularly concerned about that; what he was concerned with was the fact that Whitecross had not registered his change of address or his marriage with the embassy. He was not particularly warm or encouraging, though he made it clear he would do what he could for the Whitecrosses, because they were British subjects; he never got in touch with the UNHCR about the Chileans who were being tortured. The only advice he gave was that after three months, according to the emergency rules then in force, the Whitecrosses could expect either to be brought to trial or to be expelled; he advised them to put up with the prison as best they could.

Later, they were transferred to the main Devoto prison in Buenos Aires, and they remained there until the coup in March 1976. Then things became distinctly alarming: soldiers ringed the gaol, the prisoners were all locked in their cells, and machine-guns were set up outside. Whitecross had heard of a massacre of prisoners at the police station where they had been held earlier, and he became very worried. His fears grew because the military were starting to conduct major searches, and held everyone in the shower section, kicking and beating prisoners like Whitecross who weren't quick enough for them. The man from the embassy came again at this point: cool, correct, but not particularly enthusiastic about helping him. Whitecross explained his fears about the motives of the soldiers, and asked the man from the embassy to make representations on their behalf. He found out later that the man had tried to see the governor of the prison, but that the governor had been busy. The British diplomat left his card and went back to the embassy. Eventually, after five months, they were released. The embassy was polite enough about it all, but advised Whitecross against making too much of a fuss about his experiences by giving news conferences or making statements; it might be bad for his parents-in-law, someone said.

None of the small handful of British prisoners in gaol in Argentina during the repression has accused the British Embassy of failing to do its duty by them: it did its duty, and nothing more. When Ragnar Hagelin went to ask the embassy for help over the case of his daughter, long before her kidnapper fell into British hands, it was explained to him courteously that there was nothing Britain could do; and so it was left to the Swedes, and the French, and the Americans, and the Spanish, and so on, to make their representations for her. Women like Mrs Walker, whose husband was British and whose missing son Enrique was therefore eligible for British nationality, received no help from the embassy because, it was explained, there was no *locus standi* – no grounds for taking action. People with dual nationality received little or no help at all from the embassy. Soon, no one who had lost a son or daughter bothered to go to see the British for help; the word went round that there was no point. There was no Tex Harris there, and no Raul Castro; just a faint air of embarrassment that the embassy should be involved at all.

The priorities and interests of British foreign policy were set out most fully in the late Sixties in the Duncan Report, which emphasized that the North Atlantic alliance and Western Europe were the central areas of interest, and that other countries shaded off from there. Argentina was classed as an outer area, of a certain limited commercial interest but of little or no political significance to Britain. Once the Duncan Report had received acceptance by the Cabinet, its recommendations were enshrined as the mainspring of Foreign Office policy. Henceforth, British ambassadors would feel themselves instructed to see Argentina as a country where they should keep a low profile politically, because of the sensitivities over the Falklands, and should concentrate on trying to encourage people as best they could to buy British goods. Argentina's neighbour Chile also represented an outer area, and much the same policy was followed by the British Embassy there.

In February 1974, however, a Labour Government under Harold Wilson came to power in Britain. It was only five months after Pinochet's coup in Chile, and there was deep-seated anger in the British Labour Movement, as in social democratic and socialist parties throughout the world, at the brutality and wholesale murder directed at the left and even the centre in Chile. The anger was intensified in Britain when it became known that a British subject, Dr Sheila Cassidy, had been tortured by Pinochet's secret police. On 27 March 1974 the Foreign Secretary, James Callaghan, announced that new arms exporting licences would not be granted in respect of Chile, and that existing contracts would be urgently reviewed; and on the same day the Minister of Overseas Development, Judith Hart, said that aid of various kinds that had been sent to Chile would be discontinued, with the exception of grants for Chilean students to study in Britain. The Chilean régime was furious, and said that Britain could no longer be trusted as a trading partner, and there was a good deal of irritation in Whitehall, particularly in the Ministry of Defence, whose officials had carefully negotiated a number of contracts for warships and for overhauling jet fighters with the Chileans, and also in the Department of Trade, whose job it was to present Britain as a trading partner of the highest reliability. The Wilson government's sudden lurch into the politics of international morality gained it a good deal of credit among its supporters; but it also made it a great deal harder to take a stand on purely moral grounds, given previous practice.

As an issue, human rights in Argentina never had the appeal abroad that human rights in Chile could count on. Liberal and social democratic parties abroad had no links with, and no sympathy for, the Peronist movement, which they saw as being tainted with Fascism; and the Montoneros, though indubitably left-wing, had gained no friends in Britain and few in other parts of the world by their violence and almost indiscriminate murders. If anything, the Labour Government reacted with relief when the armed forces overthrew Mrs Perón in March 1976; the coup seemed to guarantee greater stability, and the policies of the economics minister, Martínez de Hoz, were an admittedly more extreme version of the kind of approach the British Chancellor of the Exchequer, Denis Healey, was thinking of introducing. Not even when middle of the road politicians like Raúl Alfonsín began to realize what was happening in Argentina was it easy to make contact with political parties abroad: Argentina had always been something of a world in itself, and there were few if any links between the Radicals or the Peronists and parties in the United States or Western Europe.

Amnesty International paid its visit to Argentina soon after the coup, and warned of the widespread ill-treatment that was going on, but the full extent of the military's campaign was not clear at that stage. Several of the Argentine human rights organizations outside the country were dominated by the Montoneros, who were concerned mostly with obtaining the release of their cadres from prison and with continuing their war against the military régime by political as well as violent means. And although their leader, Mario Firmenich, paraded around Havana in a uniform of his own designing, and gave press conferences in which he claimed more and more successes, the Soviet propaganda machine as a whole left him and the Montoneros severely alone. In Chile the Russians had announced that they were establishing underground radios, just as they did in Spain during the Civil War; but Argentina was not, in Soviet eyes, another Chile, and Moscow had good reasons for not wanting to upset the military régime there. Always aware of the possibility that the United States might cut off its sales of wheat to the Soviet Union, Moscow wanted to keep its lines to Buenos Aires open, just in case. And so the Soviet-oriented Communist Party in Argentina was obliged to suffer the violence of the Videla régime, while at the same time extolling it on Moscow's orders as governing in the interests of the working class, and there was no word from the Soviet Union or its allies about the kidnappings, torturings and murders that were going on daily.

It was not long, however, before reports of serious human rights violations in Argentina, objective and well-researched, began emerging in Britain and elsewhere. The left-wing weekly *New Statesman* carried a particularly accurate series of articles about what was happening, and correspondents from *Le Monde* in France, and *Time* and *The New York Times* in the United States were also providing powerful accounts of the campaign of terror there; a BBC correspondent, Derek Wilson, was arrested while covering a demonstration by the Mothers of the Plaza de Mayo.

But although there were occasional twinges of unease among Labour backbenchers, there was no intention whatever on the part of the government to raise the matter with the Argentine régime in general terms; the difficulties that had arisen as a result of the fuss, two years before, over Chile made such a thing almost impossible. What was more, Harold Wilson had now been replaced as Prime Minister by James Callaghan: a man who had some strong views about foreign affairs, having been Foreign Secretary, and who cultivated a reputation as a down-to-earth man of common sense. His view of Argentina was that it was a country best left well alone, which was precisely the view of his senior officials at the Foreign Office; and since after soundings by a junior minister, Ted Rowlands, he believed that Britain would not be able to reach an accommodation with Argentina over the Falkland Islands, owing to the strong feelings about the subject in the House of Commons, the only answer lay in playing for time – which would hardly be done by stirring up the Videla régime by unprovoked criticisms. His Foreign Secretary, Anthony Crosland, agreed.

But Crosland died unexpectedly in 1977, and his place was taken by one of his junior ministers, a protégé of Callaghan's, Dr David Owen. Owen was close to various figures within the Carter Administration in Washington, which had come into office a few months before, and he strongly endorsed Carter's human rights policy. British ambassadors in countries like Argentina which were governed by authoritarian régimes were given instructions to maintain links with democratic parties and their leaders. In Argentina itself, it was not always easy; after the experience of government under Mrs Perón there were several leaders who, though technically belonging to a democratic party, scarcely counted as democrats themselves. But there were some, especially on the Radical side, and the Foreign Office invited Senator Hipólito Solari Yrigoyen to visit London from his place of exile in Paris, for instance. Yrigoyen's credentials were impeccable, since he had been threatened and assaulted by gangs from both the far left and the far right. In 1978, Owen went further; Admiral Massera, the least savoury member of the original Videla junta, paid a visit to Britain as part of a European tour, and the Argentine Embassy allowed it to be known that he was interested in signing a contract for at least one frigate for his navy, and perhaps more. The Ministry of Defence and the Department of Trade were both keen on the deal, but Owen, after consulting his advisers, took a personal decision not to meet him. Massera, realizing that he had been snubbed, left London angrily for West Germany, where the contracts were duly signed. In Whitehall there was greater irritation even than there had been over the Chilean warships, and Callaghan himself shared in it this time.

In Britain, more than in most countries, policies endure while ministers come and go. This is particularly true with foreign policy; and diplomats tend to stay true, in their daily dealings with the countries to which they are accredited, to the fundamental principles of the relationship as they perceive them, regardless of who might happen to be occupying the Foreign Secretary's imposing room on the first floor of the Foreign Office, overlooking St James's Park. Dr David Owen made his own feelings about Argentina clear from the start, but it had no noticeable effect on the way the British Embassy in Buenos Aires behaved towards the junta. At the embassy, the Duncan Report still ruled: Argentina was an outer area power, which offered a certain amount of opportunity in the way of trade; no good would come of trying to act as a political influence there. To some extent the embassy was fortunate, in that relatively few British subjects were caught up in the repression – perhaps five in all, and most of those had been imprisoned by the previous government of Mrs Perón. By comparison, there were 16 French citizens who had disappeared, and some, like the two nuns, had been kidnapped in the most brutal fashion. British people in Argentina, by and large were there to do business, and they tended not to be the kind of people who were mixed up with left-wing political movements, or were likely to be mistaken as such.

The embassy, and the Foreign Office in London, did make efforts on behalf of the few British subjects who – like Richard Whitecross and his wife – were known to be in the hands of the military. It preferred to keep its enquiries about them private, in order not to annoy the Argentine régime; and in one case at least it succeeded. In September 1978, David Owen met the Argentine Foreign Minister at the United Nations General Assembly, at one of the innumerable bilateral encounters that are always arranged for the occasion. The main subject for discussion was, inevitably, the Falkland Islands, but Owen also handed over a note about the case of a young Englishwoman,Daisy Jane Hobson, who had disappeared in Buenos Aires. Some time later, and apparently as a direct result of the note, she was handed over to the prison service, and although she remained for nearly six more years in gaol, she did not disappear for good as so many others had.

But within the Foreign Office, David Owen's approach to

Argentina was regarded as idiosyncratic; it was, in a sense, his hobby, which the Foreign Office in general did not feel called upon to share. And since he was not a popular Foreign Secretary – he had a reputation for being short with his senior officials and ticking them off in front of others – he found it difficult to persuade people to follow his example. It was not possible for him to order the policy to be changed, because it had been set out in Cabinet, and only the Cabinet could change it. It was open to David Owen to put the issue on the Cabinet agenda, but if he had done so he would never have won; Edmund Dell, the Trade Secretary, and the Defence Minister Fred Mulley would both have opposed it in the strongest terms, and Callaghan himself – despite his personal loyalty to Owen – would unquestionably have supported them. And so the civil servants in the Foreign Office were free to follow the line laid down for them, and disregard the human rights issue as much as possible. Something of the same position had existed at the Home Office under Roy Jenkins, two years before: the United Nations High Commission for Refugees had appealed urgently in June 1976 for Western European countries, in particular, to save the lives of Argentine refugees by taking them in. Jenkins, who had established a considerable reputation for himself as a reforming Home Secretary, agreed to take in 75 people: not very many, but a reasonable figure considering that Argentine exiles had never come to Britain in particularly large numbers in the past. But the Home Office's immigration department, never enthusiastic about the occasional bursts of generosity by its political masters, was in no hurry to smooth the path for the would-be refugees; seven months later, only 13 had been allowed in, and *The Times* criticized the government for failing to keep its promises.

There were, however, always more important issues than human rights for British ministries to concern themselves with. In the case of the Ministry of Defence it was the desire to find a suitable military partner in the Southern Cone of South America, now that Chile had been ostracized; and Argentina represented a useful market, with high-spending military officers in charge of the government. For the Department of Trade, those same high-spending officers had led the way in Argentina's much-increased spending on British goods: between 1976, the year of the coup, and 1978, Argentina's imports of British goods doubled in value, and were now around 300 million US dollars. In 1978 the Chairman of GEC, Lord Nelson, led a delegation of twenty British businessmen to Argentina to drum up trade. He found that the question of human rights was irritating his hosts, and when he returned to London he made his views known in the relevant quarters. Soon afterwards the Trade Secretary, Edmund Dell, wrote to David Owen at the Foreign Office:

> Several speakers expressed concern about the effect which our stand on human rights was having, and would continue to have for some time on our trade interests there. Since then, George [i.e. Lord] Nelson of G.E.C. has written to Fred Catherwood, who as you know is Chairman of the British Overseas Trade Board, following up their discussions at the dinner. Apart from reiterating his concern over our long-term trade interests generally, he has particularly drawn attention to G.E.C.'s and British Aerospace's interest in selling the Hawk aircraft to Argentina (worth about £100 million). He believes that our decision not to receive Admiral Massera when he was in London during the summer weighed heavily with the Argentines in deciding against buying British frigates . . . I understand that you are at present considering whether or not General Agosti, Argentine Chief of Air Staff, should be invited here and be received at the appropriate level. Nelson and Catherwood both urge that we should invite him (I gather that Agosti would like to come here), as failure to do so could damage our chances of success.

Agosti, however, was not invited.

The business community in Britain had seen Argentina as a potential gold mine – a country which had been badly managed, and which needed only the smack of firm government to turn it into a highly profitable market. A consortium of British banks led by Lloyds lent the new junta 75 million US dollars within months of the coup, and there was much more to come. The British financial press commented favourably on Argentina's prospects time and again: as late as April 1979 the *Financial Times* wrote, 'For the past three years Argentina has been the darling of the world banking confraternity, and financiers have beaten a path to Buenos Aires, offering ever more mouthwatering terms for loans . . . the days of bankruptcy are over and Argentina's reserves are approaching 7 billion dollars.' Such comforting words encouraged more financiers still to follow the beaten path, with the result that by the time of the Falklands invasion British banks were owed 2 billion US dollars by the darling of their confraternity. Part of the reason for the confidence they had felt in Argentina's economic future was that it had been in the hands of someone who spoke their language – literally, since José Alfredo Martínez de Hoz had been educated at Eton.

The incoming Conservative Government resolved to renounce meddling of the kind David Owen had indulged in. Cecil Parkinson, as Trade Minister, told the House of Commons, 'I believe civil trade with other countries should be determined by commercial considerations and not by the character of the governments concerned.' A month after taking office, Britain restored full diplomatic relations with Argentina by sending an ambassador to Buenos Aires for the first time since the shooting incident involving the *Shackleton* a few weeks before the coup. This was not in itself seen as a bad thing by people concerned with human rights in Argentina; indeed, there had been suggestions that an ambassador might have had the insight and authority to point out to London the true nature of the régime in Buenos Aires. But the intention was not primarily to obtain a clearer understanding of the Argentine dictatorship: it was to demonstrate that the past was over and done with. The following year Martínez de Hoz came to Britain, met Mrs Thatcher and several of the leading members of her government and called on Britain to 'hurry up and be partners in our development'. In August 1980 Cecil Parkinson visited Argentina and met General Videla. He told him that he hoped relations would improve between the two countries after what he called 'a dark period'. Earlier, at a news conference, he had gone so far as to praise the economic achievements of the junta. 'The British people,' he said, 'admire the efforts of Argentina to reduce inflation,' and he drew a strong comparison between Britain's economic problems and Argentina's. The following month Lord Carrington, the Foreign Secretary, met his Argentine opposite number at the United Nations, much as David Owen had two years previously. This time, though, the only reference to human rights was a hope from Lord Carrington that what he called 'improvements' would continue.

None of this constitutes a particular indictment either of the Callaghan government or of Mrs Thatcher's. Dr Owen achieved little by his stand on human rights (though presumably it gave him some satisfaction that Admiral Massera did not, after all, place an order for British-made frigates which would have been involved in the 1982 war with Britain). Mr Parkinson's only achievement lay in encouraging British banks to think that a régime which came to power owing 9 billion dollars, and was to leave it owing 43 billion, was a good risk; plenty of other people made the same mistake. And yet, quite clearly, British actions during the period in which the military were in power in Argentina convinced the Argentines, not just that Her Majesty's Government had no great interest in human rights, but that it lacked the backbone to resist if its own interests – in the shape of the Falkland

Islands – were attacked. In Argentina, the decision to restore full diplomatic relations, and Mr Parkinson's ingratiating words at his press conference, were widely seen as attempts by Britain to curry favour; just as, some years earlier, the Argentines had interpreted Mr Callaghan's low-profile policy as showing that Britain was nervous of their reactions, and was prepared to ignore small-scale infringements in the interests of keeping Argentina sweet. In other words, the only practical experience that successive juntas had had of Britain was of a country which would keep quiet rather than stand up for its own interests. Ignoring the true nature of the military régime and what it was doing to its own people proved to be a highly effective way of persuading Buenos Aires that Britain would not care very much if they decided to turn on British subjects who happened to be living in a group of islands off their shores.

Compounding all this was the almost complete ignorance that existed between the two countries: Argentina imagined that Britain was too decadent and sunk in on itself to react if one of its possessions were invaded, while British MPs and leader-writers, a number of whom used the phrase 'a tin-pot fascist dictatorship' behaved as though Argentina were a small banana republic along the lines of Somoza's Nicaragua. Two countries as separated as Britain and Argentina can perhaps be forgiven for not understanding each other in too much detail, especially if they are as isolationist and uninterested in the outside world as Argentina is, and as Britain has become. But there is little excuse for the diplomatic services of the two countries to have had so little effect on the governments to which they were accredited. In London, successive Argentine ambassadors were so ineffectual that their argument about the ownership of the Falklands made absolutely no impact whatever on British thinking throughout the years that led up to the invasion. Even when the policy of the Foreign Office was clearly to find a way to hand the islands over to Argentina, the embassy made no apparent effort to support the thrust of that policy by seeking to win over British public opinion or lobbying MPs or journalists; such a campaign might at least have warned the Argentine foreign ministry of the strength of feeling that existed on the issue. Conversely, the British Embassy in Buenos Aires gave the Argentine régime, and leading supporters of it like Nicanor Costa Méndez, no reason to think that they were dealing with a government they should treat carefully or with any great respect. The mutual ignorance cost a thousand lives in the two countries, and perhaps 2,000 million pounds to their exchequers: a heavy price, in Britain's case, for the advice in the Duncan Report that Argentina was an outer area, of some commercial but no political importance.

# 20 THE END OF THE SURREALIST STATE

*'Milicos muy mal paridos,*
*Qué es lo que han hecho con los desaparecidos?*
*La deuda externa, la corrupción*
*Son la peor mierda que ha tenido la nación.'*

*(Filthy military bastards, what have you done with the disappeared? The foreign debt, the corruption, have landed the country in the worst shit it's ever been in.)*
– Demonstration chant, 16 December 1982.

It took three minutes for the forty-first President of the Argentine Republic to be sworn in at the Casa Rosada. In a gloomy ceremony, the man who took the oath was a grey-faced, unobtrusive figure of fifty-four: a retired major-general, Reynaldo Benito Antonio Bignone. He had been forced to retire by his long-standing enemy, General Galtieri, and now he had been brought out of the shadows to be sworn in as Galtieri's successor. The oath was administered by the even greyer and more sombre Army commander, Major-General Cristino Nicolaides. In the wake of Argentina's military defeat and the fall of the junta, he represented the only continuing source of power. Yet even the oath he read out was a discredited one: Bignone had to swear to commit himself to the basic objectives of the Process of National Reorganization and of the national constitution; but the national constitution had been effectively suspended seven years earlier by Mrs Perón, while the Process had all but melted away as a result of the economic disaster which underlay the military one. General Nicolaides was said to believe that Bignone's only function now was to hold the country together under the immense strains it had been subjected to, until something turned up. What that something might be, Nicolaides had no very clear idea; but he thought it might be connected with elections.

Even the military junta itself had crumbled. The Air Force representative, Brigadier Basilio Lami Dozo, had failed to turn up for the swearing-in ceremony. The Air Force had performed spectacularly well during the war with Britain, unlike the other two armed forces, and Lami Dozo believed he had earned a greater share in power and a greater say in who should be President; but he had not been given either. The commander-in-chief of the Navy, Admiral Anaya, had also threatened to stay away, but at the last minute he had slipped into the room where the ceremony was taking place. He stood quietly in the background, an observer rather than a participant. Because neither of the other services was taking part, the legal statutes relating to the swearing in had to be altered at the last minute, so that it would be an Army affair alone.

The date was 1 July 1982: by chance, the eighth anniversary of the death of Juan Perón. The war in the Falklands had been over for just 17 days. During that time the leaders of the three armed forces had met twice a day, trying to decide who should take the place of General Galtieri and how to create a formula which would bring stability and continuity. When each day's meeting was over, the individual commanders would discuss the position with their own senior officers, sounding out opinion and formulating new compromises. The position of the Air Force was made public by Lami Dozo, when he spoke to a group of reporters who were following him round on a tour of air bases: 'The Air Force does not want one of the armed forces to dominate the others. It wants a sharing of power.' Since the Air Force was traditionally the least important of the services in political terms, he was in effect demanding an agreement by the Army and the Navy to stand back and allow him to become the king-maker. Perhaps Lami Dozo wanted to be President himself, but if so he must have known that it would be unacceptable to his colleagues in the junta – despite the public popularity of the Air Force. Failing that, he wanted a group of carefully chosen civilians to take over.

But the Army would not swallow that. However badly it might have performed in the Falklands, it was still the senior service; and there were several influential Army figures who believed that there should be at least another four years of military rule before it would be safe to hand over power to civilians. The Air Force and the Navy, for their part, believed there should be a hand-over to an elected government by March 1984. In the end, the compromise came, not between the services, but between the two leading men in the Army: Nicolaides accepted Bignone's argument that there would eventually have to be an election. The constitutional crisis was over, and nobody pointed out that it was precisely that kind of argument and indecision between properly elected politicians which had caused the armed forces to step in and seize power so often during the previous half-century. The myth that the military were no-nonsense, efficient sort of people who could be relied on to take rough decisions quickly was shattered.

The surreal atmosphere persisted. In March 1983, President Bignone, the representative of a military régime which had exterminated the left and its sympathizers for seven years in the name of Christian and Western civilization, went to the Non-Aligned Conference in Delhi. There he met openly with Fidel Castro of Cuba, who had supported Argentina during the war with Britain and received Costa Méndez in Havana. But pictures of the meeting between Bignone and Castro were not shown on Argentine television: the President's press secretary felt it would be unsuitable. By this time, the armed forces were in greater disrepute than ever, and officers and private soldiers no longer walked the streets in uniform because of the insults they received. Mention of the war or of the armed forces in the cinema brought angry shouts and whistles, while one of the most popular films of 1983 was *Missing*, the more-or-less true story of an American who disappears after the military coup of 1973 in Chile. His father, in coming to search for him, slowly realizes the totalitarian nature of the Pinochet régime and the part the US Government had played in the staging of the coup. By the time the film was shown in Argentina, censorship by the military was starting to crumble, though it seems that this particular film, which deals with the whole question of people 'disappearing' and being murdered for their political convictions, was allowed to be screened in Argentina because it was felt to be anti-Chilean. The cinemas that showed it were packed even for the afternoon performances, and all around in the uncomfortable seats people were weeping openly as the film showed the father's growing understanding of the widespread nature of the political murders. When the film's characters wander through an immense glass-floored mortuary filled with dead bodies, some people in the audience could stand no more, and left. Others shouted insults at the screen. And when, at the end, the father tells an American diplomat that he has at least one right remaining – the right to go to court to sue the American Government for its involvement in the mass murders –

there was an explosion of applause in the cinema. The notion that it was a citizen's right to take his own government to court for wrong-doing was just beginning to grow again in Argentina.

In the meantime, the pressures on the military to give up power were growing. On the night of 16 December 1982 a 'march of the people for democracy' took place in the centre of Buenos Aires, with several hundred thousand people taking part. There were speeches by the leaders of the various established democratic parties, but they had been muted in tone; prosecution might, it was felt, follow if anyone went too far, so none of them did anything more than talk generally about the need for elections. But the crowd was under no such inhibition. In the thickly-packed anonymity of the Plaza de Mayo they chanted fierce accusations against the military, calling them filthy bastards and blaming them for the disappeared, the corruption, and the loss of so many men in the Falklands War. The police were in surprisingly small numbers at the demonstration, and only about thirty stood between the increasingly angry crowd and the Casa Rosada. At the time there was speculation that the military government was deliberately trying to entice people to attack the presidential palace in order to discredit the whole move towards democratic government. Whatever the truth, the Young Peronists in the crowd were more than ready to be enticed. Less than half an hour after the official speakers had finished and left the Plaza, hundreds of youths began swarming over the barriers in front of the Casa Rosada.

The thirty policemen were completely overwhelmed in the rush. Two of them were stabbed, and others defended themselves by firing tear-gas into the dense crowds. That provoked further violence. Some youths grabbed the fallen barricades and used them as battering-rams to try to force open the gates of the Casa Rosada. Others pelted the building with everything they could find: coins, stones, cobbles from the streets, the heavy rubber piping which the Peronist drummers used to beat their drums, the staves which had carried their banners. The glass shattered and fell from a dozen windows along the front of the building.

At that stage, the main force of police which had been stationed down the side-streets that led into the Plaza came charging out at the crowds in a phalanx, firing tear-gas and lashing out with their heavy night-sticks as they came. People screamed in panic, and tripped over in the rush, bringing down dozens of others with them. One man fell directly under the horses of a troop of mounted police and was trampled. Four newspaper photographers were badly beaten up for trying to take pictures of arrests, and one was nearly strangled as he tried to save his camera. During the mêlée a man in plain clothes produced a pump-action shot-gun and fired several times at close range at a seventeen-year-old who was trying to escape the tear-gas. The youth later died in hospital. His assailant walked calmly away to a green Ford Falcon and drove off.

Afterwards, General Carlos Cerda, the Under-Secretary for Institutional Affairs, said, 'I regret that demonstrations intended to reaffirm the Argentine people's democratic feeling were adulterated by well-organized activists who managed to attack Government House.' In many ways he was right; the action of about two thousand militants had ensured that one man was dead and more than sixty were injured badly, and a hundred and twenty arrests had been made. But among the military the feeling grew that the Montonero guerrillas had resurfaced, and that such things were only to be expected if the lid which had once been so firmly battened down on Argentine society were allowed to be lifted. Sixteen days before the demonstration, President Bignone had announced that elections would take place before the end of 1983. That meant that he had played the only valuable card in his hand. A military government that announces its own forthcoming departure from office becomes a little more destabilized with each day that passes; and the glum, unattractive Bignone, who nevertheless had come into office determined to begin negotiations with the politicians, found himself with no other decision to make than the date of the elections and the hand-over of power.

By February 1983, two months after the great demonstration in the Plaza de Mayo, Bignone was under heavy pressure. On 10 February the junta met for eight hours, during which the new commanders of the Air Force and the Navy, Brigadier Augusto Hughes and Admiral Rubén Franco, led a concerted attack on Bignone's record and tactics. At lunchtime, the Army commander, General Nicolaides, suggested a break in the discussions, and went off to have lunch with Bignone alone. At the lunch, Bignone offered to resign, but Nicolaides persuaded him to stay on, and when the full meeting resumed afterwards he argued strongly that another change of President would only lower the esteem in which the armed forces were held still further. The meeting ended with a tough communiqué warning civilian politicians against attacking the military government's record.

The events of the previous few months had seriously alarmed the officer corps of all three services. The hatred which the mass of the population now clearly felt towards them, the disguised but nevertheless pointed threats about what would happen to them under a civilian government, the fear of being prosecuted for the excesses of the campaign against the left, all combined to produce the demand that the junta should clamp down on signs of opposition as strongly as possible. It was a short-term expedient, but no one seemed prepared to think about the long term. As a result, an official telegram was sent off immediately by the junta's orders to a Radical Party politician, Víctor Martínez, later to become Argentina's Vice-President, ordering him to confirm or withdraw the attacks he had made on the military during a speech in Tucumán Province. He had said, 'The heroes who built our motherland did not dedicate themselves to thieving, like today's military officers.' When Martínez received the telegram he decided not to opt for martyrdom. He refused to retract what he had said in his speech, but explained that what he had meant was that the armed forces had stolen political power, not that they had stolen money or goods. No prosecution followed. The junta had also considered taking on two rather more considerable targets – a leading Peronist, Deolindo Bittel, who was later to become his party's vice-presidential candidate, and Raúl Alfonsín, who had not yet emerged as the foremost figure in the Radical Party. Bittel had said that the military had shown they knew neither how to govern the country nor to fight. As it was, the junta's decision was to let both of them off without a warning, reflecting, perhaps, that men of the stature of Bittel and Alfonsín were unlikely to back down as easily as Martínez, and that a court case in which the junta had, in effect, to defend its abysmal record both in government and in the war against Britain would be disastrous.

In the streets of Buenos Aires, meanwhile, the black market value of the US dollar had reached unprecedented heights, being quoted at its peak at 76,000 pesos. And yet newspaper correspondents noted that the junta's crisis had the effect of sending up the price of shares on the stock market. One quoted a stock exchange observer as saying, 'Look, this is paradoxical, but when there is a crisis nowadays, people think there may be a new Economy Minister, and that therefore there might even be an improvement in economic policy.' Things could scarcely have been worse or more clumsily handled than they were. It proved impossible, for instance, to get a single clear estimate of how much Argentina's foreign debt amounted to. At the end of 1982 Jorge Wehbe, the third Finance Minister in nine months, put it at US$43 billion, which in Latin America made Argentina the third most indebted country after Brazil and Mexico. In January, however, the Air Force carried out its own investigation and decided that the debt was US$37.8 billion. Wehbe replied that he must have been mistaken, and that the debt was in fact US$37 billion exactly. Not long afterwards the Central Bank announced that the real figure was US$38.7 billion. Outraged politicians demanded to know what had happened to the missing billions.

It was less easy to talk about the military's record on human rights so openly, though at about this time one of the chief offenders himself chose to speak out publicly about what he had done, in terms that showed he found nothing to be ashamed of. General Ramón Camps, the recently retired chief of the Buenos Aires provincial police, was credited with having overseen the 'disappearance' of five thousand people – a figure he himself did not, apparently, disagree with. Camps was an elaborately courteous man, who rarely refused to give interviews to foreign journalists unless there were legal reasons for doing so; his reasoning seemed to be that if only he could explain in person to people in Western Europe and the United States about what had happened in Argentina, they would understand and give up their ill-informed criticism. He was a leading supporter of the concept that the Third World War had been fought out on Argentine soil, and that world Communism had suffered a serious setback there.

He lived in what amounted to an armoury. Rifles, shotguns and revolvers were arranged around his sitting-room in places where he could presumably get at them easily, if some small spark from the Third World War should ignite in his particular neighbourhood. His mental state was fragile, to say the least; once when he was being filmed at his obsessively cluttered desk by a Dutch camera crew he became violently angry and ordered everyone out of the house because the cameraman had moved a lamp by an inch or two. Soon afterwards, however, in the most polite terms, he invited them back and the interview was duly filmed, though the lamp stayed in its place.

At the end of 1982, Camps agreed to meet a correspondent from a Spanish newspaper. He was in a bland, almost expansive mood. 'I am proud to have defeated subversion,' he said. The correspondent moved on to the subject of the fate of the disappeared: something nobody had spoken about in public in Argentina for nearly six years. 'There are no missing people still alive in Argentina,' Camps told him. 'If there are any still alive, they must be abroad.' The interviewer went on to ask if the military had fought terrorism with terrorist methods. 'Why not?' Camps replied.

Month by month the situation deteriorated. Argentina had once been the country where being poor was defined as eating steak only once a week; now soup-kitchens were opening up, and salaries in 1982 alone had lost nearly a third of their real value. There were sudden outbursts of apparently spontaneous rage: as when hundreds of people gathered in a suburb of Buenos Aires to protest about the high level of taxation. A few committed people had turned up to begin with, and the rest had joined in when they heard what was happening. The police dispersed them with their accustomed brutality. Small-scale industrial disruptions took place everywhere, leading to nationwide general strikes which were themselves aggravated by the rivalry between different factions of the CGT – the umbrella organization for the union movement.

On 28 February 1983, at the height of the unrest, President Bignone appeared on television to make a statement. 'We were watching on a colour set,' one viewer said, 'but Bignone made it seem like black-and-white.' Nevertheless he was showing the country the only way out of its political cul-de-sac: elections would be held on 30 October, and a new civilian President would be inaugurated ninety days later. 'The people will decide what their destiny is to be. These elections will pass into history as unimpeachable.' There was no immediate rejoicing, because the political parties had wanted elections to be held much sooner, but there was a very real sense of relief. Nevertheless, Bignone was heavily criticized by some elements in the armed forces for laying them open to the revenge of the civilian population once the new government was installed. These elements had already tried to overthrow Bignone, and their influence had been sufficiently strong the previous December for him to offer an extraordinary deal to the main political parties: in return for an orderly transfer of power and an agreement that the military would play no part in the election process, he asked that a number of topics should, by agreement, remain permanently undiscussed: the war in the Falklands, economic corruption, and the fate of the disappeared.

It is difficult to believe that even the politically innocent Bignone can have expected that the parties would voluntarily accept that they could never discuss the three most damaging subjects in the country's recent history. They had rejected the offer out of hand, confident that the only course Bignone could now take was to offer elections without preconditions. The sombre television performance of 28 February showed that they were right. From now on the military would have only one major concern: how to protect themselves against the retribution they expected from the country they had governed since 1976. By September 1983 they had come up with an answer: the 'law of national pacification', which pardoned not only those who carried out their orders in the struggle against what they saw as subversion, but also those who had issued the orders. In an attempt to make the law more palatable, it was extended to include many of the people who had been the targets of the military's campaign: there was to be an amnesty for former terrorists as well, though members of illegal groups who were underground or working abroad were excluded, and so were people who had already been convicted. The publication of the amnesty brought an immediate outburst of scorn and condemnation which increased the military's sense of nervousness about the future, and it was noticeable that officers who were still in positions of importance in state organizations were frequently doing everything they could to ensure that they extracted the maximum profit from their last days in office. Payments were increasingly demanded in dollars from customers and clients, at new and higher rates of extortion. Some military men decided that the time had come to put themselves and their investments out of harm's way, and they moved off in the last days of military government to Uruguay or further afield. Brigadier Osvaldo Cacciatore who left Buenos Aires with the profits of his service as the city's mayor packed in bundles of notes in a suitcase, and disappeared to Montevideo, was followed by dozens of fellow-officers; none of whom later returned, as he did.

But by this time the military were yesterday's men, despised and discredited, whose only function was to leave the stage as noiselessly as they could. All the emphasis was on the resurgent political parties. There were five main ones, two of which by general consent would fight it out for victory: the Peronists, and the Radicals, whose party was the Unión Cívica Radical. Since political activity had been illegal since 1976, the structures of the various parties had to be geared up again at short notice, recruitment of members had to begin again, and new office-holders had to be appointed to take the place of people who had fled abroad or disappeared. Newspapers and magazines, which for some months had been allowing themselves greater and greater liberties as it became clear that the military authorities were losing the will to crack down on them, sent out their reporters to question people in the street about what they wanted in the way of a new government, and one or two hired marketing companies to carry out opinion polls. The best conducted of these, carried out at about the time when President Bignone announced the date of the election, found that the Peronists had a lead of around 40 per cent over the Radicals in party terms. But in Argentina's presidential system, it was the man rather than the party which the electorate would vote for, and the identity of the man remained to be settled in a series of run-offs and primaries on the North American model. There were three main candidates on the Peronist side: Angel Robledo, a former Interior Minister in Mrs Perón's government who had the support of many of the right-wing trades union leaders; Antonio Cafiero, a one-time Finance Minister during the days when the economy was almost out of control, and who, though belonging to the nationalist wing of the party, had nevertheless been an opponent of López Rega and to some extent of the President herself; and Italo Luder, who had once served briefly as a stand-in President when Isabelita was ill, and who claimed to be the unity candidate. On the Radical side, the choice was more direct: Fernando de la Rua, a young conservative who represented the older elements in the party, and Raúl Alfonsín, who had links with Western European Social Democrats and was noticeably left of centre in the party.

Luder, as the most senior of the candidates in a party where seniority tended to mean closeness to Perón and his wives, had little difficulty in defeating his two rivals. Political correspondents, now that they had candidates to write about once more and not just officers in the armed forces, preferred to concentrate on the apparently closer race between Alfonsín and de la Rua. But Alfonsín, who had been fairly comprehensively beaten when he had sought the presidential nomination in 1972, fought an intelligent campaign in the primaries which ended in his complete victory. Not only that, the opinion polls showed that he had a distinct personal advantage over Luder; even at the start of the primaries, he had a personal lead of 19 to 11 per cent over his Peronist rival.

Luder, however, had his own advantages. For one thing, the

Peronist Party knew where its constituency lay, in the working class and lower-middle class, and had had long experience in bringing that support out on to the streets in a way which made it seem overwhelmingly great. Luder himself was a quiet, undemonstrative man with little or no crowd appeal and none of the glad-handing qualities that Peronism as a movement demanded. But he had been President for the five weeks of Isabelita's illness, in 1975; at the time he managed to impress people by his ability and by the fact that he was a distinct improvement on the woman he was standing in for. *La Opinión*, for instance, had written: 'Luder's first measures as interim president created a sense of euphoria in political circles, having opened new contacts and let fresh air into the relations of the Government with the armed forces and the Opposition.' By 1983 people wanted something different: a President who would express their feelings of profound relief at the ending of the worst period in their history.

The feeling in the early days of the southern spring was euphoric. People gathered in the pedestrian precinct of Florida Street and in large numbers, arguing about the relative merits of the candidates and the parties they supported. The graffiti and the election posters covered every possible surface. People would gather almost spontaneously and find themselves united by the traditional campaign songs to which they were continually adding new verses to express the events of the moment. The Peronists had always been the most fertile inventors of election songs and slogans, and now they found that the younger members of the other parties – and particularly the Radicals and the Intransigents under the much respected left-wing leader Oscar Alende – were using their songs and chants; in particular the one which Peronists had sung time and again over the decades:

*O le le, o la la,*
*Si este no es el Pueblo,*
*El Pueblo dónde está?*

*(If this is not the people, where is the people?)*

The period of the campaign had a curious and attractive sense of unreality to it. Most people assumed that the Peronists would win the election, and that would be repression and violence all over again. Because the outbreak of political freedom was expected to be brief, it had an extra sweetness. The memory of the last years under Peronism also persuaded middle-class people that there was likely to be an economic crisis of 1975 proportions if Luder was elected President, so there seemed to be no reason for not spending the money that might soon be worthless. The shops were thronged with customers, and the seaside resorts started to fill up even in the early stages of the season. Argentina began to take on once again the air of a country that knew how to enjoy itself.

The political spectacle enhanced the enjoyment. It was quickly clear that the race was between the Peronist Party machine and the personality of Raúl Alfonsín. He was an outgoing, ebullient man, whose heavy face and solid physical presence lent extra power to his oratory. In the light of the arc lamps of dozens of public meetings across Argentina, Alfonsín, his face sweating heavily from the heat of the occasion and the effort of putting his points over, would wave his thick forefinger at the crowd, apparently oblivious of the adoration of his party supporters who gathered in their thousands, waving their banners and their innumerable red and white Radical Party flags. Alfonsín, whom American journalists had described as the best leader Argentina had never had, was obliged to persuade people that this time he would be successful. He never appeared to suffer self-doubts about it. His election slogan was unashamedly concentrated on him and his chances, 'Ahora Alfonsín' ('Alfonsín now'), and it was accompanied by a photograph of him in a characteristic pose, his two hands clasped in a symbol of victory. But the Radical Party had never been able to defeat the Peronists in a straight fight; the only victories they had scored in recent years had been when the Peronists were prevented from running. Alfonsín and some (though by no means all) his party colleagues believed that their time had come, but the task was to persuade everybody else of the fact.

Alfonsín was greatly helped by the reputation he had built up during the Process years. There had been moments when he had compromised or kept silent, but for the most part he had been an unspoken defender of human rights and an outright critic of the conduct of the military government. And now that human rights were beginning to emerge as the central issue of the election campaign, his record as a founder-member of the Permanent Assembly on Human Rights in 1975, even before the military take-over, was a guarantee that his claims were genuine.

For a movement built on one man's personality, the Peronists' choice of the grey, lacklustre Italo Luder was a curious one;

perhaps it was a way of indicating that Perón's personality and that of Evita still infused the movement, and could not be superseded. On the other hand, it had been a responsible and intelligent choice. Luder could never totally dissociate himself from the disasters of Isabelita Perón's time as President, but he was clearly not implicated in the worst of the decisions made at the time, and had been briefly called in to take Isabelita's place partly because he was an unexciting personality who could be trusted not to hijack the movement for his own ends. The same reasoning applied to his selection as Presidential candidate now: Peronism was so divided still between left and right that it was essential to have an undramatic figure from the centre to head it. Luder was also a lawyer, and had not been completely silent on human rights during the Process; if he needed to be reminded to take his tie off and behave like one of the boys with the union bosses who would get the vote out on election day, he was nevertheless likely to be acceptable to a large section of the electorate, and especially to the middle classes, whose votes would otherwise go mostly to the Radicals. Luder's trouble was that he was not one of the boys. When he went to the small town of Santa Fe, for instance, to meet the local party machine and speak at a rally, he seemed ill at ease, the fastidious city lawyer finding it difficult to laugh and joke with the kind of tough union fixers who had once gone along with the counter-terror that had followed the guerrilla attacks on their own union's leadership, and had survived in one way or another the difficulties and hardships of military rule. Outside the hall where he had been the guest of honour at a dinner, Luder found himself besieged by people who wanted to shake his hand or slap his back, or simply grab hold of the latest wearer of Perón's mantle. And if Luder lacked the common touch himself, then the common touch reached out for him. Whether or not he found it congenial, Luder, with his mechanical gestures and his precise, unexciting way of public speaking, was the populist candidate.

But the Peronist movement had a life of its own – two lives, indeed – which made it very hard for the party bosses to control. On 17 October, thirteen days before the election, a mass rally was staged at the Vélez Sarsfield football stadium on the outskirts of Buenos Aires to celebrate the day in 1945 when the union bosses, urged on by Evita, had mobilized his working-class supporters and freed Perón from gaol. On the same day, 38 years later, three-quarters of a million people, it was later estimated, crushed into the stadium, packing not just the stands but the field itself, to the point where anyone trying to move through the crush would find themselves lifted off the ground for minutes at a time by the intense pressure of the crowd. The heat of so many bodies was intense; and the noise of the music and the ever-present *bombos* (of which there were several hundred) was magnified many times over by the immense loudspeakers.

More than a thousand people fainted, but the crowds were uncontrollable and they surged backwards and forwards like waves on the sea, breaking against the speakers' platform at one end of the stadium. In front of immense portraits of Perón, Evita and Isabelita, the tiny figures of the current leaders, themselves crammed together alarmingly, addressed the crowd.

For some time the rally went much as the organizers had hoped; the torrid atmosphere was reminiscent of the great days of Peronism, before the split in the movement became too obvious to ignore. Great sections of the crowd at any time would be jumping up and down, in obedience to the chant,

*Borom-bom-bom, borom-bom-bom,*
*El que no salta es un militar*

*(Anyone who doesn't jump is a soldier)*

or singing the hymn of praise to the founder of their movement:

*Perón, Perón,*
*Mi general,*
*Qué grande sos –*

*(Perón, my general, how great you are).*

But songs alone could not unite them. When it was announced that Lorenzo Miguel, the chief union boss and former close ally of Isabelita and of López Rega, would be next to speak, the most active and hitherto enthusiastic part of the crowd exploded into noisy hostility. For the young left-wing supporters of the Montoneros and the Peronist Youth, Miguel was as bad an enemy as the military régimes which had persecuted them, and they were as fiercely opposed to him as they and their allies had been towards the López Rega faction of the Seventies. Miguel's position in the movement was at stake, and he insisted on trying to make himself heard, but his words were drowned out despite the immense loudspeakers. Gamely, his allies on the platform chanted 'Lo-ren-zo' continually, in the hope that the chant would be taken up by other sections of the crowd; but when Miguel tried once again to speak, there was a hail of sticks and coins from the packed crowds in front of the platform. Several struck him on the face and head, and he had to cut his speech short and retire in disgust. It was not a good advertisement for a party which had to convince the voters that the old day of violent division were over.

By contrast, Radical Party rallies were mostly models of harmony and enthusiasm, if not always of organization. Alfonsín went around the country speaking to crowds that seemed to get bigger and bigger as time went past. The social differences between Radical crowds and Peronist ones were stark: the Radicals brought their whole families to hear Alfonsín speak, and they tended to drive rather than come by the hired buses which were one of Peronism's specialities.

These were, after all, mostly better-off people who had once supported the military take-over in 1976, and had turned against the military more because of the collapse of the economy than because they themselves had suffered from the campaign of terror. Nevertheless, the endless playing of songs by singers like Mercedes Sosa and Nacha Guevara preceded every Radical rally, and with Alfonsín and his party colleagues now concentrating on the human rights issue as the crucial one in the campaign, the Radical crowds themselves took over the theme and made it their own, in a way in which the Peronists could not. Peronists might have suffered most heavily under the Process governments, but they had shown the military the way to carry out its campaign of extermination. As the election campaign entered its last week, the Peronists were still ahead in the opinion polls, but Alfonsín was making his mark as a personality in a way Luder could not, and the Radicals were establishing themselves as the party of change, while the Peronists were demonstrating that they were much the same as they had always been.

Against the probabilities of a few weeks before, the Radicals attracted a crowd of around three quarters of a million people in the last days of the campaign at their culminating rally in the Avenue of the 9 July, which bisects Buenos Aires and is more than a city block wide. The red and white banners filled the avenue for nearly a mile in front of the obelisk, the monument which commemorates the raising of the Argentine flag for the first time in the city. The main street intersecting the avenue was crammed for two blocks in either direction by people who could scarcely hear, let alone catch a glimpse of, the Radicals' candidate for the presidency. But the fact of being able to bring out so many enthusiasts convinced a large part of the electorate that for the first time the Radicals were sufficiently large and well organized to be able to confront the Peronists on equal terms – and just possibly to beat them. With the confident instinct which had marked Alfonsín's entire campaign, his planners had ensured that when his speech to the rally came to an end and he stood on the platform holding up his hands in the familiar gesture of victory, the vast electronic advertisement screen that overlooked the obelisk took on the image of Alfonsín in the same gesture. The crowd roared its appreciation.

Even so, most people still believed that the Peronists would win, and they themselves, it seems, never considered the possibility that they might lose. They were, however, stung by the size of the Radicals' final rally, since they regarded themselves as the party of mass mobilization; and they had after some initial dithering, managed to arrange that two days before the election they would themselves take over the Avenue of the 9 July and draw an even bigger crowd to it. Probably they did: though press estimates of a million were more a general expression of the immense size of the gathering than an attempt at mathematical accuracy. It *felt* like a crowd of a million people, as it pushed and strained at the metal barricades and yelled and sweated its way through another evening of violent emotion. The crush, the excitement, the casualties were all worse than those at Vélez Sarsfield twelve days earlier. In the immense sea of people, two women gave birth to children, several people were crushed almost to death, there were a number of shootings, and a gang carried out an armed robbery. One man climbed the thirty-foot tower set aside for television cameramen, laid about him with his fists when he reached the top, had an epileptic fit, and was casually pushed unconscious over the side by the security men. It took an ambulance twenty minutes to get him through the crowd. On the platform in front of the obelisk were Italo Luder, who gave his usual unconvincing performance even on this most important of nights, and a silent Lorenzo Miguel, who had finally realized that it would not help the party if he made a speech. Overhead, above the heat and noise and rhetoric, a chartered aircraft flew, the lights on its wings flashing out the message 'VOTE LUDER'. But alternating with that, the lights spelled out another name: that of the rising star of the Peronist movement, who was that night single-handedly to wreck its chance of being elected.

Herminio Iglesias was the party's candidate for the governorship of Buenos Aires. Reputed to own a string of brothels, he had lost his left eyelid and his left testicle in a shoot-out which he always maintained had been connected with the underground struggle against the armed forces, and which his enemies said had been an incident in a gangland war. (When asked by a national magazine during an interview if his injuries had affected him in any way, Iglesias said people should bring him their sisters and their wives if they doubted his continuing virility.) He was an expansive character who habitually wore a ring with diamonds set in the shape of a horse-shoe, and – to the ears of the most fastidious – spoke execrable Spanish. His links with prominent supporters of the military régime had sometimes been strong, though he maintained that he had been one of the very few politicians to speak out on the subject of human rights. As candidate for the richest and most powerful of all the non-governmental posts being contested, Iglesias had been a special target of the Radicals, and his anger towards them perhaps lured him farther than he intended during this final rally, which was being watched on television by millions of viewers who would be voting in thirty-six hours' time.

Iglesias, who was adored by large sections of the party, arrived late at the rally and had to be carried head-high over the crowd in order to reach the podium. His arrival created an ecstasy of cheering and singing, and halted the speeches for several minutes. Italo Luder seemed faintly embarrassed by Iglesias's grandstanding techniques, but duly made his speech and left the platform. The crowd, however, wanted something rather more boisterous after the long evening and Iglesias, who had remained behind on the platform together with the other party bosses after Luder had left, could sense it. He stared out into the darkness of the immense crowd, and saw that some of the more violent spirits had started burning an effigy of Uncle Sam not far away from the platform. Elsewhere, held above the heads of the crowd, there were other symbols of their disapproval, including a coffin with Raúl Alfonsín's name on it. Forgetting, perhaps, the fact that the television cameras were still broadcasting the event live – or maybe not caring – Iglesias waved to the crowd to send the coffin up towards him. They did so, and Iglesias, leaning down from the platform, set light to it with his cigarette lighter.

The crowd loved it, but it was the crucial moment of the

campaign. Within hours of having to decide which way to vote, millions of uncommitted or wavering electors all over the country, having just emerged from seven years of violent and barbarous rule, saw one of the major figures in the Peronist movement perform an act which symbolized a continuation of violent and barbarous politics. The next morning people everywhere were discussing what Iglesias had done, and condemning it strongly: even those who belonged to the Peronists' natural constituency. The following day, Sunday 30 October, the election took place. By a clear margin, Raúl Alfonsín was elected President, and the Radicals had a sizeable mandate to carry out their commitment to safeguarding human rights and dismantling the last traces of military power. As for Herminio Iglesias, he was defeated in the contest for the governorship of Buenos Aires by a considerably bigger swing than was recorded nationally against the Peronist Party as a whole.

# 21 THE NEW BEGINNING

*'We'll never be afraid again'* – refrain from popular song written and sung by Maria Elena Walsh.

Forty-eight hours before President Alfonsín's Inauguration Day, 10 December 1983, hundreds of posters began to appear on the walls and hoardings of Buenos Aires. Eerie, crude, ghost-like almost, they showed simply the hand-drawn outline of a life-sized human figure, with no features and no indication of age or sex. Most were anonymous, but some – friends, perhaps, of the people who drew them – carried a name and a date. Under many of the women's names was the single word 'pregnant'. The art students of the city had prepared the posters, determined that the Disappeared, too, should be represented at the inauguration. As the new President drove from his headquarters at the slightly seedy Panamericano Hotel in an open car, standing with his wife and waving delightedly, a troop of cavalrymen in shakos riding chestnut horses behind him, he must have seen dozens of the posters at the back of the cheering, ecstatic crowds who lined his route. Now the man who had promised to bring to light what had happened to the Disappeared was about to take charge of the government.

For the tens of thousands who had lost relatives and friends, and the millions whose lives had been affected in some way for the worse by the events of the previous seven years, the occasion was a joyful one. Bells rang, car horns sounded incessantly, transistors blared out the Maria Elena Walsh song which had become the anthem of the transition from military to civilian government, and the light wind which made the hot December day pleasant caught the countless bits of paper people were continually throwing enthusiastically into the air and floated them as high as the rooftops of the city. By the time the presidential cavalcade reached the Plaza de Mayo, filled, as on so many previous occasions during the years since 1976, by a vast crowd, the bonnet of the black official car was covered with paper and the speed slowed to that of a gentle walk as the car and its outriders nudged their way through the dense pack of people.

Inside the main audience chamber of the Casa Rosada, with its heavy white and gold plaster-work, and the countless mirrors which recalled the French originals on which the architecture of the building was based, the dour figure of General Bignone, the last military dictator to hold power, was waiting to perform the brief ceremony. Behind the group was the charming, larger-than-life-sized bust, Art Nouveau in style, of a young woman who symbolized the Argentine nation itself. There was a sudden hush as the invited guests – presidents, prime ministers and foreign ministers, but also personal friends of Alfonsín's from the difficult days, and people who had stood up for human rights when it was dangerous and unpopular to do so – saw that the moment for the ceremony had come. Bignone, wearing civilian clothes for once, in deference to the spirit of the occasion, placed the blue and white sash over his successor's shoulder, and handed him the white staff of office. The oath of office was administered, and the forty-first President gave way to the forty-second. Bignone, for all his greyness and lack of political flair, had at least kept the country together in the 17 months he had been in power, and had ensured an orderly transfer of power to an elected leader. And in its way, the Argentine nation, as symbolized by the bust behind them, had shown a greater stability than most Argentines had expected, and an ability to work together which few Argentines had suspected they possessed.

For a single instant the new President stood there, carrying the symbols of his new office and yet looking more than ever the slightly rumpled provincial lawyer from Chascomús, not fully at home in the sophisticated, corrupt atmosphere of Buenos Aires politics; and then the moment passed, and the familiar smile came over Alfonsín's face as the audience stood to applaud him, and the change which had taken place in Argentine political life. The cameras of Argentine television, lingered on the faces of the guests: Vice-President Bush from the United States, Felipe Gonzalez, the Prime Minister of Spain, the French Prime Minister Pierre Mauroy, Daniel Ortega, the leader of the junta in Nicaragua. There were, too, faces from the past: María Estela Martínez de Perón, in a black and white check suit, who had returned the previous day for a brief visit from her place of exile in Madrid, and had immediately set about her leading supporters, berating them for their lack of democratic conduct and ordering them to co-operate with the new order as represented by Alfonsín – the man who had beaten them in the election. There were others, like the winner of the 1980 Nobel Peace Prize, Adolfo Pérez Esquivel, who had had the courage to speak out against the disappearances and the torture, and had later condemned the invasion of the Falkland Islands. Alfredo Bravo was there, leaning on his walking stick because of the injuries he had suffered after his kidnapping in 1976, when he was head of the main teachers' union. Not far away was Robert Cox, the former editor of the *Buenos Aires Herald*, which had been the first to publicize Bravo's case and the only one to report the great majority of disappearances. After being forced to leave Argentina, he had settled down in the United States as editor of a small newspaper, as unremarkable perhaps as the *Herald* had been, in the days before it was called upon to take its stand against the kidnappers and torturers. Now he was back, briefly, as an invited guest to see the beginning of a new system. Hebe Bonafini and Adela Antokaletz, who had stood every Thursday outside the Casa Rosada for seven years with the Mothers of the Plaza, were among the guests as well, glad at the political changes but already starting to be worried that Alfonsín would stop short of their demand that everyone proven to be guilty of human rights offences should be punished. They and the other Mothers of the Plaza had already given their welcome to another guest, Patricia Derian, who had visited Buenos Aires so often as President Carter's special envoy, and received rude and insulting treatment; for the first time, she had been received with honour. Senator Hipólito Solari Yrigoyen, a friend and ally of Alfonsín since the early Seventies, and soon to be his roving ambassador, had not been inside the Casa Rosada since the night in 1966, when he and a small group of young Radical Party aides had gathered protectively around their leader, President Illia, during the coup which the military staged because they were bored with him. Looking around him now, Solari Yrigoyen was reminded of those hours, and found himself, inevitably, considering the possibility that another Radical President could be turned out of office by the military. The delighted faces he could see everywhere in the white and gold chamber, the international attention Alfonsín was receiving, the joy outside in the streets, the humiliation of the military leadership, all made it more likely than ever before that this civilian government, at least, would run its course unchecked. But no one could be sure. The lack of fixity in Argentine political life, the desire for change, the restlessness and the willingness to believe the worst, would all, in time, work against Alfonsín as they had worked against other democratic presidents in the past. But none had quite the advantages Alfonsín possessed, even though none had faced problems quite as bad: a debt of 43 billion dollars, the world's highest inflation rate (450 per cent by the end of 1983, and double that a year later), a union system which owed its allegiance to a fractious and sometimes irresponsible political party. Most of the onlookers at the inauguration shared the anxieties: Pérez Esquivel said, 'The dictatorship might be over, but the problems it caused are still with us.' Robert Cox, struck with the pleasure of the occasion still, said, 'It's wonderful to see all the optimism about democracy, just marvellous. But they're going to need a lot of help, an awful lot.'

There were only two seats set aside at the ceremony for people from Britain, and one of those was empty. Tricia Feeney of Amnesty International, who had been in charge of a highly successful campaign to draw attention to the terror in Argentina, had been sent an airline ticket by the new government, but had been obliged, under the strict rules Amnesty imposes upon itself, to hand it back. And the organization felt it should spend its money on helping people who were still suffering under brutal dictatorships, rather than on sending her to celebrate the end of one. And so the lone guest from Britain was David Stephen who had first met Alfonsín in 1976 (when he detected 'a sort of defiant provincialism' about him), and who had, as Dr David Owen's special adviser at the Foreign Office from 1978 to 1979, played a part in influencing Owen's aproach on Argentina. Stephen had left the damp, cold atmosphere of a Northern European winter and arrived in Buenos Aires only a few hours before. He detected an air of sadness in the joy around him, because of all the disappearances and deaths; it gave the occasion a sombreness it might not otherwise have had. There was no representative from the British Government, though Mrs Thatcher had sent a message which seemed promising: 'On the occasion of your inauguration I wanted to let you know that, although we have many differences, we can all take pleasure in the restoration of democracy to Argentina, believing that it will bring freedom and justice to all your people. Today brings new hope to your country.' In a sense, though it would have been tactless to draw attention to the fact, it was Mrs Thatcher who had made possible the end of military rule and the arrival in power of an elected government. Alfonsín, whose mother's name was Foulkes and who shared, through her, a distant British ancestry, replied to the message in a way that was calculated to sound attractive to British ears: 'I thank you for your words about the re-establishment of democratic institutions in Argentina. I coincide with your appraisal of the existence of differences between Argentina and the United Kingdom. Regarding this, it would be useful to remember an old English saying, "Where there's a will, there's a way."'

Even at the time, though, the new President must have realized that the will was unlikely to be there. Argentina was not prepared to give up the demand for sovereignty over the Falklands – such a move would have been suicidal for a government which depended on the votes of its political supporters – and Britain still had no long-term strategy for the islands, and would clearly be caught between the desire not to give up possessions which had cost so much to retain, and the realization that one day, no matter how long it would take, they would probably belong to Argentina. Even the Beagle Channel dispute with Chile would be settled more quickly.

But Alfonsín, as he left his guests and made his way to a balcony to address the joyful crowds, had other problems: not least the protection of democracy from the armed forces, if they should one day feel able to challenge the civilians again. Already he had ordered the retirement of thirty out of the sixty serving generals in the army, and had appointed relatively junior officers to be commanders-in-chief of the three armed forces. As he came out on to the balcony from which so many hopeful, rousing speeches had been made through the years, from the harangues of Perón and Evita to the illusory triumph of Galtieri, twenty months before, the crowd went wild with delight. But, as David Stephen had noticed, there was a difference in the emotion; on this day, just as there had been a serenity at the inauguration itself, so there was an atmosphere of sheer happiness in the crowd outside, unmixed with the kind of ferocity which had been a part of so many gatherings in the Plaza de Mayo in the past. Even so, it had been felt better to bring ex-President Bignone out by a back exit from the Casa Rosada; the mood of the crowd, might, it was thought, change if he were recognized. As Alfonsín looked out at the sea of faces below him, there were banners of every one of Argentina's political parties, whose supporters had turned out to celebrate, not necessarily his victory, but the victory of the political process. Further across the square not far from the scene of the police attack on them some years before, were the Mothers of the Plaza, gathered under a banner of their own. Everywhere people were waving little plastic red and white flags carrying Alfonsín's comfortable features, and the same features were emblazoned across the fronts of countless girls wearing t-shirts with the words 'Alfonsín Presidente' printed on them. And for once people were looking beyond their own country's problems as they chanted, 'Argentina today, Chile and Uruguay tomorrow.' One of the three countries in the Southern Cone of Latin America had become a democracy, but the other two remained in the hands of military dictatorships. Catching the mood, and perhaps the words of the chant, Alfonsín waited until the immense noise had died down a little, and then his voice boomed out over the microphones, echoing from the walls of the Cathedral and the Interior Ministry and the colonial buildings right across the Plaza, 'We are beginning a hundred years of freedom, peace and democracy.' Such words had echoed around the square thousands of times in the past; but this time, for once, it seemed just possible that it might turn out to be true.

There were few people in the entire country who were not watching the ceremony and the speech that followed as it was broadcast live on television. Many people invited their friends round to watch, and they would sit indoors enduring the sweltering heat, joining in the clapping and singing and congratulating themselves on the new start that was being made in their country's history. Later, they would go out to one of the innumerable street parties which were organized in every town and city in Argentina, or maybe to one of the Inauguration balls which the Radical Party was holding, and which went on in almost every case all through the night and finished only when the last survivors reached the stage of final exhaustion, around midday the following day.

But the sight of so much enthusiasm and happiness was a painful reminder to some people of what they had lost. One woman, recalling it all a few weeks later, found the tears coming to her eyes as she said, 'No matter how glad I was for myself, and for the country, I couldn't forget how much my son would have enjoyed it all. He always loved that kind of thing – all the singing and the dancing. So you see there was a kind of contradiction. The whole nation was joyful, and I was happy about that, of course. But my own son should have been there, and he wasn't. It seemed so unfair. So unfair.'

Nelva Falcone, the widow of the one-time mayor of La Plata, had more cause than most people to feel the injustice. The Dirty

War had taken the lives of her husband and her daughter, and her son and his wife had been forced to leave Argentina and take refuge in Spain. She too was glad to see a democratic President inaugurated, though out of loyalty to her dead husband she voted for the Peronist candidate, Italo Luder. For her, the day represented a new departure in a purely personal way. The previous October, a few days before the election, her son and daughter-in-law returned to Argentina, confident that it was at last safe for them to do so. He found a job – not always an easy thing to do, with the Argentine economy in such poor shape – and settled down close to the house where Mrs Falcone still lived on her own, and where, as a closely knit family of four, they had all been together, before the military came to power. Gradually Mrs Falcone had been given something to live for again.

She was still, perhaps, a little too melancholy to want to go to one of the street parties on the day of the Inauguration; but as it happens she was needed elsewhere. Her daughter-in-law was giving birth to her third child, and Mrs Falcone spent the entire day at the maternity hospital in La Plata, where her own two children had been born, giving her moral support. Even at the hospital, though, the nurses wheeled a television set into the labour ward, and Mrs Falcone and her daughter-in-law were able to watch the Inauguration as it was broadcast live. It was a new beginning; and not long afterwards Nelva Falcone's granddaughter was born; a few hours younger than the new democracy itself.

# AFTERWORD

This book was completed in March 1985, fifteeen months after the inauguration of President Alfonsín. During that time democracy slowly re-established itself in Argentina on what seemed to be a sounder and more lasting basis than any previous elected government had enjoyed for half a century; though the process was far from smooth. There were some remarkable successes: Alfonsín's government reached agreement with Chile on the long-running Beagle Channel dispute, and went on, rather to its own surprise, to achieve one of the great economic turn-arounds of modern times. With an external debt of $48 billion, the third biggest in the developing world, and an inflation rate which increased by 220% during one four-week period and reached an annual rate of 1,010% in June 1985, the Argentine economy sometimes seemed on the point of collapse. But in that month Alfonsín's government replaced the peso, the value of which had disintegrated over the years, with a new currency: the austral. A three-day public holiday was called, and then on 19th June, as officials hovered nervously by their telephones at the Ministry of Finance and the queues built up outside the banks in Buenos Aires, it gradually became clear that for once Argentines were expressing confidence in their currency and their country's economic future. By the end of that day, more money had been deposited with the banks than withdrawn from them; and for the first time ever, there was a difference of only one per cent between the official rate for the currency and the black market rate. In the months that followed, the strong austral and the unexpectedly successful freeze on prices and incomes halted the hyper-inflation. The annual inflation rate fell dramatically, from the June figure of 1,010% to a mere two or three per cent a month by September. The financial press in the United States started talking about Argentina's 'economic miracle', and investing in what looked like the beginnings of a boom; though everyone knew it could all break down if the prices and incomes freeze ended and an undisciplined free-for-all were to follow.

Alfonsín was fortunate in other ways. The Peronist opposition remained disastrously divided, and the hostile line it took towards the Beagle Channel agreement was heavily defeated in a national referendum in 1985. In an all but absurd attempt to find unity, the party voted in July 1985 to appoint Isabelita Perón as its president, even though she made it clear she was completely uninterested in Argentina and divided her time between her house in Madrid and the more luxurious hotels along Spain's Mediterranean shores. But nobody could agree on a better candidate. The party was actually run by Vincente Saadi, who had been a supporter of the Peronist far left, and who lost the Beagle Channel referendum single-handed with an abysmal performance on television. In order to get the job of vice-president, he abandoned his left-wing allegiances and teamed up with the redoubtable Herminio Iglesias, who had recovered from his own electoral disaster in helping the Peronists to lose the 1983 election; together, they ensured that their party did badly in the November 1985 elections to Congress as well.

Alfonsín and his foreign minister, Dante Caputo, began opening up Argentina to the world with a series of foreign trips, partly to win economic support and partly to build up a diplomatic offensive against Britain on the issue of the Falkland Islands. It paid off in November 1985, when more than a hundred countries voted at the United Nations in favour of a motion calling on Britain and Argentina to negotiate on the islands' future. Even the leaders of the main opposition parties in Britain – the Labour Party and the Social Democratic-Liberal Alliance – met President Alfonsín and agreed with him that there should be talks and that the sovereignty of the Falklands should be on the agenda. Mrs Thatcher disagreed; and although Britain offered a resumption of trading links between Britain and Argentina, an offer which Argentina preferred to brush aside, it seemed clear that Mrs Thatcher would adhere to the line that there was no question of negotiations on the islands' sovereignty. And so Britain, which had chosen to say little or nothing about the crimes committed by the military in Argentina and had loaned Argentina a total of $2 billion during the height of the terror, still had no diplomatic relations with the democratic government two years after it had taken office; and only the most tenuous trade with a country which could just be on the threshold of a genuine boom.

There was more important unfinished business much closer to hand. 'For those of us who have had the painful privilege of knowing it intimately, this trial has been a sort of descent into the darkest regions of the human soul.' So said the Federal Prosecutor, Julio Strassera, at the end of the case against the nine men who governed Argentina from 1976 to 1982. It had produced evidence which matched in dreadfulness anything recorded in this book: the court heard evidence, for instance, from Zulema Chester, whose father had been suspected of sympathising with the Montoneros, and who was herself abducted and interrogated. 'They penetrated me with a stick that had a nail at the end,' she told the court. She had been twelve years old at the time. Another woman, Adriana Laborde, described how she had been kidnapped by the military in 1977, when she was six months pregnant. As she was being transferred from one secret prison to another, she began to give birth in the back seat of the car. Her guards would not untie her hands, which were bound behind her, and when they reached their destination they forced her to strip naked and clean the place up before allowing her to look after her premature baby.

Adriana Laborde and Zulema Chester were two of the 1,900 witnesses whom Julio Strassera selected to provide evidence against the nine men on trial. The most serious charges were laid against ex-President Videla, Admiral Massera and Brigadier Agosti, each of whom faced more than eighty separate counts of murder, more than five hundred counts of kidnapping, and more than 250 counts of torture. The charges against ex-President Viola and Admiral Lambruschini, from the second junta, were fewer (five counts of murder each) but the prosecution demanded life imprisonment for them, as for the three others. The remaining prisoners – Brigadier Graffigna from the second junta, and General Galtieri, Admiral Anaya and Brigadier Lami Dozo from the third one – were not charged with murder, and faced a relatively small number of charges of kidnapping and torture. For them the prosecution demanded lesser prison terms as a result: fifteen years for Graffigna and Galtieri, twelve for Anaya and ten for Lami Dozo.

When the trial began, in April 1985, there was much nervousness within the Alfonsín government, as much as over the fate of the austral. Scores of armed policemen were posted around the court building, and 50,000 people were encouraged to march through Buenos Aires in support of the government's policy of putting the military leaders on trial. There were rumours of a possible coup, and a few days later a quarter of a million people gathered in the Plaza de Mayo in response to Alfonsín's call for a major show of support for democracy. The fears of some major attack proved groundless, but there were plenty of unpleasant smaller incidents to show that the military were not all taking the trial lying down. Julio Strassera received a number of death threats for the way he was carrying out the rôle of prosecutor. The wife of one of his key witnesses was kidnapped and tortured, and told to give up documents that linked senior military officers with crimes against human rights. A human rights activist in La Plata was kidnapped for forty-eight hours and his captors carved swastikas and the initials of the group he worked for on his chest, back and arms.

There was growing anger in the Argentine armed forces, who had been hoping for what was euphemistically called a 'political solution' to the problem of the human rights trials: in other words, an amnesty. The military felt that the democratic government had treated them badly; cuts in defence spending meant that there was insufficient money for ammunition with which to train recruits, and the catering standards for junior officers fell. So did their wages. After decades in which the armed forces were among the best paid groups in the country, a general now received only $540 a month, and a captain $150. An elected member of Congress, by contrast, earned $1,500 a month. In spite of all the talk about possible coups, the period of the trials produced nothing of the sort. Nevertheless, in the run-up to the Congressional elections, Alfonsín felt obliged to declare a sixty-day state of siege, in which ordinary civil rights were suspended, in order to cope with a wave of bombings and an apparent plot by civilians and military men against the government. The whole affair turned to farce rather than tragedy, with the courts ordering the release of the five officers and two civilians who were arrested on suspicion of being linked with the series of explosions, and the government did not come out of it well.

At the Federal Court building, in the meantime, the trial of the nine former military leaders was continuing on its slow way. It was part of Alfonsín's strategy that after the years of lawlessness, punishment could only come through the full and fair administration of the processes of justice. For the most part it was Nuremburg without the accused, except on a very few specific occasions. For the rest of the time the nine stayed in their relatively comfortable gaols; in Galtieri's, it emerged, the walls were kept bare by his own choice except for a single out-of-date calendar, on which 2 April 1982, the day of the Falklands invasion, had been circled in red. When they were obliged to come to court, the differences in their behaviour were marked. Videla chose to wear a well-cut grey suit instead of the uniform which most of the others preferred, and he said nothing to the court – which he refused to recognise – nor to his fellow defendants. Galtieri seemed remarkably self-assured, and when the chance came for him to speak on his own behalf he pulled a piece of paper out of his pocket and read from it, 'I will wait calmly with a clear conscience for God and history to judge me.' Massera, who had seemed intensely nervous on his previous appearance in court, picking at his fingernails and his eyebrows and, continually fiddling with his papers, chose to defend himself by speaking of the subversive enemies which he claimed the military régime had defeated, and by uttering what sounded like a threat: 'The armed forces of today are as capable of defeating them as were the armed forces of yesterday.' The only man to let himself go was Viola. 'Sons of the whores who bore you!' he shouted, as the public gallery erupted into a shout of triumph on hearing the prosecution's demand for a life sentence for him and four of the others.

As it turned out, Galtieri's confidence was justified. When the court reassembled in December 1985 to hear the verdict, Galtieri, Anaya, Lami Dozo and Brigadier Graffigna were all found not guilty. Videla and Massera were sentenced to life imprisonment, Viola to seventeen years, Lambruschini to eight years, and Agosti to four years and six months. The court president, Léon Carlos Arslanian, said that he and his five fellow judges had not found a single law, whether in the Argentine or international codes, which justified the conduct of the men who had been brought to trial. But the decision he announced was a bitter disappointment to the human rights activists who sat in court listening to his words. Hebe Bonafine, of the Mothers of the Plaza, put on her white kerchief embroidered with the words 'Let the Disappeared Be Returned Alive' as a protest. When the judge ordered her to take it off, she refused, and he ordered her out of court. 'I had no other way of protesting,' she said.

There was little consolation in the thought that three of the four men who had been acquitted – Galtieri, Anaya and Lami Dozo – still faced the possibility of long prison sentences in the separate trial over their conduct of the Falklands war. Dreadful crimes had been committed against thousands of men, women and children, and those crimes, Mrs Bonafini and the other human rights activists believed, could only be exorcised by bringing home the charges against those who were responsible. The trial of the nine leaders had been significant, regardless of its outcome; it was the first time that civilians in Latin America had ever held military men legally accountable for crimes committed as the result of a coup. But far from drawing a line under the dreadful years which followed the 1976 coup, the result of the trial simply focussed attention on the efforts to bring more junior officers to justice. 1,700 cases were pending against about 300 military men of lower rank.

But the position in those cases was confused. Even the most clear-cut of them, that against Alfredo Astiz, for the murder of Dagmar Hagelin, had been tossed backwards and forwards between military and civilian courts for eighteen months or so. In December 1984 President Alfonsín intervened to order Lieutenant Astiz – as he was now styled – to be detained pending further legal process. But the civilian judge dealing with the case eventually declared himself incompetent to hear it, and passed Astiz back to the military authorities; and the Supreme Military Council promptly freed him; he is thought to have returned to service at the La Plata naval base.

Other cases dragged on against men who have figured prominently in this book. General Bignone, who handed over as President to Alfonsín in 1983, was being tried separately for the disappearance of two conscripts from the military college of which he was the commanding officer at the start of the Dirty War. The former Interior Minister was being tried for the disappearance of a young woman, Lucia Cullen. In the case of Rosa Frigerio, the young woman who was kidnapped and murdered even though much of her body was in a plaster cast after an operation, a naval captain, Juan José Lombardo, was charged. At the time of writing, General Ramón Camps, the former head of the Buenos Aires provincial police, is believed to be dying of cancer.

General Luciano Menéndez, who staged a poorly-planned attempt at a coup in Córdoba after Jacobo Timerman was released, was met by hostile crowds on several occasions when he was brought to court for pre-trial investigations. On one of them he drew a knife and had to be restrained from attacking his tormentors. His namesake, General Benjamín Menéndez, was a defendant in the trial of Galtieri and others over the military débâcle in the Falklands; and although ten of the sixteen officers on trial had the charges against them dropped, Menéndez was not one of them. Brigadier Cacciatore, the big-spending mayor of Buenos Aires, was on the run in Uruguay for only seven days before returning to Argentina. He too was charged with human rights offences. Martínez de Hoz, though free from suspicion of having brought about the murder or kidnapping of anyone, was nevertheless charged with corruption as a result of the questionable take-over of the domestic airline, Austral. He had been punished in innumerable small ways already for his mishandling of the Argentine economy: people who had once praised him highly would insult him at the few parties he attended after civilian rule returned, and when he went to the races at the Jockey Club, which his family founded, he was cold-shouldered by everybody, and had to leave in embarrassment.

General Suárez Mason, who told the last person to interview him that he was going on holiday, was the only senior officer to abscond for good. He was believed to have taken refuge in the United States, and was said by the Alfonsín government to have been the brains behind the rebellious moves within the armed forces, which resulted in the brief imposition of the state of siege in October 1985. One of the men he was supposed to have plotted with was the editor of a magazine which described itself as Nazi. Admiral Chamorro, the commanding officer at ESMA who was later posted to the Argentine embassy in South Africa as naval attaché, surprised everyone by returning to Buenos Aires. He was arrested the moment he stepped off the plane from Johannesburg, and was imprisoned pending the investigation of his part in the setting up of the Triple A murder squad, before the 1976 coup. Chamorro was strongly rumoured, while in South Africa, to be living with a former ESMA prisoner, the Montonero leader Marta Bazan. Supposedly another Montonero woman, tortured at ESMA, married one of her torturers. They were said to have gone to Mexico City to begin a new life.

As for the other people named in this book as having carried out murders or torture or kidnapping – the infamous group at ESMA described by Raúl Vilariño, for instance – none has so far been arrested, and some have probably fled the country. Vilariño himself had a brush with the law over a stolen car, and has faded from sight. On the other side of the political divide of the 1970s in Argentina, the Montonero leader Mario Firmenich was extradited from Brazil at the request of the Alfonsín government, and he too is expected to face trial. Those who had to endure the results of the war between Firmenich and the military have gradually become accustomed to the return of constitutional government, and the public mood in Argentina seems surprisingly moderate and balanced after two years of the rule of law. An opinion poll carried out in Buenos Aires in the middle of 1985 found, for instance, that more than seventy per cent of people approved of the Alfonsín government's austerity programme, even though they themselves might be adversely affected by it in the short run. That has rarely been a typical Argentine response in the past. Still, changing the atmosphere in an entire country is not an easy or a quick task. At the beginning of 1986 it looks as though President Alfonsín may succeed in doing so – just. But modern Argentine history has not been kind to democratic leaders, and Alfonsín has to contend with the national character of his countrymen and women if he is to succeed in restructuring Argentina. His one greatest asset at present is that a sizeable majority of them regard him as their best protection against a return to the kind of Argentina which the military tried to create: a country of Hitlerian *Nacht und Nebel*, night and fog, in which people could disappear without trace, and no one would dare to think so much as a subversive thought.

January 1986

# APPENDIX: THE CONADEP REPORT

On 21 September 1984 the National Commission on Disappeared Persons (CONADEP), appointed by President Alfonsín to enquire into the circumstances surrounding the disappearance and presumed death of thousands of people during the period of military government from March 1976 to December 1983, produced its report after nine months' investigation. The report was immensely long: more than fifty thousand pages of interviews and eye-witness accounts; but its findings were that an established minimum of 8,960 people – and probably a third more not recorded by the commission – disappeared during the Process of National Reorganization, and that there were no fewer than 340 clandestine gaols in Argentina during the period. What follows is a condensed version of the summary of the report which CONADEP issued.

*Prologue*

During the 1970s Argentina was convulsed by terrorism from the extreme right as much as from the extreme left – a phenomenon which has happened in many other countries. Italy, for instance, suffered for many years from the merciless activities of fascist groups, the Red Brigades, and other similar organizations. But that country never for a moment abandoned the rule of law in combating them, and did so with absolute efficiency, by means of the ordinary courts, while at the same time providing the accused with their full legal rights. At the time of the kidnapping of Aldo Moro, when a member of the security services suggested to General Della Chiesa that a prisoner who appeared to have information should be tortured, he gave this memorable answer: 'Italy can afford to lose an Aldo Moro; what it cannot afford to do is to introduce torture.'

It was not like that in our country. The armed forces responded to the terrorists' crimes with a terrorism infinitely worse than that which they were combating, since from 24 March 1976 they could operate with the power and impunity of a dictatorship, kidnapping, torturing and murdering thousands of human beings.

Our Commission was not set up to make a judgement, that being the function of the constitutional courts, but to investigate the fate of the people who disappeared during the course of those fateful years in our national life. But, after having received many thousands of declarations and testimonies, determined the existence of hundreds of clandestine places of detention, and accumulated more than fifty thousand pages of documentation, we can say with certainty that the military dictatorship brought about the greatest and most savage tragedy in our history. And although we must allow justice to have the last word, we cannot be silent about the things we have heard, read, and recorded; they go far beyond the merely criminal, coming into the black category of crimes against humanity.

From the enormous amount of documentation which came before us, it is clear that human rights were violated on an organized, governmental basis by the armed forces. And they were not violated in a random way, but systematically and uniformly, with identical methods of kidnapping and torture being employed throughout the entire country. Should we not attribute this, therefore, to a methodical pattern, established at top level? How can these crimes have been committed by evil men acting on their own initiative, when a strong military régime was in power, with every authority and every medium of communication in its own hands? How can we speak of 'individual excesses'?

*Summary of Information*

The detention centres, which numbered about 340, were found in every part of the country, and formed the indispensable basis for the system of 'disappearance'. Here, thousands of men and women, deprived of their liberty, were held once they had disappeared. They were there when the authorities denied any knowledge of them after the presentation of writs of habeas corpus, and it was in those centres that they lived out their lives at the mercy of the sadists who acted as their torturers and murderers. In spite of all this, the military authorities who themselves visited these centres assured opinion at home and abroad that the disappeared had either left the country or been the victims of their own internecine quarrels. 'I strenuously deny that concentration camps exist in Argentina or that people are detained in military establishments for any longer than the period required to investigate their cases before they are passed on to a place of imprisonment.' In fact, a large number of eye-witness accounts received by CONADEP confirms that many high-ranking military men visited the detention centres.

*Kidnappings*

Many of the incidents which are described in the information given to CONADEP are of such brutal harshness that they seem difficult to believe. This Commission, however, takes responsibility for the truth of everything which is published here.

Although about six hundred kidnappings took place before the military coup of 24 March 1976, after that date there were tens of thousands of people who were illegally deprived of their freedom in Argentina, of whom 8,960 are still missing. The statistics which are based on the information we received are as follows:

People detained in front of witnesses and still missing: 8,961
Detained in their homes in front of witnesses: 62 per cent
Detained in the street: 14.7 per cent
Detained at place of work: 7 per cent
Detained at place of study: 6 per cent
Detained in unknown circumstances: 9.9 per cent
Detained during military service, or held legally in police or penal custody: 0.4 per cent

*Torture*

Almost every single report received by this Commission mentions some form of torture. This is not accidental; torture was an important part of the overall methods used, and the clandestine gaols were designed to carry it out. In the majority of the cases which follow we have selected only the testimony relating to the form of torture used:

Mrs A.Z., (case number 1127), Argentine citizen, lawyer, was kidnapped on Saturday 20 November 1976 at 11 a.m. . . . She was submitted to the usual torture (blows, the *picana*) as well as other treatment such as the one known as 'burial': 'When people were brought here they were put in ditches which had been previously dug, and buried up to the neck, sometimes for four days or more . . . They were kept without food or water, exposed to the elements. When they were dug out they were covered with insect bites; they had been buried naked. From there they were taken straight to the torture chambers . . .' The case of J.A.M. (number 3721): 'The interrogations were shorter after that but the *picana* (electric prod) was stronger, and they forced it really violently into your anus, while they put the electrodes on to your teeth. It seemed like a bolt of lightning which struck you from head to foot, and they put a string of metal pellets in my mouth which were difficult to swallow, and which made me retch and vomit when I did . . . Each pellet was an electrode, and when the current was turned on, it felt as though a thousand pieces of glass were breaking inside me . . .'

*The Pattern of Repression*

The Commission received the testimony of several people who admitted their involvement with the task forces and other elements of the apparatus of repression. This testimony often relates as much to the overall methods used in repression as to the specific details of the kidnapping, torture and physical elimination of individuals. The involvement which they admit to relates, in many cases, to crimes which the armed forces and the security services sanctioned before 10 December 1983 as part of the fight against subversion but are separate from it (theft of cars, possession of false documents, theft and/or kidnapping for money) . . . In such cases, these witnesses did not come forward so much from moral principle – a feeling of guilt, military honour and so on – as from a feeling of having been deserted by their superior officers (case numbers 3675, 7169, 683 and 1901) and of having risked their careers or their lives in some cases during the war against subversion, while their superior officers were lining their own pockets; corruption was rife among the men in their ranks, and the objectives which were supposed to have motivated the war were abandoned. It was only occasionally that some of these men showed genuine signs of being sorry for what they had done, or of being able to make a moral judgement on it (witnesses number 7169 and 3675).

The Argentine Church repeatedly condemned the repressive methods which this Commission is investigating. Only two months after the March 1976 coup, the Episcopal Conference, in its general assembly, described the methods being used as sinful. Unfortunately, there were members of the clergy who endorsed with their presence, their silence, or their words of support, the methods which the Church in Argentina as a whole had condemned.

*Disappearance of Children and Pregnant Women*

The men who carried out the repression, in taking children from their homes or their mothers, disposed of their lives with the same cold-bloodedness they showed when dividing up their plunder. Deprived of their real identity and separated from their families, the children who have disappeared constitute now and will constitute for many years to come a deep wound in our society. The desperate, meticulous searching by the grandmothers in some cases and the fathers in others for children who have disappeared arises from a mixture of pain and distress at the thought that somewhere, growing up with no contact whatever with their families and sometimes in a foreign country, are the children they have lost. In our report we have also dedicated a considerable amount of space to the appalling cases of pregnant women who gave birth to their children in clandestine places of detention. Many of them are still missing.

*Nuns and Priests*

The terrorism of the state was employed particularly harshly against those churchmen and women who had committed themselves to helping the needy, and to those who stood out against the systematic violation of human rights. Priests, monks, nuns, seminarists, together with members of other religions, were kidnapped, tortured, and in many cases murdered. The supposed 'accidents' in which the Bishop of La Rioja, Mgr Enrique Angelelli, and the Bishop of San Nicolás, Mgr Carlos Ponce de León, lost their lives show that not even members of the Church hierarchy were free from this type of persecution. In the matter of religion, the hypocrisy of those who were responsible for the repression knew no bounds: 'Around 24 December 1976, Admiral Massera, Rear-Admiral Chamorro, Captain Acosta and several members of Task Force 3 turned up. With extraordinary cynicism, they stood in front of about thirty of us, who had our legs in chains, and wished us "Happy Christmas".' (Case number 6974). 'Before letting us lie down on the floor to sleep, the guards made us say the Lord's Prayer and the Hail Mary at the tops of our voices, and told us to give thanks to God that we had lived one more day, and also to pray that this would not be our last' (Case number 440).

*Conclusions*

*Up to the date of this report, CONADEP believes that 8,961 people are still missing, on the basis of information we have received, and collated with the lists produced by national and international human rights organizations. This figure should not, however, be considered a definitive one, since the Commission believes that there are many cases of disappearances which have not been reported.

*The system of making people 'disappear' had some of its origins in the period before the coup of March 1976. But it was from that date, on which the armed forces which seized power obtained absolute control over the resources of the state, that this system became general.

*Those kidnapped were taken to about 340 clandestine centres of detention. The Commission, in the course of its investigations, inspected a large number of these places. They were run by senior officers of the armed forces and the security services. Those detained there were held in inhuman conditions, and subjected to every sort of torture and humiliation. Our investigations have produced a list of 1,300 people who were seen in these clandestine centres, before they disappeared.

*The extent to which torture was used in these centres and the sadism shown by those who carried it out is horrifying. There is no precedent anywhere in the world for some of the methods used. We have been given evidence that children and old people were tortured so that their relatives would give the information which their captors wanted.

*The Commission has confirmed that the final purpose of the system under investigation was to exterminate the detainees and expunge their identity, in many cases destroying their bodies so that they could never be identified. It has also been possible to establish that in the cases of some people whom the armed forces claimed had been killed in shoot-outs, they were taken alive from their places of detention and killed, to give the impression that they had died in gun-battles or while trying to escape.

*Occupations of the victims:

| | |
|---|---|
| Workers | 30.2% |
| Students | 21.0% |
| White-collar employees | 17.9% |
| Professional people | 10.7% |
| Teachers | 5.7% |
| Self-employed | 5.0% |
| Housewives | 3.8% |
| Conscripts and members of the armed forces | 2.5% |
| Journalists | 1.6% |
| Actors, artists, etc. | 1.3% |
| Priests, nuns etc. | 0.3% |

*It is possible to say with authority that, contrary to what those who put this sinister plan into operation maintain, not only members of political organizations which practised terrorism were involved. The number of victims can be counted in thousands who never had any link at all with such activities, and were, nevertheless, subjected to terrible treatment because of their opposition to the military dictatorship, their involvement in strikes or student activities, their connections with intellectuals who questioned the terrorism of the state, or simply the fact that they knew someone who was considered a subversive, or their names appeared in his or her diary.

*The Commission considers that no 'excesses' were committed, if by that is meant acts which were particularly evil and unusual. Such atrocities were carried out as an everyday, commonplace part of the repression.

*Altogether the Commission gathered together 7,380 cases, statements by the families of people who had disappeared, accounts of those who had survived the clandestine detention centres, and declarations by members of the armed forces and security services who were involved in the repression. The Commission also visited various parts of the country and received information from the armed forces, the police, and various public and private organizations.

*From the investigation we have carried out we have formulated 1,086 dossiers which allow us to establish the existence and operation of the main clandestine centres, a partial list of people who disappeared and were seen by others in those centres, and a list of those members of the armed forces and the security services who were mentioned by the victims as having been responsible for the serious crimes which were recorded.

*The destruction or removal of the documentation which listed in great detail the fate of people who disappeared made the Commission's task of investigation harder. Nevertheless, the basic information exists to enable us to say that people who had already disappeared passed through the clandestine detention centres and that the answer to the question of what ultimately happened to them depends upon the willingness of individuals among those responsible for the repression to come forward.

# REFERENCES

**Books and Articles**


Barulich, Carlos (ed.), *Las Listas Negras* (El Cid, Buenos Aires 1983)

Bousquet, Jean-Pierre, *Las locas de la Plaza de Mayo* (El Cid, Buenos Aires 1983)

Dabat, Alejandro and Lorenzano, Luís, *Conflicto Malvinense y Crisis Nacional* (Teoria y Politica, Mexico City 1982)

Di Tella, Guido, *(Argentina Under Perón 1973-6: The Nation's Experience with a Labour-based Government* (Macmillan, London 1983)

Duhalde, Eduardo Luís, *El Estado terrorista argentino* (El Caballito, Buenos Aires 1983)

Fernandez, Rodolfo Peregrino, *Auto-Critica Policial: testimonio del Inspector (R.O.) de le Policia Ferderal Argentina sobre la estructura de la represion ilegitima en la Argentina* (El Cid, Buenos Aires 1982)

Gabetta, Carlos, *Todos somos subversivos* (Editorial Bruguera Argentina, Buenos Aires 1983)

Gambini, Hugo, *Cronica Documental de las Malvinas* (Biblioteca de Redacción, Buenos Aires 1984)

Gillespie, Richard, *Soldiers of Perón: Argentina's Montoneros* (Oxford University Press, Oxford 1982)

Graham-Yooll, Andrew, *The Press in Argentina 1973-8* (Writers and Scholars Educational Trust, London 1979)

Graham-Yooll, Andrew, *Tiempo de violencia* (Buenos Aires 1973)

Gregorich, Luis, *La Republica Perdida* (Sudamericana-Planeta, Buenos Aires 1983)

Hodges, Donald C., *Argentina 1943-1976: The National Revolution and Resistance* (University of New Mexico Press, Albuquerque 1976)

Honeywell, Martin and Pearce, Jenny, *Falklands/Malvinas: Whose Crisis?* (Latin America Bureau, London 1982)

Loveman, Brian and Davies, Thomas Jnr, (eds), *The Politics of Anti-Politics* (University of Nebraska Press, Lincoln 1978)

Makin, Guillermo, 'The Argentine Process of Demilitarization, 1980-1983', *Government and Opposition*, (Spring 1984 London)

Neilson, James, *La voragine Argentina* (Ediciones Marymar, Buenos Aires 1979)
Reyna, Roberto, *La Perla* (El Cid, Córdoba 1984)
Timerman, Jacobo, *Prisoner Without a Name, Cell Without a Number* (Weidenfeld and Nicolson, London 1981)
Vilariño, Raúl David, *Yo secuestre mate y vi torturar en la Escuela de Mecánica de la Armada* (Editorial Perfil, Buenos Aires 1984)

**Reports, Pamphlets and Documents**

*Amnesty International,* 'Report of an Amnesty International Mission to Argentina, 6-15 November 1976' (London 1977)
'Testimony on Secret Detention Camps in Argentina' (London 1980)
'The Disappeared of Argentina: History of Cases reported to Amnesty International, November 1975-December 1979' (London 1980)
*Asamblea Permanente por los Derechos Humanos*, 'Exigimos Justicia porque queremos la Paz la familia víctima de la represión' (Neuquen Province delegación 1978)
'Una plena actividad de la opinion publica nacional y una sustancial approximacion al estado de derecho' (Buenos Aires 1 July 1979)
*Centro de Estudio Legales y Sociales (CELS),*'Adolescentes detenidos-desaparecidos'; 'Conscriptos detenidos-desaparecidos'; 'El sucuestro como metodo de detención'; 'Los niños desaparecidos'; 'Muertos por la represión'; 'Un caso judicial revelador'; 'Uruguay/Argentina: co-ordinación represiva' (Coleccion: Memoria y Jucio, Buenos Aires 1982/3)
*Catholic Institute for International Relations*, 'Death and Violence in Argentina' (Report compiled by group of priests in Argentina, October 1976)
'Some considerations about the role played by the Roman Catholic Church in Argentina' (Report by Argentine priests, Buenos Aires May 1978)
*Organisation of American States*, Inter-American Commission on Human Rights 'Report on the Situation of Human Rights in Argentina' (Washington April 1980)
'La Contrasubversion' unpublished pamphlet (Buenos Aires)

**Argentine Newspapers and Magazines**
*Buenos Aires Herald*
*Clarín*
*El Descamisado* (May 1973-April 1974)
*El Porteño*
*La Opinión*
*La Nación*
*La Prensa*
*La Semana*
*Siete Dias*

# INDEX

**The dramatic final days of the war in Vietnam . . .**

# THE FALL OF SAIGON

## DAVID BUTLER

On April 29, 1975, the first communist tanks rolled into Saigon. The last remaining Americans departed abruptly from the rooftops, leaving behind a city seized by panic and despair.

David Butler, a reporter in Saigon at the time, recaptures the desperation and drama of those eventful days through the eyes of over 30 people on all sides of the conflict. From the highest levels of government to the streets of Saigon, this is a gripping portrait of courage and betrayal.

"A detailed and at times poignant journalistic re-creation of those terrible last 55 days . . . extraordinary vignettes . . . marvellous anecdotes".

NEW YORK TIMES BOOK REVIEW

**0 7221 2106 7 WAR NON-FICTION £3.95**